DARK WORLDS

DARK WORLDS

BRYAN KOVACH

Order this book online at www.trafford.com
or email orders@trafford.com

Most Trafford titles are also available at major online book retailers.

Printed in the United States of America.

ISBN: 978-1-4269-4747-6 (sc)
ISBN: 978-1-4269-4748-3 (e)

Library of Congress Control Number: 2010916836

Trafford rev. 11/24/2010

 www.trafford.com

North America & International
toll-free: 1 888 232 4444 (USA & Canada)
phone: 250 383 6864 ♦ fax: 812 355 4082

This is for the poets and prophets who warned me,
and for my family and friends,
and for those who goad me. An ancient Akkadian proverb says:

If I myself had not gone, who would have gone at my side?

This journey is better with all of you along. I hope you enjoy it.

1
ECHO ISO-001

Equatorial Convoy Hub Avalon,
150,000 Years Ago

Dim corridors and curving halls spanned the long winding maze that was the heart of the ship named Avalon. Though great was that heart, vast by any measure, the designers sought to multiply the imagined depth of her interior dimensions by utilizing shadows and the absence of straight lines. Their efforts reached only a limited success, however. From Ard Morvran's perspective, walking the halls of Avalon was like walking in the ribbed belly of a whale. For one thing, the ship's structural plan mimicked skeletal and muscular growth patterns. More obviously evoking this analogy was the smell. Despite the size of the place, the smell actually contributed to a subtly claustrophobic atmosphere, as did the warm mists concentrating in clouds along the walls and ceilings of the larger rooms. Generated by humi-vaporators, the mists obscured sight to short distances in the dim passageways. There was more than enough space to roam inside Avalon, but a feeling of confinement hung over the crew.

Ard paused, frowning, as if scowling would ward off the closeness of the air. He stood before an enormous hatch, shaped as the corridor like a truncated diamond. The outward slant of oblique angles left lots of room on either hand and above his head, reminding him that the designers also had in mind a different species when they'd drafted this ship.

"I'm not claustrophobic," he said to himself. "I'm just human."

As if to confirm his thoughts, he traced the high jambs of the hatch upwards to where they met the curve of the ceiling. There was something there that he had attempted numerous times to blot out, even going so far as to try and burn it off; but the organic composite the ship was made of was self-healing, very uncooperative with his efforts to efface what the designers had taken such pains to inscribe. They were words—words grown in the living tissue of the threshold. The words offended him, though no one else, for they were words of the Gremn language, which few among Mankind then knew.

ISLITH RISES AGAIN

"Up your beaked hindquarters, the dirty lot of you," he said smugly, and made as if to touch the smooth black hand-plate set in the left-hand wall. His hand hovered in place a moment, and then went back to his side. The Command Access Controls center, or *CAC*, was his least favorite place on the ship, for here he was confronted most strongly by the ghosts of the War. After all these years he still needed to psych himself up before going in.

2

The foggy emptiness of the corridor had invited his mind to churn up memories from the Old Days, and memories like these were an unwelcome companion. The emptiness wanted to be filled, and his mind had crowded it with faces and voices of people who were no longer seen or heard. These had come to him in vivid visions and dreams since the Ban was enacted. Ard wondered if there would come a day when the tormenting shadows would finally fade away. He guessed that they might, but in one of only two possible ways. One, he would wake up from this nightmare and discover that he was still in his stepfather's house on the Western Sea, and that the war had never been. Two, he would wake up from this nightmare and find out that things had gotten far worse while he was sleeping, that the sedate world Mankind had inherited under the Ban would be suddenly filled with the manifest forms of his deepest fears, and that the delusions and the dreams would crystallize into the realization that there was no end to the war they had fought—not until all the rest of them were dead.

It wasn't healthy to imagine such terrors; but he didn't need to imagine them. He had endured the attempted destruction of his race, and the terror was still alive in his memory even in these days of peaceful exile. Such was the steep price of surviving war with the Gremn. He suspected that it was because of his fears that he was still sharp, and it was because he was still sharp that the Colonial Council had not stripped him of his rank when he surrendered the military to their new limited government. It certainly wasn't because they were grateful for anything he had done.

"Are you going in, *Kanno?*"

The deep feminine voice registered in his ears almost as soon as he was aware of the prickling sensation on his neck. He got a feeling like that whenever Bec was near. Morvran turned towards the spindly blue-haired girl, the girl who never grew any older, and he was suddenly aware that the dawn of a new kinship between them was at hand. He could no longer think of her only as a trophy liberated from enemy service. Now that

3

he was past his warranty, she was probably the closest thing he would ever have to a daughter of his own.

After all that had happened, how strange was that?

"I was thinking," he said after a long pause. He turned his back to the door.

"Thinking? That's more than the Council imagines of you, I'm sure," Bec replied playfully.

Ard gazed at her a moment, revisiting the past as he did so. Bec was a living vision of another world, and not all of the memories she stirred in him were of the War. The sight of her distinctive features transported him—her pale skin, blue hair, long pointed ears, and the glittering tattoo of a flowering Ilum vine that swirled in ghostly colors beneath her eyes, all spoke of a forest he had visited as a boy. It was a forest and a time so far away that return was unthinkable.

They could only return in their memories.

Some memories could be good, then.

Forcing himself to come back, the Commander brushed a stray crumb of dinner off his turtleneck. He was still trim, but a belly was slowly forming down there—a belly that collected crumbs and displayed them in most unflattering ways.

"Well, I *was* thinking," he said. "I was thinking, why did they decide we should all dress in *black?*"

"It's supposed to boost morale?" she guessed.

"Wrong, Bec. It's because it makes us invisible, so they can pretend we're not here. We're the ones who got them exiled when we fought to protect them, but now that the danger's passed we should just fade away. *That's* what I was thinking."

"That's not exactly good for morale, Kanno Morvran."

"Then I'll try smiling."

"Better not. You never looked good with a smile."

"I'm not going in there until I look a little better than I feel, Bec, or until I feel a little better than I look."

She was grinning, but spared him a comeback. Instead, her eyes glazed over for a moment as her mind leapt to some crucial task. Looking on with quiet interest, Ard allowed that Bec was a little strange, her moods unpredictable; but then, she wasn't human. Bec was Fomorian. Her modified Null-body didn't show the marks of time's teeth, and its integration into the ship's computer by Gremn technologists had created this secondary iteration, actively participating in the control intelligence of Avalon.

"You know, Kanno," she said, coming back to him, "of the three hundred aboard, I think you are the only one left who still has the guts to walk alone on my ship."

"I never walk alone," he replied, and slapped the hand-pad on the left side of the hatch. It opened with a hiss of pressurized atmosphere, and with a blast of the soupy smell that had drenched every pore in his body since the day he'd fought his way aboard and taken the ship for the Crodah.

"After you," he said, gesturing towards the hatch. Bec stepped past him and made a left, heading for her workstation in the port hub. Ard headed straight in, and stopped at the head of a short flight of steps to look around.

CAC was sparsely manned on the best of days, and this evening was no different from any other. He counted six, with himself and Bec making eight. Their small figures moving around the dim hollow Command Access Controls center only magnified the sensations that had haunted his steps down the corridor. It wasn't easy to shake off the dread of the suffocating emptiness of the place. Avalon was so enormous that maintenance crews were often away for weeks. The entire crew occupied only one small corner on the lower levels of the Observation Chamber, and security was full of gaps. Ard knew their emotional security was also unstable, for every one of them realized this ship was not their home. It was hard to keep that fact from the front of one's mind, especially in a place like CAC.

The Commander cleared his throat. He hoped he wasn't coming down with another cold, and grimaced as his congestion brought forth a painful cough. No sooner was the sound heard than the officer of the watch, Jak, stepped away from his station and hailed him on deck. Ard waved a hand, muffling his coughs with the back of his arm, and the other officers present looked back to their consoles. Morvran hated ceremony, but he appreciated how these men and women adhered to it as a discipline. They were in a difficult place, and they were supposed to be safeguarding the lives of thousands aboard the freighters and miners that made their way to and from the planet's icy northern hemisphere. As much as the tradesmen relied on Avalon, Ard knew he was relying on the three hundred men and women under his command. Most of those who had served under him were long dead. The perseverance of the living under these stressful conditions dispelled some of the ghosts of the war he'd fought in another world.

Of course, most of his crew thought of him as a ghost of the war. They were children of Ertsetum. He spent much of his free time trying to support and strengthen the fellowship they shared in exile. Perhaps that was what represented the balance of the honor due him; for though humanity was but a tattered fringe of a remnant in these latter days, there was still something in their nature that called them to be a moral people, not *machines.*

But then there was Bec.

Ard turned his head towards the port hub to see her in her accustomed posture, arms akimbo and eyes unfocussed, staring blindly at the screen projected from the station before her. Immersed in Avalon's complex mind, she needed no console to perform the link. Bec and Avalon were one. They were also divided, and he was responsible for that.

"Nothing new?" Ard asked.

"Just a communication sequence from an inbound freighter," Bec replied without breaking her concentration.

"An inbound freighter? Inbound from where?"

"It's coming up from the southeast."

"This late?" Ard wondered. "There's no northbound traffic this time of year—it's forbidden by the Council."

"Communications says it's an envoy from the Council. I'll set them up to land in Bay 3. Do you want to go and meet them?"

Ard shrugged. "I suppose someone should go meet and greet, but I'm not leaving the Command deck right now—"

"—and walk all the way back to the Mess area and Arrivals, then back again with some stupid civilian officer in tow," Jak muttered from his station near Bec. "I don't blame you, Kanno Morvran. Make 'em come to us!"

Morvran didn't answer. Somewhere in his brain, *"Make 'em come to us"* struck a nerve, and he was momentarily awash in memories. More memories—

"Nothing else," Bec said. She returned to monitoring communications and traffic.

"About these other freighters that are still north of us," Jak said to the Commander, "I just don't understand what's going on. Are we supposed to go in after them if there's trouble?"

"That's correct, Lieutenant."

"But Avalon wouldn't survive the winter atmosphere any better than a freighter. The danger of icing in systems that were hastily improvised for this environment could bring down the entire station."

"Probably."

"We've got six ECHOs on duty, and more than twelve freighters above the line. I wonder if those guys know we can't rescue even half of them. I mean, they're all miners, so they work with payload-volatiles. They ought to appreciate the danger—"

"Enough, Jak," Morvran said. "I don't want to have to go out on a rescue mission for one of my own, either. We'll just have to do what we can do. I'm sure the payload is worth it to the miners; and yes, they do appreciate the danger."

"Didn't you do some mining, Kanno, years back?" asked one of the junior officers on the deck.

Morvran turned to regard the young man, and smiled. "Yes, *years back*. Before you were out of diapers, Eng, Avalon actually did some ore-mining."

"Mining is hard work?" Eng wondered.

"First you have to locate the unrefined ore," Morvran indulged, "and then you've got to set down and break through the ice to access the seabed. Ore usually rests more than a click beneath the surface. Drills won't work, and shafts burned by foot-light are crumbly at best. The prep takes a week, and the extraction has to be done in less than a day—or else the shaft collapses. Sometimes it does before you're ready, and no one can retrieve the bodies. Then it's off to the next shaft, and the next deposit. Ore is refined by the mining company these days, so the pay is actually decent. Back then, it was just a way of life. We were all trying our best to build a future on this new world, each in our own way."

The deck was quiet as each pondered their Kanno's words.

"The Council doesn't appreciate any of us," Jak decided, "or they wouldn't permit the miners to go into danger in the first place, whether they're willing or not. The air's too icy up there this time of year, and the companies have surplus. It's not right."

He walked away towards the junior officer, Eng, whom he was supposed to be training to use the viewer. Ard was left to wonder what it was that he'd almost remembered before Jak interrupted his thoughts. His knees ached, though, and between one thing and the other he'd totally lost his train of thought. Looking around for a place to sit, he remembered for the thousandth time that there were no proper seats here. It wasn't as much of a strain to stand up through a whole watch as he had first thought, but he might just drag in an armchair one day.

"How would that look?" he wondered quietly. "Somehow I just can't imagine an easy-chair in the middle of a Gremn Command Center."

Once again he cursed their *beaked hindquarters*, which undoubtedly had no use for comfortable seats. That isn't to say that the designers had taken no thought to comfort. Obviously, the Gremn had different ideas about comfort. They probably didn't require comfort in order to be efficient, though, and the CAC was designed to maximize efficiency. It was the most lavish and functional command deck ever to grace a vessel of its size, granting the bridge crew access to all internal systems and automations; but the crew was not needed on the deck. Here the Computer Core and workstations were the only permanent residents, and as they were the only essential installations, the CAC had been suited primarily to their presence—if not to Ard's.

The Computer Core was lord in its realm. Indeed, the name *Avalon* that this ship bore was the name of the computer that it housed—the legendary Avalon AI, which had been developed by the Gremn during the first year of the War. Ard had tamed the system to his hand by rewriting the Computer Core's drive protocols and by freeing its flesh and blood component, Bec; but it still had a mind of its own. It was essentially alive, as was the ship. Thus was Avalon treated with respect, and with no little fear and wonder as well. Some said that keeping Avalon was not unlike keeping a captured dragon as a household pet. A few of the Colonial Council said the same of Bec; but all were agreed on one thing, that though Avalon had been provided secondary drive protocols and Bec was complicit, the ship was not to be entirely trusted. Many among those who were now aboard had lost kith and kin by the cruel strokes of her intelligence. In this CAC, much of the World of Origins was once slated for conquest.

Ard cast a glance towards the starboard hub, where maintenance and engineering stations were chattering to themselves, unmanned. Avalon's bioelectric subsystems maintained the vitality of the atmosphere within, and the AI constantly checked these systems, as well as those that secured the ship from without. So much of the place ran itself that Avalon would have no trouble continuing to do its duty for a hundred thousand years after they all died; and because it could heal itself, it was sure to last twice as long before it needed serious attention. Nevertheless, Avalon's physical systems were checked and rechecked by human tenders in continuous rotation. Redundant maintenance required a sizeable crew, though most were only aboard to keep the rotation slack. And slack it was, even with only eight on in CAC at a time. The room felt empty, but it was crammed with enough marvels to keep them occupied in six-hour shifts.

The crew could not afford to let their guard down.

"We'll make them come to us," Ard mumbled, picking up the pieces of his scattered thoughts. "I wish I could remember where I've heard that before!"

"Inside the Hive," Bec said, without looking away from her screen. "You remember the Hive under Islith, where you first found me?"

Ard shook his head, his eyes startled wide.

"I asked, 'How are you going to fight them all?'"

"And I said, *'We'll make them come to us,"* Ard recalled.

Now he remembered, and he wasn't surprised that the memory came to him so clearly in this room. The prodigious space around them bulged outwards in a cloverleaf shape, and was contained under a single dome. The walls made the place look a little like a giant hollow tumor, and it was dark.

"Just like a Gremn Hive," he thought.

The three lobe-shaped hubs were distributed with one each to port and starboard and the third up front. All throughout the hubs there were strange twisted columns of the dark grey silicate that grew in accordance with the ship's self-regenerating technology, and these gave the place an appearance that was reminiscent of a cave full of stalactites—or a mouth full of teeth. The columns stretched from floor to ceiling, and supported rings of interface equipment at eye-level. Thus the officers worked standing-up. While on duty they used consoles to monitor incoming transmissions from freighters and other ships, and all other signals on the Colonial Communications Network. There were also internal security screens, and the endless maintenance-tasking stations that kept the larger part of the crew informed as to the steamy quality of their environment. Front and center, however, was the Computer

Core. The CC was a squat pyramid of bronze-colored tiers raised upon a heavy frame of gyrocompasses. The crew regarded it with awe. This was Artificial Life, the ghost of the ship, created by technologists whose secrets were lost long before the War. Avalon AI wasn't the oldest of its kind, but the gravity of its presence was considerable nonetheless. It was one of only a few such sagacious relics left over from a time forgotten by all but the poets.

And its sentience was admirable.

Mess Hall rumors that were spread by marines trained by Bec typically lauded the ease with which Avalon could find, isolate, and destroy an enemy anywhere aboard the station. No one had ever gone missing under Ard's command, but the possibility struck a chord that resonated throughout the entire crew. There was no doubt that Avalon deserved a little space of her own in the fore-hub of CAC. As for them, they would stick together. No one but Ard and Bec wandered far from quarters alone.

Ard was done reminiscing. He stepped down the flight before him into the shallow bowl at the center of the room. The Command Center, as the central station on the deck was called, was occupied by a waist-high hemisphere of eight screen-consoles that the Council Engineers had installed. These included a diagnostic display for every one of the ship's systems, plus a personal security interface. The consoles were currently offline, but with a light touch Avalon wakened her inward eye and gave him a glimpse of all her doings. The eight screens flickered to life, each glimmering with brilliant amber light. The centermost showed him a forwarded copy of the communication sequence transmitted by the inbound freighter.

"They should have landed by now," he muttered, pressing a function-icon that accessed the viewer. A three dimensional image of the ship hovering high above a frozen ocean flickered to life in the center of the forward hub—almost directly above Avalon's CC. The viewer showed that it was snowing outside, as it usually was. The world of Crodah exile was an ill-favored home, for its entire northern hemisphere was locked in a frozen mass of ice. It was in the south that the colonists made their towns and villages, and there the Council had hung up the Colonial Charter and erected a capitol of sorts; but even in the south the weather was cold and wet all year long.

The landscape around Avalon's post wasn't much to look at, but tonight the atmospheric projection on the viewer was stunningly beautiful. The sunset, a flowing tide of crimson and orange that lit the snow sideways as it swirled around the station's turnip-shaped hull, was tinged now with the dusky wine-colored hues of early evening. Nearer the top of the field of view, appearing in a rare break in the atmospheric cover, a vibrant light streaming three tails glowed ominously, a beacon in the sky. Ard knew most of the projection existed only as a data construct that was gathered and compiled by satellites, but Comet Bibbu composed so striking an image that every one of the officers on deck allowed themselves a brief glimpse from their stations. Ard was pleased. He thought it was good that they were still able to appreciate beauty in a place like this. Besides, Bibbu was a reminder of home for the few present who had seen it in the skies of the World of Origins.

His attention wavered. Bec had sent him something on his security console while he was gazing at the viewer. It was a simple text message:

UNCOMFIRMED SECURITY CODES FROM INBOUND SHIP.
ENVOY IS BEHIND YOU, AT YOUR STATION.
HE COMES UNESCORTED.

Ard studied the message for a second. He wondered why she didn't say anything aloud, since their stations were relatively close. The answer presented itself in the form of a strange voice at his shoulder.

"Kanno?"

Ard turned and leveled his eyes on the man—a curious man with slick black hair. He looked about middle age, and was rather muscular. He wasn't at all what Ard was expecting in a civilian officer. There was also something terribly familiar about his appearance—something unsettling.

As the Commander turned he also leaned forward to block his consoles, and then switched them off. His curiosity was aroused, but he wondered what had so suddenly set him off. Wasn't this a representative, the *Council-Appointed Information Dissemination Supervisor*? Though that was what the patch on his fancy blue uniform said, Ard was suddenly full of suspicions.

"You're the Council rep?" the Commander asked. "You sure got to CAC fast—and without a guide."

He could not hide the doubt in his voice.

The stranger saluted stiffly. Ard tried not to stare at the symbol emblazoned above the IDS-patch on his uniform—an eagle with outstretched wings. Where did he recall seeing that before? Averting his eyes to the man's face, Ard returned salute and took with his other hand the proffered tablet.

"Specialist of the Civilian Corps," he said, reading the report that flashed on the tablet's small screen. "This is a reply to the reports I sent?"

"The Colonial Council has received your reports, Kanno Morvran," the specialist replied, "and all of the delegates remain grateful for your diligence. Regarding your concern for our northern assets, I was carefully instructed in my briefing to request your patience in these matters. Details as to their activities will be brought to you by the appropriate representatives, to whom you may also direct any related questions."

"And when will these other reps be coming?"

"I don't know, Sir. Maybe soon."

"You don't know? Where have I seen you before, Specialist? Are you ex-military?"

"I was staffed aboard ISO-017 during the War."

"You served 017? You don't look old enough to have set foot on a real aeroship—or have you?"

"Not since they changed the name from *Combat* Hub to *Convoy* Hub, Sir."

Ard heard a quiet whisper of voices from the portside hub, and realized the others were listening in. Unannounced visitors weren't common on Avalon, but Morvran was sure this man was no stranger. He had met him somewhere before—maybe even in battle. The Commander smiled grimly, and the specialist misread him, for he smiled in return.

"I guess the change of scenery must be something new, at least, unless a thousand huffs of ice is a welcome sight for sore eyes at journey's end? How long did your trip take, Specialist?"

"It took us two days to reach you this far north, against headwinds," he said, his eyes never blinking. "And the weather suits me fine, Sir."

"You'll get used to it, if you're staying. You *are* staying, aren't you? I have lots of unanswered questions, and it would be nice to make the details known to a representative, rather than send another message to the Interior Ministry's slush-bin."

"Details, Sir? You mean the decision to call back our military assets farther north before the onset of winter?"

"There are still miners up there, too."

"You can't handle a rescue with Avalon?"

Morvran looked down on him with a cold frown. "We handle everything from equipment malfunctions to surface rescue missions from this station," he replied, "and that keeps us busy enough during the normal mining season. I'm concerned that the mining companies are losing sight of the possibility of losing another ship to the ice. We don't have many more to lose. As for the military, *my* military—"

"The War's over, Sir. There are no monsters out here."

The specialist grinned, and in that moment Ard knew the man. The moment of recognition left him stunned. There was a pause, and even the visitor—the traitor of House Gaerith—seemed to notice the hostile, brooding silence. Eyes peered at him from various workstations. The response was to his awkward comment, and nothing more. Surely no one else recognized him, Ard was certain, and he would keep it that way—for now.

"Something's wrong, Kanno?"

"What kind of game are you playing?" Morvran whispered, leaning close. "You think I don't know who you are, *Cedric DePons?*"

"I rather counted on your recognition," DePons replied quietly. He turned his head, making a cursory inspection of the triple hubs of the deck and the dozen crewmen whose shift was almost up. His eyes were mostly drawn to the viewer in the forward hub. In the very front of the room, the pyramid-shape of the Computer Core hummed and glittered.

"I'm placing you under arrest for impersonating a civilian officer," Morvran said, keeping his voice low.

He walked past DePons, awaiting him at the bottom step of the Command Center. DePons seemed to be ignoring him, though. Something was up, and intuition told Ard that zero hour was fast approaching. He caught Bec's eye as she glanced aside from her station, and he stuck his hand in the pocket of his jacket. Bec nodded, and pretended to resume working at her console.

Did she also recognize this man?

Ard closed his fist hard on the disk-shaped leather pouch hidden inside his pocket. Strangely, he sensed a stirring in its depths, as though something had come to life. Marluin had said it might be so; but it always seemed so inconspicuous an item. A gift of great value, no doubt, yet it was given with almost no explanation. Even as dusk settled on the icy world displayed by the viewer, he knew that today was the day the gift would explain itself, for there could be only two reasons DePons was here. Either he had come for the stone, or for that monster they were keeping on ice in SARA Station—or maybe for both.

"You're going to answer a few questions for me before this night's over," Morvran said, raising his voice a little. "The first is, what in *Hades* are you doing here?"

"You already know the answer to that question, I think," the Specialist replied.

Ard tapped his index finger on the holster of his pistol. "Really?"

"It will be answered any second now, Kanno."

DePons nodded towards the viewer, where several of the officers, led by Jak, were working feverishly at the CSR Terminal. The bright flash of an explosion emanated from the image of the station that hovered in the forward hub. It was the sign DePons had been waiting for.

The ship rumbled, and the vibrations of the impact rattled the decking beneath his feet. Ard leapt up the stairway and charged towards the black panel that would lock down access to CAC. Weapons fire erupted behind him, echoing loudly, but he wasn't hit. Drawing his pistol, Morvran crouched behind a column near the exit and peered out into the room.

DePons was on one knee, weapon drawn, and all around him consoles exploded and confusion ensued. The deck crew had been prepared, but half were down already, limbs twitching and flailing. Bec had collapsed motionless near her console, and he was close enough to see the probe sticking out of her neck.

The fallen were not dead.

In the confusion of the moment Ard wondered why a terrorist would deploy less than lethal rounds. The three remaining crewmen didn't seem interested in discovering the answer to this puzzle. They were busy firing blindly into the smoky Command Center, unaware that they'd lost the deck. Within seconds they were silenced.

Morvran let out his breath. Taking out a Fomorian and a whole command deck in less than a minute, unscathed—it was impossible shooting for anything but a modified person, or something else.

Something like *Cedric DePons.*

There was no longer a reason he could think of to trap himself inside CAC and fight it out with the traitor, so Ard moved quickly outside, slapping the black panel and sealing the battlefield behind him with his personal security code.

Noise of gunfire down the corridor alerted him to a new crisis, however. It seemed DePons wasn't working alone. The Gremn were here.

It didn't matter how many had come. A few would suffice. Ard knew their objective, though the Council hadn't even been alerted yet to their presence. He had kept secret the saboteur they'd captured and placed in stasis, but now the secret was out, heading directly towards him through the crew quarters; and Lír would *not* be leaving survivors in his wake.

He was rooted in place, unable to join the fight or go back inside CAC and finish DePons. His mind was reeling with a new and terrifying thought. Bec was their target all along. With Bec out of the way, Avalon's AI would take over—revert to primary protocol.

How ironic, he thought. Had he not been here before, done this before? Wasn't there anything new in all the worlds?

If something was new, it certainly hadn't anything to do with war.

2

DEEP BLACK IN THE OPEN

New Jersey,
A.D. 1901

The workmen arrived with their shovels, and the guests began to leave. Scattered groups loitered about the park in a sea of black silk and bowler hats that bobbed in the way of polite conversation amid a sighing breeze of whispered voices, an articulation in harmony with the fragrant wind in the trees. The tide of people slowly receded, leaving behind five figures beside the open grave. Of these, three were last-minute invites who had arrived late. Clearly an afterthought—perhaps an intentional oversight that served to distinguish them from the rest—their presence was regarded by many to be inappropriate, considering the circumstances.

"Art, we'll see you at home," Mrs. Morvran said. She squeezed Professor Morvran's hand as she left, and he was momentarily puzzled that she called him by his middle name. It was something she rarely did. Jonathan went with her.

Dr. Thaddeus Arthur Morvran adjusted the stiff collar of his shirt and looked down into the grave at his feet. The box below was empty, but his memory of the girl was not. Since her disappearance she had changed his life, and the life of his son. He reminded himself that this was justly so.

Looking up again he met the eyes of Colonel Albert Naruna and his wife, Talia, who stood facing him across the grave. The colonel was a huge man, his scarred face and bald head accentuating the image of a disciplined soldier. He was in full dress uniform today, and scowling with practiced confidence. The professor combed a hand nervously through his dark hair and adjusted his spectacles, knowing that it only made him appear smaller and meeker in the grim giant's eyes. Talia Naruna stood beside her husband and smiled sadly. Though he had dreaded this meeting for some time, Thaddeus felt calmed by her quiet presence.

"Your boy isn't here?" the colonel asked.

"Jonathan was here," the professor replied. "He left with his mother."

"I meant Taran," the colonel said. "Taran wasn't here. You don't think that's a little suspicious?"

Talia turned a venomous look upwards into her husband's face, but he ignored her with cool indifference.

"Taran was very distraught by the events surrounding Val's disappearance," the professor replied. "I told him about the Memorial, and I did urge him to come; but he said that he did not believe Val was dead."

"It isn't Taran's fault," Talia said, still looking up into her husband's face.

"Maybe not," the colonel replied, his own eyes still locked on Professor Morvran. "I don't think he's the only one to blame, in any case. I hold *you* responsible for this, Thaddeus."

"Me?"

"You were the one who got the ideas into her head that led to this."

"I assure you Colonel, as I have before, that Val was participating in a beneficial education—"

"Nonsense!" Colonel Naruna roared.

The last bystanders took their cue to leave.

"Women don't do those things! You meddled with accepted roles in society, and now look what's happened!"

He pointed down into the grave.

"*That's* the sum of the education you gave my daughter, and there's enough room down there for you, too!"

"Albert, please!" Mrs. Naruna said, taking her husband's arm.

"It's already done," the colonel said, glancing aside at her. Then, fixing his glare once again on Dr. Morvran, he said, "I intend to take you down, Professor. You won't get away with this. You're crazy, and you're a danger to everyone around you. The lawyers are drawing up a case right now."

Professor Morvran paled, but stood stock-still, as though he was carved from stone. "Then I'll see you in court, Albert," he said.

Colonel Albert Naruna turned, and taking his wife about the shoulders with one great arm he steered her away from the graveside; but his eyes remained fixed on the professor. Thaddeus returned his gaze until the colonel paused beside a group of people standing a little way off. Jonathan was among them, accepting the customary teasing of a gaggle of local girls who followed him, entranced by his looks and the excessive length of his dark hair. He greeted Naruna with a firm handshake.

Thaddeus stood beside the grave alone. The colonel's words slowly sank in, and he wondered if he was not in some way responsible for all this—even if he knew she was not dead.

"Now begins the search for the lamb that was lost," someone said over his shoulder.

The professor thought it was the Parish, who had said something of this sort while presiding at the Memorial. When he turned, however, he saw a well-dressed gentleman with coal black hair, slicked back so that it clung to his head like the feathers of a crow.

"Now they are both lost," the professor said. "It's good to see you, DePons."

"The machine has been disassembled?"

"There won't be a bolt of canvas left to betray its existence. I donated the engine and some of the frame to my friends in Ohio. They will be very pleased."

"That's good. On that note, I also have something for you."

DePons handed him a folded newspaper—an issue of a local paper from the previous week.

"Page seven," he said.

Thaddeus unfolded the paper and began searching through the pages and columns. He stopped suddenly, shocked by the headline.

"*Arrested and escaped!*" he read.

"He's making a name for himself, even back here," DePons said. "And that's *not* good."

"Burglary!" the professor exclaimed. His hands were shaking. "I never imagined all this would come of—"

"You might have," DePons said. "Remember, Professor, we're working with a lot of uncertainty. Everything we do has a purpose, but deviations from that purpose also have serious consequences."

Thaddeus shook his head as he skimmed the column. "I'm already living with consequences," he said.

"But you're not the primary target in all this."

"You think I don't know it?" Morvran asked, shaking the pages with emphasis. "All this has nothing to with Val Anna or Taran. It's plain, however, that the whole community believes that it does. If the courts are dragged into this, it will shine a light on matters best left in the dark."

"So, you've agreed to Kabta's terms?"

"I will not expose the Foundation. They'll find a way to get rid of us if it comes to that."

They glanced across the green towards the colonel, who nodded in their direction and gestured the firing of a pistol with a wink. He stomped away with his wife in tow, and most of the guests followed him.

"That fool and his theatrics," Morvran muttered, folding the paper. "The factions will play their games, but let's not get caught in the middle."

"The enemy of my enemy isn't really my friend."

"*We're* the enemy, DePons. If we don't manage to stay ahead, these little problems will be the least of our worries. Time is against us. Now that the lab's been destroyed, Reformation will put everything else behind schedule."

"Well, if that's all you're worried about, I can assure you the new lab's almost ready. On top of that, the calibration codes were provided without argument. As for Reformation, collaboration *has* been very beneficial, even if it leaves us feeling like we're caught between the factions. Those tests would have taken us decades and billions of dollars to perform—especially now that a stone is lost."

"Along with most of our research," Morvran lamented with a sigh. "All this we owe to the lost lamb, indeed."

He rolled the paper up and shoved it under DePons' arm, patting the man's shoulder with mock affection.

"What happens if the lost lamb finds *them* first, Cedric?"

DePons nodded agreement. "It *is* becoming dangerous," he said. "In the world they are from, we are accounted nothing but tools in a war that goes on forever. All our history is but a long sad record of their sojourn here and there. I can't even manage to keep our heads above water without the aid of their

22

defectors; and it's obvious I'm only getting help of any kind from the factions because they need something I possess."

"Then let's hope she comes to us first."

"We also have something *she* wants."

"You hope to convince her of our goals, Cedric? If she is what you believe she is, then even Taran may not be enough."

There was a pause as these unsettling words passed through the air between them. Somewhere a crow was calling. Professor Morvran shivered.

"So we find her," he said quietly. "We find her and contact her, even if she comes to them first. Then we try to convince her that we're the good guys."

"And she'll do what? Look, she's only one part of what they need, Thaddeus."

"Yes, the most important part," Morvran replied. "But what happens if they retrieve both Regulus *and* her?"

DePons looked up from the grave, his eyes hollow and dark, as dark as his hair. For a moment the professor almost thought he saw the other man's pupils dilate until there was no more white left in his eyes.

"Then we're in trouble," DePons said, shaking his head. His eyes were clear, sparkling now with thoughts that the professor wished he could get at.

"What of this other stone, then, the one you've been hiding from me?"

"Regulus? I shall continue to press my contacts. They are still willing to cooperate, even after the fiasco at the lab; but how long this will last I won't dare guess. If it turns out that collaboration is no longer desirable with the FTI group, I will at least learn what we need to know to survive what's coming."

"I do not envy you," the professor remarked. "You'd better be careful. That Kabta fellow is a murderous monster."

"Maybe. In any case, he's informed me of the existence of another Location. It's what I came here to tell you."

"Where? Is it accessible?"

"Wales. It's rather close to the Island, in fact."

"You're joking."

DePons held his gaze. "Fain must've known," he said.

"He never told me anything," Morvran replied. "And now that he's gone, we'll never beat them at this game."

"We might keep them from getting what they want—maybe win back some bargaining chips in the meantime. We might even be able to undo their plans, Thaddeus, or turn them against each other, and thus endure a little longer."

"And you want Taran to help you do this?"

"What choice do we have?" DePons asked. "Without him, we'll never regain the girl. He's all we have, and I'll need your help to get to him."

"Why? You know where my young housebreaker is hiding?"

"The question is not if I know, but if they also know. It's only a matter of time."

"What are you saying, Cedric? That Taran's now an interest to them?"

DePons turned a grim look on his friend. "I have no reason to doubt that they have known longer than you or I about the Morvran family and its secrets, Thaddeus. You have obviously never used the stone yourself, yet someone's disappeared. It doesn't take a genius to figure out what's happened. Taran is the heir, and he's the one they will be looking for. If he had not gone underground when he did, I fear he would already be in their hands."

"He's safe, then?"

"I have someone watching the group he's taken up with. I'll set up a meeting, and we'll pick him up directly. In order to make this less stressful for Taran, I want you to be there."

"I don't know how much I can help, Cedric. I'm probably responsible for some of the poor choices he's made."

"Don't listen to Naruna," DePons said. "He's found a way to get to you, to make you realize that you have no place in his game. So what? He's no more than a pawn himself."

"Even so, he did have a point," the professor replied. "I made it too difficult for them both. I thought they weren't ready for what Fain wanted to show them, and I failed to warn them. I failed my own son, Cedric, and he felt compelled to leave."

DePons rested a hand on his shoulder. "I seem to recall another Master Morvran vanishing from his home—after Fain revealed his secrets to you at *my* bidding. You didn't fail Taran. We both failed him. So, will you come with me?"

"I will go with you to the city, though I doubt much good will come of it—and it won't be easy for Mrs. Morvran!"

"Is that all you're worried about?" DePons asked with a smile. He threw an arm around the professor and ushered him away from the grave, even as the workmen approached to bury the empty casket.

"Taran's in New York?" Mrs. Morvran bellowed. "He's in the *city*? I thought you said he was living with his Aunt Moire! How long have you kept this secret, Art?"

Thaddeus winced at hearing his middle name again. The two men had stopped by the house long enough to explain that the professor had to leave within the hour. Mrs. Morvran didn't pleasure Mr. DePons with her usual cordiality. She was ruffled enough by all that was happening to suspect her husband was up to something, and would have been happier if Thaddeus stayed home—that is, until he told her that he was going to New York to see Taran.

"I sent him to the city two months ago," Thaddeus said. "I didn't want to tell you until he was settled, Marge. I set him up with a publisher's office, and for awhile he seemed to be doing well. It wasn't much, but he needed to get out of here. He was working for small pay; but the business must've flopped. I'm going there to see to it he's back on his feet, and when I come home we'll take a little trip."

"And how does Taran being in trouble amount to us going on a vacation to Moire's?"

She put down the chicken she was preparing and faced him, crossing her arms, a gesture which surprised Mr. Morvran almost as much as the use of his middle name. It wasn't like her to be so hostile; but then, she was naturally perceptive.

25

"I was just now informed by Mr. DePons that Dr. Westrom's daughter is getting married," he answered with a nervous smile, gesturing to Cedric. DePons stood by with his hands folded behind his back. He did not seem inclined to speak.

"You remember Violet?"

She turned in silence and began sliding spices beneath the chicken's loose skin. The professor watched her for a moment, and then he said, "Well, she's agreed to come by today and help you pack for our trip."

"Talia came by while you were out," she replied. She spoke without turning, but Thaddeus could hear the strong emotion in her voice.

"She told me she was forbidden to visit anymore," Marge said.

"Don't you worry," he replied. "Violet will keep you company until I return. And if that pompous fool Naruna shows up, I have no doubts you are capable of standing up to *him*."

She turned her head slightly, and he saw that she was smiling again.

"Taran will be alright," he consoled. "I will tell you all about it on our trip."

"Yes, you will," she replied in a firm voice. "You had better leave at once to go and see to it that our boy is set straight. I have enough trouble with the other one, with his talk of joining the Army—no offense, Mr. DePons."

"I shall make Taran write a letter to you before I return," Thaddeus replied. The two men turned and left.

3

STEALING A THIEF

New York City,
A.D. 1901

Taran had indeed fallen on hard times. He wouldn't give up looking for Val, though he searched the surrounding woodlands and the town from May to the end of June. His father brought him away to the University and had set him up with work, but that soured quickly. Taran's mind was never on task. Though he was promised they would never stop searching for her, he knew that Val was still alive, and he couldn't care less about anything else. With no way to find her, though, he despaired.

He was turned out of his job, and left his campus apartment the same day with only a change of clothes. Taran didn't wonder if his own disappearance would eventually be hailed back home as a sign of his involvement in Val's. It made him sick to imagine the cruel eyes of Colonel Naruna reading along a newspaper column to find even a shred of evidence against him. He had treated Taran like a criminal on the loose. If that's how the Colonel truly felt, it wasn't very kind; but it might have been prophetic. He only wanted to disappear, like Val, and a life of petty theft seemed big enough to hide under.

It soon became clear that disappearing in New York would not be a problem, though his conscience would make trouble enough. So Taran discovered that his moral sense sharpened even as he violated it, like those senses that sharpen when night steals away the use of one's eyes, and becoming invisible to others he discovered that it was not easier to hide from himself the things that he did.

A month went by, and when it was over few of his former acquaintances would have recognized him. Though it pained him, he threw himself into this transformation with a will, for it was only in being knocked about on the streets that he felt he had disentangled himself from the past, and from Val. Once in awhile, he almost allowed himself to forget about her entirely. It was impossible, though. Somehow, Val had become his conscience; if lost for a time, she was never completely forgotten.

Thieves do not work alone, and Taran did not desire to make friends, yet there were others who relied on him for sustenance and secrecy. Such is a thief's world. His most common acquaintance was a young woman named Drusilla, a close confidant of the Big Man, the fellow for whom he had twice robbed the houses of wealthy folk. The Big Man liked Taran, because Taran was smart—he knew what to look for, and had a knack for finding more valuable possessions. Taran had brought the Big Man some antiquities from the last house he burgled, and that made him important in his present company.

Taran hated robbing houses, though. He dreaded thinking what might happen if there was someone at home when he broke in, and for this reason he carried no weapons. In his heart he knew that what he was doing was wrong, and that he would eventually be shot or arrested. When he finally was arrested, he explained to a judge that he only wanted food, and that he had chosen to lose himself in acquiring necessities like food in dangerous ways. What troubled him most was that he could not explain to himself why he felt this need to disappear, or what he was proving by choosing a dangerous path. He did not wish to examine his deeds too closely, for fear that the kinder heart of his youth would reemerge and shame him.

It was the shame he felt after his first hearing that prompted him to assault an officer and make his escape. Shame, it seemed, was not a virtue in itself. Then again, neither was anything else that he did.

There was no real meaning in the path he now walked, though there was a pattern. Previously, his entire life was ruled by a purpose. He did not yet suspect that this purpose still held him, and would not let him go so easily. Nor did he admit to himself the quiet nagging doubt that told him his purpose had something to do with the stone he gave to Val. Never in his wildest dreams would he have come to guess that his adventures were only beginning, because it felt to him like his life had come to an end.

And that is how he came to be living under the bridge.

Taran thought of the Big Man's girl as a sister. Drusilla treated him like trash, but she was the only one whom he trusted—almost. He told her where he lived, which was either unwise or hopeful, but probably both. So it was that she was the only person in New York who could find Taran on any particular day. Presently she found him asleep on the pile of filthy blankets he called his bed, housed deep in the darkness under the bridge he called home. She was usually sent to wake him up around noon, but he had been out late the previous evening while luring the policemen away from his lair. It was mid-afternoon when she popped her head in through a narrow culvert in the wall.

"Get up, you lazy mop-headed toad!" she greeted.

Taran yawned and stretched, and flinched when his face was struck by a soft glob that dripped from above. Something was dribbling down through a crack in the ceiling, and had wet the front of his shirt. For a moment a peculiar double vision dazzled his eyes, and he saw another place before him. It was a kind of dark tunnel that dripped, and there were tall diamond-shaped doors on either hand. A sense of danger thrilled through him, and he sat up sharply; but then the vision faded. He saw a face in the dark by the culvert, a face framed in wild hair.

"Lazy!" Drusilla said, louder now. She thrust a candle through the mouth of the culvert before her, and Taran was saddened to see the puffy bruise around her eye. He suspected the Big Man hit her when he was drunk—which was often.

"You okay?" he asked.

"Shut up, Toady!" she hissed. "You think I can't stand a little beating? You gonna tell me that I'm a lady, and that ladies ought not to be hit?"

"Something like that," he replied, sitting up and wiping the glop off the front of his shirt. "One day you'll meet a real nice guy. He won't hit you."

"I can't stand it, you're so nice," she said, and spat on the ground. "You up yet?"

"What time is it?"

"It's three o' the clock. I'm late comin' here. Police walkin' round your house like they lookin' for somethin' they lost."

"Great. If you'd come any later, Drus, you wouldn't have been able to get in. I lock the grate about four to keep out the rats."

Drusilla smiled. "You sayin' I'm a sewer rat? An' what does that make you?"

"I don't know. What am I supposed to do tonight?"

"Nothin' for the Old Man. The police still lookin' for you. You supposed to lay low until nightfall. Then you goin' to this place."

"A house? I told him, I don't like robbing houses."

"Well, you goin'," she said, stabbing a folded piece of paper in her hand with the butt-end of the candle. She crawled through the culvert and handed him the page. Taran took it, and the candle, and unfolded what was probably a map.

"Anything I'm supposed to look for?" he asked, squinting at the page. There was nothing clearly visible on it. The Big Man liked to write in pencil, and the marks were too faint to see in the light of a candle.

"You'll read it outside," she answered. "He says you'll find what you're lookin' for on the page."

"I doubt it. Whatever I'm looking for can't be found in this world, Drus."

"You crazy," she muttered, and leaving him the candle and the map, she crept back through the culvert and disappeared into the darkness. Taran watched her fade away, and shook his head sadly.

"Maybe I am going crazy," he said to himself.

When she was gone, Taran tucked the map into the pocket of his pants and changed into his only other shirt. He then took the trouble to move his pile of blankets farther away from the crack that was dripping in the ceiling. Examining it in the light of the candle, he was relieved to see that it was only rainwater thickened by some kind of reddish algae. He wondered about the dream he had glimpsed upon waking. There were no tunnels or diamond-shaped doors under the bridge. The vault he was in was a cavity in the foundation, accessed by a grate.

After a meal of dry bread and a bottle of boiled water, he exited his lair by the grate, and paused to look back through the culvert into the darkened cell. There was nothing inside that he felt attached to.

"Why do I get the feeling I'll not be back?" he wondered.

He left the extinguished candle by the grate, which he locked, and combing his hair with grimy fingers he stepped out onto a little path that led up towards the busy streets along the river. There were indeed a few helmeted police officers about, but no one seemed particularly interested in one more tramp standing by the water. That alone gave him a small feeling of vindication. As a tramp he was one of many. He was invisible. He could disappear into the crowds, and that was just the way he liked it. Little did he suspect that this desire to remain unseen was rooted in his purpose. He would have to learn harder lessons yet before this became obvious. For the time being, Taran felt a strange kind of freedom that only the homeless truly appreciate. He smelled the air, detecting among all its strange aromas the scent of sausages, and decided that he would *buy* something to eat tonight, which he did as often as he could. It seemed important to him that buying his food took precedence over stealing it, and there was change in his pocket tonight—change from someone else's purse, of course.

The noisy bustle drew him into the crowds, and he was off. While he crossed the bridge and headed south along the street, Taran thought of all he had gained by his twisted fate. Theft had given him a place to live, and new companions, though he could have improved upon both. The Company—or the Troop, as they liked to call themselves—was a small band of crooks. They shared what they could find in richer men's pockets. In a time of corruption in the den of despair, it was a kind of living, and not much different from publishing. The few in Old New York who looked down their noses at the trade most likely did so from the prospect of the standards and principles that stood them on loftier grounds, upon their success, which in turn was the source of his income. It was a system forged in most ancient times, and was not likely to change soon—certainly not if the Big Man could help it!

He kept his face downward-turned, avoiding the sharp glances of the men of the watch. He did not fear falling into their hands, now that he knew escape was possible; but they did make him feel unsettled. He almost wished things could have turned out differently, that he could be like one of the flock the police guarded from wolves like himself. The thought that he was regarded as someone dangerous actually filled him with fear, for stealing had not left him completely impoverished of morals, nor of the knowledge of good and evil. Taran suspected that was even true of people like the Big Man.

Horses and hacks clattered by on the cobblestone streets. Taran unfolded the map. The sun was still high in the west, since it was then late summer, and in the daylight he was shocked to see that he hadn't been given a map at all. It was a letter, and it was addressed to him. He was on a busy street, yet despite the danger of being spotted by police he stopped to read. The loopy handwriting spelled out words that he would regret before the day was over.

11 August, 1901.
Taran,

I will meet with you tonight. Your colleagues (a rustic bunch—it would do you good to choose better company) have assured me you will be contacted this very day. I've made it clear to them that they had better not contact you henceforth, and as that would be difficult for them to arrange from their new vantage behind prison bars, I am afraid you are out of work once again.

Perhaps you are wondering why you should not tear up this letter and choose to do things your own way? I remind you that none of us chooses the good or evil that will befall us. We can only choose to meet our lot in life, Taran, and do with it what we can. It is time for you to pick up the pieces of your tragedy and do something better with them. If you do not believe that Val is dead, you show it in strange ways.

I know that she lives. Does that surprise you? I also know that you've given her the stone amulet. Her disappearance and the stone are linked. The stone has whisked her away, Taran. It was a stroke of good fortune, whatever you may believe, and now I've begun my own search. I think there is a way to call our lost lamb home, and that is what I want to speak to you about.

If you would be so good as to come out of hiding, I will inform you of some honest work with which you could assist me. It involves travel to Europe. You will labor beside my associate, Mr. Cedric DePons, whom you have already met. And though it is against my better judgment, there is something else which integrity begs me now to share with you, which concerns my life's work and the Morvran Family Legacy.

Your loving Father

"I don't believe it," Taran muttered. "But how could he find me out here?"

"He sent us to do that," said a voice behind him.

Taran turned, and saw a policeman standing behind him. Beside the officer there was a man in formal attire. Taran immediately recognized his face, and his slicked-back black hair.

"Mr. DePons!" he said, his own face growing pale with dread. The recognition of DePons had brought with it a sharp memory of the night of Val's disappearance.

"Taran! You look...well."

"How in the world did you find me?"

"You Morvrans aren't easy to keep track of, but you'll recall I once worked as a detective of sorts."

"So you said."

"Your father and I set up this meeting."

Taran wondered if he should try to run. He supposed the police had as much to do with this meeting as anyone else.

"It's alright," DePons said. "You aren't in any trouble. I discovered your whereabouts last week. The details are unimportant."

"And what about him?" Taran asked, nodding towards the policeman. He'd been preoccupied by the officer, his eyes glued to the man's every move. Last week, he'd assaulted this same officer to make his getaway after the hearing.

"I'm off," the policeman said. "Have a nice evening, gents; and stay out of trouble young man!"

Taran's jaw dropped as the man walked away, never once looking back.

DePons said, "It was a nasty knock on the head you gave him, but no harm done. No hard feelings, either."

"But, what about the—"

"The stolen property? It turned up in the possession of another man. Once returned, the offended parties didn't care so much who took it, or how you got into their houses. They dropped the charges when the situation was explained. The *Troop* has gone to prison for the thefts they ordered, and you were an agent of the law hidden among them, instrumental in bringing them to justice."

"Me?"

"We couldn't have done it without you, or so the story goes. Will you come with me?"

"What happens if I don't?"

"Then you will no longer be under my protection. There are some powerful people who think you had something to do with Val's disappearance, Taran, and your father and I cannot stop them from pursuing the course of Law."

"You mean Colonel Naruna?"

"If you come with us now, we will do what we can to protect you, just as we were able to help you out of your current difficulties."

Taran remained silent, for he knew he was trapped. There was a sound of footsteps behind him, a familiar stride, and a familiar voice that said, *"You face a difficult choice, Son."*

Taran knew his father's voice, and turning he saw him exiting a storefront nearby. He felt a momentary flood of relief before blushing red with shame.

DePons immediately turned and began walking down the street, and Mr. Morvran fell into step beside him. The two passed him by without a word. Taran hesitated a few moments, and then he quickly followed.

"It was foolish, Taran," the professor chided. "You might have been hurt. Tell me, how did this happen, this transition into a *criminal?*"

He did not turn to face him as he spoke. Gazing at his father's back, Taran sighed, saying, "It's complicated."

"You mean you can't rationally explain it, or that you're too embarrassed to share the details?"

"Take your pick."

"Indulge us," DePons said. "We got you out of this, after all."

"Well," Taran began, "one day I had a job, and the next day I didn't. So I went to a coffee shop and ordered a piece of pie at the counter."

"You stole the pie?" DePons asked.

"I never got the chance. Some guy got up and immediately accused me of lifting another man's five-penny tip. I left in a hurry when someone shouted for the police."

"You ran?" his father wondered.

"I was surprised. Nothing like that had ever happened to me. The police seemed to be following me everywhere after that, but I was just scared. Still, I had to eat, and I felt like I had some justification, so I lifted fruit from a vendor."

"And how did the gang become involved?"

"Some other thief saw me stealing, and took me to a man who promised to protect me if I stole things for him. Things kinda went downhill from there."

"Well, how about I get you a better job under real protection—or has stealing become too easy?"

"It's not like that, Father. But what could I do? I mean, I'm not looking for a lot of money, but the city's no easy place to find gainful employment."

The professor turned then, and quickly shoved a fat envelope into Taran's hand. They resumed walking. Taran tucked the envelope into his pocket and stared ahead, numbed, as he felt the wads of banknotes inside. With trembling fingers he counted the bills, turning his head only twice—once to glance down and see the denomination of the notes, and again to see if anyone had spotted him; and then he realized that it did not matter. He would not be going back to the bridge tonight, not with over ten *thousand* dollars in his pocket.

"What's with the money, Father? Where'd you get it?"

"It's ours," DePons replied.

"It's the Foundation's," Mr. Morvran clarified. "There's also a ticket."

"A ticket?" Taran wondered. He shuffled his fingers through the pile of bills again and detected the thick cardstock on the bottom.

"It's a mail-steamer ticket," the professor said, "first-class, aboard Olympic."

"*Olympic?*" Taran said. "What's so important in Europe? And how in the world did you get the police to agree to all this?"

"It's not something to discuss in the street," Mr. Morvran replied, slowing his pace.

"We could get a room with some of this."

"Yes, and that's where we're headed now; but even a room's not safe, Taran. The business we're in is something of a secret."

"So it's not less dangerous than stealing," Taran replied sharply. "How does it involve Val?"

DePons turned his head and flashed Taran a withering look. "Hush!" he whispered. "Even if you can't imagine a better life than sweeping streets, chimneys, and other men's pockets, you might now be decent enough to listen when you're spoken to! We don't know who might be watching—"

"What do you mean? You make it sound as if we were in some kind of danger."

The two men ahead of him shared a silent glance.

"This isn't about antiquities or physics, is it?"

"I seem to recall," Mr. Morvran replied, "you were quite fond of history and science yourself—before you started a life of crime."

"I was dragged through every one of your boring journals, and forced to learn eight ancient languages," Taran retorted. "You killed my love of history by trying to make me a historian—by trying to make me into Fain!"

"What are you going on about?" DePons replied hotly. "He made you the most overqualified crook on the circuit!"

The men laughed, keeping their backs turned towards Taran's unhappy glare. DePons glanced back only after a long moment, and riled by the look he saw on Taran's face he decided to continue his jibe.

"Well, let's look at it from your perspective, then. You can't get a job in any useful profession in this town. First question they ask is, 'what are your qualifications, sir?', and then you've got to say, 'Oh, let's see. I can organize notebooks. I can draw little pictures of jars and bowls really well. I can point out the location of all the ancient kingdoms of the Egyptians on a map of the Nile and recount the history of a myriad extinct cultures and civilizations. And, oh, I can speak to those who've been dead for thousands of years. Besides this I am also well versed in nineteenth century physics and astronomy.'"

"What's your point?"

"His point," Mr. Morvran said, "is that if I was able to get you a job with that publisher, you could have gotten a job in antiquities—or anywhere else, for that matter."

Taran squinted at his father as though he had just suggested he fly to the moon. "There are no jobs in antiquities. Just *professorships*. It's the new wave. You study and study until you've stopped doing useful things, and then you teach other people how you did it."

"And what you've been doing this past month is useful? How, may I ask?"

"I'm not becoming *you*," Taran fumed. "I don't care about your life's work, Father. I've already messed up my own."

"That's where you're wrong," Mr. Morvran said. "You *didn't* fail. You succeeded where all others failed, and you showed true spirit!"

"I built an airplane. Big deal! Someone was bound to do it!"

"There's much more to it than that, and you know it. Really, Taran, your antics would have your mother in tears!"

"Mother doesn't know?"

"Of course she doesn't know; but she will be getting a letter from you before you leave the country."

"So you're sending me off to do what? To tidy up some notebooks with Dr. DePons here? And what's this preposterous attempt at coddling my interest by taunting me with some kind of *family legacy*? The only family legacy I've ever known is farming, and look where that's got us!"

The two men stopped walking. Professor Morvran turned to face his son, and said, "It has to do with the amulet you gave to Val. It's special."

"So, am I going to Europe to find Val, or to find your amulet? And how are we supposed to find anything from three thousand miles away?"

"You don't care to find her?"

"I'm past that, Father. She's lost—and I wish I was, too."

Thaddeus placed a firm hand on his son's shoulder. DePons walked a few steps away, scanning the street for watchful eyes.

"Please understand, Taran. Val's disappearance was more than a vanishing trick. The Foundation, the group that funds my work at the University, is giving us a lot of money to help find her. That is a noble gesture, don't you think? You *will* go to Europe, to our family's old estate, and there you will assist Dr. DePons, whose forensics talents will lead us in the right direction."

"And what's the Army got to do with this?" Taran asked.

"Do you see me wearing a uniform?" DePons asked.

"DePons isn't under Army command," Mr. Morvran explained, "though he is in command of some of the Army's most valuable assets."

"He's a contractor or something?"

"With your father's help, I develop technology for future weapons," DePons said quietly.

"At the lab in the university?"

Again the two men shared a troubled look.

"There was an accident at the lab," Mr. Morvran replied. "It was destroyed shortly after Val's disappearance."

"The Army has accepted a plan for us to set up a laboratory on the Morvran estate," DePons said. "It's an island, and it's secret."

"A secret island lab? I don't suppose Mother knows about this, either?"

"Of course not!" Morvran said, almost shouting. "Do you think I want to send her into conniptions?"

DePons was smiling.

"You will go to the Location and work with Dr. DePons, Taran."

"Can't I go home for a little while first?"

"It would be most dangerous for you to return home now. Naruna has his eye out for you. As a matter of fact, I'll be selling the house and moving your mother very soon. She doesn't know that yet, either, so we'll leave all mention of it out of your letter."

Taran felt a chill rising in his stomach, and wished he was very far away. Strangely, he was not comforted by the realization that his wish was about to come true.

"It isn't because of me that all this is happening, is it Father? Is it because I gave that stone to Val?"

"It's the result of a number of factors, not least of which stem from my own choices. Don't you worry about it! For the time being, think of this as a chance to find a new life in a new world."

Taran gave his father a deep look. A feeling came to him then that he had really turned a corner. A new adventure was beginning, and at the end of it was hope. Maybe not the hope of seeing Val again, but it was hope of something.

"I suppose I should thank you, Father," he said. "Considering the circumstances of my arrest, and the consequences; but I'm still not sure about all this."

"Wouldn't it be nice, Son, to really believe in your work?"

Taran was lost in silent thought a few moments. Then DePons snapped his fingers and leaned his head towards the road, indicating an urgency to get moving again.

"You'll be going without me," Mr. Morvran said as they walked side by side.

"You'll come eventually?"

"Of course! And DePons, too. In the meantime, we've got a mess to clean up here."

"Wait, if neither of you are coming with me, how am I to know where to go?"

"You will meet my assistant tomorrow morning before Olympic casts off," DePons said. "You will be well cared-for. Don't worry."

"I'm worried," Taran said. "I've never been anywhere before, and you're sending me first class on the world's best steamship for a foreign port and an island with a secret lab."

Thaddeus wrinkled his nose in deference to Taran's rakish essence. "If that's a first-class ticket," he said, "then we've got some work to do before you leave!"

4
FACTIONS

Jerusalem,
A.D. 2006

He stared down on the row of stones and smiled. If the smile
he wore was mostly amusement, at least one small part was
nostalgia. After all, the artifacts in this room were things he
had a personal connection to as a boy. Now, as a man, they
still stirred memories; but the significance attached to them by
others was downright silly.

"Who would have thought, of all things, that *these* would
survive?" he asked himself quietly. "Even the old crackpot who
made them would have laughed!"

"What was that?"

Shubalu turned towards the voice and saw a woman standing beside him. Her presence surprised him a little, for though she was wearing high-heels he hadn't heard her coming. He noted the heels and her excessive makeup with mild curiosity. And who could miss her ridiculously short black skirt? He was not intended to miss the skirt; indeed, every detail of the woman's physical appearance cried out for his attention.

"Sorry. I was talking to myself. I do that sometimes."

"Ugly stones, aren't they?" she asked.

Shu looked away from the woman's short skirt and eyed the contents of the knee-high platform before them. Eight basalt standing-stones were arranged in a gentle semicircle, flanked on the right by a small stone lion carved from a solid block, and on the left by a seated figure. Between the seated figure and the lion, in front of the stones, there was a rough basalt slab—an offering table. It was, as the display announced, an arrangement of sacred objects found in a chapel of the Lower City of Hazor.

In *his* Lower City, not far from the spot where he looked on battle for the first time.

"This whole hall is for Hazor?" the woman asked.

"Mostly. There are other things, like the anthropoid coffins along the wall on your left. They're rearranging the museum, you know."

"Makes it difficult to find what you're looking for when people keep moving things around," she replied. "At least some stones are easy to find. You're Israeli?"

Shu kept his eyes on the display. Her questions were not idle chitchat.

"I guess so," she said, answering herself. "I can tell from the accent. You can also tell from mine that I'm not."

"It *is* Israel," he said, allowing a little gruff annoyance to leech into his words. "It is, in fact, the *Israel Museum*. Should you not expect there to be Israeli's here?"

"I was just curious," she said, and walked away.

This time Shu heard her heels clicking loudly on the dark slabs. He rubbed a hand through the stubble on his head as she walked towards the display of anthropoid coffins to his left. Was he being too suspicious? Like everything else in that room, it was a matter open to interpretation. Just as he had smiled and laughed at the significance they tied to the cultural artifacts displayed before him, others would undoubtedly laugh at the significance a living leftover from that culture tied to a strange woman's questions.

Probably she was one of Lír's people, but he had come here to meet with an old friend, not the usual contact. Either way he had missed something, and he was getting nervous. He couldn't understand what they were waiting for. So he stood still and stared at the standing stones, and he smiled. He smiled because *this* was something he understood quite well, though no one else did, and that gave him a feeling of confidence. Wasn't that always the way with things these humans felt attached to?

Was he becoming more like them?

How could it be avoided? He was, in fact, half human himself. The only real difference was that he had been in the black water, and his life would be sustained indefinitely—at least until he was slain. Like the monstrosities displayed around him on the glass shelves, he was an artifact, a relic of something that could no longer be understood for what it once had been; but he understood, and that was how he knew.

He was also *Gremn*.

Daylight streamed in through the opaque windows behind the display, highlighting a particulate rain of dust in the air. Shu fixed his attention on the stones in front of him, and particularly on the seated figure, trying to discern the features time had eroded. The face that once was proud looked less kingly now. The gilding and ornaments were gone. He was so engrossed in reverie he wasn't aware that someone once again stood beside him. Turning slightly, the figure bumped his elbow.

"Sorry," said a voice. Shu knew this voice, and the man to whom it belonged.

"It's good to see you, Shimeon," he said, turning.

"In the flesh," Shimeon replied, offering a hand. Shu took it, and pumped his arm a couple times in greeting.

"Sorry I'm late," Shimeon began. "Zabli couldn't verify your identity. This is her first time out, so we're teaching her the tricks of the trade."

Shu looked towards the anthropoid coffins, but the woman in the black skirt was gone. "*Zabli*, huh? I thought you worked alone."

"They're one of *his* pet projects," Shimeon said, beaming. "Zabli's special. I took her on as a favor to him."

"So you owe him favors, do you?"

"I don't owe anything to anybody, Shu."

Shu raised his eyebrows at this.

"Don't give me that look," Shimeon said. "You've worked with me yourself. You ought to know."

"Oh, I know; but that was long ago, Shim. I was just thinking that she looks a lot better than I do. You might not owe anything to anybody, but you certainly thought you owed something to *yourself*."

Shimeon laughed aloud, and clapped Shu on the back. "You're right!" he said. "She does look a lot better! And she's not some measly half-breed, like you."

"She is *Féth...Fiada*," Shu pronounced in a halting fashion.

"You've been practicing your native tongue, Shubalu! Yes, in the Old Words the power to change was called *mist-lording*. Zabli's a shape-changer, a more versatile agent than those who must learn to deal with security while wearing only *one* face and form."

"We all have talents," Shu replied. "You said it yourself; she couldn't identify me. So, what've you been up to now that there are no more Romans to fight? I was in shock when I received your coded message. I haven't seen you in so long—"

"There is always someone to fight," Shimeon replied. "Look, they were good times while they lasted. We're still okay, right? I only wish you'd seen it through."

Shu looked away, and he stuck his hands deep in the pockets of his jeans. Shimeon frowned, and looked at his feet. He was a big man with a wide face. This was his favorite shape—one he'd worn for two thousand years. Back then, as now, everyone in the country was a soldier. The memory of standing with Shim in battle stirred strange sentiments in Shu. He looked up again, regarding his friend from the well of deep memory that all the Gremn share, and struggled to keep his mind on the impersonal aspect of the business at hand.

"Well, Mr. Bar-Kochba?" he asked. "What's Lír got to say?"

"I will be brief. I know that you have a plane to catch in Cyprus—"

"Still trying to keep one step ahead? You'll never catch *him.*"

Shimeon looked up shyly. "We don't need to fight each other, Shu," he said.

"Of course not, Shim. I'm not a Roman. Then again, I'm not exactly a Gremn, either. Just a *measly half-breed,* like you said."

"It was meant in jest," Shimeon said in submissive tones. "Do you want to hear what I've got to say, or—"

"It was not in jest that *he* plotted to divide the Gremn from each other," Shu snapped, surprising himself by the anger stirring deep inside.

Shim frowned. "Shu, it's ancient history. It happened long ago. Besides, he's done nothing short of a miracle in trying to reunite the factions since then."

"History doesn't just *happen,* Shim, and you know it. Everything that's *happened* was carefully orchestrated. There's no coincidence. Lír set out to bring war between the two factions so he could push his own plan forward. He unites only those who think the way he does so that he can fight everyone else."

"You think he wanted war with his own kind all along?"

"Are there factions?" Shu asked.

Shimeon blinked, offering an innocent uncomprehending stare.

"There are, Shim, and those factions produced human governments that serve the purpose of continuing our war. I was born in Canaan, whose people suffered greatly because of the Gremn infiltration."

He waved his hand at the idols arranged in the display.

"Among the Gremn, powers are consolidated and reconfigured meticulously. We've all had lots of time to make our plans, and to carry them out personally over centuries. These people lived in a much smaller frame of reference, and Lír took advantage of them without mercy. Think of all the human governments on this planet that were contrived to serve his purpose—like Rome. You and I fought against that one together, Shim, and we lost."

"I have not forgotten it."

"The Crodah have no history of their own, Shim. Neither do we. He began it all, and I *hate* him for what he's done. We're all just tools in his war without end!"

"There is an end to all things, Shu."

"Yeah? Like there was an end for *Ard Morvran*? All Lír ever wanted was the thing he carried, and since he's lost it he would kill all the rest of us to get it!"

"It's not the same thing!" Shim said in a tense whisper. "Where'd you hear about that, anyway? That was long before your time!"

"Someone told me."

"Your uncle doesn't know the whole story, Shu. He wasn't there; and I never mentioned all that to you when we worked together."

Shu stared.

"Shu, where did you hear the name, *Ard Morvran*? Did DePons tell you?"

Shu shook his head, and after a long pause Shimeon checked the room again. "You know who he was?" he asked.

"I know he was Commander of Lír's captured ship. I know all about *Avalon*. After Morvran got away, you were trapped inside with Lír."

"So it's Avalon, eh?" Shimeon asked. "Kabta's finally gone inside?"

"That's what you want to know about?"

"It'll do for starters."

Shu eyed him evenly, unblinking.

"Have I not been fair in trading information with Kabta before?" Shim asked. "I've heard from those you're used to dealing with that you have much to learn about these kinds of negotiations. I promise, what I have to say will leave you in my debt. All I want to know is, has he gone inside yet?"

Shu frowned. "We went inside, but there have been problems with the security system. It's still active, so I suppose the Computer Core wasn't shut down before you left."

"Of course not, Shu, and you would know it if you'd really been inside. The CC codes were known only to Lír and a select few, and once the CC was powered down only those left behind in molecular stasis were given codes that will raise all of Avalon's systems again."

"We found no one. We checked the SARA-station."

Shimeon met Shu's eyes and stared at him quietly for a few moments, and Shu hoped his bluff would not be called so soon.

"Sorry, Shu," he said, "but you're a terrible liar. They're there, believe me, and their dendrites haven't migrated one nanometer in 150,000 years, so they're probably status-recoverable. There was also another person, someone maybe we shouldn't have left. She can answer all your questions, if you ever get inside."

"We're trying."

"Now I know what *you* need," Shim said with a wink.

"Lucky for me you're feeling generous today?"

"Yes, I am! So, you're fishing for anything I can tell you about security, the computer core, access codes, or anything like that."

"You really would tell me all that?" Shu asked.

"You *are* a pup, aren't you?" Shim asked, shaking his head. Then, in a lower voice, he said, "But if you really are going in, there's a manual airlock somewhere on the Command deck—somewhere real close to CAC. Look for the damaged rectangular hatch on the south side. It's the only one damaged, because Avalon was told to ignore it."

Shu stared hard into his face.

"Maybe I want *you* to get inside," Shim said. "Maybe there's something inside that some of us think should not have been left behind, like a message in a bottle."

"And you trust me?"

A cloud passed before the sun, casting a deep shadow across them. The room was still empty, and Shu was not surprised—though he was a little anxious. They'd obviously made sure the meeting would not be interrupted; but Shimeon continually glanced over his shoulder as if to confirm this. Shu turned his head to the left, and caught a glimpse of a female security guard standing on the stairs above the anthropoid coffins. She winked at him. He turned away quickly—he liked her better in a skirt and heels.

"This thing left behind, is it the *person* you spoke of?"

"Yes, Shu. It's a person—but there's something else. There's a *virus*. It was something Magan was working on when we first arrived. You remember Magan?"

"Magan's dead, and I already know about the virus."

"What do you know about it?"

"Its mutated form is carried, but not spread, by both Crodah and Gremn. It was released as a failsafe to assure General Lír's cooperation, since all of the Gremn on this world have already been exposed to it, and all on Iskartum would surely die if it made its way there—"

"Your facts are confused, perhaps intentionally. The mutation of the virus originated on Iskartum, and was accidentally brought back by a team Lír sent several centuries ago. It's the pure form of the virus that's aboard Avalon, in stasis. It's the pure form we need."

"I get it. The virus is a threat to whoever doesn't control Avalon," Shu said.

"Surely Kabta knows this, though the story he fed you reveals his own involvement in the manipulation of the factions. I guess that doesn't seem so surprising to you. After all, he did kill your father."

Shu held back what he was about to say, and hoped that the pause did not reveal too much of his doubts.

"I've already given you something useful," Shim said, digressing. "Maybe you'd like another bit from the worktable, like last time? Perhaps you'd like to know if Lír plans to interrupt your class trip to the bottom of the Atlantic, or why he's moving so many pieces here in the Middle East so soon after you disturbed the Hazor site."

"Why are you willing to tell me anything at all, Shim? You know this meeting is dangerous for both of us."

"I tell you what Lír wants you to know. I also tell you what I want you to know, and that's the way I play Lír's game. I told you how to get inside, and I told you about the virus. One of these pieces of information is a gift from Lír, and one is from me to you—between old friends."

Shu considered this. He suddenly realized that Shim was leading him on to something else—something he might divulge if Shu guessed right.

"Is Avalon a trap?" he asked.

"Listen carefully," Shim said, raising one index finger and lowering his voice to a whisper. "I asked to set up this meeting, and promised that I would pontificate about the virus and try to sway your allegiance."

"It won't happen, Shim."

"I know it, but he still thinks you're important."

"That's ridiculous. I'm a Gremn-Human who can't even do half the job of the least of his agents. You're the one leading him on to pursue me, aren't you? Why?"

"I do speak well of you as often as I can; but it's because I don't want anything to happen to you, old friend. You've been a bit sloppy, I'm afraid, and we've had you followed closely from time to time—close enough for capture."

"And making Lír believe I'd gotten sloppy because I was interested in playing two sides was what kept me alive?"

"Well, it's more than just that. He knows Kabta wants access to Avalon, and that you've acquired a new friend at Hazor who possesses a key that opens the door home. I just put it into his head that you might lead her to us, if we came to you in the right manner."

Shu tried not to show his fear. If Lír knew about Val Anna, it was only a matter of time before he found a way to get to her—with or without his cooperation.

"Avalon leads back to the World of Origins, Shu, and perhaps to the end of this miserable war as well. Comet Bibbu sent a hefty download of information to Avalon this time around, and it's got the old general in high spirits, if you can imagine that."

"The comet?" Shu wondered. "You mean the link?"

"Yes, it was a link Lír set up for his private use, long ages ago. I overheard some of the communication—"

"You mean you were spying on Lír," Shu said.

"Listen! That comet only comes around every hundred and twenty years or so, but when it does it points the way home. That's pretty vital to directing a Viaduct to the World of Origins. Now that we've lost Narkabtu, Bibbu is the last chance we have to find the road home—unless your pretty friend can summon a Viaduct all by herself?"

"The last time we tried that, she was displaced for thousands of years."

Shim nodded. "But she wasn't the one who initiated that transit, I hear."

"How would you know? You were in stasis on Avalon at the time."

"And you didn't even know the Gremn existed," Shimeon said with a grin.

"You're obviously leading me in order to get something, Shim; but I'm telling you, there is no way Lír will take her from us."

"Of course," Shimeon said with a sigh and a smile. "She trusts you! I only wish you trusted me, like you used to. I'm telling you all these things because I am required to, but I did not come here only to do his bidding."

Shu regarded his old friend oddly for a moment.

"You trust Kabta?" Shim asked.

"I trust him. He rescued me, and he has never hidden things from me."

"I trust Lír because he *can't* hide things from me. His communication with Avalon via the comet is something I've used to our advantage."

"You *were* spying on him!"

"I can sometimes tap into what he's thinking, especially when he's in the black water. Avalon's AI resides partially in Lír's mind, or else I'd not have access to his waking thoughts. His dreams are interesting enough."

"His dreams?"

"While the sleeper sleeps, Avalon's consciousness has shared its awareness with the AI of your Uncle's ship at Hazor. I think the two of them have recently been wandering off-world in the mind of your old friend, Kal Nergal."

"You know where he is?"

Shimeon's grin widened. "He's in the World of Origins, and he can help you."

"How?"

"Well, you have two of the stones, and Avalon has a Viaduct Chamber that can fix Nergal's location in the World of Origins. Because he's still connected to the Auriga via the AI, and because the Source is talking to Avalon, Avalon should be able to find Nergal."

"Run that by me again?"

"Look, it's simple. It only requires the cooperation of two people. First, you need the one who holds the stones, someone who is strong enough to bond with them. Then you need another—someone who could link Avalon's AI to Nergal in the World of Origins."

"Who could that be?"

"Weren't you listening? She's the one in stasis, the sleeper in SARA station."

"You're telling me all this for free?"

"Think of it as back-pay from the old days."

"I thought you owed nothing to anybody, Shim."

"I owe you my life, many a time," Shim said, his voice edged with sincerity. "You know this. And chances are, *if* you have access to the stones, and *if* there is another way off this world, you might just pull me out of the fire again."

"What do you mean? Are you in some kind of trouble with Lír?"

Shimeon's smile faded. "You give Kabta my greetings," he said, "and make sure he listens to what I've passed on to you, because even if I'm blowing smoke in your eyes there are those among us who are still capable of seeing beyond *factions*. Maybe you can't, yet. I hope you can at least see that our heads have led us astray far too long. There are many on both sides who're saying it. We still have to think of the future, a future that rests now on your success. All you have to do is get inside, get the sleeper and the stones to the Viaduct Chamber, and she'll do all the rest."

"That's it, huh?"

"Don't get saucy with me, pup. You'll have to make Kabta believe the airlock is the only way in, because it is. If Gremn and Crodah are ever to make it back, and if the Ban is ever to be lifted, you must pass through. You must go in the stead of those of us whose hands are bloodied by this War."

"Right, Shim. It only took us 150,000 years to find a stone and this girl. Now you want me to lift the Ban, too?"

"You'll find a way, because you have *her*, you have the stones, and you have a good heart. Don't worry about Lír. He'll ask how I did, and if I acquired your allegiance. I'll tell him you escaped my wiles."

"Lír's always hiring these days, huh?" Shu asked with a grin. "Tell him I said hi. There's always next time."

"I hope so," Shimeon said, nodding. He now openly wore a vaguely frightened look.

"Next time," Shu repeated. Then he decided to shake Shim's hand once more. Shim gripped his hand tightly, and stepping closer he held out a small electronic tablet. Shu took the device and examined it suspiciously.

"Take this with you, Shubalu," he whispered. "You will need it to access the Viaduct Chamber near SARA station on Avalon. Be careful of that sleeper—she has no love of our kind!"

"Shimeon," Shu said, "He won't let you get away with this when he finds out. Maybe *you* should consider coming with *me*."

"Just hurry!" Shim said. "We'll be watching."

5
DEEP MATTERS

North Atlantic UAMC Facility,
A.D. 2006

Val stood alone in the long corridor of the ship, entranced by the loneliness evoked by her surroundings. The hall ran straight before her and behind her. She chose to keep walking, to keep going forward, as she did every night she dreamed this dream.

Fear stalked her steps, but she eventually ended up at CAC. The hatch was open, but there was no one inside. The CC was active in the forward hub, though, and the Source was aware of her. She tried to hide her thoughts from it, but it spoke directly into her mind.

"Proceed to the Viaduct," it said.

Val obeyed. She walked around the port hub and approached the CSRT, a column-shaped console, and came to a halt in front of a raised ring of rushing light. The Mirror gave off no noise, but radiated an awful sense of violence and turmoil. It was like watching a hurricane trapped inside a soap bubble. Val was terrified that it might open at any moment and draw her inside.

"Proceed," the Source commanded.

An interceding will compelled her to stay, however, and Val's resolve was strengthened. Just as she was thinking of turning around and leaving the chamber, though, she clasped something hidden beneath the folds of her dress—something sharp that was pressed against her thigh. Fumbling through her clothes she removed a knife from its sheath, noting with dismay that it was dripping with blood. Val was repulsed. She wanted to fling the knife away from her, but the blood was already running down her hands. She turned, awakened by a quickening sense of dread, and saw behind her a figure standing in the dim red deck-lights.

"Nunna!" she cried. But as soon as she said it, she thought this could not be so. Though the woman's face was hidden, Val could see that she had long white hair.

The woman ambled unsteadily forward. Her head was hung forward, facing the floor, so that nothing of her features was visible. Val wondered what she was looking at. She turned her eyes towards the floor in time to see something skittering between her feet—something like large centipedes with hard shells on their backs, and with hundreds of tentacles sticking out in front. Several of the creatures were heading towards the Viaduct, and presently they disappeared inside. When they were gone, Val returned her gaze to the woman, who had stopped only a few feet away.

Her face was still downturned, and now Val could see that she was looking not at the floor but at her chest, where blood was spreading downwards in a great black apron across her abdomen. The woman stumbled suddenly, and pressing a hand against her front she moaned. She then lifted her other hand outward blindly, as if reaching for something she knew was there. Val stood her ground, but moved her head back as the woman's fingertips brushed her chin. With that touch, the stranger lifted her face.

"Morla?" Val wondered.

It was Morla; but it was Morla changed. She was more beautiful somehow than before, yet her face was pale—as pale as a corpse's. Her hair flashed silver in the red light, radiance streaming from it in a glorious corona.

"I told you," she said in a hoarse whisper. *"You will be the death of me!"*

Val awoke from the dream in a sweat, her heart pounding. The first thing she did was roll out of her bunk, and as soon as her feet touched the cold metal deck she knew where she was. The room-lights sensed her movements and turned on. She blinked her eyes and went quickly to the footlocker at the end of her bunk. Throwing it open, she tossed aside the neat bundles of clothes until she came to the bottom, and there she saw the knife. She knelt and thrust forth her hand to grasp it, but before she got half-way she paused and looked at her fingers.

There was blood on them.

Val drew back her hand, and grasped it with the other. She rubbed the two together, and then the blood was gone—vanished. Was it all in her mind?

"There is a time coming when there shall be no more secrets between us," a voice whispered.

Val dreaded that voice. She had heard it in her dreams since the day she was a little child. Now it was stronger. Now it spoke to her when she was awake as well.

"I fear that hour of truth, because when it comes the old alliances will be forgotten, and there may be fighting between those of us who are left—a slaughter among friends. You should be prepared."

Val reached into the locker and drew out the knife.

"Brisen?" she asked aloud. There was no immediate reply, though the lights dimmed and flickered.

She sat on the floor and stared at the blade. Cold and brown and grim, it lay in her hand. The length was lesser than her forearm, but it was heavy, being one solid piece of bronze. A curved leaf-shape was the edge, and the hilt bent comfortably in her hand. Where the metal of the hilt joined the base of the blade there was no guard, only a narrow flan. Val gently traced the contours of the ancient weapon with her fingertip, marveling at the keenness of its edge.

Then the air grew close, and her breathing was labored. Something brushed her as it passed through the room—a spirit, perhaps, or a ghost from the past. Val knew her only as Brisen, the Woman in White; but she longed to know who Brisen really was, and why she spoke to her.

"Now we are drawn closer to something that has been hidden from our kind and from the Gremn since the Beginning," the voice said. *"That is surely a secret worth discovering, and you shall discover it."*

"I don't want any more secrets," Val answered, speaking into the air. "Morla said that when we get close, the trap will be sprung. She said it was not a trap of Gremn-cunning, but of some greater evil. Something sleeps in the dark—a Shadow of shapeless malice. It feeds on hatred and strives against unity. I don't have the strength to face such an evil alone!"

"You are not alone."

"My friends have gone on to some other place," Val replied. "Morla is gone and Nunna is dead, and so is Ibni the King. All that is left to me are the Gremn."

"Not even this is a coincidence."

Val gripped the knife tightly. "What if I don't want this job?" she asked. "What if I choose to end my life and be rid of it?"

"You safeguard the past and future of all our worlds by what you protect. If you perish, then the stone's purpose shall never be fulfilled."

The tone was final, unmoved.

"And if I choose to sacrifice myself, the lives of others would be robbed of purpose?"

"It is a perilous road, and a difficult choice. It is the Lost Road, where all of you are joined in purpose. Even while you are apart, you are still trapped within the destiny of the stone. You dream its dreams, as you have always done."

"It dreams of the death of my friend," she replied. A tear ran down her cheek.

"Your friends will find you again; your tasks shall reunite you. You shall regain all that was lost in the Dark Worlds."

"What about Taran? What about my family? I don't even know where I am!"

"Beware," the voice said, fading now. *"Doubts are a weakness easily exploited by the Shadow. Trust rather to our promise, and you will see the Road to its end."*

There was a soft bump as the air handlers turned on. The room-lights flickered again. Val awoke, finding herself in the center of the room on her knees, clutching the knife to her breast. She had tears upon her face, but her mind was clouded. Had she been speaking to someone? Was someone else here? She had dreamed inside a dream, and awakening she knew not which world was real.

While she wondered about this, the room's hatch opened behind her. Val's soul shivered at the creak of the heavy hinges. She lifted her face, still streaked with tears, and was embarrassed to see Shu standing in the corridor.

"Shu!" she said, dropping the hands that held the knife so that it was pressed against the floor. She knew she hid nothing from him by doing this.

"Bal-Ona," he greeted. "Or should I say, *Val Anna?*"

"Val, if you please," she said, wiping her face and covering a bare shoulder. "You're speaking English!"

"Of course. You haven't dressed?"

His eyes had widened perceptibly. Val suddenly realized she was wearing the same gown she wore the day they parted, thousands of years ago.

Wearing Morla's gown, holding Morla's dagger...

She didn't inquire who he was speaking about when he said, "You look like *her.*"

It wasn't something she could respond to, so her attention shifted to Shu's own costume—strange attire by any stretch of the imagination. It was clearly a type of military armor, close-fitting and complicated; but it was nothing like the field-uniform her father had worn. The lower portions of his legs were covered with plates of dull metal, also camouflaged, as were his feet, arms, chest, and hips. Under all this he wore a camouflaged jumpsuit. There was a similar suit stowed in her footlocker, but she'd left it untouched—mostly because she detested the idea of wearing pants again.

"What in the world are you dressed as?" she wondered. "It's like a knight's costume."

"Designed for a different kind of warfare, though," he replied, looking down on his trappings.

"I wouldn't even know how to put it on if I wanted to. It looks like you're ready to be shot out of a canon!"

"Likely so," he said with a grin. "Actually, it's battle-dress, like armor but nicer to wear. It's a blend of nanomaterials, carbon fiber, and a new composite—pretty high tech stuff. It'll stop a bullet or a bomb. I'd like to see you put one on when we have the chance. I'd rest a lot easier knowing you're safe—"

"What's that stamped on the chest?" she asked. "It says UA MARINES. And that other symbol, what's that mean?"

Shu touched the round silver seal opposite the military logo on the right breastplate of his armor. "I'll explain these; but first I want to make sure you're okay."

"If you're worried about the knife—"

"I wasn't worried about that," he replied. "I was thinking that maybe you were finding it difficult to cope with the changes. A lot has happened to you."

She made no answer. They stared at each other in quiet sadness, he standing on the threshold and she kneeling on the floor. Val noted how much taller and stronger he was than she remembered. He was growing some hair, trimmed short on top and shaven on the sides. He was now a warrior, whom she had last seen a frightened boy.

Had she also changed?

Val drew out the dagger and cradled it in her hands.

"It's the same one he used to take her life," she said.

"Her name was Nunna, wasn't it?"

"You remember?"

"How could I forget? She used it to stab my father, and then she came at me, too."

"She knew she couldn't kill him with this. She meant to try and save us."

"She used that to cut my bonds," he said quietly, staring at the blade. "More than that, though, she brought me to an understanding of who and what I am in a way that no one else could. If it wasn't for this knife, she wouldn't have died; and if she had not died, none of us would be free, and Kal wouldn't have done his part. My father would have killed us all down there, for nothing more than vengeance against his brother."

"Morla told me the knife belonged to an assassin who was hired to kill her in her hometown, after she was made chief-priestess there. She brought it with her to Hazor."

"And you brought it through the Mirror?"

"I don't know why. I hope it's no trouble."

"Tell you what," he said. "You keep it for us both, as a memento."

Val nodded, and rising she took the blade back to the footlocker. She laid it among the bundles of clothes, atop the sheaf of papers that Nephtys had given her to read. Her eyes glanced at the cover sheet.

"*Retrospect*," she read, wondering at the irony of the name. When she turned around to face him again she felt suddenly weary, as if a great task had been finished; but she knew there was more yet to be done.

"Better now?" he asked. "I'm sorry it took me so long to catch up with you. I was delayed, tidying up our trail. There are many people looking for you. If you've rested, we're having a meeting to decide what to do next. Afterwards you'll need to suit up."

Val cast a glance aside at her bunk. Its sheets were still tucked neatly under the edges of the mattress.

"Couldn't sleep?" he asked.

"Knowing that we're thousands of feet below the surface of the sea didn't help."

"DePons tells me that you were pretty out of it when you arrived—*totally unresponsive,* as he put it."

"I wasn't feeling well. It's like I'm in two places at the same time. I remember only bits and pieces, starting with the flying machine—"

"Helicopter."

"The *helicopter.* I remember it landed on the deck of a ship. Then there was an island, another flight, and afterwards a boat."

"You were on the boat for a week. You were sick."

She shook her head, dazed. "I guess someone must've been looking after me."

"It was one of the scientists, Hannah Aston."

"Hannah? I do remember speaking to someone while I rested on the boat."

He raised his eyebrows.

"I don't remember what I was saying. Don't worry. If it was anything to do with the Gremn or Auriga, she probably thinks I'm loony."

"Do you remember the descent to this place?"

"Only one thing: a ladder that led into a small vehicle, and a sealed hatch above."

"The ships we use to dive here are special craft that travel submerged. They're called *submarines.*"

Val thought quietly about what he was saying, and then she asked, "These ships travel *submerged*—like an ironclad?"

"No, Val. They are *completely* submerged, just like this station."

"I know we're underwater, but where are we exactly?"

"We're currently docked with a substation complex in the North Atlantic. We call this one *Main Office,* or just *Substation 12.* It is a very secret place."

"I skipped the tour," she replied. "I'm still a little dizzy. I ate and bathed, but sleeping is out of the question. Every time I close my eyes I feel like I'm somewhere else."

"The transition will be difficult," Shu said. "Of course, I've never been through a Mirror myself. Another of our marines, Abdaya, has traveled that way. He says it must've been pretty rough—the device was old, and not in best operating condition. He warned me that you might experience auditory and visual hallucinations. It's called Displacement Syndrome. Don't worry about it, though. Apparently, the effects wear off with time."

"Great," she said, massaging her temples.

"I hope you feel up to a few answers. You really shouldn't worry."

"And you really should try knocking before entering a woman's room," she said, looking up with a smile. "I suppose I'll get my answers first, and then rest."

"Actually, we're ready to make a move today. The others are already here. We're just waiting for you."

"The scientists are here?"

"Yes. They'll be granted an abbreviated counsel; but of yourself and your journey you are specially bidden not to speak while we are in their presence."

"I think I understand," Val said. "It is not known that you are—"

"Mention of the *Gremn,* the Mirror, and the stones is strictly forbidden," Shu replied.

Val placed a hand on her chest. The stone hung on a cord beneath her dress, its warmth spreading like a flame. It seemed aware of her.

"Would they believe me if I told them the truth?" she wondered.

"Their questions and yours will be answered; and yes, they are the sort of people who might believe what you have to say.

Remember, they saw you appear from the side of a buried spacecraft."

"I had almost forgotten. It must have been quite shocking when I came through that way."

The walk down the windowless corridor was not very interesting. There was no roll or pitch, or any sense of movement as there might be aboard a ship. Her dizziness made up for it. As they walked, Shu filled her in on a few other interesting items of information.

"The UAMC is a military organization," he began, "but there's more to it than that."

"UA MARINES," Val said. "That's the logo on your uniform. What's it stand for?"

"*United Aerospace* was a division of the Foundation Technologies International group—that's the people who found you at the Location."

"The people who came in the flying machines?"

"The *helicopters*," he said, stooping under a low bulkhead. "Anyway, the company's interests have made it the target of some pretty aggressive competition. We needed protection, not least because we covet privacy. We forged a relationship with the United States Army and Marine Corps, and in a trade of advanced technology for secrecy and protection we produced a private army—the corporate army of the FTI, which we call the UAMC. It's a small group, but we've got the most advanced weapons ever made by the collaboration of Mankind and Gremn since the days of the War."

"*Wait*—Crodah and Gremn are working together?"

"A lot has happened, because of you. Only a handful on either side knows about it, and the collaboration has almost no chance of long-term success. There are only a few of us who believed it would be of any value from the start—people like Cedric DePons. He became the head of our research division, but he's also the Field Operations Coordinator; hence his code-name, *FOX.* We think he'll be helpful in facing-off with

Lír's group, since he's been doing that for the US Army since the—well, for a long time."

"Oh," Val said, pausing.

Shu stopped beside her and smiled. "I know," he said. "I'm not explaining it very well. I guess I should start with the basics before I get into all the rest, huh?"

They were approaching another hatch at the end of the corridor—a door with a wheel in its center. They stopped, and leaning across her Shu reached for a small metal box mounted on the wall to the left. He pulled down a recessed switch behind a plate covering the box. A hissing and banging sound escaped the hatch in front of them as it cycled through a depressurization sequence. The door did not immediately open.

"Beyond this door is one of twelve laboratories that are run by the Foundation and protected by the UAMC," he said. "Only a few Outsiders know this place exists—Americans, mostly."

"The Army?"

"No. You might run into a few American soldiers on our ships and choppers, but none have ever been down here. Those I was thinking of are members of a secret weapons division within the US government—something that didn't exist in the days of your disappearance."

Val frowned. "My disappearance?"

"Welcome to the future, Val. For those of us who had to arrive upon the long road, this seems just like any other place. Things are about to get a little confusing. I'll try to help you fit in as best I can, but I'm afraid you're in for a bit of adventure—or, a bit more."

He gently rotated the wheel in the center of the hatch and yanked it open. Then, offering his hand, he led her through into a rather strange-looking room she had seen once before. Stepping over the threshold, Val was momentarily arrested by the brilliant lighting. It was warm in here, and the walls were dove-grey in color. There was a strong smell of seawater, for the space in the center of the room was a pool cordoned off by a metal rail. From the water there projected an orange metal tube, which rested close beside a jutting section of decking.

"This is the airlock. The tube there opens into a submersed vehicle cradled below the Station—the same that brought you here yesterday."

"Where do these other hatches lead?" she asked, looking around the room. There were six hatches along the four walls.

"Other quarters," he said, pointing, "the galley, a recreation and exercise area, offices, and public bathrooms—the toilet and showers, I mean."

"A toilet underwater," Val said, marveling. "How far ahead am I? I am *ahead*, aren't I? I'm not in my right time, anyway."

"You are about one hundred years ahead."

"You know this for certain?"

Shu heard the sadness in her voice, and gently he said, "We know your starting point. There is someone with us who was there, who knew your father and Mr. Morvran—and who knew Taran Morvran, your friend."

Val felt sick. "They are all dead?"

Shu looked down the corridor, and then turned to gaze into her face. Val met his silent gaze and suddenly realized that he also knew this kind of pain, and worse.

"I've lived many centuries now," he said, "and I've lost lots of people who were my friends."

Though she felt grief-struck—and even a little angry—she could find nothing to say. She refused to believe that Taran was dead. She still felt him in her heart. He *must* be alive, somewhere.

"The funny thing," he said, bringing her back, "is that we couldn't figure where you'd cross our path again until we knew when you disappeared, and then a stranger came to us who knew of a curious disappearance. The name *Morvran* was tied to the incident. It was a bolt from the blue, as they say. The man was Cedric DePons, the same who directs the UAMC."

"Mr. DePons seems very familiar," Val remarked. "He knew Mr. Morvran, and Taran?"

"One hundred years ago."

"So he's Gremn?"

"Not unless he's able to hide it from us. He looks young."

"And he helped locate me?"

"We knew that Hazor was the place you'd arrive, but the timing was key. As for where you were in the transition of all those years, not even DePons knows for sure."

"I was inside the stones," she said, touching the artifact through her dress.

"Inside?"

"I can't ever go back to my right time, can I? I had hoped—"

"No, Val. That's the problem with displacement. Abdaya or Breaker could explain it better than I, but the basic idea is that there are very few who can use the stones without incurring a displacement. You or I could try to force a Mirror to open wherever or whenever we desire, but we'd probably only end up sending ourselves somewhere else, like what happened when Nergal sent you and Morla out from the *Auriga*. We could end up anywhere, or anytime, and if we dragged the stones with us on the journey—"

"I think that's what I mean," Val said. "It has something to do with purpose. I did bring the stones with me, but I came through the stones instead of the stones coming along with me, if you get my meaning."

Shu glanced aside at her and shook his head.

"I don't really understand it either," she confessed, "but that's what I have heard over and over again in my dreams."

"The stone speaks to you?" he asked quietly.

She hesitated. For some reason, she was reluctant to speak of Brisen.

"Is it strange that they should speak to me?" she asked.

"There are stories about them. I don't know what is *not* strange about the stones and the Mirrors. Even among Gremn, these things are regarded almost as magical. Suffice it to say, it's a wonder you arrived here at all."

"I wonder how DePons knew I would arrive at Hazor when I did."

"I also wonder, but only Kabta knows his story. Now come." He touched her slender arm gently, but it was like touching steel. She did not move.

"I don't want any more surprises or secrets," she said.

"Not everything about this day should be an unpleasant surprise," he replied. "There are friends waiting for you down the hall. One of them has been waiting to see you for a very long time."

That seemed to rouse her again, and Shu pointed ahead of them. There, on the other side of the pool, Val saw that one hatch now stood open. It led to a larger corridor. Shu offered his hand, and together they walked through the airlock, past the pool. Val shivered, for the air above the dark water was chill. She knew that Shu was trying to cheer her heart, but her mood remained grim, and it did not improve much as they made their way along the short corridor ahead. Twenty feet or so past the hatch, they came to a halt before an ordinary panel-door, stained dark red.

"Go in," Shu said.

Val took the knob in her hand and turned it. The door opened silently, so that she could hear low voices speaking. Then everything was hushed. Val looked into an oval room that was set up like an office, though it was larger than any office she had ever seen. Three people sat in overstuffed chairs around a circular table lit cunningly from panels within its surface. The rest of the place was dark. There wasn't much to it except some cabinets and consoles against the near wall. The rest of the walls were curved downwards under the domed ceiling of the substation, sloping gently outwards towards the floor, and there were heavy braces running along all their smooth surfaces.

At first she could not see the faces of those at the lighted table, and this made her a little frightened. Then someone leaned forward into the glow, and Val, recognizing at once that she was among friends, bowed her head in silent greeting. Kabta rose from his place, his face beaming a welcoming grin.

"Our dear lost lamb!" he said.

Across from Kabta the two scientists, Ford and Aston, also rose—though it was immediately apparent by their nervous gestures that they didn't understand why everyone was standing on ceremony for a strange girl dressed in something that looked like a nightgown. Val thought how they must have wondered about her since her appearance at the ship in the ruins, and she was suddenly moved by a desire to befriend them—especially Miss Aston, who had taken care of her on the boat.

Their brief salutations concluded, Shu passed her up and led her to the table. Pulling aside a large chair he gestured for her to sit. She did, and when she was settled Kabta also sat, followed by the two scientists—still exchanging confused glances. Shu did not join them, but walked to the door, which he shut behind him as he left.

Val looked hard into Kabta's face, but he was much the same as before. For Kabta, thousands of years had passed since they last spoke together.

"When we parted," he began, "I was so busy that I must have forgotten to say farewell."

"It's good to see you again," she said. Val was bursting inside to know how he had survived his battle with Nurkabta, his brother, but her curiosity would have to wait.

"You've met Mr. Seijung Ford and Hannah Aston?" he asked.

"Of course. They were on the ship. Miss Aston helped me through the worst of my transition, for which I am very grateful."

Hannah smiled and nodded, but Ford was frowning.

"She sounds American," he remarked.

Kabta looked at Val, and nodded.

"I am," she said to Ford. "I'm from New Jersey, actually."

The scientists could not have looked more surprised. Val smiled sweetly, trying not to appear smug. In her heart she was thinking how she would feel in their situation.

"Her story will take some time to tell," Kabta interjected. "I was hoping we could save all that until we were settled about our current situation, and the tasks for which we have been assembled here."

"That's fine," Ford said. "We'd like to know more about this Station, and about the real work of the Foundation."

"You are already familiar with some of the Foundation's work via your contacts at Columbia University," Kabta replied. "We were first interested in Hannah's work, which was to identify archaeological sites of ancient human cult activities, specifically those established in association with natural electromagnetic anomalies and with clear stellar orientation. Your concurrent development of satellites that could pinpoint magnetic anomalies on the planet's surface—or below it, as things turned out—was more on the application end of things. I suppose you've guessed a little of the Foundation's reasons for investing in both your projects, now that our first task is finished."

Ford and Hannah looked blank.

"You identified candidate Locations for anomalous activities, which led you to the buried spacecraft, and to Val."

"*Is* it a ship?" Ford asked. "But how could you know what it is, if we've only just found it, and if you haven't been inside?"

"Isn't it obvious?" Hannah asked with a glance towards Val. "Someone's been inside. I think the Foundation knew all along that there was something down there, too. What I'd like to know is why you assembled all these resources to find her—your *lost* lamb. If you don't mind me asking, when did you lose her, and how did you know she would appear in such a peculiar place?"

"Such a sharp mind graces you, Miss Aston," Kabta said. "As I recall, your parents exhibited similar intelligence and curiosity."

Hannah recoiled, surprise and fear crossing her face in a single moment.

"Yes, I knew them both personally. The Foundation funded your father's excavations and your mother's quantum research until they also could be taken under our wing. I have to say, their disappearance in these waters was a hard loss to endure. I hope you understand why none of this was ever mentioned to you before."

"Why?" she asked, struggling to recover her poise.

"We were testing technology aboard ships in this location before the habitats were constructed. Locating Val was our primary objective all along, because she has successfully completed a test of those technologies—a test your parents began."

Ford asked, "Are you going to tell us about these experiments, or explain your plans for the stuff being salvaged from the Hazor site?"

"I'll keep it short and simple for now by explaining to you our basic purpose," he answered. "We're bringing parts of a device from the ship here to study. We'd like you to take a look at them with our top engineers and physicists, Mr. Ford. Every bit of the wreckage we recover must be examined in detail, and I'd like you on the team we've assembled for that task."

Ford blinked behind his glasses. "Is it alien?" he asked.

"As far as we know. It could also be something developed by an ancient human civilization."

"You've been experimenting with it for awhile, right? It's this technology that was able to bring a girl from New Jersey to a sealed excavation area under an ancient city. What is it, pieces of a quantum transport device?"

Kabta smiled at him. "Something like that. DePons will lecture you on the finer points. On the off-chance that it was developed by ancient humans, Miss Aston will be busy investigating the ship's cultural origins. I thought that might interest you quite a bit, Hannah. It was something your father was working on."

The scientists didn't return his smile. They looked at one another in silence.

"I need to pose a question," Kabta said. "I'm almost certain that I will get a favorable response, now that you know a little about our work, but it is necessary to ask before all is revealed. Will you two join our efforts here until we have the answers we seek?"

Ford shrugged, "I'm game," he said. "It would be pretty stupid to say no to an opportunity like this."

Hannah Aston looked across the table at Val. "What about her?" she asked. "She's obviously a part of this. What is she, some kind of guinea pig?"

Noting Val's confusion, Kabta explained aside, "It's an animal used in scientific experiments. I think what Miss Aston is really asking is whether or not any of you will be free agents in our association."

He leveled his eyes on Hannah. "As you have no doubt guessed, going home is not the first and easiest option on this table. This is a secret location in international waters, and our work here is known only to select elements of the United States military."

"How do you keep it hidden from satellite and radar?" Ford asked.

"An easy trick," Kabta said. "All will be revealed in time."

"Why would we want to know *everything*?" Hannah asked. "I only wanted to know a few things. I certainly don't want to know it *all*. As long as we don't know where this place is—and no one outside would believe us about a buried spacecraft—I figure we could refuse your offer and go home. Right?"

"Or are you saying that we can't refuse your offer?" Ford wondered. "You wouldn't hold us against our will, like this girl, would you?"

"Val Anna is a close friend of mine, and she is otherwise alone in the world," Kabta said. "Though I am sure she wishes the circumstances brought upon her by past events had left her in a happier place, I am not holding her against her will."

"Then she could leave?" Ford said. "Can we leave any time we want?"

He didn't answer, so the group sat in silence for a moment. Hannah frowned, and said, "If this is a job interview, I'd like to know more about the employer before I agree to any terms."

Then Kabta said, "I have a fierce policy of anonymity, which I've already broken in meeting with you. I just wanted to make things a little less formal; but it's obvious that this level of secrecy is the cost of your protection. There are competitors who would bring you to harm if they knew you were in my fellowship, if only to get to me."

Turning towards Ford he said, "I assure both of you, I have no hostile intentions of holding you against your will. I'm only thinking of your safety. I would have preferred that we could work together, however—"

"Who's saying I won't take the job?" Hannah asked.

"You *will* then? Both of you?"

"Yes," the two said in perfect unison.

"Good," Kabta replied. Then, rising from his place, he walked towards the door and opened it. Shu stood aside, and nodded towards the scientists within.

"You will be briefed again later today," Kabta assured them. "Now you must go and prepare for departure."

"Departure?" Ford wondered.

"You will each be sent to a separate substation to work with other members of our team. They will tell you all you desire to know about our work—about *your* work, I mean. There will also be discussions of financial remuneration, recreation, and all additional benefits."

Ford and Aston rose hesitantly to their feet, each looking to the other for support. Val could see that they weren't the best of friends, and was mildly amused by their uncertainty.

"You'll be just fine," she said, giving them her best smile.

Aston smiled back, and headed towards the door with Ford in tow. After each had shaken Kabta's hand, they exited the room and were met by another armor-clad soldier Val hadn't seen before. Shu shut the door behind them. The sliding bolt clicked loudly, and Val knew then that she was about to get some real answers.

6
GEOMECH

Hannah Aston gripped the edges of her seat and tried to calm down. She wasn't used to being in tight spaces, and the minisub was very small. She had amazed herself when she'd crawled head-first down a deep crumbling hole under Hazor; but now things were different. Now she was caged in a fragile bubble, and the environment outside was as dangerous as outer space.

The more she tried to tune out her fears and relax, the more she was distracted. Claustrophobia brought on feelings of suffocation. The knowledge that there was less air to breathe caused her to breathe more rapidly. Worse still, she knew the feeling she wasn't getting enough air was due to the strange mixture of gasses they breathed. The gasses were not at their normal atmospheric concentrations at sea level; nor were they at the accustomed pressure. That made every sound sharp and tinny—the hissing of valves on the pair of tanks behind her head, the plunking tock of the sonar, and the hum of the sub's rotors vibrating the decking beneath her feet.

Hannah wished they had let her stay with Ford. She shut her eyes and swallowed. Really, this ride along the seabed was as smooth and gentle as the one that had brought her down from the boat. She hoped she wouldn't embarrass herself by passing out. The tall armored man who drove the minisub looked like he would know how to take care of her if she panicked. He hadn't spoken a word since the hatch was sealed.

An anxious half-hour passed. The lights inside were low, and the air chill. The minisub was designed for a maximum of three occupants, but was cramped even for just the two of them. Hannah shifted her legs uncomfortably, and then she heard the sound of the rotors change pitch. They were slowing down.

"We're almost there, Miss Aston," the marine said, breaking silence at last. "You can open your eyes now."

Hannah leaned to her left and tried peering out of a very small round window near her shoulder, but everything outside was dark.

"I can't see anything," she said. The sonar began pinging faster.

"There's another substation above us," he replied. "This one is larger than Station 12, though, and you'll be the only one on board for awhile."

"I'll be totally alone? I'm not qualified to be down here at all!"

"You needn't worry about a thing. You'll see. I'll show you around for a few minutes, and then you can relax."

"What am I supposed to be doing?"

"I'll introduce you to the computer. It'll make sense. Trust me, okay?"

"I'm having second thoughts."

"So have we all. We're here."

He turned off the sonar with the flick of a switch, and shut down the forward rotors. A smaller whining noise vibrated through the floor, but there was no sense of buoyancy. They weren't floating; the belly of the sub was resting on a kind of cradle, which was rising upwards like an elevator. Artificial light trickled in through the sub's windows—light from a room above. Then there was a rumble and a loud clang, and everything was still. Her chaperone squatted upwards from his seat and pulled down a cage that guarded the hatch above his head.

"We'll take a walk and see the sights," he said, turning the wheel to equalize their pressure. "Afterwards, you can take a shower and change."

"And you'll give me some sort of assignment?"

"Not me, Lady," he replied, popping the hatch open and wiping its rim with a rag. "I'm just an equipment warden, and you're a scientist. Down here in Substation 6 you're your own boss. Trust me, remember?"

"Do you have a name?" she asked.

"They call me Breaker, but it's my job to fix things," he replied, offering his hand.

He seemed pleasant enough for a marine. Hannah took the large hand in hers for just a second. There was something unusual about his touch, though, something that made her shiver. Breaker stood up on his seat and lifted his feet to the rungs built into the sub's walls. Reaching upwards, he pulled himself out of the narrow top. Hannah waited for him to clear the hatch, and then she followed.

Everything was identical to Substation 12—identical to her own eyes, at least. The large rectangular airlock was brightly lit, with a pool in the center that had room for several subs to dock. There were closed hatches everywhere, two on each of the long walls and one on either end.

"Watch your step," Breaker said as he knelt by the edge of the pool. He offered his hand again, but Hannah pretended not to see it. She pulled herself up and out of the minisub and flopped indecorously onto the metal decking beside him. As she pushed herself up into a kneeling position, she noticed the docking clamps that kept the minisub from rolling around on its belly while the divers got in and out. If not for such clever devices, Hannah was sure she would've ended up in the freezing water. The water in the pool was only as deep as the sub, though. A metallic pressure door below was raised and lowered to admit the passage of vehicles in the dock.

"How far are we from the nearest substation?" she asked, standing.

"About two miles," Breaker said, rising beside her.

Hannah looked up at his tall form, and wondered how he had ever fit into the minisub. Was he taller now than he looked before, or were disorientation, fatigue, and the stress of travel joining forces to make her loopy?

"I suppose I don't get my own minisub," she said, "as if I'd know how to use it if I did. What am I supposed to do in case of emergency? Swim?"

Breaker smiled. "There's a ring-tunnel that attaches each substation," he said, pointing to one of the doors, "but it's very dangerous to go in there. It would have to be quite an emergency. The corridors aren't protected, and the atmospheric ventilation is very poor. Someone could go in and wait it out until a rescue team arrived, but it's doubtful that a...that *anyone* could make it very far inside the tunnel. It was designed as a conduit for the experiments, and for general maintenance of the habitats."

Hannah looked at him with a worried expression. "Experiments?"

"It's completely safe," he said. "We could leave a *kid* down here by itself for weeks. You have food, hot and cold running water, lights, air, and a recreation room. We keep the video library fully stocked, and there are plenty of books. It's been used as a kind of retreat for FTI Company members from time to time."

"There's no phone, I suppose."

"Is there anyone you would like us to contact?"

"No. My parents were lost when I was a child, so I was raised by my Aunt. She passed away several years ago. There's no one who'd notice I'm missing—except the IRS."

"Don't worry about it. The reason I asked is that we have a general order about outside communications."

"As in, there are none?"

"That's correct," he said, turning towards the nearest long wall of the airlock. "This place is a well-kept secret, Miss Aston, and we need to keep it that way."

"I didn't sign any ND agreement."

"Because you're a part of the secret we'd like to keep. Your voluntary cooperation is essential to the delicate balance the Foundation must manage between its assets and the outside world."

"No pressure on Kabta, keeping such secrets. What about you? Do you have any family or friends on the outside, or are you going to tell me that the FTI and UAMC are all you've got?"

"Absolutely," Breaker replied, grinning widely. "And who would trade this for *anything*?"

Hannah thought for a moment, and realized he was right. She would be stupid to let her fears get the best of her now. There was so much to learn and do down here. It was the chance of a lifetime.

It was just that she had a nagging sense that something was wrong.

"Come on," he said, waving for her to follow, "I'll show you around. This station has a name of its own, by the way. It's called the *Geomechanical Laboratory*—Geomech for short. I think you'll like it here, once you settle in and figure things out."

They quickly walked a circuit of interconnected passageways, beginning at one of the hatches in the airlock. The rooms were surprisingly spacious. There was an exercise area and toilet that could have served a national league team. They passed by several offices, a medical facility, and a kitchen that was fully stocked with microwavable meals—she was assured no stoves would function correctly at this depth. Near the kitchen were the crew quarters, including four private rooms, each with a cot and a few Spartan furnishings. Her own room was a little larger than the rest. She noted a footlocker inside, which she was told contained a change of uniforms and some toilet items. She was more interested in the outfit laid out on her bed—something that looked like gear for a riot squad built over a blue and black jumpsuit. A logo of an eastern dragon was emblazoned artistically across the right thigh. Hard plates covered parts of the arms, legs, ankles, back, and chest.

She wasn't given much of a chance to investigate before she was led away to a laundry area, where a sign proclaimed *"Undergarments Only"*. The very last hatchway in the corridor brought them back to the airlock, but there Breaker turned around and led her back to a door near the crew quarters—one of several doors he had left off the tour. A plaque near the latch displayed one word: ARCHIVE.

"I'm sure you have many questions," he said. "This is the place where they may be answered. Take a look."

Hannah opened the door. Inside the darkened room were banks of LED monitors and consoles. The lights flickered on as soon as they entered, as was the case in the rest of the station, but here they weren't so bright.

"It looks like a television broadcast hub," Hannah said.

"You're referring to the data consoles? They're not as busy now as they once were. Geomech was the first station built down here, about ten years ago, and back then it was home to the team that studied the soil and rock formations along this stretch of seafloor. Their job was to figure how best to anchor and arrange things, and now that we're done with all phases of construction we occasionally use the place as a lab of sorts, for experiments. Its primary use is as an interface hub for the massive amounts of data collected and archived by the company, from all our projects all around the world."

"An ultra-secure location. I guess corporate espionage isn't much of a problem."

"That's what the marines are here for."

"You mean you *do* have threats from outside, even down here?"

"Anything's possible, Miss Aston. Everything's here—from finances and construction to developing technology; the minutia of every project FTI is running. We take security very seriously."

"Including the work Ford and I have done? Can I access any of that here?"

"You can access all of your own work from this station, and you'll receive updates from all other project personnel as the work progresses. Even your parents' stuff has been uploaded."

"My parents' work?" she wondered, staring. "You mean the work they did for the FTI group?"

"Yep. I'm told you'll find it all very useful and engaging, though I'm sure there are restrictions. I don't know much about it myself, really. I'm just a repairman."

"Where is the Computer Core?" she asked. "There are so many systems aboard this habitat, and most are automated, but I haven't seen a single computer anywhere among all these consoles."

"The CC is isolated in a vault, in a special substation."

"How could a single system govern so much?" she asked. "There's got to be more than one supercomputer here, right?"

"No. There are no supercomputers. The system is quantum."

"You have a *quantum computer*?" Hannah wondered, her eyes squinting with incredulity. "No such system exists!"

"Who says? Quantum computers are being used and developed by every great nation on the planet. Just because you've never seen a unit on the shelf in an electronics store doesn't mean that it doesn't exist. The Foundation has been working with quantum computers for more than a decade."

"And no one knows the Foundation exists."

"Good, you get the picture. Let me show you one more thing."

He walked towards the far end of the room towards a padded office chair at a workstation. Hannah followed.

"When you're refreshed and you want to begin, just place your hand on this biometric scanner," he said, pointing to a plain grey pad in the countertop beside the keyboard. "It will initiate an interface program that was prepared specifically for you. The briefing will answer your questions, when you're ready."

Hannah stared at the scanner and nodded.

"If there's nothing else I can help you with right now, I'll be going. Expect a visit from our support personnel once a day at 9 a.m. We'll be sending a team to work with you, but that might take a few days to set up. In the meantime, I'd rest up and get to know the place—watch a film or something. Then, when you're ready, listen to your briefing."

"Yeah," Hannah said, distracted.

Breaker shook her hand again, and then he left. Hannah listened to his footsteps retreating down the corridor, and heard him close the hatch to the central airlock. The air handlers clunked as they pushed warm air through the room. Hannah continued to stare at the console before her, and at the banks of video screens rising towards the eight-foot sloped ceiling of the habitat. Though she had wanted a shower and a change of clothes, she doubted she would leave this room before she listened to the briefing. It wasn't very long before she placed her palm down on the biometric scanner at her workstation.

Almost as soon as she placed her hand on the pad, the wide screen in front of her flickered to life, showing the seated figure of the man she had met in Substation 12—Kabta was his name.

"I trust you have refreshed yourself and are acquainted with your home away from home," he said. "I have recorded this briefing in order to rest your anxieties about the quick transition you've agreed to make. I assure you, Miss Aston, once you have become familiar with our work, you will find it quite exciting. For myself, I am confident your commitment to this project will be secured as soon as this briefing is over."

"We'll see," she said, talking to the screen. It wasn't her habit to talk to her computer, but she was feeling more anxious now than she had been in Kabta's office.

"Back at the University, you were led to suspect that the FTI group is dedicated to the development of new satellite technologies, but that is only one small part of our work. As you have recently discovered, we are also interested in unlocking the secrets of the past—specifically, ancient technologies. Your father's work here added to our knowledge the existence of extinct civilizations that were far more advanced than those of most recent times. You have unknowingly advanced his research by helping us uncover some proof of his theories. Now we need your assistance in completing the picture that has begun to take shape."

Kabta paused. He was sitting in a padded chair like her own, but now he rose to his feet. The camera followed him as he walked towards the far wall of his office. There he looked at the darkened wall as if it was a window, and folded his hands behind his back while he talked. Hannah thought this very strange.

"The ship that was discovered beneath the mound of Hazor in northern Israel is being investigated by our science teams even as you watch this briefing. Soon, pieces of that ship will be arriving, where your friend Dr. Seijung Ford will help study them in the nearby Lucius substation. We are doing everything we can to keep the discovery a secret from the world's governments, and this requires the presence of a special unit of corporate marines called UAMC. Some of them you have already met. I assure you, they are moral men who were hand-picked by myself, and they would never hurt you. However, with all these scientists and soldiers down here, I thought you might require a little more explanation as to our current location. FTI didn't just choose this spot for the purpose of hiding our research from the rest of the world. There is something else here that you need to be aware of before we proceed. When you're ready, press the large switch under the console."

The screen went blank. Hannah searched beneath the console with her fingertips and quickly located something like a flat switch. She pressed it. There was a low groaning noise, and the walls shook. Slowly they slid down along the slope of the hull, revealing as they did a massive window dressed with a network of sturdy cross-braces. Meanwhile, the screen came back on and Kabta continued speaking. Now she could see that he was looking out of a window similar to the one that had opened in front of her.

"They're acrylic, several feet thick, and can easily withstand the tremendous pressures of the deeps."

Hannah wasn't conscious that she gripped the tabletop until her knuckles cracked.

"Behind these windows, Miss Aston, you see the darkness. For a long time, that darkness is all that was known of the world that existed before modern Man began to write history; but now there is a light—"

As she listened, she saw lights appearing in the deep darkness beyond her habitat. At first they were small pinpoints in the far distance, but soon larger lamps were lit and the sea-bottom appeared in a wide swath stretching perhaps several miles. At the end of the path she saw a hill, backlit by bright lights so that its round shape rose like a titanic black ball. A fine rain of grey-green material was coming down.

"Welcome to the true Underworld," Kabta said. "Let me briefly introduce its geography, starting with the habitats. The substations are twelve in number. Among these are a geothermal power plant, and reactors for the production and purification of clean air and drinking water. Food is brought a couple times a month from the surface support fleet, but no one else knows we're down here. We're well hidden. Six of the twelve substations are located beneath a shelf of rock on the seafloor."

Craning her head to look upwards, she saw only darkness. The lights weren't strong enough to illuminate the rock shelf. She did notice clusters of lights to the left and right sides of the window, though, stretching away in a gentle arch and connected by a stout tube along which lighted cables hung. She guessed these were the other habitats.

"The habitats are connected in a ring-shape by the tube. The tube itself is pressurized, but you wouldn't want to walk through it from station to station except in an emergency—the distance between habitats is quite far. The tube just protects the cables and machinery that maintain the stations. In order to get to them, you'd have to get in a sub and dock in an airlock. However, in the event of an emergency you have been given a key that permits access to the tunnel."

The figure of Kabta turned, and the camera followed him back to the table. He continued, saying, "Just beyond the edge of the rock shelf, resting at a depth of about eighteen thousand feet, the Foundation made contact with another bit of the past that remains unknown to the rest of the world. It may be only coincidental that ancient legends speak of the island of Atlantis or the city of Avalon that were lost beneath these seas. You will find that most of us don't believe in coincidence, however."

Hannah looked on the rotund peak outside the window, and then she realized that it wasn't a hill at all. Her heart began to beat faster.

"It's a second ship, Miss Aston, far larger than the first, and completely intact."

"You knew it was here before we went to explore Hazor?" she asked the screen. The recording paused, as if Kabta had heard her, and then continued.

"It's hollow, and heavily shielded. There is atmosphere inside. We have recently found a way in, and will be sending a science team to explore. I will make sure they keep you and Mr. Ford informed of any significant findings. Meanwhile, though we're not certain there are any more than these two ships anywhere on the Earth, we will continue the search. You must be aching to know who made them, and if there are surviving cultures in the Earth today that are descended from the makers. I believe they must have left more traces of themselves for us to discover. You will be given access to all of your father's research, including inscriptions and artifacts. New data regarding the non-metallic composition of the hull and some of the technology we've studied so far will also be made available to you for comparison with the Hazor ship. This is secondary to your real task, however. I'm asking you to spearhead the search for more candidate locations at ancient human cultic sites; I'd like you to concentrate specifically on South America, where your father made his most impressive discoveries. When you feel reasonably certain that we have a strong candidate, we will assemble a team, led by yourself, that will travel to the next Location."

The screen went blank.

Hannah sat for awhile, looking out the windows. She couldn't figure this was a cultic site at minus eighteen thousand feet. There were other factors that weren't adding up, but Kabta had gotten one thing right. She was hooked, and she would cooperate willingly. She wasn't so sure about Ford, though, and wondered if he also had listened to a briefing like this. Maybe he was stationed with others—Ford wouldn't do so well on his own, she thought. He always needed someone to talk to in order to think. Then again, so did she. She would've talked to herself, but she had the uncomfortable feeling that someone was watching her. As if to confirm her suspicions, the console in front of her flicked on automatically.

The screen displayed an animated series of concentric circles, all revolving in opposing directions around an off-center sphere consisting of still more rings. Arrested by the dizzying clockwork motion, Hannah leaned closer and noticed, in the innermost quadrant, one unmoving circle. Drawn in the middle of this focal point was a sphere budding three orbs, and this contained a triangle.

It all defied interpretation. She was wondering if it was nothing more than a screen-saver, when twelve icons suddenly appeared, each in a series of very peculiar characters arranged around the outermost circle. The whole look of the thing and the arrangement of its parts suddenly took on a familiar appearance, bearing eerie similarity to late nineteenth and early twentieth century *Tangka* coins from Tibet—though those bore only eight symbols. The symbols here were not Tibetan characters, or letters from any other language she knew. There was a wireless mouse next to the keyboard, and as she passed the cursor over the strange letters English labels appeared; but these were just as mysterious as the symbols.

MAIN OFFICE
STOW
HORUS
GEOTHERM
REGULUS
CC
GEOMECH
LUCIUS
ARMS
UAM BARRACKS
SIRIUS
ASSEMBLY LAB

She figured the twelve names must refer to the twelve substations. Hannah lingered a few moments over the label GEOMECH, and decided to try clicking it. The adjacent symbols lit up briefly, but nothing else happened. She tried several others around the rotating rings, to no avail.

"The user interface must be limited by my biometrics scan," she said to herself. "So, there are still secrets you're keeping from me, Kabta."

Then she noticed something that made her really curious. Moving the mouse across the screen, she passed over the sphere in the center, and another label appeared.

AVALON

She clicked on it. The concentric rings stopped revolving. A menu appeared below the central sphere, displaying twelve more English icons.

>**Command**
>**Hydroponics**
>**Maintenance**
>**Power**
>**Deep Black**
>**Computer**
>**Interferometry Array**
>**Mobile Recovery Unit**
>**Security System**
>**Health Office**
>**Mission Control**
>**Salvage & Assembly**

The icon labeled Security System caught her eye. Hannah clicked it, but nothing happened.

Just as she was becoming truly frustrated, she noticed that one of the screens on the left-hand wall had turned on. This screen displayed the contents of the folder she had just opened. Several other screens had also turned on along the right-hand wall, which showed folders she had accessed earlier. Her attention was riveted to the Security System file, however. She got up and went to the screen, and touching it she was permitted access to a series of dated files. Pressing the icon closest to the top of the list opened a document on the same screen. It was brief, and she scanned it quickly. Part of what she read gave her pause, however.

>*The tragedy of our first dives from surface craft*
>*reminds us that Avalon is aware and active. There is*
>*no established contact-protocol for this situation, and*
>*no procedure for predicting an AI's interactions over*

such a long period of time; still, no previous contact has led us to believe that it regards us as a threat. System specifications recovered by our agents revealed that the CC controls a nanoswarm—perhaps a series of swarms—as a defensive measure. The swarm's behavior was designed to be instinctual, but more than this we do not know. Sightings of a quick-moving mass on sub and station sonar may or may not be schools of fish. It appears that Avalon has kept its distance, and so have we. Once we attempt to move in and open the ship, however, preemptive hostilities will almost certainly ensue, for keeping proximity seems to be one of the system's initiatives. Testament to this is the fact that small planes and surface craft regularly disappear in this region of the Atlantic, often in violent winds that come with a boiling of the seas. Wreckage cleared from the site during construction of the habitats included vessels contaminated with trace particles of non-native metals and ceramic substances, though testing these materials produced no intact swarm-components...

Hannah stopped there, and thought of things she had not thought of since she was a small girl. She thought of the day she was sent to Auntie's house because her parents were out to sea on a U.S. Navy vessel. Months later she learned they were never coming home. Now, peering out of the acrylic windows, feelings of insecurity reached through the water from the dark hill in the distance and shook her violently, knocking aside the confident assurance that had kept her going all these years—alone yet unafraid. She trembled, wondering at the news Kabta had passed in so carefree a manner. Her parents ended up drowned in this place while experimenting with an alien ship the FTI called *Avalon*.

How did it come to have that name?

Hannah turned away from the report she'd been reading and investigated the screens on the other side of the room. One of these displayed a file-tree labeled *Interferometry Array and Beam Control.* She scrolled through the list of files, noting that the headings looked like titles in a physics textbook. On the screen below this was an open menu.

"Schematics?" she wondered, reading the title. She went to the screen and touched an icon labeled LUC. Her touch brought up engineering specifications of a ring with associated structures—the ring of habitats around the ship. The plans were dated to the 1980s, and the name Anna Aston appeared on the bottom of each document. Her mother was obviously a key figure in planning and constructing the substations. As she began to read the details of the specs, Hannah soon stumbled upon a rather interesting fact.

The ring connecting the substations was a *particle collider.*

Walking back to the center console, she plunked down and spun the chair lazily a few times, taking a leisurely look around the room and the screens. The suspicion that she was being watched increased, but she saw no cameras. When the chair came to a rest, she saw that the screens all around her had gone dark again. The lights dimmed. She was about to get up and find the showers when the center console displayed one line of text:

THE STRANGER WHO CAME OUT OF THE SHIP DOESN'T BELONG HERE. SHE IS FROM THE PAST.

Hannah looked at the screen, and thought about the slender girl with red-brown hair whom Kabta called Val. She wished she knew more about her. All the days she tended her aboard the ship, Val mumbled strange words over and over, sometimes in ancient languages that Hannah barely knew. How could this girl know them? Was she really from the past, or was she dutifully playing a part assigned to her by Kabta?

Leaning over the keyboard she typed, "Who is this?", and pressed *enter.* The words she typed appeared on the screen below the message. She had no idea if there was an open program, or if someone would receive what she typed, but she felt she had to try something. She was a little surprised by the instant reply.

I AM DR. CEDRIC DEPONS.

"Cedric DePons?" Hannah wondered. "Why does that name sound familiar?"

Then she remembered. DePons was the man she had met at Hazor a week ago—on the day Val appeared. Kabta said he was someone important to the UAM paramilitary organization.

VAL ANNA IS STILL ON SUBSTATION 12 WITH KABTA. I WOULD LIKE TO ARRANGE A MEETING BEFORE SHE IS BROUGHT TO AVALON, BUT I DON'T KNOW IF THERE IS TIME. I WILL BE IN CONTACT WITH YOU. KEEP IT A SECRET FOR NOW.

"When are we meeting?" Hannah typed.

There was a brief pause, and then one word.

SOON.

"What's the rush?" she wondered, speaking aloud.

The screen went dark again, and the walls began to slide back up to cover the station's windows. Hannah watched until the ocean was completely shut out, and then stood up and headed for the door. Her mind was full, and she needed something to eat. She had neither showered nor changed her clothes for two days, and this itself was a major milestone in her experience. Something drew her eyes back to the console before she entered the corridor, however—some warning sense. There were words on the screen in front of the empty chair, and they made her shudder.

WE MUST RECOHERE THE STONES, OR DARKNESS WILL AGAIN COVER THE FACE OF THE EARTH.

7
LUCIUS

Ford leaned against a table and waited. Watching the hangar was making him nervous. It wasn't just the coffee, either, or the fact that he hated being alone, or that he hated waiting.

It was a feeling—a sense of danger.

And Ford wasn't normally an anxious man. At least, that's what he was telling himself at the moment. Despite the fact that he was in the hands of the Foundation and dressed like a commando, there really was nothing to fear. It was just a hangar in a sub-base, cluttered with junk—

Over the past half-hour, he had come to realize the stuff on the deck wasn't just junk. Nor was this really a hangar. It was only a room the size and height of a hangar. After that, comparisons failed. For one thing, the room was nearly twenty thousand feet below the surface of the Atlantic. It was also a clean laboratory environment, the kind where satellites and spacecraft were assembled. Breaker called it *Lucius Station*, but the name meant nothing to him. He realized that he'd been thinking of it as a hangar for no other reason than that this dispelled some of the terror it evoked.

Rust-streaks stained the far wall, and somewhere a cable clanked rhythmically against the hull. He forced himself to take a sip of cold coffee and relax. He focused on what was near at hand, a rather gummy blow-dryer and a few loose files on the table. The files contained reports about trivial expenses, like food, laundry detergent, and shipping costs. Though curiously out of place, these items didn't hold his interest for very long. The pieces of wreckage clustered around the center of the room intimidated him, though. Pieces of what seemed to be oxidized metal hung in gurneys suspended by motorized carts—huge carts, grown-up forklifts the size of ore trucks. At first glance, the twisted chunks of debris might have been the remains of a plane crash. In the briefing, Kabta called it the *carcass*, and it looked just like one.

Where was he supposed to start?

He wished he'd asked that question before, but when Breaker showed him how to suit-up and left him in his quarters to don his outfit and watch the briefing, all Ford learned was that Kabta wasn't going to tell him anything he wanted to know.

"You've settled in your quarters yet?" a voice asked from behind him. Ford turned his head and saw a soldier coming through the door from the airlock. The man was a giant by anyone's measure. He wore a lab-coat—open at the front—over armored battle-dress, and he'd slipped white plastic bags over his boots and a mask on his face.

Ford stifled a laugh. *"You invading a maternity ward?"* he mumbled.

"What's that?" the behemoth asked, sidling up to the table with a swagger that would have been more threatening if it wasn't accompanied by the swoosh-swoosh of his bagged feet.

"Are you guys commandos or something?"

"Didn't you listen to the briefing?"

"Of course I listened to the briefing. I just don't understand why the Foundation's housing a corporate army down here. That part seemed a bit vague to me."

"You're not wearing a mask or gloves. You showered before coming in here?"

Ford looked him up and down. He didn't feel threatened, but he was insecure enough right now to mouth-off at just about anyone. It was Hannah's habit of hanging around and keeping him out of trouble when this mood took him, but Hannah wasn't here.

"I showered," he said. "I dressed. I even washed my glasses. You want to know what else I did in the bathroom?"

"Calm down," the marine said, holding up his gloved hands in mock surrender. "Just wanted to make sure you were comfortable."

"You wanted to make sure I was comfortable? Why? What does it matter that I'm comfy? If they wanted me to be comfy they would have sent me to an industrial park in California and offered me a pretty assistant to point me in the right direction; but they dropped me into the abyss with *Attila* instead."

Ford pointed towards the man's massive chest, where a patch proclaimed his name, *Hun.*

"That's pretty clever, Mr. Ford. Actually, everyone calls me that."

Ford turned his back to the man. He began to wish very strongly that he would go away, but he was also curious. Maybe the marine would answer questions that a Foundation scientist would not.

"So, Attila," he said, glancing aside at the table. "I don't suppose that's your hairdryer?"

Hun patted his shaven head. "It's Nuta's. She's a good kid, though a bit of a slob. Until you guys showed up, she bunked in Lucius."

"This is supposed to be a clean environment?" Ford asked, eyeing the dryer.

"Not that she'd know it, but yeah."

"So is this place primarily a bio-lab, or an engineering station? I'm an engineer, but all I see is a chemical locker."

"The stuff you're looking for is on the far side of the room," Hun replied, waving towards a row of steel benches and glass cases lining the far wall. "Someone will be in here once a week to make sure the place is stocked. If you need something that's not on the shelf, just type it up on the interface in your quarters and we'll send it along right away. I think you'll find everything in order, though."

"Maybe I would," Ford muttered, "if I even knew what kind of lab this was."

He looked away across the bay. The floor stretched exactly one hundred and fifty yards to the far wall. He knew it was one hundred and fifty, because the space was marked in a grid with numbers. Ford appreciated the attempt at precision, but he couldn't tell if the wreckage was arranged on the grid according to any specific pattern. It seemed very haphazard.

"Stripping technology off these broken bits will be like cloning a live pig from a piece of burned bacon."

"Did anyone tell you that this is all they're bringing out of the buried ship?"

Ford turned around again. "This is all they're bringing out?" he asked. "Why?"

"I don't know why. Maybe Kabta figures they'll have better luck with the other ship. You know about the other ship, right?"

"From the briefing, yeah. But they haven't gotten inside yet—"

"It's the other ship that the Foundation is more interested in."

Ford knew he had learned something important, but he managed to appear disinterested. "Anyway," he said, "The real question is how they got this stuff down here. We only arrived at the buried ship about ten days ago, and I just got here yesterday."

"There was a team ready when you were there. You must have just missed them. They went in while you were flying out."

"And they went in and grabbed—what? The first thing they could find? Why'd they choose one piece over another?"

"I don't know what any of it is," Attila said. "Spaceship parts, I guess. You're supposed to figure that out."

Ford thought Attila was playing him. The man wasn't as dumb as he looked. "Right," he said. "I'm supposed to figure it out. I don't even know what it's made of."

"Looks like metal."

"So does a pencil, if it's painted silver," Ford said, looking at the nearest gurney. "Those pieces there look like there might be oxidized metal on them, but there are ceramic structures beneath. See, where the breaks are?"

"Actually," a new voice said, "the surface isn't metal at all. It's full of exotic amino acids."

A man had entered the room behind Attila—a man Ford vaguely recognized. He was also wearing a white lab coat over combat gear. Attila stiffened and saluted him as he approached. The officer returned the salute informally, and Hun departed without another word.

"Hey, another guy whose head isn't shaved," Ford said with a smirk.

"Cedric DePons," the dark-haired stranger replied, offering his hand to Ford across the table. "Don't let my marines frighten you."

Ford took his hand cautiously. "We met at the site, right?"

"Yes. Quite a find, and we have you and Miss Aston to thank for that."

"Even though the Foundation is less interested in the buried ship we found than the one outside this station?"

DePons shrugged. "From what I hear, the two are equally prized. Hannah's looking for more as we speak."

"More ships?"

"Kabta didn't elaborate."

"But he told you exactly what I'm supposed to be doing here?"

"Yes. I'm here to help you."

"I thought you were the head of the UAMC," Ford said. "Don't you have security duties to attend to?"

"Of course, but these are light in comparison to what you've got on your plate. Besides, I think you'll come to appreciate my input. I was once a fine engineer. And this isn't the first time I've seen some of these things."

Ford's astonishment was plain, and DePons grinned.

"Let me explain, Mr. Ford. I used to work for a secret weapons division in the United States Air Force, and long before that I headed a project for the Army that was called *Reformation*. In both these posts I saw very interesting things come out of archaeological excavations in the Midwestern United States and South America. The military was only interested in the technology we dug up, but probably the most fascinating things were the inscriptions."

"Inscriptions?" Ford wondered. "I'm not trained in that sort of thing. I'm a scientist."

"Right. Let's have a closer look at those structures you identified as *ceramic*. That should serve as a decent explanation."

DePons led him across the floor to the nearest hunk of debris in the room, a behemoth slung on cables between two huge lifts. The piece had few identifiable features on its surface. It was knobbed and oval, and bent slightly in the middle—and it was huge, measuring more than fifty feet across.

"You're probably wondering how they got it here," he said in answer to Ford's inquisitive gaze. "The answer is easier than you'd guess. All these artifacts were transported to the bottom of the sea aboard Lucius itself."

"It's mobile?"

"Not like a submarine, though. The whole station is a pressurized freight-elevator. We cable it to and from a surface ship. That's what made it possible to construct the other substations, and to bring such sizeable pieces as this to our labs."

He gestured towards the debris in front of them.

"It looks like rotten fruit," Ford said. "Smells like it, too."

"That's natural decay of the living tissue that once covered the parts within," DePons said. "Think of it as a cocoon. Once this was disconnected from the rest of the ship, it began to putrefy."

"It was living tissue?"

"A regenerative flesh that protected the underlying mechanical components," DePons replied, snugging up his latex gloves. Ford watched with great interest as he carefully peeled back a thick layer of the brownish-grey stuff that looked like rust. The surface beneath was smooth and grey.

Ford wrinkled his nose at the folds of flesh in DePons' hands. "Smells gross! What's all that stuff underneath?"

"We'll find out. The really interesting item is here, on the broken end."

He released the flesh and went over to stand beside the ragged edge of the wreckage. Ford followed him, and where DePons probed the carcass with his fingertips he saw several pale white projections in the cross-section.

"They look like ribs," he said. "Are they structural or mechanical?"

"Probably both," DePons said. "In any case, they're ceramic, just as you guessed, but I'm guessing there's more to it than that. Ah! Look closely, there."

He pointed to some scratches on the end of one of the pieces. Ford pushed back his glasses and leaned in towards the surface, and he saw that the little scratches formed a clear pattern. There was a bold triangle, and inside he could just make out the shape of tiny letters.

"FTI!" he exclaimed. "What in god's name is this? Is this some kind of joke?"

"No jokes, Mr. Ford."

"I'm looking at a piece of ancient spacecraft—or whatever it is—"

"—that bears the company logo, in English," DePons nodded.

Ford tried to calm himself down, but he was starting to feel like he was being made a fool of.

"A real mystery," DePons said. "Like I said, there are interesting inscriptions to be found on some of these pieces. You should see some of the others."

"But the wreckage has only been here a matter of hours. How did you know about the inscriptions, unless you put them there yourself?"

"Like I said, I've seen things like this turn up in archaeological excavations before."

"It's not possible!" Ford exclaimed. "It can't really be ancient—unless maybe the company took the name after they found the inscriptions?"

"What do you find so impossible, Mr. Ford?"

"Time travel, for one thing! And an ancient civilization with a modern counterpart in corporate America for another. I mean, how could a spaceship built by the Foundation be buried under an ancient city? And if the logo is a coincidence, how'd the ancient people come up with Latin letters? It's all impossible!"

"I must admit," DePons said in a more confidential tone, "some company members have been less than forthcoming. I have been working on small-scale salvage operations for the Foundation for a decade, and before that I was doing the same for the United States. Mostly we've run into little scraps of things buried in sites of ancient human occupation; but lately we've run into stuff on a whole different scale. Some of this might actually be salvageable, and then—could you imagine what we might learn?"

"You're a scientist of some kind? You said you were in the military."

"I am a scientist," DePons said, "and I am also an old soldier. It takes all kinds!"

"How's Hannah dealing with it all? Does she know about this?" he asked, pointing to the inscription.

"She will come to know about it when the time is right. Miss Aston is working in a substation all on her own, trying to piece together another list of candidate locations using your EM satellite system and her own archaeological expertise."

"She has a habitat all to herself?"

"Kabta respects her deeply, and felt it was important to give her some space. She has a great mind, and I believe she will be able to make the connections that will enable her to figure some things out on her own—given enough time."

Ford lowered his eyes. He had thought the Foundation selected Hannah because of his recommendations. It was beginning to seem like they needed her more, and that he was only an afterthought.

Leaning closer to Ford, DePons whispered, "I will bring news from Miss Aston, and send messages back to her if you wish. Communication between the two of you has been all but severed, by Kabta's orders. Also, further communication between the two of us will only be face-to-face. If you absolutely need to set up a meeting, use the main console and send your inquiry to *FOX*. This will be coded so that it looks like a maintenance request."

"Why the cloak-and-dagger?"

"There are always security risks, even here."

"Are you disobeying someone's orders by showing me this stuff and talking to me?"

"There are others who think you should be left to find your own way without my interference. I thought you'd appreciate a head's-up, though it's technically against the rules. Like I said, time is crucial, and the more you know at the start, the more you'll accomplish in the time we have down here."

"You make it sound as if we're moving out soon."

DePons projected a somber look. "Remember," he said, "I am the head of Kabta's security, and as such I am capable of making informed decisions. You can trust me or not."

Ford nodded.

"I'll also try to set up a meeting between the three of us and the girl."

"The girl?"

"Val Anna. I'd like to confer with all three of you together; but we'll have to keep that a secret for now. I'll bring it up with Kabta later, when nothing else is going on."

"What else is going on?"

"Your integration. While you are settling in, you'll report directly to Kabta. Keep in mind that the Foundation is very particular about keeping us so focused on our work that we may miss the big picture. Keep your eyes and ears open."

He turned and began walking back towards the submarine bay.

"You're going?" Ford called after him.

"I want you to take a close look at each of the pieces," DePons said over his shoulder, "especially that large one in the back."

Ford looked away towards the far side of the room, and saw something big that looked like a rusty aircraft folded in half.

"Is there something special about it?" he asked.

"I noticed it when they loaded it into the bay, back at the port of Haifa. It's covered with thick folds of this organic goo. I exposed a small surface and saw a panel labeled *PCU*."

"PCU?"

"There's no current recorded inscription matching it in our database. I want you to check it over, and see if you can distinguish something significant in each of these components. Look at everything—down to the very chemistry of the materials—and start with that particular piece."

"So now I'm a chemist, too. Is this your assignment for me, or is it Kabta's?"

The hatch slammed shut. DePons left.

8
PANDORA'S BOX

Val tugged at the corners of the armor they'd hung from her narrow shoulders. Her slim frame bowed beneath the unaccustomed weight.

"The scientists will be safe," Kabta said.

Val asked, "Safe from what?"

"Lír will be looking for them. Though they weren't wary of us, they are exceptionally clever people, ranking superior to many of the best among Gremn technologists. I set them the task of finding the ship so that—"

"It was all just a test?"

"Well," he said, closing the armory hatch behind them, "we hadn't lost track of its location, you know. It hasn't moved much in the last 150,000 years. You must understand, Val Anna. It was a test of skill. There were bits of technology at that location we meant to recover; and here we have the necessary equipment to reassemble some of it. I could have arranged for all this to happen by many other means, but I wanted to see what our friends were really capable of. It was a difficult test, asking them to locate something that has remained a secret even from modern nations with nearly unlimited resources. I don't believe that even Magan would have performed so well, given the chance."

"Why is that?"

"The Gremn are skilled at maintaining what they have and what they know, but we did not make these ships. The truth is, we never completely understood all that was made by those who came before us—much the same as it is with the stones. Therefore, though they know nothing about the Gremn, Ford and Aston do not understand less than Magan, who was a Gremn. The test was an exercise in judgment and skill, not in loyalty to the Foundation, about which they know little enough."

"We certainly don't undervalue the contributions that anyone has made, human or not," Shu said.

"What contribution am *I* making?" Val wondered.

The three left the armory, Val tramping along noisily between Kabta and Shu.

"And Mrs. Morvran made fun of *Arctics*," she lamented, trying not to shuffle. Her legs were covered below the knees with casings that looked like exaggerated imitations of feet. Each legging, Shu explained, housed a power supply for the suit, though why the suit needed powering was left a mystery.

"You will be missing it when it comes time to take the armor off," Kabta warned. He had also been outfitted on their way from the conference room, though in much heavier gear.

"I wish you would have taken my advice and worn the helmet as well," Shu said. "Be thankful you won't be asked to don a fully equipped CM9 suit."

Val frowned. The leggings were sleek and surprisingly light, but they made her trip. Likewise troublesome were the units encasing each arm from elbow to wrist. Packed with instruments, these made her arms feel like clubs. She also wore chest armor, borrowed from the lone female among the contingent of marines, gleaming brightly with a bluish hue.

"It's not that I don't appreciate it. It just seems like all this was fit for someone else—someone of greater substance."

"There is no such person in the world today," Kabta replied.

They both looked at her. At that moment, as unobtrusively as she could manage, she was attempting to adjust the form-fitting jumpsuit while she walked. It rode up her backside, clinging like a glove.

"I don't recall *Alice's Adventures in Wonderland* requiring her to dress quite like this," she said glumly.

"Good analogy," Shu said. "Only, in this tale you're less like Alice than the rabbit."

"Or the queen," Kabta interjected. They both looked aside at him, puzzled.

"I'm not going to war, am I?" Val asked.

"I hope not," Shu replied. "You have that knife?"

Val patted the leather-clad pommel. The dagger was in a hip-sheath, its lower limb belted to her thigh.

"You won't have to use it," Kabta said.

"I didn't intend to. It was Morla's."

"A memento?"

"Something like that. Since the day someone accidentally emptied a tub of wash-water over me, I've been made to dress in other people's clothes and carry their oddments across time and space."

Kabta placed a hand on her back. "Nevertheless," he said, "you are the reason we have done all this, and your decision to transport the stones to the World of Origins is now our primary objective."

They walked on a few paces in silence. Shu interrupted their quiet thoughts with a question.

"What about rebuilding Auriga?" he asked. "Nephtys said *that* was our objective."

Kabta shook his head. "The reconstruction of some parts of the Auriga is indeed a priority, but only as far as it advances Val on her quest. Auriga will not be raised from its tomb, because even if that was physically possible, the ship is so badly damaged that it could never leave the surface, much less reach space."

"But you are trying to reassemble pieces of Auriga?" Val asked.

"Yes. We have the means of stabilizing the quantum field of Auriga's engines. That will be Mr. Ford's next test. If he and DePons are able to make progress with that, we could probably raise Avalon."

"But you obviously have no intention of bringing this ship to space, either," Shu said. "So, why bother with Auriga's engines at all?"

"We might need them as backup to power the CSR Terminal aboard Avalon if Avalon's engine cores are dead."

"You'd jump-start Avalon to power her Mirror?"

"If Avalon can't do it herself."

"So that's why I'm here," Val said in a low voice, "to go through the Mirror, again."

"That's no small feat," Kabta warned. "What we are attempting by entering Avalon and making transit against the Ban is something that no one has dared before. It is very dangerous, yet I believe we have little choice. If we don't do anything, there are Gremn in this world whose design it is to destroy or enslave the Crodah. So, we must try despite the danger. Besides, you are needed there."

"Me?" she looked from one to the other. Shu shrugged, but Kabta held her eye.

"Indeed, you," he said. "Or did you think this business would end upon the completion of a successful transit? Much time has passed in the World of Origins since the Ban was enacted. You will come to understand that your role as a warden of the stones carries with it other responsibilities."

"Never mind that," Val said, waving her hand in the air. "I still don't understand how we'll manage the transit. Shu says none of us is able to direct the stone to our own will, so how am I supposed to use the CSR Terminal? Won't I just end up displacing us all again?"

"Maybe, but your timely arrival here has convinced me that it is not beyond reason to try. There will be consequences. We'll deal with those when they come."

They continued along the passage towards the airlock. Val lowered her eyes and pressed a hand to the hardened chest-plate that protected both her and the secret stone. In her mind the words Kabta spoke at Hazor echoed with a weight of doom, when he said, *"I hold myself loyal to you, and every Gremn under my command will follow your word. You are the true leader of our expedition. The Morvran-stone was passed down to you for a reason, and I will not argue with Purpose."*

She still wasn't entirely convinced that purpose was a part of the equation. Kabta never explained his comment.

He stopped at a hatch just ahead labeled DIVE POOL, and placing his palm on a black panel beside it he began to turn a wheel in the center of the massive door.

"This talk of the World of Origins has jostled my long memory," he said.

Shu asked, "What have you remembered?"

The wheel in Kabta's hand clanked hard against a lock, and he pushed against it. The sound of pressure whistling between one hall and the next came with a mild popping in Val's ears.

"When I was young," he said, "my father was one of the Gremn technologists at Islith—a position of high honor among our folk. He was one of those trained to develop the technology of the Ancients, which required mastery of a wide array of skills. Many marvels were crafted in those days in Cipa, the mighty city on the Karn River. The Guilds marketed all sorts of interesting things there—engines, stasis tubes, weapons, and even ships. The items were sold piecemeal in auctions to Gremn and Crodah alike, who studied them and rebuilt them. Of course, that was what led to the War."

The hatch was unlocked, and Kabta pushed it aside as he continued talking.

"On this world, the discovery of these ships would likely also have led to war. Maybe it will yet."

"But no one else knows about it, right?" Val asked.

"There are Gremn who might be willing to reveal a location to human authorities, just to stand back and watch the results."

"But they won't be able to make use of the CSR Terminal," she said.

Kabta stepped through the hatch, and the others followed.

"I did learn that the sequencing of this device was something mediated via Avalon's CC, which required a kind of key. That key is a person living inside Avalon, sleeping in stasis. Such a person, if recovered, would be more devastating to mankind than the discovery of atomics."

Shu looked troubled by this news. Val misunderstood his expression.

"We can't just leave it all here, then," she said.

"Of course not," Kabta replied. "Measures have been taken to assure no trace of our presence or of Avalon remains after we complete transit."

The lights inside the chamber flickered on as they advanced. Val looked past Kabta at the still water in the pool. She smelled the strong odor of seawater, and shivered from the cool touch of moisture in the air. As the three stepped together towards the pool and the waiting minisub, she experienced a brief moment of disorientation—a parting effect of the displacement, perhaps—and turning towards the darkened hatchway behind them, a double-vision filled her eyes with a curious sight: in place of a hatch she saw a dark crypt, like a cave, and in it a young man was reading by candlelight.

The air handlers came on with a clunk and a whir. Drawn shut by pressure, the hatch clanged behind them. Val felt a dull echo in her heart. The image of the young man reading, only a second ago so clear, vanished as swiftly as it had come.

"Don't worry," Shu said, touching her arm. "We're only going halfway to the UAM Barracks and Armory, and when the others have joined us at the rendezvous point we're going straight to Avalon."

The sub's hatch was recessed like a manhole-cover in the end of a tube that stood up a couple of feet from its orange domed roof. Going before them, Kabta knelt down beside the tube and unlocked the pressure seal by turning the wheel set into the top of the hatch. Val thought the whole device was very clever, though she recalled the sub being very small inside. When the hatch was open, she eyed the narrow aperture poised at the water's edge and tried to think of something else.

"We'll be taking along two small teams to expedite our search," Kabta said as he lowered himself into the sub. "They're the most reliable of my warriors. I just hope we can fit three subs into an airlock designed for EEVs—and I hope our informant wasn't lying about the manual airlock."

Val tried to dismiss this comment from her mind. She fumbled with her new gear while Kabta prepared to undock the sub.

"Stop fidgeting," Shu said. "How's the weight of the armor?"

"I hardly feel it."

"I think you could have gone with a light-gauge back-plate. I don't like to think you're unprotected."

Val rotated her shoulders to stand straight. There was thick padding over her shoulder blades, but the light armor in front was still uncomfortably inflexible. The stiff collar around her neck poked at the bottom of her chin, too; but she felt safe enough. The warmth of the stone hanging from its cord was an added measure of reassurance. She could feel it pulse from time to time with tremendous power, as if it was a living thing aware of what went on around it.

"Sure you don't want a helmet?" Shu asked.

"Gremn marines don't wear helmets," she said. "Why should I?"

"Gremn marines don't die unless their heads are cut off or they're completely burned."

"You've managed to survive without a helmet, and you can't regenerate like they do. Besides, Kabta said we're not going to war."

"We don't know what we're up against," he said, waving her towards the edge of the pool and the waiting sub.

Val approached the sub-hatch and sent one foot down inside towards a narrow ledge. Kabta was in the left-hand seat, and she was to take the right. As soon as she was settled, Shu came down the hatch and sealed it above him before plopping down between them in the pilot's seat. A few practiced moves of his hands upon the complicated control-boards, and the lower gate of the dive pool began to descend beneath the sub's belly, drawing them down into the water under the station.

The floor of the sub vibrated gently. Val watched the small round windows go dark, and then their movement stopped. Even before she heard the rotors whine and they began their slow journey through the deeps, her stomach was churning with fear and anxiety. No one spoke for a long time, and she was left to ponder the strange turns life's road had taken since the day she climbed a ladder to the loft of a barn.

They were inside the sub for half an hour when lights became visible through the window beside her. Val had been dozing a little, but she roused herself when she saw a kind of road appearing in the lights—an illuminated path that led away towards the dark hill that was Avalon.

"The Lost Road," she whispered, remembering something that seemed oddly on the edge of consciousness. *"The Lost Road leads Mankind and Gremn back from exile, together."*

"Track lights are on," Shu said, adjusting the sonar. "We'll rendezvous with the others in a few minutes. They're now in visual range. Let's keep an eye out."

She turned her head to look through the central portal. Two distinct beams of light slowly approached their position like a horse-drawn carriage making its way through deep fog. Another pair of lights appeared much farther behind the first. Shu slowed their forward momentum until they hovered in place. His eyes darted from window to window, and Kabta was doing the same.

"What's the danger?" she asked. "What are you looking for?"

"No one's sure," he said, almost whispering. "Avalon has a security system that was activated by Lír before he left. It's completely autonomous, and will respond to any perceived threat to the ship."

"And you're telling me this now?"

"We've come pretty close to the ship in recent months, though this is as close as we've ever been since first setting down and laying out the cables for the lights. The theory is, if we move inside its perimeter and contact Avalon, we'll not get much warning. Then again, we might just slip by it unnoticed."

"What is it?" Val asked.

"Let's hope we don't find out. DePons has developed a weapon—though I hope we don't need to use it."

Without taking his eyes off the oncoming minisubs, Shu lifted his hand towards a flat red button near the console in front of him. It was under a protective plastic shield.

"Careful!" Kabta said, speaking so suddenly that Val was quite startled.

"What is that?" Val asked.

"Do you know what *electromagnetic radiation* is?" Shu asked.

Val thought she had heard of something like this in her studies, but as she searched her memory she was surprised to find the clear answer emerging from another source—from the obscure and faded trove of knowledge that had been granted to her in the black water.

"It is energy radiated in waves, formed at the speed of light, by electric and magnetic fields."

"Good," Shu said, nodding towards the oncoming subs. "You see them? At this range, the device fitted to our hull can produce an electromagnetic pulse capable of disrupting all electrical activity aboard those subs. The radius isn't huge, but the effect is powerful and immediate."

"Unfortunately," Kabta said, "the pulse would also disable this sub, leaving us helplessly stranded without air until rescue arrives. Of course, no one knows we're here. We need to keep our distance from each other—and from the substations and Avalon itself."

"The pulse wouldn't harm us?" Val asked.

"No," Shu said. "It will only damage electrical components."

"So whatever it is, it's electrical?"

"Maybe."

"They're here," Kabta said.

The first two beams of light approached their position and stopped about fifty yards away. Shu turned on an instrument that clicked, and started up the rotors.

"We read your signal, Sub 1. Lead the way," said a booming voice from the open com-link. Val heard the voice coming from somewhere near her head, but turning she could not discover its source.

"Make sure you stay in formation with a good distance between us," Shu replied.

"Copy that, Sub 1."

Shu turned them towards the right and adjusted their course so that they were heading along the lighted path towards Avalon. Val watched as the muddy grey bottom slipped along beneath them; and though at first she was fascinated, the novelty soon wore off. It wasn't until they left the overhanging shelf of rock that more signs of life began to appear. Sea-stars and fish like large tadpoles moved out of the way of billowing clouds of silt raised by their rotors. And all the while, so slowly that it was at first imperceptible, the dark hill before them grew larger and larger until it filled the whole field of view. Just when Val thought they must be so close that they would soon crash into its black surface, she saw something glowing a great distance ahead. When she realized that it was the sub's head-beams, and that they still had that far to go, she was astonished.

"How big *is* it?" she asked.

"About ten miles across," Kabta said. "Our ring of habitats surrounds it completely."

"It must've taken a long time to construct the habitats."

"Not really," he said. "Money gets things moving very quickly, and the Foundation has good resources at its disposal. Decisions are made with a single purpose in mind, so the governance of those resources goes largely unquestioned. The only real obstacle was to gather enough of us together in one place to build this without anyone discovering us. The entire project took less than ten years, and Avalon has rested here with its secrets for much longer than that. Now the time has come for the door to open. This is our time."

"Our time," Val repeated softly to herself. She felt suddenly drowsy. A steady parade of images began trickling into her mind, some familiar and others utterly alien. Most notably among the latter were a burning city full of tall buildings of glass and steel, a crowd of terrible creatures that looked like men—but were not, and last of all a thing like a turnip flying high above a snowy landscape. While she imagined these strange things, Val was no longer aware of the others beside her. Nor was she aware that there was a minisub, or that she had been under the sea. Confusion and terror gripped her, and a sense of being completely disconnected from her physical body brought on a rush of panic that actually awakened her.

She was back in her seat.

"Still in the black water, are we?" Kabta asked, looking on.

Val lowered her head and massaged it. Slowly the disorientation wore off, and she opened her eyes—aware only at that moment that they had been closed.

"What just happened?" she asked.

"There is a possibility that as we come closer to the secrets of the thing outside the window, you may experience changes."

"What kind of changes?"

"Apparently, the Source buried some things deeper in your mind than the knowledge of language, which has already worn off. What did you just see?"

Val shook her head. "I saw lots of things," she said. "The last thing was *that*."

She pointed through the forward portal towards the ship.

The glow of their beams on Avalon's hull seemed a little closer. Val could definitely see details of its surface. What seemed at first to be a dull black featureless mass rising from the seabed was now a gently sloping shell incised with complex patterns of metallic bars, disks, balls, and tubes. Here and there, panels covered the surface, panels in regular geometric patterns. She tried to take in the view upwards along one side of the ship; but even if there had been adequate light, the view was restricted by the tiny window.

"Straight ahead," Kabta said. "There's a rectangular patch of hull that looked a bit out of place on our previous scans. If such a thing exists, I'd guess that's the manual lock."

"I wonder what Taran would have thought about all this?" Val said to herself as they came nearer the structure. "He's long dead by now, I suppose."

Shu glanced quickly back and forth to either side, taking his eyes off the path for only a moment as he read the mood of his companions.

"I do not believe that we have heard the last of the name *Morvran*," Kabta replied.

This was said as they drew so close that it was necessary to turn down the sub's lamps. Just as Kabta leaned forwards to examine an oddly dented patch of hull through the forward portal, something knocked the minisub sideways.

The sound of the impact was shockingly loud, for they had been speaking very softly up to that point. Shu cut power to the rotors at the helm. All three were staring at the portals, but there was nothing to see, for they were as black as pitch.

Val asked, "What hit us?", but then she saw Shu reaching for the red button.

Kabta reached over and cupped one hand over the plastic panel. "Not yet," he said calmly. "Beware any threatening moves."

"Sonar's out. We're drifting. Should I try to power-up and see if we can break free?"

"No. Let's sit still awhile."

Then the sub stopped rocking to and fro. Val stared out her window at a black mass that boiled with movement and flickered with light. A disturbing thought came to mind, and a memory of the black water in the stasis tube.

"Is it alive?" she asked.

"The black water lives, yes," Kabta replied. "It's really not water at all, but a swarm of microscopic electromechanical entities."

Then, seeing her confused look from the corner of his eye he added, "It's a swarm of billions of tiny machines, each much smaller than a red blood cell."

"They were inside me?" she asked, staring out the window.

"They still are."

"Sub 1, respond," hailed a voice over the com.

"Sub 1," Shu said into his microphone. "Halt your approach. We're being probed."

"Acknowledged, Sub 1. Standing by."

"It hasn't cut off our communications," Shu said. "That's hopeful."

Kabta said, "It's observing us."

Val was still looking out into the dim murky brew. "There must be an awful number of them if we can see them at all," she said, "—and if they can actually hurt us."

"Things like this were designed long before the War," Kabta said. "I'm afraid I don't know much about them. Down here, it must lay dormant in the mud until something comes by. If it perceives that we're a threat, my guess is that it won't stop at looking in at us."

As if in response to his words, the hull of the little sub creaked as it was stretched and flexed by the swarm. Then, as quickly as it had arrived, the black water was gone. The portals turned grey, and then they could see their lights reflecting off Avalon's hull again.

"Pick up and resume," Kabta ordered. "We've been released."

"And we haven't drifted far," Shu said, "only a couple of meters. In fact, we're right in front of our target area."

"Sub 1, this is Sub 2. Security has cleared the area. It's completely disappeared. We're moving towards you now."

"Where'd it go?" Val asked.

Shu glanced at her, and said, "I don't know, but something must've gotten its attention."

On the other side of Shu, Kabta was pulling a box on a long cable out from under his seat. The box was covered with small switches and a tiny tab that he rotated easily with his thumb. Val heard a whining noise.

"Well, this is certainly the place," Shu said. There was a note of disappointment in his voice. "It looks like we won't have much trouble opening the lock."

Val squinted through the tiny window. Just a little to the right of their position was a rectangular panel of the ship's hull.

"The lower part of the panel," he said. "You see it? It seems out of alignment with the panel below. It's twisted slightly outwards."

"That panel's more than two feet thick," Kabta said quietly. "This isn't a breach. It's just a little scrape."

Val said, "There are no controls or switches on the outside. Maybe Lír's people forced the door closed behind them when they left, and damaged it."

"Great!" Shu griped. "Even if we do get inside I don't see how we can seal it shut behind us and restore atmosphere to this section of the ship. We don't have suits capable of diving at these depths, so we'd have to set up an artificial lock outside the door. With the security system active, I don't see how that's possible—"

"I've been wondering," Val interrupted. "Can't you guys… go *outside* to work the lock?"

They both stared at her.

"If I understand correctly," she continued, "you can't physically drown. Is that right?"

"We can't drown," Kabta replied, turning his attention back to the control unit in his hands. "At these depths we would be compressed to the point of immobility, however. And though we are capable of drawing oxygen from the water, it is not enough to keep us active for long periods. Besides all this, there's the security system to worry about. So no, we couldn't go out and work the airlocks manually. That's why we brought *this*."

He pushed a thumb-tab on the remote. Val saw a long jointed arm with a pincer-gripped claw move into view through the portal in front of them.

"Cheer up," he said. "This would have been a real short trip if we hadn't found a way to lift the edge of that panel. As Val noted, there are no controls on the outside. I've been thinking all along that we might have to blast it open, and I doubt the security system would have reacted kindly to that. Besides, you don't know what's inside the dock. There may be a separate control for closing the door and evacuating the water from the lock. Think of it as a *gift*."

Val said, "You think the security system opened it for us."

"Yes. We were meant to get inside."

"And how would Avalon know that?" Shu asked.

"Because *she's* with us," he answered.

Even as he spoke, he maneuvered the robotic arm so that the claw contacted the hull of the ship. There was a dull clank and a scraping sound, and a little cloud of grey mud slid down the sloping hillside of Avalon's hull. Kabta rotated the claw into a vertical position and slipped the pincer-grips under the panel. Val was about to ask how he intended to lift the massive panel upwards by leverage, since the sub itself wasn't locked in place, but then she saw something spinning inside the claw. The whine of a motor grew steadily louder, and the pincers moved slowly apart. The claw contained a screw-jack.

"It's opening," Shu said.

Val stared out the portal at the widening gap, and a noise like the creaking of a great gear vibrated through the minisub. The door had already opened about a foot along the entire length of the panel, and a slim line of darkness was appearing beneath.

"How far can the jack open it?" she asked.

The panel bounced suddenly, and their windows were filled with muddy silt. Then something bumped the front of the sub, and the interior lights flickered.

"It's back?" Val asked.

"Check on our location for Security," Shu said into the com.

"*Sub 2 to Sub 1,*" came the reply. "*Except for a lot of mud, the area's clear.*"

They stared out the portal in front of them, but everything looked black.

"Turn off all the lights," Kabta ordered.

Shu flicked a switch, and in moments they saw lights ahead of them—lights that grew steadily in intensity across the darkness, illuminating a wide space inside the huge hull of Avalon. Soon the light was so bright that Val couldn't look directly into the window any longer.

"It's open," Kabta said as he returned the arm control to its stow-position beside him. "That bump was the door hitting our bow."

"The lights are on and nobody's home," Shu replied. "I have clearance above and below—I think."

"Take us in, then, and tell the others to follow slowly."

As they moved forward, Val felt a little tug in the back of her mind. There was something forbidding about this entrance, she thought. It was like another she had seen. She wished Shu would hurry up and get them inside.

In the end, the entry took more than an hour. The three minisubs jostled one another inside the airlock. Everyone was tense, for their backs were to the sea and the security system, and the door was stuck open. They had spent ten minutes just finding the manual pressurization switch inside the dock, which confirmed Kabta's suspicion that there was a way to evacuate the water from the airlock. The rest of the time was a frustrating exercise in manipulating the robotic arm.

Val watched as Kabta and Shu switched seats and tried different tactics with the arm and its clumsy claw. The marines had communicated nothing since taking up places on either side of them. Val could only imagine the conversations in the other subs.

"How do we even know it's the right switch?" she asked.

The room was about the length and width of an Olympic-sized pool, and it was completely bare of any and all devices except for the recessed lever in front of them.

"It's the only thing here," Shu said, his voice edged with frustration. "It's got to do something."

"Have we checked above or behind?" she asked.

"Escape vehicles would have hung from the ceiling. It would be impossible to access a manual switch to open or close the dock from any other position, and even if it could be reached, I wonder if we'll be able to manipulate it without more specialized equipment than a robotic arm. I wonder what the EEVs used—"

"There must have been some way to close the outer door from inside as well," Kabta said. "We know it's possible, because we know that Lír's people left in two groups, years apart. I just hope the switch wasn't only accessible from the other side of this door, inside the ship."

While he spoke, Shu moved the arm so that one large pincer sank down into the horizontal ratchet-shaped handle in the wall. He closed the claw—imperfectly, because of its size—and brought his hands off the controls for a moment.

"One more time," he said. Then, less gently than his previous attempts, he drew back the small tab in the center of the control unit with his thumb. Val saw the pincer bounce once off the handle, as it had done countless times before, and then miraculously reconnect, drawing the handle down as Shu followed through with the arm and throttled the rotors. The portal was obscured by a cloud of mud, and Shu let off the engine.

Then they heard a sharp *click*.

Everyone held their breath. Through the cloudy water they saw the dock's lights flicker, and then there was a shuddering boom. The sub began bobbing up and down, but they couldn't see what was happening. The portals were dark with mud.

"Get the arm out of the way!" Kabta shouted, slapping Shu's shoulder. "Pull it back, or we'll be hung up!"

The sub jolted wildly as Shu pulled back the controls. They crashed down hard, and then they were left rocking steadily back and forth for awhile. As the motion grew less, light filtered in through the portals. Drips appeared in the central window.

"We're sitting pretty," Shu said, grinning. The sub rested on its belly.

"How can we tell if it's safe?" Val asked, squinting through the portal.

"Avalon is capable of manufacturing atmosphere from base components," Kabta said, looking at an instrument above his head. He was still in the pilot's seat, having switched places with Shu.

"The inner atmosphere looks like it's breathable, but there's no way to know for sure until we pop the hatch. How's the pressure?"

"Sea-level," Shu said.

Kabta stood up in the pilot's seat and pulled down the cage that protected the hatch. As soon as he was about to start turning the pressure valve, a rapping noise startled them from above.

Shu smiled at Val across the tiny compartment. "I guess the air's alright," he said. "The others are already out!"

"Fools throw caution to the wind," Kabta said, easing the valve against a sharp backflow of air that gusted in his face. The air smelled strong and sour. Val and Shu wore expressions of revulsion.

"Get used to it," Kabta warned.

"What is that?" she asked. "Is something dead?"

"There are a few more things left to explain inside on our way to CAC," he replied. "I want you two to stay sharp. This place is exceedingly dangerous."

Val wondered, "Is it more dangerous than the thing waiting outside?"

9
AWAKENED SERAPH

Hannah Aston was thinking, "This station is dangerous," but she knew the real danger was outside. She'd discovered the switch that let the widow-shields up and down, permitting her a view of inky black depths studded with distant glowing lights. Her eyes strayed through the window towards the giant ship, dimly backlit against the eternal twilight of the deeps.

"I wonder what's inside," she said through a mouthful of dried mango. "I wonder if anything's alive in there, and if it knows we're out here watching."

Hannah absently turned something in her fingers—something that dangled by an alligator-clamp from a strap on the front of her jumpsuit. It was a blank white plastic card with a magnetic strip along one side. No one had explained to her its use, and she hadn't seen a card-reader anywhere in the station. Stranger still, there was no apparent reason for locking doors and keeping marines posted if no one else knew they were here.

These mysteries and many others distracted her thoughts in the hours since her arrival. She had washed, but taking a shower miles below the surface of the ocean did little to ease her mind. Dressing in the jumpsuit—an armored deal built for Wonder Woman—was no less a matter for contemplation. She wondered what the Foundation thought they were going to run into on a scientific outpost that could justify suiting everyone up in protective combat gear. The answers were either inside the ship or out there in the water. They sure weren't in the data she had access to in the archive room. That only raised more questions.

Hannah plopped her bag of trail-mix on the counter. She wasn't hungry anymore, and her sense of adventure was swiftly ebbing away. She noticed the outside lights had turned on again, but the whole area was looking quite a bit darker than before. Turning her attention back to the console in front of her, she brought up the schematic map displaying the ringed layout of the station complex. To the west of Geomech was a station named Lucius. That was where Ford was sent. She clicked the symbol for Lucius Station, and then looked around the room. A display on the right-hand wall brought up a dialogue box with fine print. She already knew what it read, because she'd gotten the same message before: *Mobile Recovery Unit.*

She'd dug deep enough to determine that Lucius was a large station that was able to be detached from the ring for transport to the surface and back. It was utilized for the storage and study of recovered technology. Geomech was used as a particle collider lab, and housed an Interferometry Array. Hannah didn't know much about particle accelerators, but she thought they were pretty well shielded and operated at extreme low temperatures. Such high-end toys would have been useful in developing a quantum computer system. Whatever its purpose, the accelerator's beam-tunnel was the ring connecting all the stations. She felt the tug of curiosity overcoming her apprehensions—her sense of adventure wasn't all gone yet.

"Man, I wish could find a way into that tunnel and visit Ford!"

Of course, the marines were probably watching them closely, and they'd find out if she left Geomechanical Station on an exploration mission. She wondered if they'd be angry, or if they'd report her to DePons. The thought of conversing with him face-to-face after his strange messages left her with a sinking feeling. She certainly didn't want to do anything to set him off. Then again, she'd only received a general warning about the ring-tunnel. One way or the other, she decided that she wasn't going to be doing much work until her curiosity was satisfied.

"It would take a hundred years to explore just one of these ships, and they've found two. I think the search for a third can wait a little longer."

She paused in the act of rising from her chair. Maybe what he said about darkness coming over the face of the Earth was an analogy referring to something else. She certainly hoped this was the case. For the time being, the darkness outside the windows was a little more disconcerting. She popped a leathery dried apricot into her mouth and watched as a cloud of silt blew up around her little world inside Geomech Station, noting with rising apprehensions the gravelly sound it was making as it blew across the windows.

That was when the alarms went off.

A brassy honking blast and shrill ringing erupted from the corridor, and to this was added an explosion followed by the thunder of rushing water. Hannah leapt to her feet, but froze a moment for sheer terror and stared at the windows. The greyish cloud of silt had become a solid wall, pressed flat against the acrylic. In the darkness she saw a face, a monstrous face looking in at her, its open mouth twisted in a horrible grimace—a face like a Chinese mask. The will to move momentarily left her.

Then, with a rush and the sound of scraping metal, the whole room began to twist and bounce. Sharp jets of water streamed in around the windows, and where they struck her exposed skin they stung with more than cold and pressure. Black spots clung to her.

Hannah needed no further persuasion to find the exit. She dashed through the archive hatch and pushed it shut behind her, spinning the round handle of the locking mechanism wildly. There were red lights flashing in the corridor, but she hardly noticed. All of her focus was on the hatch, which shuddered suddenly beneath a ringing blow. She let go of the lock and backed away. The small portal set in the surface of the hatch showed that the Archive had decompressed. It was completely flooded. The interior lights flickered and went out.

The lights in the hall flickered, too, and then faded to a steady red glare. The alarm continued. Hannah ran along the passage towards the airlock, and when she reached it she sealed the passageway closed behind her. The dive pool was empty. There was no minisub in it, but that was no matter. If the thing in the water could smash the station, it could obviously make mincemeat of a minisub.

She wondered if it was from the ship.

There were more noises of water in the passage outside the airlock. She thought she was lucky to have sealed the hatch in time; but the ceiling was beginning to buckle, and most of the hatches in the room were spraying water. Then the lights went out completely, and the alarm was silenced. The station groaned. Hannah's eyes began to search the room, and now her mind was thinking through the panic. She'd just remembered something important.

Breaker pointed out the little door across the dive pool when they entered the station. It was a simple metal door with a horizontal handle in place of a knob. She suspected the tunnel was behind it—the tunnel that connected Geomech to all of the other substations. Chances were, there might be nothing behind it now but water; but she would have to try it to find out. What else could she do? The hope of rescue was quickly retreating.

Was she going to die here, so close to where her parents died when she was a child? She gave it no more thought. It was the tunnel, or nothing.

The chamber was pitch black, and the water continued to come in; yet she strode across the room with a will. That door was going to open if she had to beat it down with her fists.

But first she had to find it.

She managed to avoid falling into the pool, and spent only a few moments feeling the wall with her hands before finding the edges of a doorframe. The door was impossible to budge, though, even when she set both hands on the latch. In the process of prying back the handle it broke free in her hand and hit the deck with a splash. It wasn't until that moment she realized she was standing in a few inches of water. Panicked, she ran her hand up and down the door until it rested on a large box where the latch had been. She then remembered the plastic card hanging from the front of her suit.

The habitat shuddered again, as if something was pounding on it from outside. Water was raining down from above. It hammered against the hatches with crushing pressure. Hannah knew the whole station was falling apart, but she forced herself to take breaths and think clearly. Her hand clutched the box in the wall next to the door. It was probably like the card-reader on an ATM. She plucked the card from her pocket and slid it through a groove in the side of the box.

Nothing happened.

Struggling to remain calm, she inserted the card one way and another, and then tried flipping it around. It occurred to her that if the station was without power, the door might not be able to read her key. Worse, it might be nothing more than a key to the pantry. She decided to keep on sliding the card anyway, and was surprised when a green LED lit up. There was a buzzing from the latch. With no handle to pull, she inserted her fingers into the socket where it had been, jiggling things around blindly. Miraculously, something clicked. She pulled, and the door opened slowly against the rising waters.

The area within was small. Hannah slipped inside with a little cascade of water and pulled the door shut behind her with the help of a wheel on the other side. As soon as it was closed a light turned on, illuminating a square room standing between the door and a larger hatch ahead. Lamps were set in the walls to either hand, and on the left-hand wall there was a sign.

USE BREATHERS IN MAINTENANCE TUNNELS.
RECHARGE BREATHERS AFTER USE.
CHECK BREATHERS OFTEN.

Hannah saw what appeared to be a pair of light hazmat tanks with a mask and harness on the wall. The two diving classes she'd taken on a vacation in Sinai weren't going to help her much, because this kind of equipment wasn't intended for underwater use. If the tunnel was compromised, she wouldn't last more than a few seconds.

Tossing these thoughts aside, she took up the tanks in her arms. They were heavier than they looked, and the facemask was rather large, but she felt a tiny bit better. Reaching to one side she found a valve, and turned it while holding the mask to her face. Chill air gusted against her skin, startling her and refreshing her in the same moment. Taking a second more to adjust the mask and wipe the plate, Hannah pulled back her hair and tied it off in a knot so that it stayed out of her way. It was time to go through the inner door.

Turning to examine this second hatch, she noted that it was sealed like all the others by a wheel-lock. She began to spin the lock counter-clockwise, even as the door behind her leaked. In moments the hatch was open, and Hannah plunged through into total darkness.

She was inside the tunnel.

The irony hit her that this was where she said she wanted to be only a few minutes ago. Now that she was here, though, she wanted very much to leave. It was a very unpleasant place, pitch black and cold. The grating beneath her feet splashed with every step. She could see nothing. For a time she paused and wondered if this was really safer than waiting in the station; but then she felt the water rushing past her boots again, and turning she slammed the great hatch shut, wheeling its lock round clockwise until it clanged loudly. The sound echoed around her, and even seconds later she heard fainter echoes returning from the left and the right. She was thinking of the map she'd seen on the console in the workstation.

"Was it left or right?" she asked, walking straight with hands outstretched. In a few seconds she came to a sloping wall covered with conduit. She knew the Computer Core station was to one side and Lucius was on the other. Too bad she couldn't remember exactly which was which. Her best guess was that the Computer Core was right, so she turned left.

"I wonder what's going on," she muttered. "I hope Ford's doing better than I am."

Walking with her right hand on the wall to guide her, and her left out before her to prevent her from walking into things, she set one foot in front of the other and began a blind journey through the dark.

It was very quiet in the tunnel. There was no sound of decompression, or of water. Only occasionally did she detect the hum from an electrical panel. The panels were lit with tiny red LEDs, but they were so small that they illuminated nothing. It was just enough to read the gauge on her air-tank. For about twenty uneventful minutes she went on in this manner before she began to notice a drop in the gauge's needle, and then Hannah began to wonder if she needed the breather at all.

"It's a collider," she thought, "so there's radiation, and probably some residual toxic gases. Maybe the warning was for those who would be exposed on a regular basis."

She kept the mask on.

Eventually, though, she began to hear something strange. For a long while she'd noticed her ears becoming more attuned to sounds, probably because her vision was restricted. Now she heard a sharp crackling and hissing noise coming from her right shoulder. Pausing, she patted the rough padding on a strap of harness there. Her fingers found a small bulge, and a pocket, and exploring this Hannah removed a plastic clip with an earbud and a short protruding wand. It was a radio. Fingers trembling, she attached it to her ear and listened, and amid the static she heard the sound of voices. All of her senses were instantly back to sharp focus.

"Blow the CC!" a voice was shouting. *"We can't let it use our system to access the link!"*

Hannah tore the mask from her face.

"Hello?" she said, hoping beyond hope there was a vibration-actuated transmitter somewhere on the device. Her hopes were not completely dashed.

"Is someone else on this frequency?" the voice demanded.

"This is Hannah Aston," she said. "I'm inside the tunnel!"

There was a loud burst of static, and the transmission went dead.

"So they're in trouble, too," she said to herself, replacing the breather.

She spent a moment fiddling with the clip to make it fit more comfortably around her ear. This led to two discoveries. The first was a small dial in the side, a tuner. All was static, but in the center of the tuner she made her second and more useful discovery—the tiny bubble of a microswitch. Depressing this, she was rewarded by a cheery gleam of light from the wand. Though dim, in that dark tunnel it shone like the sun.

"Hello?" she said louder, rotating the tuner-dial click by click. No one responded.

The realization sank in: rescue wasn't coming. In that hopeless moment she almost cried; but something else woke up inside her. She wouldn't lay down and die yet, and certainly not all alone. She would find Ford, or at least find out what happened to him.

The stout pipe to her right led her on. There were great bulges in the pipe—magnets for the particle accelerator. Powerful magnets could interfere with transmissions, she reasoned. She would need to locate a place where there were none, and then maybe she could take off the mask long enough to send a message that someone would hear. If she could do this before running out of air, so much the better. Hope quickened her pace, while claustrophobia began to quicken her pulse.

In the back of her mind, Hannah worried that Lucius Station might already be flooded before she got there. She was sure that more than half an hour had passed since the attack on Geomech began.

Who attacked them? Was it the thing she saw outside the window?

She was more concerned now what she would do if Lucius was destroyed. All she could think of for a backup plan was to keep walking the circuit, even if only to discover—should her air last so long—that this tunnel was all that remained.

Just then she reached a sealed hatch on her left.

The hatch opened easily enough. It closed behind her, but she didn't lock it. The chamber within was exactly identical to the one by which she'd exited Geomech Station, with a door in front of her that presumably led to Lucius; but now she realized that there was no card-reader on this side of the door, only another breather hanging on a hook to the right. Hannah tried the wheel-shaped latch, but it was locked. She kicked the steel door in frustration, but it didn't even shudder in its frame. Things were looking bleak indeed, when suddenly she heard a sound from the other side of the door—the sound she had been dreading.

It was the sound of rushing water.

She removed her hand from the latch and stretched it out before her. The door was icy cold to touch, and condensation was forming on its surface. In that moment, the thought occurred to her that Ford was already dead; but before she had a chance to consider what that meant she heard a tremendous crash followed by a buzzing noise from the door-lock. The wheel spun. The door burst open and a figure fell through, and with him came a wall of water that knocked her backwards violently. She collided with the hatch behind her, and then she was underwater. The icy cascade was bone-numbing. She'd never been in water so cold that it actually *hurt*.

Hannah rolled to one side and stood up, breathing hard. Her mask was seated firmly on her face, but it was beginning to fog over again with the temperature differential. It was therefore through a very cloudy faceplate that she glimpsed something beyond the open door.

It was too foggy, and too impossible to be real.

"It's after me!" a gravelly voice croaked beside her. "It's coming!"

It was Ford's voice. Hannah turned briefly, noting that he was struggling to stand amidst the water that had filled the room to their waists. He'd spent more time in the water than she, and was already very weak. She wiped her faceplate to no avail, but it seemed his face was covered with a tar-like substance that leaked from his eyes and open mouth.

"We've got to get away from it!" he gasped.

He fell to gagging on whatever it was that seeped out of his face, and Hannah reluctantly looked back into the substation. Her eyes were drawn by a fury of fuzzy movement within. The dim figure of a titan lumbered in the flickering lights, splashing about in a spray of foam as it slammed its forearms against the deck and dashed its body against the bulkheads in a frenzy of destruction. A long head jutted forwards from its torso, its bottom ending in a beak, and in the head were eyes that glowed green.

Her faceplate fogged even worse. She pried it up to rest on her forehead, but got no better look because the lights inside the station started flickering on and off. Ford's hand closed on her arm.

"Please!"

The situation was becoming quite serious. They were almost chest-deep in water.

"The hatch!"

Hannah pushed past him and reached to pull the hatch shut, but though she set all her strength to the task it closed very slowly. Just as she was about to set it firmly in the seal, a brief flickering of the lights within and of the little LED on her radio revealed movement on the threshold. She paused. A hand and arm thrust suddenly inside the hatch, preventing her from shutting the door.

Hannah leapt back, gasping with surprise while the arm pried the door back a little. It wasn't much—just enough for her to see people standing very close, two people, just on the other side. Ford must have noticed her hesitation, and he staggered towards the door; but Hannah was unnerved. The hatch began to open wider. A cloud of glistening grey smoke drifted through the opening, and standing in the smoke were the shapes of two people. Though their forms were indistinct at first, they quickly resolved; and now she saw their faces returning her gaze of wonderment and alarm, for these were people she had known.

They were her parents.

In the midst of that moment of doubt, Ford attacked the door with a strangled cry, yanking it hard by the wheel until the lock clicked. Hannah actually shoved him aside, and would have opened it again had he not grabbed her shoulders and held on to her. She was shaking, shivering with cold and the terror of what she had seen, and when she looked at Ford's face she was not comforted.

"We'll drown if we don't get out," he muttered, coughing on tarry sludge. "This station is separating from the ring!"

Then there was a soft knock at the door behind them, and the latch began to move. It was stopped by the lock, but Hannah reached out and grabbed it, holding it steady.

"*Not real,*" Ford said, and nodded towards the hatch.

The water was chest-deep.

She nodded in reply. Though all her mind and body was in confusion, she returned to the hatch leading to the tunnel, and together they pushed against it with all their strength. It was stuck.

Hannah ducked beneath the chill surface to brace herself against one of the walls, and then pushed with her legs. After a few intense moments she heard a sucking noise. Water coursed around her limbs, dragging her towards the hatch as it drained from the antechamber into the tunnel. Ford slid down to his knees and fell face-down on the floor beside her. Hannah reached with numbing hands to raise him up again.

"Come on!" she cried. "If that door behind you opens, the whole tunnel will decompress!"

As if in answer, the center of the door crumpled outwards towards them with a mighty blow. Water began to spray into the antechamber. Hannah dragged Ford towards the tunnel, but as they went stumbling side-by-side out into the dark there were shouts and screams behind them.

"They're not real!" Ford grunted, his smudged face very close to hers. "Don't you trust me?"

Hannah froze. Was this really Ford with his arm around her?

"Come on, Aston," he mumbled weakly in her ear.

She thrust him suddenly to a sitting position against the near wall. While he gasped in surprise she ducked back inside the airlock.

"Aston!" he shouted.

She reemerged seconds later with another breather in her hands.

"Here!" she cried, dropping it in his lap. Ford was too startled to do anything but sit and stare at her as she pulled the door shut. It banged loudly, and she sealed it with a few turns of the wheel.

Her eyes swiveled towards him, and momentarily she wondered if she hadn't made a terrible mistake.

"What's going on?" she asked, her lips trembling. "What was that thing?"

"Is it locked?" he asked.

In the slender beam of her light she saw a large wrench clamped against the tunnel wall. Hannah took it down and wedged it between the spokes of the wheel-lock and the frame of the hatch. No sooner had she finished this than the entire ring shuddered violently. Her ears popped, and the hatch groaned eerily with the force of decompression. Lucius had separated from the complex.

"Locked!" she said, dropping to her knees in a pool of water.

Another voice spoke nearby, startling them both. It was a calm feminine voice, prerecorded, announced from a small speaker above the hatch.

"*ZRP Protocol initiated,*" the voice said. "*MK-4000 Nuclear Depth Bomb activated. All personnel are requested to evacuate immediately beyond NDB range.*"

"What in Hades would they need a Nuclear Depth Bomb for?" Ford asked.

Still kneeling before the hatch, Hannah slipped the faceplate from her head and let her tears fall silently.

A few minutes passed before she was aware that Ford was trying to stand up. She turned and crawled towards him along the grating. He was still oozing a little bit of black syrupy liquid from his face. His glasses were gone. She noted no sign of trauma in his pupil dilation—his eyes just seemed a little darker than usual.

"Wipe off some of that gunk," she said. "I'll help you put this breather on."

He wiped his face on his arms, and she pulled on the mask, adjusting the straps tightly. The goo continued to drip, though a little less now.

"Looks like you found oil," she joked, opening the valve to his air-tanks. He was immediately refreshed, though he had to prop open the mask to cough.

"Remind me to ask Kabta for a fair share," he replied.

"Do we get paid anything for this?"

"You're shaking," he said.

She was surprised by the gentleness of his hand on her shoulder. They were both in hypothermic shock, so there was less romance in their sudden embrace than the perceived need for warmth. Ford held her only a moment, and then let go.

"Thanks, Hannah. If you hadn't banged on that door, I wouldn't have discovered the way out of there before Lucius separated. You saved my life."

She couldn't remember the last time he'd called her by her first name.

"Don't get all dramatic on me," she said, pushing him farther away. "There's a nuclear bomb here somewhere. I haven't saved anyone's life."

Ford patted her armored back with a firm hand. "Hey," he wondered, "how come you got armor on *your* jumpsuit?"

"It's not like either one of us is more important to the Foundation than the other."

"—Not so sure about that," he said, coughing.

"What's all that stuff on your face?" she asked. "And why did Lucius detach from the ring?"

He looked towards the hatch and shook his head lamely. "It was all automated. Some kind of toxic compound was in that thing from the buried ship."

"Is that what made me see *them?*"

"No. I saw them, too. I can't tell you what they were, but I can tell you that they weren't real people. They came from the smoke."

"Smoke?"

"Don't know. It looked like smoke, or oil. The crazy robot-thing was real enough, though, and whatever this black stuff is, I feel like I've been *drinking*."

"Great. We have a long walk ahead of us to the next substation. Can you make it?"

Ford nodded.

"I'm afraid I have only a little air left in my tanks. I hope *I* can make it."

Rising, she took his arm and helped him up. Then, together, they set off into the darkness. While they shuffled along, Hannah wanted to ask him more about what she had seen through the door, but she decided it could wait. Besides, talking would only waste whatever air they had left.

It was another half hour before they began to suspect they were the last survivors. They passed a hatch with the word ARMS on a sign above it. The lock wouldn't budge, and there was no breather tank on the wall. They kept walking, and in another half-hour Hannah began to feel very faint. She stopped and unslung her air-tanks.

"I'm out," she said, her jaw chattering.

"Take off the mask," he replied. "You'll dose yourself with CO_2."

Hannah obeyed, and was instantly struck by the fact that there was more air inside the tunnel than there was behind her mask.

He reached up and removed his own mask, and his features were almost completely obscured by the black water. Hannah's hands trembled as she reached to turn off his valves, and then she wiped his face with her hands. The goo was slick, and smelled like chicken-broth.

"It doesn't hurt," he said, blinking. "It feels like a really bad cold. Kind of gross, huh?"

Hannah frowned.

"Hey, can I see the light on your earbud thingy a moment—?"

He broke off his question, turning abruptly to look down the tunnel. Hannah followed his gaze, but she could see nothing beyond the reach of her lamp.

"Voices," he whispered.

"Is it the radio?" she wondered. She reached for the tuner, but got nothing more than static.

"Not a transmitter," he insisted. "I hear voices nearby, coming from that direction. Can't you hear them?"

Hannah listened, and soon she could hear them, too. She was suddenly overcome with fear.

"What if it's coming back?" she wondered. "What if it got through some other hatch into the tunnel?"

Then they saw distant flashlights. Ford stepped nearer to her, and together they waited.

The marine approached without friendly greeting, contrary to what one might expect among survivors of a catastrophe. He came upon the pair of scientists cautiously, weapon raised and ready. Hannah knew what he suspected, and it worried her. He was staring at Ford's face.

"It's good to see we're not alone," she said.

"You escaped," he replied. He did not sound relieved.

"Is that you, Hun?" Ford wondered.

"Yeah. What happened to you?"

"We were attacked, as if you didn't know."

"We were all attacked. CC station was destroyed by an explosion, and then everything just kind of went to pieces. The Barracks are flooded. I've just come from there."

"Lucius and Geomech are flooded, too," Hannah added. "And there's a bomb."

"Kind of sucks, huh? You must be freezing. Why aren't you wearing your breathers?"

"They're out of air," Ford said. "Why aren't you wearing yours, Attila?"

The mood lightened up, and Hun lowered his rifle. "The air's thin," he said, "but we should be okay for a little while.

We didn't have enough in the Barracks for all of us, and we decided to get out in a hurry."

"All of us?" Hannah wondered. "There are other survivors?"

"Yes, dear," a feminine voice said. Hun stepped aside as a black-suited figure strode out of the darkness.

"Nephtys?" Hannah wondered.

Her skirts were rumpled and her fair hair a mess, but Nephtys looked otherwise as fresh as she was the day Hannah had led her down to the buried ship at Hazor.

"Are you both alright?" she asked.

"We're not in great shape," Ford answered. "I guess everyone else is dead."

"There was no loss of life, Mr. Ford."

"Where are Kabta and DePons, and the other marines?"

Nephtys looked over her shoulder as DePons made his way into the light.

"I apologize for all the excitement," he said to Ford. "This is hardly what I had in mind for a second meeting with you two. As for the others, they weren't in any of the stations when the attack came. They've made it to a safer place. They're probably waiting for us there."

"A safer place?" Hannah wondered. "What about the nuclear bomb?"

"Miss Aston," he said, looking her way, "I told Kabta that you should have been better warned of the danger. It was against his wishes to reveal overmuch our security issues, though after this incident I suspect he will be persuaded to divulge a little more. I can see by his current health crisis that Mr. Ford has already glimpsed some of the complexities of our delicate situation."

"It's not permanent," Nephtys confided. "The black water will make you uncomfortable for only a few days, dear, and then you'll feel normal again."

Ford frowned. "That won't matter if we're blown to atoms, will it?"

DePons walked to Hannah's side and took her hand gently.

"Don't worry about a thing," he said to her. "Even if the substation is fully flooded, the ballast tanks on Lucius will bear it straight to the surface. We timed it so the NDB would go off while the station is still at a half-mile depth. We'll be well out of range by then."

"But we'll still be stuck in here!" she cried, pulling her hand free.

"I doubt the Armory is actually flooded, and if it's locked I can easily get us inside. There are two minisubs there. We'll be off this station in just over half an hour, which leaves us plenty of time to meet with Kabta and finish this business."

He waved his hand in the direction they had just come. Ford shrugged, and turning he led the way back towards Arms.

"Where are we going to meet Kabta?" Hannah asked as they walked

"You know," DePons replied, winking slyly.

10
GHOST MESSAGE

Val stood in silent wonder of the place and wrinkled her nose. Avalon was no less forbidding a sight to see than its stink was to smell; but while their adventure ushered them deeper into the ship's dark cavernous depths, the rank odors wafting along the passageways grew somewhat less conspicuous. Maybe it was because the short walk to CAC was full of other overwhelming sensations besides smell. Her eyes, nose, and ears took in what they could, but there was little in Val's experience to compare the place to. Having been aboard a Gremn ship before she expected something more familiar, but Avalon was unique.

Kabta and Shu went before her, and four other marines walked behind. Though none spoke even a passing word to Val, she wondered if she hadn't met some of them before, thousands of years ago in the heart of Auriga. Kabta introduced them by their names this time: Sheb, Abdaya, Malkin, and Hanuta—the last being a freckled young woman with pink hair. Their silent presence reassured Val, for these were among Kabta's trusted inner-circle; but even they looked nervous when the large corridor narrowed suddenly around them.

"Slow down," Kabta warned from the front.

Before he was finished speaking, bright blue lights automatically flickered on, blinding their startled eyes and washing the passage in misty brilliance. A single spotlight was fixed on Val, following her slight movements like an eye.

"Another probe," Shu said quietly. "I don't see any auto-guns."

"Avalon's curious about her, no doubt," Kabta replied. "Let's keep moving. The CAC is just ahead."

The light tracing her steps was beginning to hurt her eyes, but the hall soon came to an end at another hatch, and there the beam turned off suddenly with a sharp click. While her eyes adjusted, the others paused to look at something like writing just above the door. Val could no longer comprehend the Gremn language, though.

Kabta stepped up to a panel set into the left-hand wall. He set his hand gently on its smooth black surface, and with an abrupt groaning sound the doors slid apart. Lights were on inside, but the CAC appeared very gloomy.

Val's face paled as her recurring dream was recalled before her waking eyes. "The system recognizes you?" she asked.

"It recognizes any Gremn," he answered, peering into the room. Then he paused, considering.

"Please don't touch anything, Val Anna, or we may all be destroyed. You and Shu follow me. The rest of you post guard here."

They left the marines outside and went in. The layout was identical to the CAC of Auriga, having hubs on both sides and one in the front that housed a large pyramid, the Computer Core of Avalon. There was a CSRT console standing before the Core, and something unfamiliar on the deck between them, a wide round platform only a few inches high. Besides the CSR, there were few other consoles, and no handrails anywhere—no distinctly human touch to the appearance of the place. This was a curiosity to Val.

"I thought you said the ship was inhabited by a group of Crodah for several years," she said. "The buried ship never passed into Crodah hands, yet it seemed less strange than this place."

"It's as though Avalon was kept up for the Gremn," Shu remarked. "Or maybe the Gremn erased all traces of the Crodah occupation?"

"Avalon and Auriga were two very different ships," Kabta replied. "Both were controlled by an artificially intelligent source, but Avalon's AI and much of its technology are far older. Avalon is virtually unchangeable. Morvran's crew may have tried to make things more homelike, but the ship's capable of regenerating components switched out by human hands."

As he spoke he prodded a hunk of the ubiquitous stinking membrane covering a support truss with the toe of his boot. "Everything wrapped in this artificial flesh is actively preserved by Avalon," he said. "The ship's a living thing."

"It's a story my father told me," Val said in a quiet voice. "It was a ghost story, from one of his long sea voyages. He told me that he served aboard a ship where everything seemed to be alive, controlled by a secret intelligence that wished harm upon the crew. I suppose that's what it must have been like aboard this ship."

The others were hushed by her words, and exchanged curious glances.

"What's wrong?" she asked.

"Nothing," Kabta replied casually. "That's actually a very good description of what it was like. You couldn't even hang a picture in here. The walls would push out the nail."

Small red and blue lights cast a ghastly pallor over the ochre-stained walls, and air pulsed above their heads in misty tendrils. To Val, this seemed less like the sophisticated control center of a fortress than the heart of a vast sleeping beast. She wondered what would happen when Avalon awoke, and patted the haft of the dagger—Morla's dagger—in its sheath on her hip. The blade didn't make her feel safer, but looking where Kabta stood she suddenly revisited the events of her last adventure in the CAC of a Gremn ship. The dagger was a real connection to those events, and to the friends she had already lost.

Kabta descended the stair towards the bowl-shaped center of the room, and paused at a bank of consoles. These had a familiar look about them. They were like the consoles surrounding the tube of black water in the Archive of Auriga.

"I suppose the viewer would be the best place to start," Kabta said.

"Where is it?" Shu asked, looking around the surrounding hubs.

"Forward hub. It's the round platform in front of the CSRT."

Val followed Shu around the port hub towards the front of the room. She glimpsed the smooth columns to her left with awe—columns like twisted termite mounds. Consoles glimmered there, but as she moved past them she realized they were completely immaterial, floating in the air just above the fleshy surface of the columns.

"Projected images?" she wondered.

Shu passed these wonders by with only a glance, stopping when they'd reached the round platform on the floor of the forward hub.

"We're here to locate something specific," Kabta said as he climbed another stair to join them. "The bad news is the volume of information stored aboard Avalon is enormous. The good news is we won't need to worry about going through it all, because we don't have access to more than a small fraction of it."

Shu asked, "How do you know what we're searching for is even accessible, then?"

Kabta gave him a strange look, narrowing his eyes.

"We know that we'll be displaced if we actually succeed, Uncle."

Val noticed the tension in Shu's voice. Kabta noticed, too.

"I will show you why I have decided to pursue this course," he said to Shu. "I want you to see something I've held onto for a very long time. I can think of no better place to share it than this, because it was here that all Gremn and Crodah began our exile under the Ban. Here aboard this command deck an unforgiveable atrocity was committed, and what we all thought would bring an end to the war only brought about a new, lasting conflict."

He held in his hand a small metallic rod. Val thought it looked like a cigar in a tinfoil wrapper, only a little stouter. Kabta pointed the rod at the platform in front of them and pressed one end with his thumb. The CAC's lights dimmed almost to total darkness, and the air above the floor shimmered. Then they saw a wonder. Val looked upon what had been in her mind only a little while ago, an aeroship projected in three-dimensional clarity.

"This is Avalon. Though, you might also say it's the way Avalon *remembers* itself, since the ship recorded this viewer-image many ages ago."

Val's astonished eyes took in the sight of a thousand miles of ice. Cloudy tendrils of snow blew through the air before her face, wreathing the image of the ship. She shivered, though the room was quite warm.

"Its purpose was quite different from that of the ship where we met," Kabta said to her.

"That ship was full of weapons and armories," Val remembered.

"Yes, and also a powerful AI, an archive of our knowledge, and learning machines. But Auriga was more a transport than a warship, and Avalon's purpose remains shrouded in mystery."

"I thought it was a fortress."

"That is what the Gremn made of it, though whatever it was before the Gremn received it from the hands of the Ancients, no one knows. Many Gremn dwelt here in days of peace, and most of them were technologists. In those days Avalon was a fount of scientific discoveries. Our search for new ideas and technology led us ultimately to division, when the Gremn learned to change their bodies and became superior to the Crodah in more than mind only. It was aboard Avalon that the first of us were changed. We used black water stasis tubes to do it. I think the discovery of these devices left behind by the Ancients was what brought about the desire to create a race of perfect warriors. Success in this enabled us to enslave the Crodah, but the Crodah resisted."

"The war began with a gift of technology," Val said. "Why did the Ancients give away this technology and the stones, if they knew we would make them into weapons?"

He regarded her keenly.

"Speaking of weapons," Shu said, looking on the enormous ship with wide eyes, "how'd the Crodah manage to capture this fortress, and how'd it get here?"

Kabta sighed. "Once there was a hero of the Crodah," he said, "a man who with only a handful of skilled warriors came and destroyed the Gremn hive at Islith. In the aftermath, Islith's fortress, Avalon, traded hands a couple of times in the matter of an hour—so short a span for so horrible an event."

"What happened?" Val asked.

"Destructive weapons called atomics were deployed by both sides from this command deck. Much of the World of Origins was affected in the ensuing firestorm. The war jolted to an abrupt halt, but only because there were so few left to fight. Avalon with a small fleet of Crodah vessels was sent through a

Viaduct to Ertsetum, while the Gremn were stripped of almost all our technology and exiled to Iskartum."

Val stood in thoughtful silence for a few moments, staring at the holographic image above the viewer. "But you didn't lose everything," she said. "There was the Auriga, and also another ship, somewhere else in the Earth."

The looks of surprise on both the Gremn were answer enough to her suspicions.

"You wouldn't have asked Hannah Aston to look for a third ship if it didn't exist."

"It is called Aries," Kabta replied. "It was an advanced warship we brought with Auriga when we traveled to Ertsetum."

"These two ships were not sent here by the Ancients, like Avalon?"

"No."

"That means the Gremn also have more than one stone in this world."

Shu shifted uncomfortably beside her. She realized this was news to him as well, though he'd had thousands of years to figure it out on his own. Across from them, Kabta's stone-cold expression revealed more than the Gremn thought he was hiding.

"You see more clearly than I anticipated," he confessed. "Lír held the stone Agru aboard Aries. My brother and I held Narkabtu on Auriga. There was then no clearer purpose to my mind than that we were given Narkabtu to drive the engines of our ships and Agru to lead us."

"What became of this stone, Agru?" Val asked.

"It was lost, perhaps with the Aries."

"The Ancients gave the Gremn the two stones they needed to continue their conflict with the Crodah in exile?"

"I believe there was a reason for this other than to continue the war," he replied. "Four stones there were in this world, two for the Crodah and two for us. Narkabtu of the Gremn you hold, though Agru is lost. Qashtu of the Crodah you also hold. That is two of the three required to return against the Ban."

"What of the fourth, the second stone brought by the Crodah?"

"It was also lost, somewhere on the South American continent. We followed it closely for a long time, even up to the day that Avalon fell. It was named Regulus, and was held by the keeper of Qashtu, the commander of this vessel. He was a warrior named Ard Morvran."

Val mulled his words slowly, wondering that she felt no surprise.

"Maybe it's difficult to imagine," he continued, "but your meeting up with one of Morvran's direct descendents and receiving Qashtu from him is part of a plan neither Gremn nor Human. We are all a part of a longer story than any of us can fully appreciate—even those of us who have been around for awhile. For it all began in the days before the War, even in the days of the Ancients."

"—if you believe such bedtime stories," Shu remarked.

Kabta nodded his head. "Not much is known of them outside of legend," he admitted.

Val said nothing, but she could not repress the memory of the evil cloud that had suffocated her on the wall at Hazor. The Destroyer was one of these Ancients. She was suddenly very interested in their plans for the stones, and for her.

"Why would spiritual beings need stuff like this?" Shu asked, waving his hand around the forward hub. "They were probably just people like us, but more intelligent."

"I remind you, Nephew, the Ancients are those who enforce the Ban. You forget that those of us who were exiled, who dwelt in Syrscian during the War, faced one of these creatures at Gilthaloneth when the Ban was pronounced. Your father and I both stood before him, and the memory of it still weighs heavily upon me."

Shu's smile faded at the mention of his father. The three gazed quietly at the viewer. Val disturbed the silence with a question.

"Don't we all share the consequences equally?" she asked. "I think this is the purpose of the stones. The stones came to

Ertsetum divided, but I brought them here inside one stone. Now they are gathering together again, just as we are, so that we can find a way back to the place we were banished from."

Val felt a throb of heat against her chest, and she knew that whatever the stone was it stirred when she considered it. Or was it because it considered *her*?

Kabta said, "This wisdom graces you, Val Anna. It was with you on Auriga, and I see a glimpse of it again now. You hold a secret that binds us all together. That is why I pledged to protect you."

Shu looked at his uncle, and the rising agitation that had hardened his features melted away.

"Lír's people believe the Ban will be lifted if we take the stones from the Crodah and make our return," Kabta said. "But there is no faction, no government of Crodah or of Gremn, and certainly no forceful ambition, that could ever succeed in lifting the Ban. It's immediate effects are felt in displacement."

Val's stomach tightened. "That's because of the Ban?" she asked.

"That *is* the Ban."

"Then how do we beat this?" Shu asked. "Val says the Ban will only be lifted if the stones are returned, but we'll end up being displaced under the Ban if we try a transit out of here."

"As unfair as that may sound," Kabta replied, "it is even more complicated than you yet realize. It's time for us to take a look at the other side of the situation. This image of Avalon isn't what we've come all this way to see."

The shape of Avalon floating in a snowy sky disappeared. In its place was a grainy field of grey arranged in an oblong sphere. Val and Shu both frowned, clearly unsure of what they were seeing. Kabta began speaking again, and it was immediately apparent that he had only been building up to an explanation.

"It is beyond our ability to merit forgiveness for the waste of what was once most beautiful. Something more is required than our efforts to correct our misdeeds."

"Like what?" Shu asked.

"We must participate in an experiment of trust, blindly, with no more guidance than a few words I once heard from the mouth of an Ancient in the city of Gilthaloneth—and this."

He spread out his hands towards the grey transmission bubble that hovered and glittered in the air before them. An uncomfortable stillness settled over the three. Val and Shu exchanged confused looks, but Kabta was gazing steadily at them.

"Val Anna," he said. "You know that I have eagerly awaited your arrival twice now, at intervals of thousands of years. Have you not guessed how this was possible?"

"I have no idea," Val replied.

"What if I told you I had news of your transport long before you and I first met?"

"It couldn't be the time-viewing capabilities of Auriga," Shu stated. "But for the brief time Kal-Nergal awakened it, that device has never worked. How could you know when she would appear?"

"I simply told myself," Kabta replied. Then, seeing their puzzled faces, he smiled. Before them, the grey orb above the viewer went dark, and blue static appeared in its place.

"Let me explain," Kabta began. "It happened upon the very day that Magan met me at the hill of Hazor, the day I was betrayed by my brother—the day Avalon fell. It was an event that convinced me, however slowly, of the priority to recover Avalon and attempt this transit. It was the day the comet appeared."

There were lines shifting across the static, and faintly they descried among these lines the shapes of people moving.

"On that day," Kabta continued, "the sky above the hill of Hazor cleared—a curious omen in the ages of endless winter in Ertsetum. I saw a shining comet hanging in the heavens, and I received this very curious message."

The instrument he held hummed quietly, and there was a hiss as brighter light leapt suddenly from the viewer's surface into the air before them. For a moment nothing more happened, and then the air flickered with distorted projections.

"This message was broadcast over our secure link—the link with Comet Bibbu which was thought to be severed. It was not transmitted by the Crodah. The message uses a quantum frequency the Crodah could not hack, and still cannot. No one else could broadcast or receive this message, because it employs my own security codes. Stranger still, users of these devices are all identified by their biometrics. Though I had no knowledge of it, I had sent this message to myself."

Shu frowned. "You sent a message to yourself 150,000 years ago? What does this have to do with your foreknowledge of Val's arrival ten days ago?"

"Patience, Nephew," Kabta said, watching the image resolve. "As I said, *I told myself.*"

The silvery shapes above the table were becoming clearer to Val. "Who is that I see?" she asked.

But the answer presented itself when the static suddenly cleared, and ghostly figures began to assemble themselves from the light, cast in the ring before them in three dimensions. Val and Shu both looked on in shocked silence. Front and center, Kabta's own face was easily recognizable; but there were others in the image. There were three seated in front, two on either side of Kabta, and several others standing behind. The projection was fuzzy, and the faces indistinct, but the identity of the three people seated in front was obvious—if also ominous.

"It's *us*?" Shu wondered.

Val squinted at the ghostly reflection of herself. "How can it be us?" she asked. "I don't remember this happening before. And who are those others behind us?"

"I can hardly see them," Shu replied. "The one on the left is U.S. Air force, by his uniform. I can't place the one in the middle or the lady on the right. Is she wearing a white dress?"

Val was suddenly struck by the absurdity of what she was seeing. "This was sent to you *how* long ago?" she asked.

"150,000 years before present. The northern hemisphere of this planet was frozen in ice. There was no United States, much less the land for it to exist—"

"Much less a U.S. Air force to defend the land that didn't exist," Shu added, staring at the uniformed man.

"Who is he?" Val asked. "I think I know him."

"That's Cedric DePons, our joint UAMC and UAD commander-in-chief," Kabta replied. "You two met at Hazor—and also when you were a small child."

Shu shook his head. "That can't be right," he said. "You never told me Cedric's story, but it seems he gets around too much for an ordinary human. He can't be from Val's time if he's still around today!"

"But he's in the picture!" Val said, gesturing with her hand.

"So are we all," Kabta said, his voice growing quiet. *"Listen."*

The seated image of Kabta addressed them in ordinary English.

"You are receiving this transmission by a cooperative effort of Gremn and Crodah. We do not know in what frame of reference our message reaches you, if it reaches anyone at all, but it will hopefully come at some suitable juncture. I, Kabta of House Gremn, speak on behalf of those with me in Ertsetum, whose utter displacement resulted from the misuse of the stone Regulus. Decoherence has rendered in this world some rather dire circumstances, a calamity from which we shall likely perish in short time. Thus, we who once were enemies have been forced to band together to survive. Return now is impossible for us, for all the other stones entrusted to us have vanished. We assume this is good news, that they are being recohered due to collaboration elsewhere among the Dark Worlds. News of this event has come to us by the dreams of Val Anna, who first arrived via the Auriga's Mirror on the eve of the dissolution of the Canaanite kingdoms, and a second time upon the comet's first transit of Auriga after the formation of the state of Israel. We trust you

> *will support her in her quest to recohere the stones and
> return against the Ban, wherever her journey takes her,
> and we look forward to the completion of her task, for
> only when Regulus is recohered and vanishes from our
> world will our suffering end."*

After a few more moments, the image froze, and Val stirred from her amazed silence with a question.

"Is it from the future, or the past?"

"Neither," Kabta replied. "The message, like these unfortunate counterparts of ours, originated in a Dark World. The sequence of events within their frame of reference is obviously the same. Past and future, however, are irrelevant."

"And what's decoherence?" Shu asked.

"Displacement is something that occurs as a manifest symptom of decoherence," Kabta explained, "decoherence being the result of matter from one side of a vacuole coming in direct contact with matter from the other side."

"Matter coming in contact with matter from the *other side?* What other side?"

"When one travels through a Mirror-device to places far-off, time as well as space is compressed; but matter must first be disentangled from the current frame of reference if it is to arrive at a new location. This transfer of matter across compressed space-time is called decoherence by the Gremn. What the message claims is that there's an entire decohered *world*—or maybe many of them—that was created as a result of the activities of the stones."

"That defeats all I know about life and purpose," Val said. "How could there be alternate realities?"

"It's not an alternate reality. It's a Dark World, a reflection, like this world we are in now."

"Will this decoherence happen in our world, as it has in theirs?" Val wondered.

"That's the real question, isn't it?" Kabta asked. "I personally feel that we have begun to defeat it. We've already accomplished much in reuniting just two of the stones. What's more, recohering Qashtu and Narkabtu has had an effect on our counterparts—those stones vanished in their world. Nergal's activation of a Mirror on our side, however, may also have had something to do with that."

"What did you do when you received this message?" Shu asked.

"You appreciate the irony, then?" Kabta said with a smile. "When I received this message through the comet's link with Avalon, I wondered if Avalon itself had not fabricated the entire thing to lure me into rash deeds."

"But aren't we about to do the same thing?" Shu asked. "You still haven't explained how this will work now, when it obviously hasn't worked before. Nergal messed everything up when he displaced himself and Val in transit from Auriga."

Kabta's look grew stern. "I think you and I both know there's another way to access the lost road," he said. "Regulus has caused some trouble on their side, but thanks to Nergal we only need the two stones we have."

Val looked from one to the other, and then back to the viewer. "Can we get a closer look?" she asked.

The image slowly zoomed as Kabta manipulated the control. They were now able to see past their seated counterparts, and each quietly examined the central and right-hand figures.

"Do you recognize him?" Kabta asked, pointing towards the short figure in the center.

Shu shook his head. "No," he said. "I've never seen him before, unless he's a shape-shifter. Val?"

Val's face went very pale. She suddenly recalled seeing this face before, in a gloomy subterranean chamber beneath Hazor.

"I *do* know him," she said. "And so do you. He's the young king, Ibni. Don't you see?"

Shu leaned forward, eyes wide with wonder.

"But that's not all," she said. "We also know the girl. The weird bluish hair makes her look different, but the woman in white is *Nunna*."

151

Kabta nodded. "Who has seen a specter in the moonlight and not felt its fear?"

"Ghosts?" Val wondered. "You mean to say that Nunna's really dead?"

"Of course she is."

"So if you die in one world, you live on in another?"

He narrowed his eyes. "That I do not know. What I do know is that there was more to Nunna than anyone was aware of, and the proof is before your eyes."

"How could there be more than one of her?" Val asked.

"And of *us*?" Shu added.

"The appearance of our own counterparts in the message is simple, if grim," Kabta said. "The Dark Worlds are a consequence of our misuse of the stones. The worlds, like the stones, were all divided from one, and so are we."

"They are *divisions* of us?" Val wondered.

"And now we've got to get this stone from their side, somehow, or we'll all be further divided," Shu reasoned. "It doesn't get much worse than this."

"Oh, it does," Kabta replied. "But thanks to Kal-Nergal, we can ignore these complications for now."

They both stared at him.

"We don't need Regulus. We need Nergal, who is somewhere in the World of Origins, and we need the one who can fix his exact location. That is as good as having an open door for our transit."

"What about the third stone?" Shu asked.

"When all this is accomplished, Regulus will come to us—it will be recohered."

"Now I know why you didn't brief the others on this plan before we came here," Shu said, running a hand through his hair.

"Who can pinpoint Nergal's location?" Val asked.

"The Source."

"The *Source*?" she wondered, her voice pitched with alarm. "How do we contact the Source? Isn't Auriga's CC dead?"

"The Source and Avalon were linked until the day Avalon fell. In their long ages of isolation afterwards, however, the link was reestablished somehow via the comet. The two AIs began to talk again, and they still do. The Source did not expire with Auriga, but resides now inside Nergal. Avalon is still linked to the comet, as is the Source. In order to establish a location for the World of Origins and complete a transit, however, we also need the assistance of one other person, someone here on Avalon."

Kabta looked sternly at Shu, but Shu said nothing.

"What is it with you two?" Val asked, exasperated.

"His contact with Lír's man revealed something that he thinks I do not already know."

Shu sighed.

"Besides what I have already told you, he was likely informed of the presence of Avalon's control entity in stasis. With the help of this flesh-and-blood pilot, we could access the Viaduct Chamber even without security codes—"

Just then, the marine named Abdaya crossed the CAC towards them. His expression was serious, but Val couldn't tell that he was upset about something until he spoke.

"I've received a transmission, Sir," he reported. "There was an incident. It seems the security system has attacked the substations. A PCU was simultaneously activated in Lucius, which initiated separation and ZRP Protocol. All survived. Attila has them holed up in the armory for now, but the air's getting thin in there. One of the scientists may have been injured—"

"Lucius is ascending?" Kabta asked.

"The station's ascent was uncontrolled, and it's fully flooded, so it got hung up underneath the rock shelf above the ring."

"Or was that also the work of the security system?" Shu wondered.

The marine nodded. "I suspect so. The NDB is active, with less than two hours remaining."

"NDB?" Val asked.

"*Nuclear Depth Bomb*," Shu replied with a slow exhalation. "It's part of the Zero Residual Presence Protocol, which prevents Gremn technology from bobbing around on the surface for cruise ships to bump into. Detonation is set at two hours from ZRP initiation, which should put Lucius a half-mile below the surface; but now it's right outside."

"I calculate a high probability the NDB will completely destroy Avalon," the marine added.

"Then what are they waiting for?" Kabta asked. "There are subs docked in Arms. Tell Attila to get them over here, *now*."

The marine snapped a salute and turned to leave.

"Ab!" Kabta called. "Abdaya, take Val Anna with you to settle her friends Aston and Ford in the corridor outside. I'll hunt for the Chamber access codes here with Shu. If we find nothing in another half-hour, we'll head for SARA Station regardless."

"So much for jump-starting the drives," Shu said. "Without the accelerator and Auriga's cores for backup, we'd better hope Avalon has the power to initiate transit."

"This is all sooner than expected," Kabta replied, "but now we are in Avalon's hands, and it seems that Avalon already knows of our plan. The ship's AI may in fact be leading us into a trap by limiting our choices. Let us hope that it will help and not further hinder us, or none of us will get out of this alive."

11

THE TRAP CLOSES

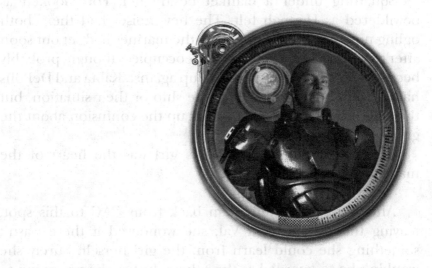

Resting against a ribbed wall of the passage, Hannah shivered in her blanket. The curving corridor twisted away before and behind her, confounding both imagination and scientific curiosity. Hannah was frightened, for this place didn't seem much safer than the substations. While Ford rested beside her, Val paced before them, looking out into the vast dark tunnel like an explorer in the deepest cave in the earth, shining a flashlight the marine had given her. Near at hand it revealed only surfaces glistening with foul excretions. The dim beacon failed altogether less than fifty feet away, dispersing in clouds of mist. From beyond the wall of vapors came sounds of air moving and water dribbling, and occasionally an alarming rattle of noise that echoed from farther away. It was now about one hour after their arrival, and the rumbling, which at first had been so faint that Hannah thought she imagined it, rose suddenly to a thunderous crash and distant flicker of flames. Then, ominous silence. Val flicked off the light, and they waited in the dim twilight of softly luminous consoles, projected here and there onto the layers of tissue growing on the walls. Another boom rumbled down the ribbed passageway, drawing a startled gasp from all three.

Squatting under a blanket beside her, Ford looked as bewildered as Hannah felt. The new noises had them both ogling nervously in the direction the marines had set out soon after they'd arrived. Val seemed preoccupied, though, probably because she knew what they were up against. Kabta and DePons hadn't told them much about the ship or their situation, but they did make an attempt to clear up the confusion about the girl.

Hannah had no doubts. This girl was the heart of the matter.

After Kabta escorted them back from CAC to this spot, leaving them alone with Val, she wondered if there wasn't something she could learn from the girl herself. Surely she wouldn't be so guarded as the others. Just as she was going to break the menacing silence that followed the previous crash, a new clamor erupted even closer at hand.

"Sounds like a real war down there!" Ford said loudly, startling them both.

Hannah looked closely at him. He hadn't spoken a word since they left the substations, but now he was looking downright cheerful—if not a little bit drunk.

"Are you alright?" she asked.

"I don't know, Hannah. Still a little giddy."

"Sounds like it's stopped," Val said.

Hannah strained to hear something in the deep silence. There was nothing—not even the ceaseless irritating drip that had punctuated the previous hour's sitting.

"Maybe it left," she said. "Too bad this smell doesn't go away. It reeks like a carcass!"

"Try breathing through your mouth," Val suggested.

Hannah took an experimental breath, and retched.

"The taste's as bad as the smell!"

"You'll get used to it."

"Are *you*? What about this rust? Is it dangerous?"

Val turned her light on again, and shone it on the nearest wall. At first it had seemed the walls were covered with rust where the dull grey and black surfaces, slick and fleshy, gave way to rougher vivid red hues. The red also appeared wherever the walls bulged into protruding structures, twisted ribs curving gently to meet the high arched ceiling. Val walked to where Aston sat and placed her hand against the wall's surface. It was warm to touch, and surprisingly stiff—like a tensed muscle beneath a layer of skin. She took her hand away and shone the light on it, revealing a red stain.

"It's not rust," she decided. "It looks like algae."

"Whatever it is, it *stinks*."

"It's warm. It'll keep you both warm until you dry out."

"I hope there's nothing infectious growing in here."

Ford peered out from his blanket. "It's a protein-silicate composite that continually regenerates. DePons says it keeps everything working, and protects their technology from decay. It won't hurt us."

"If it's alive, what does it eat?" Hannah asked.

"Maybe it filters nutrients from the atmosphere surrounding the ship," he said, "in this case, from the sea. It's actually based on plant life, but not of any plant from this world."

Hannah turned away from him to examine the wall, touching its damp surface, and flicked her fingers to release a small quantity of gooey stuff into the air. She wiped her hand on the blanket in disgust.

"Alien plants?" she mumbled. "Just being this close to it is absolutely vile!"

"You two were in Columbia University?" Val asked, changing the subject. "I've been to New York, but that was very long ago."

Ford lifted his eyes toward her, and Hannah thought for an instant that she could hear him speaking. His mouth wasn't moving, however.

"It's different now," she said. "*Very* different."

"So he told you—"

"DePons told us the Foundation brought you here from more than a hundred years in the past, though I still don't understand how you then appeared in a spacecraft buried beneath thirty-five hundred years of human occupation at Tel Hazor."

Val offered no explanation.

"They also said you are the official leader of this expedition," Hannah continued. "I was wondering if you'd give us a few hints as to what Kabta's up to in that fancy room, and why we've got to wait out here with whatever-it-is making all that noise down the hall."

"New York must be a wonderful place," Val said, completely avoiding her inquiries. "I've been told there are many more people, and the buildings are extremely tall."

Silence resumed for a few moments. Hannah asked, "Is everyone you knew…gone?"

"The current year is 2006," she replied gently. "Everyone I knew must be dead. If they are not, I do not think they would know me. It must be so, for it was all done in the stone. I just…I just keep hoping that maybe this is all a dream. I'm sorry, Miss Aston. What Kabta is doing in CAC—the control chamber down the hall—is looking for access codes we require to enter certain portions of the ship. He's better acquainted with the technology than anyone else. We're in his hands now."

"I guess that's what's bothering me," Hannah said.

Ford chuckled, and said, "A man's in charge—look out Hannah! I don't think they've got a hotline to the ACLU down here!"

"Shut up, Ford! I meant I'm bothered by the fact that he knows anything at all about this place."

"I suppose we aren't meant to know how he got experience working with alien technology," Ford said, still grinning from his joke. "Aren't you the one whose parents were abducted by aliens in the Bermuda Triangle—*ouch!*"

Hannah withdrew her elbow from his side, eyes glowering. Ford shut up.

Val studied Hannah curiously, and asked, "If you were at University, you must be older than me—unless you count all the years between."

Ford bit his lip. Hannah elbowed him anyway.

"Ouch! What was that for?"

"How old are you?" Hannah asked, turning back to Val.

"I'm only eighteen."

"I'm twenty-three," Hannah said.

"It might interest our anachronistic friend," Ford said, eyeing Hannah's elbow, "that the lifespan of Americans has increased significantly since the early twentieth century."

The women stared, confused by his comment.

"It began when we put away the self-destructive habits and lifestyles of an emerging world culture," he continued, speaking rapidly. "We began to pursue a common purpose, and thereby discovering their own purposes for being—their niches in society—individuals began to live longer and fuller lives, resulting in the technological advancements that've made it possible to preserve the body to even greater age. Of course, that also doubled the planet's population over just a few generations. Why are you looking at me like that, Aston?"

Hannah shook her head and asked, "What *are* you going on about?"

Ford gave her a look of annoyance. "Weren't you listening?"

159

"You've never carried a non-technical conversation for more than a couple beats. Now you're spouting *human anthropology?* It's the strangest guff I've ever heard from your mouth! When did you ever start caring about people's purposes or lifestyles, anyway?"

There was a sound of footsteps approaching, and they all turned in the direction of CAC. As Shu approached them, he said, "He's been in the black water. It's already begun to change him."

"Black water? You mean the stuff that was oozing from his face? I thought Nephtys said it was harmless."

"Dr. DePons says Avalon's security system compromised the substations because Mr. Ford awakened the *Seraph*. The ship's AI then attempted to bond with him, to use his mind. Kabta thinks it might have given him something useful."

Ford roused himself to an upright position. Shu came to stand above him, looking down with undisguised loathing.

"You can choose to do whatever you want," Shu said. "Flip a few switches on a hunk of debris in Lucius, see what happens. I mean, they were just switches in a box under a flap of smelly skin, right?"

Ford shook his head. "What are you—?"

"I'm talking about choices, Mr. Ford. It seems that since your fiasco on the substation, you have come to believe in a self-determined purpose—that human choices ultimately govern things like lifespan. Don't you think that's a little ironic?"

"How's it ironic? It's a fact."

"If I was referring only to the consequences of poor choices, we would all agree. However, considering our situation, I think it's safe to say that an intelligent agent of destiny has graciously intervened in order to overrule your poor choices, sparing us the consequences altogether. Despite your idiocy, we're all still alive and moving steadily towards our long-term objective—for now."

"He's saying it's not your fault," Hannah interpreted.

"And what agent performed this miracle?" Ford asked sourly. "You're not saying I'm lucky, are you?"

"No, I'm not. No matter what you might have chosen to do, the outcome already lay within a trajectory appointed for us. We were guided in a quiet way, protected from poor choices."

"You're talking about a god, then? Something that grants us the ability to choose, and then takes it away totally or partially, provided me with the opportunity to wake up that crazy robot so we could all end up here? Even if I believed it I'd still have to wonder, if there's someone pulling the strings, what's the point in granting Mankind the power to make choices at all?"

"Good question," Shu replied with a smirk. "I've often wondered that myself."

Ford looked suddenly pale. Shu stepped closer.

"To answer your question, Avalon was the agent of destiny working to limit your choices, and it is Avalon who preserved us in order to move us forward to the end it has contrived for us. Avalon is a living and intelligent machine that has been drafting its plan for millennia. It sent out the black water to attack the substations as soon as our minisubs crossed the line. It did this because it knew we would be forced to abandon the stations and come here, where it could continue to use us to carry out its plan."

When silence had fallen, Hannah asked, "What is the black water?"

"It belongs to this ship," Shu answered, turning to face her. "The foundation has determined it's a swarm of nanoscale machines programmed to infiltrate the human nervous system, utilizing the human mind to hold information. Besides that, it apparently lowers the hurdles on normal physical limitations."

"And it's inside of him?"

"I no longer need glasses," Ford said happily, "and I feel like I could knock over a mountain!"

Hannah was clearly dubious. "You're saying that some kind of information was dumped inside his head, and *that's* why he's rambling on about destiny and purpose?"

"It buried ideas deep in his psyche," Shu explained, "ideas about life and existence that make it easier for his mind to become integrated into the Computer Core—or that's the theory."

"But you can't possibly believe some kind of swarm got into his body and fixed his eyes! Couldn't it be a natural reaction to the trauma we've been through?"

"Now this is *truly* ironic!" Ford replied with a startling laugh. "The skeptic is miraculously healed, but his explanation to the believer is met with skepticism! How can I convince you? What would you like to know?"

Hannah was silent.

"See how fickle?" he asked, clearly delighted. "Offer her the answers, and she asks more questions. Ask her what more she wants to know and she settles right down—"

He stopped short. Hannah's elbow was aimed at his side.

"I think we'll skip Mr. Ford's convincing proofs," Val said. "I've also been in the black water, Miss Aston. He speaks the truth about its effects on human physiology; but there are other more alarming changes that it may also inflict upon his personality. These changes are, as Shu says, a method of integrating him into the artificially intelligent CC."

"You know about computers?" Hannah asked. "But you're from the past!"

"Yes," Ford replied, "she is from the past—and every computer aboard this ship predates the earliest civilizations you've studied as an archaeologist. Doesn't it make sense now? You've just got to—"

"I've just got to believe?" Hannah asked, her voice edged with frustration. "Seijung, if anyone else in the *world* were telling me this stuff I'd have told him where to go by now! You can't expect me to understand all this in a minute, you know! I haven't been changed in any *black water*!"

Val knelt beside her, and said, "Those who enter the black water learn many things, some things that are useful for them to know, and other things over which they have no command.

Ford was given more information than he is consciously aware of."

"But I am master of myself," Ford insisted. "I am perfectly aware of everything I am doing, and I make my own choices!"

"That remains to be seen," Shu said. "You were not given psychological conditioning alone, though. You may also have received access codes."

"Access codes?" Hannah wondered. "Access to what?'

"Part of the ship is currently sealed off, and we think that's just where we need to get."

"Something put the keys to this ship inside his head?"

"And then gave us a good reason to use them."

"I have no idea what he's talking about," Ford said.

"The knowledge, if it is there, is latent," Shu explained. "He isn't conscious of the content."

Hannah asked, "How would you get it out of him, then?"

"I don't think we can. It would be dangerous for him, and Kabta thinks whatever is inside his head might be sabotaged."

"By the ship?" she wondered. "Why would it do that?"

"DePons suspects Avalon is using Ford as a vessel for information, that it's installed something inside him that it wants moved in the direction we're being herded."

Ford blurted out, *"How can you be certain I have any useful information inside my head at all?"*

Everyone stopped and stared at him. Ford covered his face with a hand, but looked up in startled surprise when the one person who started chuckling was Val Anna.

"Thank you, Mr. Ford, she said, recovering some of her composure. "It's been a long time since I've felt what it's like to laugh! But you really ought to hear what Shu is saying. The link established within you serves only Avalon."

Their smiles faded. The air became suddenly very tense.

"Whatever knowledge or physical power is gained in contacting the black water," she said, "you will not easily evade the AI. It is merging with you, and its thoughts are becoming your own. You must take care not to allow the link to control your conscious mind."

Turning to Shu she said, "Kabta's half-hour is almost over, and the bomb is still active. We'll have to proceed without the information he seeks."

"What about him?" Shu asked, turning towards Ford.

"We'll all keep a sharp eye on him, just in case something changes."

"You're suggesting I would betray my friends?" Ford asked. The smile was gone, and he seemed himself again.

"Speaking of friends," Shu deflected, "it appears a visitor tagged along with you when you fled the substations. He's also partly to blame for Lucius' separation and the bomb's activation."

"A visitor?" Hannah asked.

"I'm sure you must've heard him banging around? I was sent to take a quick look while Kabta finishes up in CAC, and you're coming with me—that means you, Mr. Ford."

Leaving her blanket behind, Hannah followed the others through a cavernous dark space. The corridor curved, ran straight, and turned to no obvious design; but the closed diamond-shaped doors and dim projected consoles assured her of the fact that Avalon was no haphazard construction. She found herself longing for a regular rectangular door or a bit of carpet. At least the floor was flat, though it was of the same fleshy design as the walls and squished underfoot.

When they had walked almost a quarter-mile they found a hatch on their left that was torn open. The doors had been knocked out of it, and lay crumpled against the far wall of the passage.

"This was the door to the supply closet outside the airlock," Shu said, examining the wreckage. "Looks like it headed in Abdaya's direction."

"What did this?" Hannah asked, surveying the smashed doors.

"Something nasty," Ford said. "Shouldn't you warn the other marines?"

"They already know something's up. Trust me; those five are ready for anything."

Shu stepped past the hatch into the room, and the rest followed. They had all passed through this place on the way out of the airlock into the ship, but the scene was greatly changed. What was once a supply room full of rows of ordinary metal shelves was now a mess of smashed and twisted debris. Beyond this, the slender beams of their flashlights revealed a massive tear in the far wall where the airlock door once stood.

"Great," Shu said. "We can't possibly pressurize that chamber with seawater now!"

"It appears that filling the chamber won't be a problem," Ford said, pointing into the airlock. In the dock, the minisubs bobbed in a few feet of muddy water.

"Looks like the outer doors were damaged," he noted.

Behind them, Hannah asked, "This was a storeroom?"

She stood amidst the ruin of battered shelves, most of which were trampled flat. She had noticed the shelves on her way in. She remembered that they were all laden with strange bundles, scattered now like leaves in the wind.

Ford said, "These look like pressure-suits and helmets."

"The airlock was probably always a weak point," Shu said. "It looks like they stowed this gear here so they could suit up in the event of a disaster; but none of it's any use to us now."

"Do you think it was trying to depressurize the airlock *and* flood the ship?" Ford wondered.

Hannah said, "Surely so sophisticated a ship would have a safety measure preventing the accidental release of a pressure-door?"

Just as she finished speaking, there was a loud bang and a plop from the water near one of the subs. In the flicker of the lights they saw a narrow stream jetting across the room from the outer door as a new fracture formed. They retreated back into the storeroom, where the sound of dripping was notably louder.

"The PCU really tore this place apart," Shu remarked. Then, noticing Hannah's curious glances, he said, "It was a *Personal Combat Unit,* the mechanical warrior Mr. Ford awakened on Lucius Station. We had one in the wreckage brought from the buried ship. It must have been what the Foundation calls a *Seraph* model, which would explain the scorch marks on the far wall."

Everyone turned towards Ford, who was backing away from the airlock. He stopped abruptly when his heel came down with a snap on a bit of broken metal shelving, and seeing that they all looked at him he became suddenly defensive.

"I only did what DePons instructed me to do," he said. "How was I supposed to know it would go nuts and follow us around?"

"What's done is done," Hannah said. "Let's talk about this PCU. Is it some kind of robot?"

Shu continued to stare at Ford. "The Combat Units aren't just mechanicals," he said. "They're massive suits of armor, and they require a pilot. I don't know how pressing switches could possibly animate it, unless there was already someone inside when Mr. Ford was working on it. If that's weird, how can we say it got into the dock? There's no sign of a breach, other than the fractures in the outer hull we encountered on our way inside."

"Could it have gotten inside with the last subs?" Hannah asked.

Ford said, "In the mud on the bottom of the dock it would have looked just like a big piece of wreckage. Anyway, I didn't notice anything, and neither did the marines."

"It may have been invisible," Shu said. "It was invisible to sonar, anyway."

"It can turn invisible?" Ford asked, his voice strangely edged with delight.

Shu gave him another stern look, and he appeared suddenly sullen and confused.

"Sorry," he said. "I'm sorry about this whole mess."

"If I hadn't seen the thing with my own eyes," Hannah replied, "I might have thought you really were to blame. But this is too complicated a mess even for you, Seijung. If the machine needs a pilot, then someone else must've been waiting inside for you to start it up."

"Someone *is* inside," Val said. "We're dealing with a person, not a machine; but *who*, I wonder?"

Hannah asked, "What'll the marines do if it finds them, and what about us?"

"We'll have to deal with it when the time comes," Shu said. "Let's go back to CAC. After I report the situation to Kabta, we'll all set out together for SARA station and the Viaduct Chamber."

He began walking towards the outer passageway, and the others joined him.

"SARA?" Hannah asked. "Viaduct Chamber? You've already got names for what's inside this ship?"

"The Foundation's had experience with this technology for a very long time," Ford said gloomily. "They were using us to locate more, and to rebuild whatever they couldn't find intact."

Shu gave him a hostile glance, but Ford paid no attention.

"It's okay, Shu," Val prompted. "Every one of us was able to guess that much already."

"Is this *Viaduct* the bit of technology you said you need to access?" Hannah asked.

"What else is there left to guess?" Shu wondered.

"Yes, it is," Val replied. "The Viaduct is very important. Now that the dock is destroyed, it may be our only chance of escape."

Hannah raised her voice, and asked, "What does it *do*?"

"It transports."

"Like…a teleportation device?"

"It's a bridge to other worlds and times," Val explained.

"And that's how you—"

"I suppose all this makes my brain pretty valuable right now," Ford said. "If we can't risk plugging me into the computer, or if the information just isn't inside me, what will we do?"

Walking briskly ahead of them, Shu muttered quietly, saying, "Then we'd better hope there's some other way out of here in the next hour or so."

As they walked, Shu pushed the pace hard until he and Val were farther ahead of the scientists, but not quite out of earshot. He slowed until she caught up to him, and said, "I'd better go first from now on."

"So now you're my bodyguard?" she asked.

"So long as you don't mind. Actually, I doubt anything will happen. Just don't *touch* anything. Have you got your comm unit on?"

"My what?"

In answer, he reached over and pressed a small plastic blister on the shoulder of her armor. There was a click followed by a brief hiss of static.

"We'll keep it on monitor, as per orders," he said. "Just in case you need it, though, you can speak to everyone else by holding down the switch. Squeeze twice if you want it to stay on, and once more to turn it off."

"Thanks," she said.

"What's up? You seem nervous."

"Nervous? I feel like I'm back on that other ship."

Ford touched Hannah's arm. He was also eavesdropping.

"Kabta asked me to keep an eye on you," Shu said.

"And how is Kabta?" Val wondered.

"He's still on edge because he knows almost as little as you or I about this place."

"I meant, what about the things you're hiding from Kabta?"

Shu pulled a grim look on her, and shook his head.

"It's that bad?" Val asked.

"Let's just say I have many uncertainties. Maybe that bomb will go off before we can do anything about it. If we open a

Viaduct down here, things could turn out far worse. Maybe it's a good thing we can't get access to the Viaduct Chamber codes."

"Are you saying you have the codes?"

"Val, if we use the Viaduct, we'll be doing just what Lír's man told me to do."

"And did he tell you anything about Kal-Nergal?"

"He said exactly what Kabta said."

"Isn't that good news, though?"

"Nergal didn't exactly turn out to be a good person. Fixing him as our Location could bring us to a worse end than displacement."

"I'm sure you will make the right decision, Shu," she said.

"I hope you're right."

They walked in silence for a few moments. Hannah wished she could ask just one of the thousand questions spinning around inside her head, though she doubted she'd get anything like a straight answer.

Just then, Val said, "I wonder what ever happened to Morla, and if Nergal made it through. Do you ever think about them, Shu?"

"All the time."

"Do you think they're alright?"

His reply sent a chill through Hannah's being.

"I don't think they died when they went through the Mirror, if that's what you mean."

12
CONSPIRACY FACT

They walked on until they passed the place where she and Ford had left their blankets, and then continued until they reached the eerie blue-lit threshold of CAC. Hannah followed the beam of Val's flashlight towards the inscription in the wall above the hatch.

"*Islith rises again,*" Shu read.

"What's that mean?" Hannah asked.

"It's ancient history."

"I'm an archaeologist."

Val gazed quietly at the symbols.

"Look," Hannah said, "If you're afraid of answering me just because you're not sure how much I know—"

"You don't know anything."

She glared at his back, fists clenched. Shu turned slightly, and noting her agitation he sighed.

"Sorry," he said. "Val's the leader here. If you've got questions, just ask her, alright?"

"I've never seen symbols like those before!" Hannah exclaimed, pointing up at the wall. "How can a *stupid marine* like you read them?"

"You know," Ford remarked quietly, "Kabta said the substations would be home away from home, and that our anxieties would be allayed when the work began. He was right about one thing, at least. It *is* exciting."

The oblique comment brought their argument to a halt. Hannah turned questioning eyes on him, but Ford didn't seem to read her puzzled expression.

"He may be stupid," Ford continued, "but he knows more than you or I about this place, Hannah."

"What do you mean?" she asked, her voice still knife-edged with frustration.

"He means, the AI is giving him glimpses of content," Shu said, "probably for the purpose of generating suspicion and creating division among us."

"What kind of suspicions?" Hannah wondered.

"About the nuke, for starters," Ford replied.

"What about it?"

"Kabta knew we'd get stuck in the substations if the PCU woke up," he said. "The NDB was meant to clean up all the loose ends, including us."

"That's ridiculous," Shu said.

"Why do you think Kabta would do such a thing after helping us?" Hannah wondered.

"He's an alien," Ford replied. "So's he."

He pointed at Shu, who stared unflinchingly.

"He's too stupid to be anything but human," Hannah muttered.

To this Shu chuckled. "So, you've been abducted by aliens, Mr. Ford?"

"You're *not* human," Ford insisted. "How do you explain your first-hand knowledge of this ship?"

"Because some of us have been around for as long as it has."

Ford stared back at him, frozen with quiet shock.

Turning to Ford, Hannah said, "The last thing we need down here is hysteria. It's the most ridiculous thing out of your mouth yet on this trip, and I don't want to hear another word from you, Seijung."

"He confessed!" Ford snapped. "Avalon says it's true!"

Hannah gave them both a warning look. Ford turned his head towards Shu, who only shrugged. Val walked to the door, ignoring the spat, and set her palm upon the panel in the wall beside it.

"I don't think you should be touching that," Shu warned.

The doors opened.

"Avalon's not what we've got to worry about," Val replied. "Let's try to work together, shall we?"

She stepped inside, and Shu followed, leaving Ford and Aston upon the threshold surveying the dim interior with wide eyes. There was movement from the lower central portion of the deck. Kabta stood there. He looked up warily at the two scientists.

"See?" Ford whispered. "He knows!"

"Paranoid fool," she said, following Val.

"Where are DePons and Nephtys?" Val asked when they all stood together in the Command Center of CAC.

Kabta turned his back to them. *"Maintain silence,"* he said.

For a moment, Hannah thought he was talking to Val, but then she saw that he held one hand over the side of his face. There was a wireless device in his ear. She had left behind her own unit in the minisub.

"You have your orders," he continued. "Team One proceeds to the Observation Chamber. Team Two is now to move towards the location of the crew quarters. That's on this level. Team Three's going up and up, to the Data Storage Center. I guess you two will know what you're looking for when you find it. Everyone falls back to SARA within the hour. That's all for now."

He turned towards Val. "You didn't see them pass you in the hall?" he asked. "I sent them to search for Data Storage."

"They must've passed us by while we were checking out the airlock," Shu said. "Have we given up on our guest?"

"Hun confirmed it was a PCU—a Seraph model," Kabta replied. "It was brought to the substations with the wreckage, as you well know. If proper precautions had been taken—"

They all glanced at Ford, who shrugged weakly. His face was turning a sickly shade of green.

"I see no sense pursuing it," Kabta continued. "So long as it doesn't turn on us, I suppose it's safer to leave it alone. We'll try to stay out of its way."

Shu flicked a switch on the rifle that dangled across his chest. "Maybe there's an armory on board," he said.

"I couldn't find one nearby, and we've got nothing on us capable of taking the thing down. Those AR-15s will only prompt it to engage."

"If it wants to take a shot at me, maybe I want to take a shot back."

"Travel weapons-ready, then, if it makes you feel better. In any case, we shouldn't stay here long. We're running out of time."

Kabta started up the steps of the Command Center ahead of them, turning once to glance in Hannah's direction.

"I apologize for your accident on the substation," he said to her. "Have the two of you had enough time to digest our situation?"

"No!" Hannah said, speaking more sharply than she intended.

"I'm afraid there's nothing else we can do but get moving. The longer we stay in one place, the more likely we'll never get out of here alive; and our chances are slim as it is. How's the airlock?"

"Leaking," Shu said. "The PCU totally destroyed the lock and the doors. I would venture to guess that the minisubs were also damaged, though I didn't really check."

"It hardly matters. If the doors are damaged, the subs are useless. There's no getting out of that airlock, and even if we could move the subs they're just too slow to make it out of range of the NDB. The only chance we've got is the most dangerous, and unless it has been guiding us on this path all along I'm not certain Avalon will let us slip away even that easily."

"So, we're going to this Viaduct device, and it will take us somewhere else?" Hannah asked.

"I thought you couldn't get to it without hacking my brain," Ford said. He looked worried.

"Rest easy, Doctor," Kabta replied. "I found a place to do that while you were gone. There's a SARA Station on the other side of the ship. It's equipped with a chair. We'll head to SARA now."

"What's this SARA?" Val wondered.

"Sleep, Animation, Recovery, and Arrest," Kabta said.

"There's a chair?" Ford wondered. "How's a chair supposed to help me?"

"There's no time for lengthy explanations now, Mr. Ford. Suffice it to say, it's a very special chair. It's designed to enfold the occupant and stabilize his or her alert functioning so as to facilitate integration into the ship's AI."

"The thing that came into my body—that black water—was developed in order to make humans work with the machines on this ship."

"That's correct."

"Will *integration* hurt me?"

Kabta weighed his words before responding.

"The unique features of human brain functioning are easy for the AI to mimic. The ship has a personality. It will make the process as easy or as painful as it pleases, and I am not completely in control of it. Avalon will decide."

"So," Ford mumbled, "no promises I guess."

"It's your chance to save us all," Shu said with a smirk.

"It's *your* job to be a hero. I'm just a scientist."

Kabta looked at him with genuine pity. "There is some chance that it will strain you to a point where mental recovery is prolonged," he confided, "but the SARA Station is equipped to handle just such an event. The chair is a device that was actually designed for human use."

"Then, whoever made these ships knew about us before they arrived," Hannah said. "I wonder why they abandoned them here, or why they came in the first place."

Ford arched his eyebrows, hearing the mild note of accusation in her voice.

Kabta chose not to reply.

As they left, Hannah noticed Val and Shu lingering behind the rest of the group. Shu's hand went to the zipped pouch on his chest, from which he produced a small tablet PC. Val spoke to him quietly. They both seemed concerned. Val was looking at Ford, gesturing towards him as they spoke. Shu nodded consent to what she was saying.

Hannah pretended not to notice the exchange. She gripped Ford's arm absently, but he pulled free of her with a grunt.

"What's bothering you?" she asked.

"The same thing that's bothering you," he answered.

At that moment, Shu and Val passed them up. Val asked Shu, "Have you made your decision?"

"Yes," he answered. "I won't let anyone get hurt. I promise I'll do what needs to be done, if Kabta takes it that far."

Hannah and Ford glanced at each other. Uncertainty slowed their steps, but they followed everyone outside to the passage. As soon as they joined the group, a tall dark-skinned marine appeared in the corridor before them. He was alone. They were all surprised by his sudden appearance—even Kabta.

"Malkin, what are you doing here?" he demanded. "Where's the rest of your team?"

"Abdaya and Hanuta stayed behind in SARA. We would have called, except you insisted on transmission silence. As soon as I left, it seemed to me something followed."

"Something's down there," Shu said, looking off down the dark corridor. He unslung the rifle from his shoulder.

"*Sleepers,*" Malkin replied, casting a wary glance over his shoulder. "At least one slipped away from us."

"What are sleepers?" Val wondered.

"Captives kept in the SARA Station, submerged in black water," Kabta answered.

"Whose captives?" Hannah asked.

Ford tensed suddenly. "They're captives of the Gremn," he said.

Everyone seemed surprised by his answer.

"*Gremn?*" Hannah wondered.

"He's in the link," Shu whispered to Kabta.

"Then we'd better get him to SARA before he becomes a target," Kabta replied. "I feared some of these stowaways might reanimate when we started poking around in the data."

"There's something alive aboard this ship?" she asked, "after all this time?"

"Yes," Kabta answered. His eyes held hers for a long moment.

"They're alien?"

"They are *Gremn*," he answered. "The black water has linked Ford to the ship, and what the ship has told him is true."

Hannah surveyed his stoic figure, the firm set of his jaw, and the icy flint of his eyes, and she asked, "These Gremn are perfect look-alikes, are they? You can't tell them apart from humans?"

"Of course not."

"The sleepers might know the access codes we've been looking for," Shu said, interrupting them. "We won't have to put Mr. Ford in the chair if we can capture one alive."

"Isn't that lucky?" Ford wondered.

No sooner had he spoken than there was a rumbling noise in the distance.

Malkin and Shu turned instinctively, dropping to one knee and leveling their rifles towards the gloom ahead. The others gathered behind them.

"Sounds like a train's coming," Hannah said.

The squishy deck trembled beneath her feet. She turned to Ford, but he was backing away. A light of recognition was in his eyes, reflecting the light of a much larger pair of eyes that blazed like a green flame in the dark far ahead. Tremors shook the corridor. Something screeched and rattled like the collapse of a barn; but there wasn't time to guess what was coming.

Kabta moved first. Reaching back with one hand he pulled Val forwards. With the other he simultaneously waved everyone else on—towards the gleaming eyes.

"There's a hatch up ahead. Move!"

Everyone set out at a jog. Running on the jelly-slick surface was tricky. Hannah held onto Ford's hand, and tried to see ahead in the pale narrow beam of lamp-light thrown from Malkin's helmet. The distant green lights disappeared suddenly. Hannah stopped, hearing a door sliding open to their right.

"Get inside!" Kabta shouted, pushing her into the dark after Val.

She let go of Ford's hand, but he was shoved in right behind her. Stumbling hesitantly over the threshold, she followed Val, who moved the beam of her flashlight around the bare little room. Beside her, Ford was muttering to himself in a state of panic. Whatever he was feeling, he no longer looked like a man who'd recently boasted of superhuman strengths.

Kabta waited the second or two that it took for the three of them to enter, and then he followed. Malkin and Shu came last, backing in so that their rifles were trained on the corridor even to the very moment the hatch slid shut.

"That went smoothly," Shu said. "Maybe it didn't notice us."

"Stay very still," Kabta warned.

It seemed that Shu was right, though. There was no sound from the corridor, and no sign of trouble—until an explosion rocked the room.

The shockwave pushed them all flat on their backs and echoed with fierce intensity. For a few moments Hannah thought she was deaf, but then she heard dully the clang and boom of footsteps, and a rushing intake of breath.

The room shook again, but the door remained intact. Hannah glimpsed Shu in the light of Val's flashlight, and she was amazed that he was able to keep calm. He picked himself up and knelt beside Malkin facing the door, his body slack and his hold on the rifle relaxed. She tried to imitate their stamina, rising on unsteady feet. Even Val looked shaken. Ford was crouching beside them.

"What now?" he asked, his voice a higher octave than usual.

Val turned around and resumed her lamp-lit search of the room. It was square in shape, glistening wet, and completely empty; but there was a rear exit—a doorway slightly smaller than the hatch opening into the main corridor.

She gestured to Kabta with her light, and pointed towards the exit. Kabta moved his head to her ear, and speaking loud enough for Hannah to hear he said, "The rooms on this side are all joined by a rear corridor. It won't take us all the way to the SARA station, but it'll get us close enough to make a dash for it. I don't think the PCU will be able to follow us there, though it could track us to where we need to pass through the corridor again. We just need to—"

Before he finished speaking, their ears were assaulted by another thunderous boom, and with a squeal of twisting metal the hatch to the corridor buckled inwards. The misty air was full of the smell of burning flesh. The walls around the frame of the hatch literally bled, wounded by the impact. Hannah stumbled backwards into Kabta, her hands over her ears.

"Come on," he said, steering her gently towards the exit.

She didn't immediately respond, except to drop her hands and gaze in wonder at the imprint of a fist in the middle of the locked doors. It seemed impossible that anything could have done that much damage with one blow of a fist. Shu and Malkin were still crouching at the ready, just yards away. Hannah felt Kabta's grip on her arm tighten.

"Are you coming?" he asked. "Come on, Mr. Ford, you too. No time for drama."

Ford was blinking in the smoky air, gagging on the stench.

"Hurry!" Shu called back. "He's breaking through!"

The hatch bent under another tremendous blow. The whole wall groaned.

They made for the exit, which now stood open. As soon as they had filed in Kabta joined them, pausing at the door to peer back into the room.

"Fall back," he called to Shu and Malkin. "You won't do any damage to him with rifles."

"How do you know it's a *him*?" Shu asked, retreating through the door. "The pilot, I mean?"

Kabta waited until Malkin passed them up, and then he stood facing the crumpled doors on the opposite side of the room. Those in the passage also looked, so that several points of light converged on the breach. There was another blow, and this time the doors parted a little. Hannah glimpsed something moving in the other corridor—something big.

"We know this pilot," Kabta said.

Shu looked sidelong at him. "It's got to be one of our men," he agreed. "Who else would have had access to Lucius Station?"

"That's not what I mean. I don't think he's one of ours, but we do know him."

"You think he's one of Lír's men?"

"No, I don't. I feel certain he's not trying to kill us."

Then he paused, and strained as if to listen. Everyone stood quietly, hardly daring to breathe, while from across the way they heard the last thing they expected to hear.

"Is it *crying*?" Malkin whispered. His own voice was ragged, for the sound was quite terrible to hear; and soon it filled them all with fear. It was a nightmare noise, a scratchy squealing sound that was unmistakably weeping.

"This must be a trick," Shu said. "It probably hopes to lure us back into the room. Let's get out of its way, quickly, before it sends in fire after us!"

"Hush!" Kabta said. "Listen!"

Then they all heard, hollow and low, the faint sound of words echoing eerily. The voice was hollow and scratchy. It was like listening to a conversation from the far end of a tunnel.

"Don't lose hope!" it said. *"Don't lose hope!"*

The voice died away then into more weeping, and finally receded to a dull inarticulate rumbling. After a few more minutes, complete silence descended on the dim and stuffy corridor. They waited, listening to drips that fell from the ceiling. This passageway was drier than the one they'd fled, but then a drop of cold water landed on her nose, and Hannah was awakened to the realization that they were still on the bottom of the ocean.

"If it gets worked up again and knocks down a few more walls, we might just become a permanent part of the seabed," she said to Ford. Ford, however, had turned and was walking down the corridor on his own.

"I agree with Kabta," Val said to her. "It's not trying to kill us."

Kabta shut the door behind them. There was no more noise from the PCU—not a sound—and the silence put everyone on edge more than the attack. Hannah wasn't so sure the pilot of this machine meant no harm. Hadn't he tried to flood the ship at the airlock? He'd ripped open the substations while they were still inside, too. Just what were they up against here? In her mind, over and over again, she kept hearing the echo of the weeping words they'd heard.

"Don't lose hope."

The group walked on for awhile in silence, each lost in their own thoughts; but Val had fallen back again to walk beside Shu. There was only room enough for two to walk abreast in this passage, and they were alone behind all the others. Hannah wished she could continue to spy on their conversation. The whispers echoed a little, but only enough to overhear just a few teasing words.

"You alright, Val?"

"You're still protecting me?"

"Just worried."

"If Kabta's been worried about the stones being carried by someone who's compromised by the black water—"

"I don't care. I trust *only* you with the stones."

Hannah was puzzled. What did they mean about the stones? The next words she heard made her wish she'd decided to mind her own business.

"You have no thoughts of vengeance against us, Val. In fact, I think they're with you because you'll save us all—all of us under the Ban."

"Not by the stones themselves. Martial exercise isn't what they're for."

"Maybe *that's* why they're with you."

"I hope your trust in me isn't misplaced, Shu. I only want things to go back to the way they were."

They spoke lower. Hannah couldn't understand what they were saying anymore. Soon they stopped talking altogether, and she had only her own fears and doubts left to ponder. The only problem was she couldn't think straight. The minutes were counting down, and she kept imagining what it would be like at the very end, just before the bomb's pressure-wave hit Avalon's hull.

The passage felt strangely still, and just ahead Ford and Kabta slowed their pace. The dark-skinned one, Malkin, was walking right beside her now. Hannah was tempted to talk to him. He was so imposing a figure, though, that for a few moments she could only stare.

"You have a problem?" he asked, catching her gaze.

"We can't destroy that thing with guns, can we?" she wondered.

"It seems not," he answered. "Anything that's able to rip open the substations, walk across the ocean floor at three-point-five miles depth, enter this place without being seen, *and* punch through bulkheads like they're cardboard probably won't be killed by bullets or grenades. I doubt a tank round would dent it. What we need is an atomic rail-gun."

"What's that?"

"Something I cooked up for the Foundation a few years back," he replied. "Wish I had one now—though it wouldn't be good to use it too close to an outer wall of the ship."

"You're from Kenya?" she asked, noting his accent.

"Been there. No more talking, okay?"

He picked up his pace and walked past her, leaning towards Kabta to whisper something in his ear.

"So many secrets in this place," Hannah sighed.

Just ahead, Ford and Malkin were standing before another large hatch while Kabta turned a wheel-lock and jerked it open. Everyone cringed at the grating squeal made by the door, but there was no other sound from the outer corridor.

"This is where we have to rejoin the wider passage," Kabta said in a low voice. "Now listen. We now have less than an hour before detonation of the NDB. We're running out of time, so we can't afford to play it safe and take cover if we're attacked again."

He fixed his eyes on Hannah.

"Just keep going straight, single file, and keep the pace. No talking, and lights out. You men cover our rear."

The flashlights were off. Shu and Malkin stepped quickly by them, and no one dared whisper as they dashed out into the main corridor, weapons leveled. Once they had taken positions on either side, Kabta led the others out quickly, turning to the right.

"Quietly, now," he said, moving on at a quick jog.

Right behind him, Hannah thought she saw a glimmer from his face, and she wondered how he could see anything at all. The mists reduced her own vision to just a few feet. Ford kept apace of her now to the left, and Val was on her right. Shu and

Malkin fell in behind. They went on almost without incident for a long while, until they heard a crash far behind them.

"Keep moving!" Kabta said.

For a terrible moment they jogged on while listening to echoes of distant rumbling. Hannah's heart raced a bit faster than her feet, for she'd been keeping an eye open for convenient escape-routes and doors for quite some time. There were none, and had not been any since they left the smaller passageway. There was no going back or hiding, like Kabta said.

Shu ran up to Kabta's side to report. "It's definitely following us again," he said, "but it's coming slowly. I wonder if it's cloaked."

"We're all invisible in this soup," Hannah remarked. "How does it even know we're here?"

"It can read the thermal signatures of our footprints," Shu replied. "It can probably hear us—even at a whisper."

"How much farther?" Val asked, panting.

"We're almost there."

13

SARA

The corridor ended abruptly about a thousand feet ahead upon the threshold of a great round room. What they saw there was a startling departure from the twisted ribbed passageways behind. The space was like a vast shallow bowl covered with green growing grass. Light fog covered the lawns. In the center, like an island in a sea of mist, there was a garden of fruiting trees and flowers, lit from above and below with a rich golden light.

"Do I hear birds?" Hannah asked.

"The Great Ships once had many such stations," Kabta said. "I suppose the Makers who designed Avalon saw the need for a touch of homely beauty."

"Well, it doesn't fit," she remarked.

"No," Val agreed, "but neither do we."

Mostly in colors of grey and reddish-brown, the organic architecture of the chamber cupped the green arboretum like a natural dell. Vines climbed the walls, where here and there were carved cotes for the many birds they saw. Val had no doubt the walls themselves were engineered to consume the waste of the host creatures—the wardens of this garden—and to befit their needs in return over many millennia. As her eyes went upwards along the inside curve of the mighty dome she descried level upon level of halls and interconnecting chambers, until finally, a thousand feet above, they ended at a great tangle of vines dangling from a massive hemispherical lamp filled with clear bubbling water.

"Whoa!" Ford exclaimed. "It's like *Biosphere*—except it works!"

Shu said, "We're on the ground floor. Crew quarters were straight across on the other side?"

"According to the logs I recovered in CAC," Kabta replied. "But Morvran never occupied the other levels of the ship. He probably didn't want to spread everyone out too much. Avalon *is* a security nightmare."

"And where is SARA?"

"We're going straight across and up one deck. We should arrive at SARA in a little while."

He started out into the chamber.

Val followed Kabta, and Hannah stuck close to them both.

"I think the pilot wants something from us," she said, speaking timidly.

Kabta regarded her with an expression that Hannah read as discretion. "The PCU pilot may have been kept alive in that unit for thousands of years," he replied, "so if he's only recently awakened he must be terribly confused."

"But he's following us for a reason, right?"

"He's certainly interested in us," Ford said, coming to her side. "I mean, if he knows what's about to happen to this place, he's got to be as interested in getting out of here as we are. Maybe he thinks we know a way out."

Val was quiet for a moment. Then she said, "I think he's after *me*."

Before Hannah could ask her to clarify, they reached the trees. There was a kind of dirt-path before them, winding in through the foliage. It was very much like a real garden outdoors—albeit a very foggy garden—complete with a gentle breeze in the leaves and a golden light falling from above. Malkin pushed ahead suddenly, and whistled softly. A marine stepped out onto the path before them. He was wearing a helmet that sported a swing-down arm with a pair of night-vision goggles—at least, that's what they looked like. Malkin strode forwards to meet him.

"Sheb?" he hailed.

Hannah recognized him—the one nicknamed *Breaker*, who led her on a guided tour of Geomech Station. He turned in her direction, acknowledging her presence with a nod of his head.

"Team One reports no trouble," he said to Malkin.

"We've got enough trouble on our tail," Malkin replied, looking back towards the tunnels. "I am certain the PCU is heading this way, though I cannot see him yet."

"Take Sheb, fall in behind us with Shu, and cover the rear," Kabta said to Malkin. "The rest are ahead?"

"Hun and Abdaya are standing by at SARA," Sheb reported. "Nuta's here. Want her in back with me?"

"No. I want her up front. She can cover Val and the other two."

Sheb turned around and clapped his hands. Another marine appeared, literally from nowhere. Hannah noted that she was just a girl in appearance, her hair dyed a vibrant shade of pink.

"Neat trick," Ford muttered in her ear. "I think it's that suit."

As the girl approached, Hannah studied her armored jumpsuit. It was the same as Val Anna's—a distinctly different armor than that worn by the other marines. The suit shimmered slightly when the girl turned sideways.

"Good to see you, Nuta," Kabta said, patting her head affectionately as he took the lead. She favored him with a smile and walked beside him on the path beneath the trees.

"What's wrong?" Ford asked, noting the way Hannah stared after them.

"Never mind," she replied, following.

They entered the garden, and the smell of it was a heavenly escape from the stink of the ship. There was no trace at all of the harsh odors of the tunnels, and there were birds singing. Spying their bright green and red plumage, Hannah thought they were of a variety of parrot. She wanted to ask if the species was alien to Earth, but there was a strange hush as they walked the path.

"These plants aren't tropical or sub tropical," she said, breaking the tension with an effort. "I don't recognize any of them."

"There are some here that are closely related to the ones you already know," Kabta said. "Here you will find oak and maple, and ferns and herbs; but most of these plants are species found nowhere on Earth."

"They're alien?" Ford asked, coming up behind them.

"They were brought here."

"So, are oaks and maples alien to Earth?" he asked.

"Apparently."

"And we're also an alien species?"

Kabta did not answer.

No one dared ask any more questions for a time, but each fell to studying the strange flora and fauna around them. Hannah thought it beautiful, but also sad, knowing that all she saw would soon be destroyed by either the PCU or the bomb.

She took in several deep breaths, scenting flowers sweeter than any rose. The fruits looked good to eat, and while they walked Kabta picked several and handed them out. They looked like apples. No one asked if they were safe to eat, but after wiping the bright red surface on the front of her jumpsuit Hannah took a hungry bite. She was surprised to discover a taste far sweeter than expected, and only a little bit tart. A couple of the fruits filled her empty stomach.

Shu walked up from the back of the line to share water from a small bottle with Hanuta.

"We've all got fluids enough for the time being?" he asked.

"Ford and I don't have any equipment," Hannah said.

"Right," he said, handing a second bottle to her. "Guess I'm the only one, unless you were able to scrounge up some 150,000 year old food for us, Nuta."

"Actually, Team Two found some small store of supplies in quarters. We've brought it all to SARA."

"Does SPAM last that long?" Shu joked.

Nuta smiled at him. "I don't think we're going to get a chance to find out, Bro," she said. "I don't plan on staying down here long enough to enjoy a meal!"

It took another half hour to reach the other side of the garden, and a little while after they reached a pair of tunnel entrances in the curved wall of the chamber. Hannah held her breath as they stepped inside the right-hand entrance, hoping to keep some of the freshness of the garden with her as they reentered the stinking passageways. Her effort was in vain.

At the end of a short tunnel they encountered a stairway that snaked upwards along the outer wall of the round room, and as it was open on the left-hand side this stair offered a view across the garden-lands below. Kabta proceeded, walking slowly and cautiously, often peering out towards the garden. Hannah followed his gaze. She thought she saw the glimmer of something moving along the hazy green paths under the trees.

She asked, "Is it still following us?"

"Yes," Kabta replied.

The tunnel they entered upon reaching the second level was like those below—gloomy and smelly. They walked along a wide passage for about an hour before halting at last before a hatch like that of the CAC. It was an important door from the look of it, yet it stood open. Hanuta and Val continued inside, but Kabta stopped in his tracks, bending towards the ground. There, just within the shadow of the doors, lay the bodies of two men. Long homemade knives were clutched in their hands. They were dressed in rags, riddled with gunshot wounds.

Their heads were missing.

Kabta studied the scene with a grim expression. Just behind him, Hannah Aston stood and stared at the carnage, trying not to cry or look foolish. Her legs shook, though, and she was afraid she might pass out. In a surprising display of gentleness, Ford took her shoulder and walked her past the bodies towards the dark chamber beyond. Hanuta stood just inside the threshold, waiting for them with a pair of folded blankets.

"Here," she said. "Your clothes are still wet. These are from Breaker's pack. I think he uses them as floor-mats when crawling under things he fixes. They're kind of old and smelly, but better than nothing."

The temperature inside the room was chillier than the garden. Hannah reached and took one of the blankets, wrapping it around her shoulders. It was made from an insulated canvas material that crinkled like plastic.

"They're recently dead," Hanuta said to her, noting the pooled blood with a nod of her head.

"Yeah," Hannah replied, looking very pale. She thought Nuta was smiling at her.

"Just don't look at them," Ford said weakly, taking the other blanket.

Hun stepped out of the darkness of the open doorway, pausing to hand a canteen to Ford. "It's best not to think of them as human," he said. "Right, Nuta?"

Hanuta didn't reply.

Hun tugged his cap down over his brow. "Well, here comes the Dynamic Duo."

Malkin and Sheb had returned. A few moments later Shu also arrived. Hun stepped over the pool of congealing blood to join the others by the bodies.

"These were the sleepers?" Kabta asked.

"Two of Lír's technologists," Hun reported. "Abdaya confirmed their identities."

"Why'd Lír leave them?" Shu asked.

"Insurance," Kabta replied.

Hun grinned. "Maybe," he said. "Or maybe they were left here because they didn't get along with Lír. They attacked Breaker and me inside SARA."

He turned his arm to display a bloody smear near the shoulder, where his skin was exposed. Hannah had already noticed the blood, but his skin wasn't broken.

"Caught us off guard, and stabbed with improvised daggers. Guns only slowed them down, so we took their heads."

Hannah was staring at the smear of blood on Hun's shoulder. *"Took their heads?"* she whispered.

"Not human," Ford whispered back. He nudged her to move on, but she resisted, wanting to hear more.

"Well," Kabta said, "they're dead now, and they're of no use to us."

"There are still some others in stasis," Hun added. "I counted seven pods that are still occupied, and there are probably more. One I found apart from the others. It's definitely putting off stable life-signs, but I can't identify what's inside."

"I want all four of you with Hanuta keeping a perimeter," Kabta ordered. "Where's Ab?"

"I sent him looking for DePons and Nephtys when they didn't show."

"They'd better be back soon," Kabta said. "Let's keep moving."

The marines turned and entered the station. Hun paused again before passing them by. To Ford he said, "Be careful, Doc. This place is really dangerous, so no flipping switches this time."

He left, melting into the shadows in less than five paces. Hannah was amazed at his stealth, for he was huge, yet his swift steps over the metal decking made no more noise than a stalking cat.

"Let's see what Avalon's got to show us," Kabta said, urging them inside.

The dim light of the round room was extinguished suddenly as the doors closed at their heels, leaving them in near total darkness.

As Kabta led them farther in, flashlights were turned on, revealing a room filled with rows of metal cylinders slanting steeply upwards out of the floor. Each of the tubes leaned at an identical angle, and was covered with untidy coils of hoses and cables. Light from overhead lamps and glowing panels was sparse. It was a spooky place.

Hannah's eyes searched the room, flitting from oddity to oddity like bats in a cave of wonders. She was mostly absorbed in the strange tubes jutting from the floor. There were thousands of them, and all were similar in appearance, being composed of a central tube more than three meters long, angled forty-five degrees, meeting the floor at a spherical mass and flanked on the left and right by smaller supporting structures covered with pipes and cables.

"*Kabta!*" someone shouted.

Shu swung his rifle around, and in the glow of its mounted beam they saw DePons and Nephtys standing about a hundred feet away in a clearing among the rows of tubes. Abdaya was with them. Shu lowered his weapon only after Kabta gestured for him to do so.

"What did you find?" Kabta asked, striding towards them with everyone else in tow.

"We were in Data Storage, and made our way here via an inner shaft," DePons said.

"The elevators are working?" Shu asked. "We might need a quick escape-route."

"We've run into a PCU," Kabta explained. "But let's not get too far ahead of ourselves. I want to hear the news before we proceed."

"We found something interesting," Nephtys said. "There was a recorded transmission from the day the ship went down. The transmission is brief, but it's very significant."

"It's from Morvran," DePons clarified.

"Morvran?" Hannah thought.

Why was that name familiar?

Nephtys held up one hand, and in it there was a small metallic rod. She clicked the end of the cigar-shaped instrument and aimed it at the floor between herself and Kabta. When the projected hologram of a man's face appeared before her at eye-level, Hannah tried her best not to look alarmed.

"Who's he?" she asked, gaping.

The image was blue, and slightly garbled with transmission lines. A progress indicator shaped like a cube was slowly rotating at the bottom of the projection.

"Kanno Ard Morvran," Kabta said. "The Foundation believes he was a human who was in command of this ship, and one of the first to come to this world."

"Right," she replied, gazing at the flickering image. "So, how old would this message be—and how did you download it into that thingy?"

"It's 150,000 years old," Kabta replied.

Hannah was shocked. More than twenty-five times had passed the span of years from the building of the pyramids to the present since the day the image was recorded. She fixed her eyes on the scarred face of the man, and was instantly lost in his deep brown eyes and straight dark hair. It was terribly familiar, like an old photo she remembered from some other place.

The cube stopped, and widening suddenly it became a bar filled with scrolling numbers. The man in the image began to speak, and though his words were badly obscured by static, the message was clear.

"... Kanno Ard Morvran to Colonial Council and all vessels in the fleet. You should have received by now an automated ... from Convoy Hub Avalon. Sadly, I must confirm ... Avalon ... I repeat, Avalon was lost today to a Gremn attack, and all aboard are dead or ... alone escaped, and am ... to submit my full report. For now, there is no recommended military action. If my experience in these matters is still esteemed, I beg ... send a general order to all military and commercial transport vessels to withdraw south of the winter line ... likelihood of further incidents ... The Gremn have access to Avalon's Fomorian. If they are here with ships of their own, they will be capable of networking a large scale assault. Worse, they will ... ships through deep space to our world if they use Avalon to contact comet Bibbu's existing network. The Council ... have to say before taking any other action, for today's events will have a lasting effect on our race in exile."

Then the image froze, and the message ended.

Ford spoke first. "I thought this was a prehistoric message," he said. "Why was he speaking English?"

"There was Akkadian in there, too," Hannah said. When Ford looked at her quizzically, she pulled the blanket closer around her and said, "I definitely heard Babylonian. Specifically, the name of the comet, *Bibbu*."

"The Babylonian culture wasn't around 150,000 years ago, either."

"The roots of all language and culture may have been firmly established in a people who came here from somewhere else," Kabta offered.

Hannah asked, "You're saying they came here with a developed English language, and though their societies later collapsed these and other forms of language somehow reemerged?"

"Hate to interrupt the history lesson," Hun said, stepping out of the shadows where he'd been lurking. "You all know there's a bomb ticking above our heads, right?"

Nephtys clicked the remote-device, and the image of Ard Morvran disappeared. "He spoke of a *Fomorian*," she said. "If it was captured alive, it's probably in here."

"Our unknown sleeper," Kabta said, nodding. "This is good news at last—especially for you, Mr. Ford. Where's that tube you said was all by itself, Attila?"

"It's down this end," he said, pointing past DePons and Nephtys.

"The Fomorians were modified creatures," DePons said to Hannah, answering her unformed question as they walked. "The gist of it is they were modified specifically to be soldiers and machine-interface modules, though the archived records we searched told us something else very strange about the Fomorians themselves. They were designated as *incorporeal entities.*"

"What's that mean?" Hannah asked.

"*Ghosts,*" Ford replied with a grin.

"Ghosts of what?"

"As strange as it may sound," DePons continued, "these Fomorians were thought to be the spirits of green growing things."

"*Spirits of trees?*" Ford muttered, pushing his finger up the bridge of his nose to adjust the glasses that were no longer there.

"That's what the crew of this ship believed, anyway," DePons replied.

"But if it's a ghost, why does it have a body?" Hannah asked.

"Whatever corporeal form it possesses," DePons said, "was assimilated with the Fomorian in a black water stasis tube—one of these." He waved his hand around the room.

Ford seemed to lighten up. "So, it's a shrub in the body of a super-soldier that can link to the computer on an alien spacecraft. I suppose this gives new meaning to the term *green technology*."

Hannah gave him a dark look, but he only smiled.

"Whatever the creature referred to in the message may be," DePons said, "if it's still alive, we have a chance of linking to this ship's AI."

"You think Avalon will give us a chance to escape?" Shu wondered.

"I think whatever we find inside that tube *is* Avalon," DePons replied.

"Either way, it sounds very dangerous," Hannah said. "This is a hostile ancient life form from another world, kept in some kind of stasis for hundreds of thousands of years. Wouldn't it just try to kill us if we wake it up?"

"I'm with her," Ford remarked. "It doesn't sound smart, fooling around with this thing—even if it turns out to be nothing more than a shrub."

"It could save you a visit to the chair," Kabta said, fixing his eyes on Ford. "And in the case that the access codes to the Viaduct Chamber aren't inside your head, that Fomorian may be our only hope of opening the Mirror device and escaping."

Ford seemed to sober suddenly. "In that case," he said, "let's get Snow White out of her glass coffin and hitch a ride on the magic Mirror out of here."

"Clever, Mr. Ford," Kabta said, leading the way towards the far side of the room. Everyone else followed, with the marines fanning out behind them.

"See," Ford whispered to Hannah, "aliens *like* my jokes!"

"Whatever," she said, allowing a slight smile. Her smile faded quickly though, for in the near distance, just beyond the last row of stasis tubes, she saw one standing alone in the soft glow of lamps above; and she sensed a change that threatened their fellowship loomed now very near.

14
FOMORIAN

As they neared the far side of SARA station, Ford and Aston fell back to the rear of the group. Closely examining the tubes as she walked among their legions, Hannah stopped suddenly and asked, "You know what these remind me of?"

"What?" Ford wondered, pausing beside her.

"They look like coffins."

"That's so weird, Hannah. You're just upset about those two dead guys—which is perfectly understandable, considering they're not human, and they have no heads."

"Actually," she said, "I'm more upset about the nuclear bomb than headless aliens that look like humans."

"What about alien marines working for an international technology consortium that's 150,000 years old? That ought to at least take second place."

She grunted appreciatively, and continued walking.

"So, it's not nonsense anymore?" he asked.

"Oh, it's all nonsense," she asserted. "Especially the part where we go looking for a forest-spirit transplanted into an artificial biomechanical body, who's supposed to open up a door to another world so that we can escape from the nuclear bomb—if the aliens don't take off all our heads first. Remind me, please, why did I agree to work with this madman and his crew?"

Ford smirked. "It was my charm and inescapable magnetism."

"No," she replied bluntly, picking up her pace.

"Well, I suppose we were both lured by the prospect of exploring the unknown; and here it is in all its glory."

He looked around and sniffed the fetid atmosphere. Hannah kept walking.

"Wait up!"

She pretended not to hear him, but slowed her steps when the passing gleam of a marine's flashlight shone upon the nearest cylinder—one of the last in the final row. A figure was dimly visible through the glistening material that shielded the central pod.

She stopped, and Ford bumped into her. Both stared, transfixed by fear and wonder.

Ford asked, "Did it just move?"

The shape of a hand appeared suddenly against the inner face of the tube, bumping loudly and startling them both.

"I guess they really are still alive," Ford said. Then, looking back at the rows upon rows that stretched out in deepening gloomy fog behind them, he wondered, "How big is this place?"

Hannah looked up at the tangles of cables hanging from the shadows above. The room was cavernous. She shivered, despite the comfort of the blanket. As they set out to catch up to the rest of the group, she focused on the lone stasis tube ahead, and on the wall emerging from the darkness a couple hundred feet beyond. The sight of an end to all of the echoing dark space through which they'd passed was a strange comfort, though the rectangular hatch in the wall's face looked more ominous the closer they got. It was surrounded by panels illuminated with dull flickering lights, and in the hatch's central panel, the number *32* was glowing.

Why would a door in a place like this bear Arabic numerals?

Hannah and Ford caught up to the others just as Kabta approached the isolated pod. The light coming from overhead lamps seemed brighter here, Hannah thought. The space around them was framed by large pieces of equipment—machines that looked like giant pistons or shock-absorbers.

The stasis tube wasn't as impressive as its surroundings—but then, none of them were. Like the others, it was coated in slick verdigris, and was dripping all the length of its underside with small stalactites of stringy organic material. Cables stretched to the ceiling above, umbilical cords feeding whatever remained within. Hun shone a light through from the other side, and Hannah saw a silhouette through the glittering surface.

"We saw another one back there," Ford said. "It was alive."

Hannah squinted into the pod, trying to make out details of the sleeper. "We can see through this material," she said. "What is it? It's not glass. Is it some kind of metal?"

"It borders on translucence only when light shines upon it," Abdaya noted. "I'm not sure what its composition is. Magan could have told you, but he's dead."

"And this guy's not?" Breaker asked, gesturing towards the stasis tube with his rifle.

Abdaya stepped forward and rapped his knuckles against the hard surface, eliciting a ringing tone.

"The only way to find out is to pop the top," Hun said.

Kabta glanced at his wrist. "We're down to minus fifty minutes. Abdaya?"

"There's no interface on the device itself."

"Anyone bring a can-opener?" Breaker asked.

"We can't risk exposure by cutting her out with plasma torches," DePons warned.

Ford startled them all with a loud clapping of his hands.

"What was that about?" Hannah asked. Her voice was edged with irritation and fear.

"Maybe they installed a *Clapper*," he replied with a smile.

"Begging your pardon, Doctor," DePons said to Hannah, "but your friend appears to be suggesting we attempt to access the pod by general voice commands."

Ford smiled at her.

"However, it's extremely unlikely that the level of technology evidenced here would respond to a simple *Open Sesame*."

"What about *Islith rises again*?" Val asked. Then, to their utter astonishment, the cylinder pulsed briefly with a light like a camera strobe, and there was movement and noise from within.

The marines moved as one, making a circle around the tube. As they readied and leveled their weapons, Hannah shouldered her way between Malkin and Breaker. Ford and Val also found places in the line. Shu took the center, training his sights while fluid drained from the pod's central cavity by some internal mechanism. Then the cables above jerked, humming in a discord of tones. The light inside flashed once more and then went dark. After a pause of several seconds, a sharp hiss drew their attention to the front of the cylinder. Glowing lines appeared suddenly in its surface, tracing an oblong area in the front between a pair of supports. The material was evaporating before their eyes, and in another few moments the pod was open.

"Stay back!" Shu warned.

Everyone complied; but though their eyes strained in the dim light of lamps and flashlights, all they saw within the pod was mist. Slowly the vapors drew aside.

"Good grief," Shu said, lowering his weapon perceptibly.

"What *is* it?" Ford asked.

But by then everyone could see, and fear gave way to stunned surprise. Hannah had never imagined such a creature. Her ears were long and sharp; her eyes surrounded by a faint glimmering tracery of floral patterns. The eyes were open, and gleamed like chips of ice, hard and blue. Her short hair was also blue, cobalt like the deep sky over the sea on a clear summer day.

"Beautiful," Hannah whispered.

"Could we get it something to wear?" Shu asked. "Maybe something to tie it up, too, before it wakes up?"

"If no one else will cover her, I will," Hannah said.

She removed the blanket from her shoulders and stepped forwards to the stasis tube. Before anyone could stop her, she was leaning over the mouth of the pod. Then, with a suddenness that stunned them all, a pair of dark slippery arms, thin but inhumanly strong, snaked out of the cylinder and grabbed her. She was twisted around and pulled within.

Everyone moved towards the pod, but all they could see was a tangle of arms and legs inside. Then, as suddenly as it had begun, all movement ceased. Hannah lay still, held tight against the body of the pod's occupant.

Shu's weapon was back up in the instant Hannah was grabbed, but Ford reached aside and pulled down the barrel. He locked eyes with Shu and shook his head.

"*Sleeping Beauty's* just taken her first prisoner within seconds of awakening from 150,000 years of hibernation," he said. "Let's just take it easy, huh?"

"Take it easy? It'll kill us all!"

"It's just a shrub, remember? And if you shoot Hannah by mistake, I'll kill *you*."

"As if you could," Shu replied. Then, to Kabta, he shouted, "We need this thing alive?"

"If we can get her to the Chair, Ford won't have to risk using it himself."

Shu kept the muzzle of his rifle down. "If things turn ugly," he said aside to Ford, "I'm going to do what needs to be done. *Stay out of my way.*"

Inside the pod the Fomorian shivered, her eyes wide and bright against the black filth that covered her body. Hannah did not struggle against her, and seemed in fact to be moving freely in her choke-hold. Then, with a chilling moan, the creature released her and eased back into a relaxed position. Hannah immediately crawled out of the pod, leaving the blanket behind. She was dripping with black foul-smelling fluid. As she stepped out of the tube, Val reached to take her by the hands and helped her stand on shaking legs. Everyone else stood back, looking into the blue staring eyes of the creature within.

"It's still dangerous," Nephtys warned.

"Deceptively harmless," DePons said. "She might be run-down after all this time in stasis. I hope we can get what we need from her—if we can safely secure her."

"Both those objectives may be a bigger problem than any of us anticipated," Kabta remarked.

"She does look pretty bad," Hannah said quietly, turning around to face her attacker. "We're running out of time. Do we have anything at all to revive her?"

Shu looked from Hannah to Kabta, who nodded. He jogged away towards the entrance with Hun. After they left, Ford came forward, standing beside the pod across from Hannah and Val. Though he was still trying to act cocky, his face was stretched in an expression of amazement. Val understood what he was thinking.

"It's the same," she said to him. "It's the same black water you and I were in."

"I wonder what it's done to her."

"What do you mean?"

"I wonder if it's made her, you know—"

"Crazy?" Hannah supplied. "Crazy like you?"

"I was going to say *confused*."

"Maybe we should all just back up a little," Nephtys warned.

Hannah disregarded her, and leaned again over the opening of the pod.

"What are you all so afraid of?" Ford wondered. "She was probably just a little freaked out. We need her up and out of there fast, or we'll never make it in time."

"I strongly advise caution," Nephtys replied. "If it's the NDB you're worried about, Mr. Ford, know that this girl may be far more capable of exercising large-scale destructive power than a nuclear bomb."

"What do you mean?"

"She commands this ship's security and life-support systems—and its fusion cores."

"She may also be carrying a virus," DePons said, looking at Hannah.

Hannah wiped the black slime on her arm with the back of one hand. "I don't think she meant to hurt me," she said. "It seemed like a response, a reaction to being awakened."

She reached inside and gently wiped the girl's face clean with the edge of the blanket, arranging it so that it covered her. The cleaning revealed more of the tattoos of vines and flowers beneath her eyes, and around her long graceful ears. As Hannah began to dab at the arms, the Fomorian gave a little gasp and convulsed. Everyone else stepped back a pace.

"It's breathing again," Kabta said. "Give it a moment, Miss Aston—"

The girl suddenly sat bolt-upright, and with wide eyes and open mouth she let out a horrendous rasping shriek. A circle of rifles stared back at her as the marines snapped to readiness, cringing slightly at the piercing sound—a sound no human larynx could have produced. Hannah staggered backwards, hands clapped uselessly to her ears. The cry went on for what seemed a minute, and the entire chamber shook. Showers of sparks rained down, and then all was dark again outside the glow of their flashlights—and still she screamed.

Shu came dashing back even before the scream was finished, and tossing the first aid kit to the ground he raised his rifle. Ford didn't argue with him this time, and even Hannah backed up; but it was soon apparent there was no need for alarm. The girl's voice gave out with a gurgling sound. A moment later, she fell forward across the front of the pod and began to belch forth quantities of the black water with painful gagging noises. Hannah was back at her side in an instant, holding her shoulders.

"Puking Caesar's ghost!" Ford exclaimed, kicking the first aid kit towards Hannah. "What do we do with it now?"

Hannah unclasped the case and removed a tube of oxygen and a mask. When the girl started gasping, she covered her face with the mask and rubbed her back gently.

"It's possible this is a trick," Shu said.

"Careful, Miss Aston!" Breaker warned.

The choking stopped suddenly at the sound of their voices.

"Better?" Hannah asked, looking into her face.

She grabbed Hannah's hand, removing it and the mask. Awareness of the others gathered around the pod slowly dawned on her, and covering herself with the blanket she sat upright. Sharp eyes raised towards Kabta and ears pulled slightly back like a cat's, she bared her teeth and growled. It was not a sound they expected to hear from such a perfect mouth. What surprised them more was what came next.

"*Warad Lír!*" she yelled, her voice raw and edged with wrath.

"She names him *Slave of Lír*," Hannah said aside.

"Babylonian?" Ford asked.

"Yeah. You got smart in that black water?"

"Those words aren't in *my* Scrabble dictionary," he replied. "Who's *Lír*?"

"La tapallah," Kabta said, holding up his hands. "Do not be afraid!"

"Warad Lír!" she said, jabbing a finger towards him. *"Aweelum shu, wardam shuati, namkoor ilim ishriq—"*

She fell to retching again before she could finish. Hannah didn't move to help her this time, but pulled her hand free and backed away towards Ford and Val.

Interpreting, she said, "That man, that *slave*, who stole the possession of a god—"

The girl heard Hannah speaking, and turned to observe. When she saw Val standing there beside her, she slowly calmed. At first she looked afraid, and then she shook, pulling the blanket closely around her body. With deliberate and painful movements she pushed herself up into a kneeling posture inside the pod, and bowed her head in Val's direction, her hair dangling forwards in greasy blue knots around the long arch of her neck.

"Sinnishtam shiati!" she said, choking. *"Rubum sha ishpurakkunuti, zaerum darium sha sharrutim!"*

Gasping for breath, she lifted her face to say more; but the strain was too much. Her eyes rolled back in their sockets and she pitched forward, rolling fully out of the pod onto the deck. There she lay in a pool of the black water, unmoving.

Hannah stepped forward again to tend her, translating as she did.

"She calls Val the *great one* someone sent to us, *the seed of everlasting kingship.*"

"Is that all?" Ford said, smirking at Val. "A friend of yours, Miss?"

But Val said nothing. Instead, she went and knelt beside Hannah.

"I think she's dead," Hannah said.

They rested a short time after that, passing water bottles while Kabta talked to Nephtys. Ford and Shu were sitting beside the pod, having their own discussion while the marines looked on anxiously. Hannah and Val sat on either side of the Fomorian. She had exhibited no signs of life since her collapse.

"A verbal passcode kept the pod sealed tight for ages," Ford said. "And Val opened it with an English translation of a Gremn phrase. Then *this* creature emerged speaking Babylonian, calling Kabta a slave and a thief. I'm a little confused. I think the rest of us deserve some explanations."

"It's the black water," Shu replied lamely. "The conditioning transfers information back to a Source, which transmits to all creatures that've been in the black water. It enables a sharing of languages."

"Then why didn't the creature speak English to start with, and why can't I speak Babylonian?"

"My name is Bec," said a voice from the floor.

Everyone turned to where the Fomorian lay. Val and Hannah helped her sit up. They'd cleaned her with one of the blankets while she lay unconscious, and the other was draped around her now like a cloak.

"Could you keep the light out of her eyes?" Hannah said, waving her hand.

Shu lowered his rifle, and the other marines did the same.

The Fomorian's eyes were fixed on Val.

"Bec?" Hannah wondered.

The girl turned her head to take in the startled glances of the others, pausing lastly upon Kabta, who stood to one side with Nephtys and Hanuta.

"You said I should not be afraid," she said. "Why have you awakened me, Kabta?"

Kabta made no reply.

"You two know each other?" Hannah asked.

"Bec is my given name," she said to Hannah. Her voice was still rough, but she spoke without halt, and with only a gentle lilting accent.

"What's your real name?" Val asked.

"I am a *Null-User*," she replied. "I am Avalon. My teacher called me his *little one*, which is *Bec*. Whoever I was before is lost to me, Bal-Ona."

"How do you know that name?" Val wondered.

"I know many things about you!"

Bec looked aside at Kabta, who returned her icy gaze with a frown.

"They are afraid of me," she said. "That is good, for they have much to fear."

"Why do you say that?" Val asked.

"They only want the one thing, *ina qaqqadim*." The last she said very quietly, tapping her own head.

"What do they want inside your head?" she asked in a whisper.

"Bal-Ona, Belutki bael hulqim."

"What?" Val asked.

"You are...the owner of a lost object," Bec whispered. "I know your secret. *Belutki lusharrih, adi baltat.*"

"She names you *your lordship*," Hannah said, leaning across Bec. "That's an ancient royal title! What gives?"

"I will glorify the Empress so long as she lives," Bec stated, bowing her head. "I will protect her."

"Tall order for so short a girl!" Ford quipped.

Bec turned her head towards him and smiled. Hannah could feel his terror as he squirmed under that gaze.

"What he means," Val said, "is that we are in terrible danger right now. Avalon is beneath the ocean, and it's going to be destroyed by a bomb."

"Lír has a bomb?" Bec asked, seemingly puzzled.

"Lír is gone, and many ages have passed since you were detained here."

Catching her eye, Hannah saw the flicker of a light deep inside. It was like a spark of red-hot metal. Val took the girl's small hands in her own.

"Bec," she said, "these people are our friends. They wish to bring all those together who were divided by the war."

"Be wary, Bal-Ona! They want to put one of us in the *Chair*. That person is Kabta, Lord of all the Gremn on Ertsetum. I recognize him, and he knows what I am. Don't you know what I am, Lord Kabta?"

Kabta folded his arms across his broad chest and nodded.

"Lord of the Gremn?" Hannah wondered.

"Told you," Ford whispered. *"Even the shrub says it's so!"*

"This is going nowhere!" Shu griped. "We've only got forty-five minutes left!"

Val grimaced at him, and turning to Bec she said, "I know it's hard to understand, but much has changed since you were captured, and the Gremn are a changeable folk. I have heard of what was done to you in the past, but the war ended long ago. The time has come for us all to go home, together."

Bec looked into her face, considering. The hot glare melted away from her eyes, but they were still very grim. "Bal-Ona," she said, "I had a dream about you when I was sleeping. You came to me and explained many things that were happening in the world, and in time. Marluin was with us, and we were in the High Place in Gilthaloneth. If I did not dream this dream, I would have killed all of you or died trying. I am sorry if this sounds cruel to you, but you don't remember what the Gremn did to our people."

"Well, this Gremn didn't do anything to your people," Shu said angrily, and walked away.

They all looked after him.

"Small warrior," Kabta said, "please try to understand. There are Gremn who were born on this world who have only ever fought other Gremn. We are here with Crodah, ordinary humans, and Shu is half-Crodah himself."

"Half—" Hannah stammered, her eyes staring at the floor in front of her.

"Then it is the Gremn half that's so ready with a weapon," Bec replied hotly. "I would not have known such a thing to be possible as a half-Gremn half-Crodah person, and I will not say this brings me joy, Lord Kabta, for I have *not* changed. Nor have the designs of the Gremn, I think. Do you pretend to me that your plans are different now than they were before?"

"My plans have not changed," Kabta replied, "though now my goal is different. I intend to return to the World of Origins, but now I will go without victory over the Crodah, and I will only go the way that was prescribed by the Ancient in Gilthaloneth, by the Dyn Hysbys you name *Marluin*, who said that Gremn and Crodah must recohere the stones and return them. We must do this, or all the worlds will go dark."

"What's this all about? Ford asked.

Hannah looked up to see DePons smiling at her.

"Whatever you claim to be, Lord Kabta," Bec said, "I am a Fomorian. Experimentation with viruses and other biological and chemical weapons was practiced upon us by the Gremn after we were given artificial Null-bodies. Your technologists intended to use our Null-bodies to perfect their virus before releasing it."

"I wonder," Nephtys said, "wasn't it the Crodah who first subjected your people to all this testing?"

Bec turned to consider her. "A female?" she wondered. Then, seeing Hanuta beside her, she displayed wide-eyed curiosity. "*Two* females! Gremn females are as rare as Fomorians, or so it was said; yet I believe it was also said among your kinds that females are always right. In this case, the adage was mistaken, and so are you."

Nephtys blinked surprise.

"It was the Gremn who began it," Bec said. "That is why my folk and all the Forest People chose to ally ourselves with the Crodah. We knew that our survival and theirs were entwined, and the Gremn would not stop until all the Crodah were dead. Thus was Galaneth wasted by the Fire, and my people were unable to leave the forests and go to the city Gilthaloneth."

She lowered her eyes sadly.

"I still don't understand why they needed you to interface their technology," Ford said. "Couldn't they just use keyboards and consoles?"

Everyone looked at him. He offered a sheepish shrug.

"The *Null-Users* were trained to infiltrate Gremn hives and ships," Bec answered, lifting her gaze to meet the eyes of the circle of curious stares. "It is because we are good at adaptation, faster than any other kinds of people or machines. The Gremn captured us, and incorporated the unique patterns of our minds into their computer design, and thus the AI of each Gremn ship was granted its special personality via a Fomorian drone. I am Avalon, and Avalon is me. I am of spirit, and I am this ship's soul. We are one."

There was a pause. Everyone looked at the small girl wrapped in a blanket, and she gazed back from behind the stray locks of her short blue hair. Silence filled the empty spaces of the vast chamber.

Shu had been listening from a distance, and still stood apart from the rest, glowering in the shadows. Bec turned her attention towards him, but said nothing.

Hannah asked, "If we could get off the ship, where would we go?"

"To the World of Origins," Bec answered. "Didn't they tell you that's where they wanted to go all along?"

"No, they didn't," she answered, glancing at Kabta. "I just don't understand how we're going to get off the ocean floor, let alone to another world."

"She is the one who travels through the stone," Bec said, looking at Val. "She will bring us from this place."

"Val?" Hannah wondered.

"Can you not see the light on her?"

"No, I don't understand—"

"—It is as our trees promised in Tryst, in the ages that our people walked there unhindered before the War, before the sacred groves were cut down and the dragons came. In the days before the Galanese came out of the East and Gilthaloneth was still held by the Ancients, a promise was made. The exiles will return, together. *She* will lead them."

Bec then rose up on steady legs beside the pod where she had lain asleep for so long. They watched as she looked at the machine and wrapped the blanket closer around her slender figure. There was a hush that could be felt, and leaning forward with an intent look, Bec gazed into the eyes of tall Nephtys.

"The Gremn don't know the meaning of my words," she said, "but these words are well known to those of us who once protected the Aerfen, and the stones which are the source of its strength. My words were given to me before any of your farthest ancestors were born. Now that I am the last princess of my people, perhaps the very last of my kin, these words are mine to guard and to bring to fulfillment."

"What words are those?" Nephtys asked, her voice softening.

Bec paused briefly as she inspected each of the faces gathered around her.

"It is a catechism," she replied, "the catechism of the stones. We must bring it back with us to the World of Origins. It is the key to the discovery of the Dark Stones, which were lost, and to the recovery of the Aerfen, the weapon that ends all wars."

"I thought this wasn't about weapons," Hannah said. She gave Kabta a sour look.

"We will bring Bal-Ona to the Chamber now," Bec said. "Engine cores are operating at acceptable levels. I am initiating vacuole capture. The Mirror will soon be active."

"We're just going in?" Ford asked. "I thought we needed access codes."

Then, without even turning her head, Bec pointed straight at Shu.

"He has them," she said.

Shu sighed, and fishing in his pocket he produced the tablet computer, holding it up for everyone to see.

"How'd you know?" he asked.

"I know it because you have thought of little else for several minutes now," Bec answered.

"You know my thoughts?" he asked, striding towards them.

"I know only the thoughts that you desire to make known to the others."

"Right," Shu said, lowering his gaze. "She's right. Shim gave it to me. He said we'd need the codes to access the Chamber, and that we would also need Val Anna and a sleeper that was left behind in stasis. I just didn't know if what he gave me was some kind of trap, and when you started saying the same things, Uncle—"

"There is no deceit in you, and no harm was done by this," Kabta said. "But you could have saved us time; and what if we had tried to use Ford?"

"I wouldn't have let anything happen to Ford," he replied, looking aside at the scientist. "Even his life must have a purpose, I suppose."

"Thanks, *idiot*," Ford said, folding his arms angrily.

Bec regarded Shu closely. "You and I are not so different, after all," she said, holding his gaze. "We now belong to one purpose, and are called by one stone. We will be brought together in one place, to protect her. That is why you will need me to go with you."

She turned and patted the chest-plate of Val's body armor, and met her eyes with a knowing look. *"Lia Fáil,"* she said solemnly, "Stones of Destiny they once were called; but to find their destiny they must reside in you, as you reside in the one."

"To this end have we pledged to protect her," Kabta said. He stepped towards Bec, offering his hand.

Bec looked at him suspiciously. Kabta towered over her by more than three feet, but she appeared undaunted.

"Maybe it's strange to you to receive kindness from the hand of an enemy," he said, "but I promise that I will do all I can to help you accomplish your mission. We shall put away the past, Fomorian, and let no talk of agendas or secret motives keep us from our one purpose."

Bec cautiously took his great hand in hers. *"Lumnum ay ikshudanni?"* she asked. *"What is the evil that has befallen me?* My eyes are opened, Lord Kabta, and I will agree to this strange alliance. We must journey through the Dark Worlds, through the stones, and only Bal-Ona can merge the worlds without recourse and return to the World of Origins. We must do this quickly, for Avalon has decided that the explosive device outside the ship will be sufficient to bring about its end. We have less than twenty-five minutes. Shall we proceed?"

15
CATECHISM

They followed Bec towards the hatch, and Hannah noticed that all the marines walked in front now. Ford noticed, too.

"They're no longer concerned about the PCU?" he wondered.

She wasn't sure.

He lowered his voice so only she could hear, and he said, "A few minutes ago they were ready to kill her, and now that she's complicit she's like one of us."

"They haven't threatened Val. I don't think they mean to harm us."

The sound of her voice was hollow in her own ears.

"Except for Val and DePons, none of them are human," he replied. "What do you think they'll do when they no longer need us, Hannah? I don't know about you, but my own confidence is wavering."

She hated to admit it to herself, but Ford had a point.

Val walked in front of them with Bec. The Fomorian wore a makeshift tunic fashioned from a fresh blanket. With holes cut for the arms and a belt around her waist, she posed a strange figure indeed. Walking unshod in this rough raiment, she put on a determined look very similar to Val's when Hannah first saw her under the hill of Hazor; and like Val did then, the Fomorian glimmered now with light, with a soft glow that fell all about her like rain. It was a strange thing to see. Hannah thought at first that it must be a reflection of some other source of light from above, but before long the illumination grew in intensity, canceling all doubt. The light was definitely coming from Bec.

"Bioluminescence?" Ford wondered quietly.

"I don't know," Hannah replied. "We saw the same thing under Hazor."

"Yeah, but I wonder how the trick is done."

"Trick? Isn't she a spirit?"

"What? Like in *A Christmas Carol*?"

"I can't imagine," Hannah replied honestly. "It just seems—"

They stopped in front of the hatch. Val and Bec stood staring at it, and Hannah felt a sudden heaviness wash over her being. Into her mind crowded a terrible fear of crossing the darkened threshold of that door. The fear told Hannah that if she crossed over she might never return to the world she had known.

Shu approached the door with tablet in hand. Beside it was a small console set in an illuminated panel.

"All I have is a 32-digit numerical code," he said. "That's all that's on this thing."

"Input the code," Bec said.

"You can't just open the door for us?"

"This security protocol was established before I was integrated into Avalon."

"There are doors even the AI's not allowed to open on this ship?"

"She's running the Mirror for us," DePons said. "Just input the code."

"What if this is a trap? What if the code sets off some kind of self-destruct sequence that she can't stop?"

"Then we'll die sooner."

"Great," Shu said, gazing at the console. It was all in Gremn characters. "This is just *great.*"

"Should've studied," Breaker taunted.

Then the screen cleared before he had a chance to touch anything, and he was looking at a glowing numeric pad with standard Arabic numerals.

"This is the limits of Avalon's clearance at this console," Bec stated. "The Mirror will be active soon."

"Thanks, Bec," he said, typing in the code.

"You are welcome," she replied, her face betraying both curiosity and confusion.

As soon as Shu had entered the final digit, the hatch door slid open, revealing a chamber beyond. A bright white light was emanating from the interior walls. Blinking in that light, Hannah found herself suddenly overwhelmed by strange sentiments. She heard whispers among the marines. DePons said something to Ford, who looked like he was about to start another argument.

Ahead, Val shook off whatever everyone else was feeling and set one foot before the other. Bec followed her, and Hannah came next. A tremor ran through her as she passed the threshold. It was no longer a fear or suspicion. Like her parents before her, she was never coming back.

The Viaduct Chamber was a perfectly spherical space, and here the walls were smooth and radiant. Though the outer wall adjoining SARA Station was flat and covered with organic deposits, all surfaces herein were curved and clean. The round shape of the room naturally drew their attention to the center, and to the chair. It looked like a cross between a hospital gurney and a half-folded deck chair, Hannah decided.

As Val walked farther into the room, the others followed silently, hushed with awe. It was very much like entering a temple or a church, for in the air there hung the profound sanctity of a quiet that none dared disturb. After Ford and DePons had passed within, Kabta and Shu came, then Nephtys, and finally the group of five marines. They stood and gazed in wonder at the gleaming walls, perfectly formed, polished, and completely featureless—that is, except for the reflections.

Strange shadows were reflected in the walls, shadows that kept moving when everyone around her paused. Hannah couldn't decide what they were reflections of, for they were all smoky in appearance, but they almost looked like people.

Bec stopped in the center of the room and faced Kabta. The door behind them shut with a hiss. They all watched in silence as the chamber sealed itself. Hannah's heart sank, for now she was turning another corner, plunging ahead into deeper waters, passing ever farther away from the life she had known.

When the interior surface of the hatch was perfectly contoured to match the rest of the sphere, leaving no line to betray the presence of a door, Shu turned back and touched the wall. A startling electric discharge jolted his hand, singeing him.

"What's that about?" he asked, wringing his hand.

"Like the cylinders," DePons said, "it appears the aperture is sealed by a powerful electromagnetic field."

"Great," Ford replied. "How do we get out of here?"

"There's only one way out of this room, Mr. Ford, and despite my extensive experience in working with the Gremn, I'm beginning to have second thoughts about it."

"Come on, DePons! You'd rather stay on the bottom of the ocean in an alien spacecraft that smells like cheese, with a bipolar robot running loose and a nuclear bomb about to go off?"

"That depends. Will you be staying, too?"

"Stop talking," one of the marines said behind them.

Ford turned and saw Hun standing there. "Attila, I thought it might be you. You want to know how I thought it was you?"

"Quiet, Ford," Hannah said. "This is a special place. I don't think we're supposed to be talking."

Hun said, "He's not even copasetic. How's he supposed to know when to shut up?"

"*Copasetic,*" Ford mocked. "That's a mighty big word for someone whose shirt-collar is larger than his hat size."

"You wanna talk about irony," Hun fired back, "how about we discuss how your ego's even bigger than your mouth?"

Hannah hushed them with an exasperated look, and when silence resumed they were suddenly aware that someone else was speaking. Bec's voice was so low that at first no one heard her; but after a moment she repeated herself, chanting a beautiful dirge-like verse, and all of them were amazed. It was a lovely but frightening experience, for Bec's childlike voice uttered strange words that sounded wondrously fair, and the things that she sang of formed images that were projected on the walls of the chamber.

First Hannah saw a forest, dim and foggy. The image moved very rapidly from a bird's-eye view to ground level, and there it was confused with many other sights. There was a floating city—a shining hill of metal in the clouds. Then there was another city on a hill above a dark blue lake in a desert, a white city rising level upon level until its mighty summit lifted wings to the sky.

In the sky there were three moons, and one of them was the Earth.

The chant finished suddenly, and on the chamber's walls was a dark field of stars and what appeared to be a lone comet with three tails. The faint radiance that came from Bec now increased as all other lights were extinguished. The glow streamed from her in tendrils of radiance, like a coronal garment. The Fomorian stood thus in their midst and chanted one last verse in a mix of English and Babylonian.

> *Mul'hungá, Agru the fighter, which is Aries.*
> *Mul'gigir, Narkabtu, Gift to the Gremn-Under-Ban,*
>   *the Chariot.*
> *Mul'ur, Kalbu, the hound of Great Strength.*
> *Mul'Babbar, Kakkabu Petsu, the blessed White Star of*
>   *Jupiter.*
> *Mul'hul, wicked Lumnu, the witch of Mars.*
> *Mul'ellag, Bibbu the Lonely, the Comet.*
> *Mul'sipazi-anna, Shitaddalu, Beautiful Orion.*
> *Mul'ashiku, Ikû the Far-Ranging, the Last Pegasus.*
> *Mul'lugal, Sharru, the Hidden Lord Regulus.*
> *Gír'tab, Aban Zuqaqipu, the Scorpion, most precious*
>   *of gems.*
> *Mul'pan, Qashtu, Gift to the Crodah-Under-Ban, the*
>   *Heart of Venus.*
> *Mul'dara, Dim Da'ummatu, the Dark Star, First and*
>   *Last, the Dragon's Heart.*
>
> *These, the Twelve, shall endure apart as one.*
> *Hidden by the Ancients, reunited by the hidden;*
> *May all hold fast their legend until the end.*

The ancient catechism finished, Bec became still, and her stillness fell upon them all, full as it was of the presence of some restless and watchful being that had come at the behest of her song. No one dared speak out. All stood facing the center of the room, where they saw the chair. It had a flat surface and a back, but the back tilted forwards at a sharp angle. The whole thing rested on an armature that rose from the floor.

Bec then extended her hand towards Val, who seemed to understand the gesture. She reached back to untangle the cord from the hair at the nape of her neck, and pulled out the stone from her suit, holding it up in the palm of one hand. Everyone stared at the dark glittering disk—even the marines broke their candor and gawked like schoolchildren. Val withdrew her hand a little before their greedy eyes.

"You hesitate because you feel the weight of the Holy Jewel," Bec said.

Her voice was alarmingly loud, and the stone responded, first spinning rapidly on its cord and then jolting to a sudden halt with a cool light and a soft ringing tone. Hannah saw in its face a blue tracery of whorls and loops that glowed from deep within.

"It is a very sacred thing," Bec said to Val, "and it is right that you remember the reverence in its unity. It has been betrayed by mortal vessels, and thus was it divided by a divided people, and all the worlds were divided within it. Do not fear now to unsheathe its brilliance, Bal-Ona, for the hour is approaching in which the stone's purpose may be fulfilled. It longs for its counterparts. They must be gathered together in you. Now, go to the chair."

Val trembled visibly, and taking the stone in the palm of her hand she proceeded towards the chair. Hannah longed to walk with her and provide some sort of support, though she sensed this was something Val was expected to do on her own.

"Not alone," she mumbled, and stepping forwards from the circle she came to stand on Val's right. Bec joined her on the left, and each took one of the girl's arms in their own. It was a day of strange happenings, Hannah decided, but above all else it was now apparent that a new thing was happening—an event long-awaited. Val grimaced, probably thinking that it had waited for her. As the sense of doom intensified, so did Hannah's doubts. Those doubts took awful shape just as they reached the chair.

There, when the three stood at last beside the high seat, Val cried out and clenched her right hand, holding it away from her. A gasp went out around the chamber, and all looked on in amaze, for the stone burst suddenly into blue flames, and then sank into the living flesh of the hand that held it.

Bec let go of her at once, but Hannah was dragged to the ground as Val fell to her knees. It happened so quickly, right before her eyes; yet Hannah clutched the girl's wrist while Val rocked to and fro, hissing with apparent agony. Beneath her fingers, Val's arm burned suddenly with an intense scorching heat, so that she had to let go.

That was when the walls began to shake.

"The PCU's trying to break in," Shu muttered.

No one moved. Bec stood still and silent, her eyes closed and head bowed in an attitude of intense concentration. Val was still incapacitated, but her writhing agony lasted only a few more moments, and then she seemed to calm, letting out her breath in an awful rush. Hannah placed a hand on her back and helped her to her feet, where she stood unsteadily, casting about with a dazed look in her eyes.

"What's happening?" she asked in a groggy voice.

The wall behind them shuddered under the hammer-strokes of a giant, again and again. Shu looked to Kabta, who nodded. The marines nearest their point of entry knelt and took up firing positions, though there wasn't even a door visible to aim at.

Val hardly noticed all that was going on behind her. She was looking down at her hand, where the stone had vanished along with the pain. Hannah kept one hand on her back to steady her as Val turned towards the chair.

"It's for navigation," she said.

"How do you know?" Hannah asked.

Val didn't respond. Instead, she began to climb onto the seat. This would have been a trick for anyone to do alone, for the chair was at waist-height and balanced very strangely. Hannah knew it was up to her to help, though she didn't have a clue what they were doing; so she steadied the girl's shoulder while Val straddled the seat and leaned forwards. No sooner was she situated than the wall of the chamber buckled, dented inwards by the force of an explosion in SARA Station. At last,

Val seemed to awaken to their danger. Her eyes widened with fear.

"I'm here," Hannah said, patting her knee.

"The Mirror is opening, but a location has not yet been determined," Bec stated.

"Sixty seconds!" Shu yelled, glancing over his shoulder. "You can do this, Val!"

Stooping atop the chair, Val tried pushing against its forward-leaning back, but this produced no results. She sighed, frustrated and fearful, and sagged her shoulders forwards a little. Just then some other mechanism sprang into action, and with a crackle of static her body was jerked violently backwards against the chair. Hannah stepped back, unsure how to help. Val's arms stretched out towards the seat in front of her, but could not reach. Her legs would not move. She was held in place by invisible bonds. When she struggled a little, trying to sit lower, the chair responded by tightening its hold.

The wall behind them rippled, and the hatch reappeared.

Bec's eyes flew open, and she faced the breach. One moment the hatch appeared, and then vanished, only to reemerge. The wall continued to buckle under the strong blows of the monster outside. Bec stiffened suddenly, and turning briefly towards Val she spoke one word.

"Relax."

The chair's invisible restraints seemed to ease up, but just then her lower body was unfolded quickly beneath her as the chair swung upside-down, suspending her facing the floor.

"Is this right?" she asked.

Hannah knelt down beside the chair and grinned up at Val, giving the thumbs-up.

"Thirty seconds left," Shu said, keeping his voice calm. "Whatever you girls are doing, please do it *fast*."

The wall behind them burst into flames.

Hannah turned in time to see Shu knocked flat on his face. Several of the other marines also hit the deck, beaten down by the force of an explosion. The wall where they had entered was torn suddenly aside like a veil. The hatch was opening, and great hands were reaching inside to tear the doors asunder. DePons was right in front, down on his knees, trying to pull Ford out of the way. He reached to grab Shu also, shouting something Hannah couldn't understand. Then they disappeared—all three of them. It was as if they had never existed.

Kabta was still on his feet. Turning around towards the chair, he caught Hannah's eyes and winked. Then he also disappeared, and all of the marines and Nephtys vanished with him. She was alone with Val and Bec—and the PCU.

The walls were peeling back like foil, and into the opening lunged a massive metallic head shaped like a bird's. The sounds of tearing metal stopped suddenly, though, and an eerie silence fell. All was completely still. A hand on her shoulder warned her, and a look from the Fomorian's eyes pierced her soul. She now stood shoulder to shoulder with Bec, and there was something comforting about that. The soft radiance that came from her was warm, and the air was sweet. Hannah could hear something now, something like the distant ringing of bells.

She was calm.

"Steady," her thoughts said, speaking directly into Hannah's mind. *"She is binding us to herself, in the stone."*

"She's doing it?" Hannah asked.

"I'm doing it?" Val echoed.

The PCU's green-glowing eyes were fixed on Bec, as if it too was soothed by the sight of her.

"Whatever you're doing, do it quickly," Hannah muttered.

"I don't remember how!" Val complained, shaking her head. "Kal-Nergal did it the last time, and he had help from the Source—"

As soon as she said his name, a blurred image of a red desert swirled around them. Hannah gasped. Below her feet—and in front of Val's face—there appeared the figure of a man walking in the heat of a parched and windy wasteland. Then everything changed. Darkness rushed all around them in a vortex punctuated by the ringing of bells, and then a voice broke across the thunder, silencing everything in an instant. It was Val's voice.

"*Gilthaloneth!*" she shouted.

Hannah stumbled forwards into empty air, and fell on her feet with a crash. Wherever she was, it was very dark.

"Val?" she said. Then, turning around, she saw Bec.

The Fomorian stood a little away from her, glowing still, and still wearing the blanket. There was nothing else around them she could see.

"Did something go wrong?" Hannah asked. "Where are we?"

"Don't move," Bec warned. "There is a pit before your feet."

Hannah could see nothing in front of her. "We're not in the ship anymore," she guessed.

"We are in a bad place."

"If it's not exploding, I'll take it."

Bec moved slowly, and Hannah could see that she walked the edge of a circular pit that was more than ten feet across. When at last they stood side by side, Bec took her hand and tugged her towards the darkness behind them.

"Walk quietly," she whispered. "I do not know our *when*. If it is now, we are safe; but if it has already been, we are in terrible danger."

"You know this place?" Hannah replied, allowing herself to be led.

"It is *Tref Toghail*, a meeting of the worlds, which is located in the cave below. We are beneath the *Cnoc Ddraig*."

"The Dragon's Mound?" Hannah wondered. "Sounds like a fairy-tale. What kind of place is this?"

"The Great Mound's location is not fixed to one place or another," Bec said. "It has a tendency to move. However, you are right to guess that we are not currently in Avalon. We are no longer in Ertsetum."

The ease with which she said this chilled Hannah.

"I do not know why the others are not with us," Bec continued, "nor why we have come to this place. Perhaps it had something to do with the detonation of Kabta's weapon."

"Well," Hannah replied, "at least we made it here safely."

"That remains to be seen," Bec said.

They walked through an open space, and then through a tunnel. At the end, Hannah was disappointed to see that they had not yet entered free air—though the smell was somewhat better than the interior of the Gremn ship.

"Smells like a cave," she remarked.

"The smell of Wyrm is not here. By this token I would guess we've come in our right frame of reference to this place, and thankfully there is little for you to fear."

"That's good," Hannah said.

"Still, there are other spirits present than myself, and they know I am near."

This was *not* good, Hannah decided. She wasn't sure about this creature's claims of being a spirit, but she couldn't deny the fact that she was terrified by the possibility of meeting up with unseen villains in the pressing darkness.

"I wish we could see."

Then, as if summoned by her words, a gleaming disk appeared high above in the distance. It was a mirror lit from some other source, and the world it illuminated was more sinister than any Hannah had ever seen or imagined. She knew now that they were no longer in any place on Earth.

They stood in a cavern of vast proportions, hard beneath the wall of a shining black tower. The tower was a quadrilateral tapering towards a pyramid at the top, where it nearly touched the natural stone ceiling of the cavern. Its surface glittered like darkened steel, and the eyes in its face looked out upon still more wonders.

"Is it a city?" she asked.

"It was a city in the northern wilds of the World of Origins, not far from the forest where my people once dwelt. Gremn lived here, slaves of the sorcerer who made this place."

"A sorcerer, huh?"

Hannah surveyed a plaza that stretched before them, filled with broken and ruined columns. It surrounded the central spine, the Dark Tower, like a maze. Farther off she saw the huddled shapes of stone-built houses and paved streets. Bec tugged her by the hand, leading her down from the tower in the direction of the disk of light that burned high above.

"This mound was once very evil, and it will be evil again when the prophecies are fulfilled that were spoken long ago. Wicked things always dwell here; yet there will come a hero who shall take away the Tower and all the darkness. Then this place of crossing to the Dark Worlds of Ertsetum shall be forever closed."

As they walked through the lair, the darkness wavered and broke before them, and resumed in their passage. The glimmering Fomorian was as an angel in the depths of Hell to Hannah Aston, leading her through a nightmare few of the children of Mankind had ever seen. They walked for almost an hour, passing through haunted streets and courtyards before coming at last to a place illuminated by the light of day. It emanated from a large doorway ahead.

They approached the gate with high hopes, but Hannah paused when she came to a massive heap stretched upon the pavement. It was an iron door, enormous, yet broken in ruin and rusting to bits. Passing carefully over this hurdle—Bec in bare feet—they came to the threshold, and there they paused again to consider a few strange characters inscribed upon the doorsill. Bec stood beside her and read them aloud.

"Behind the gate is the beginning of the world, and before it the world's end."

Hannah craned her neck to take in the scale of the massive gate. "What's it mean?" she asked.

A breeze blowing through the gateway ruffled Bec's makeshift dress. "It is an evil thing that anyone should desire their own will to be set above that of others," she replied. "The one who wrote these words believed that it was his destiny to save Mankind by changing the past and the future in the stones. He was wrong about everything, yet his defeat still awaits him. Who can say what will become of him, or of the one who is lured here to try and succeed where he failed?"

They exited the gate to a paved courtyard, and stood in the sunlight of a dying day. The clouds were red-lit from below, yet that glimpse of the daystar after her sojourn in the deeps was the most refreshing sight that Hannah Aston had ever seen. Then she realized, this wasn't her sun, and it wasn't her world.

Bec let go of her hand suddenly, and stretched like a cat rising from long sleep. Hannah watched her yawn, pointed ear-tips waggling.

"It is green here!" the beautiful girl said, her voice rising. "It is not like the green in Avalon. This is better!"

"It sure smells better," Hannah remarked.

Bec turned a surprisingly impish smile on her. "You Crodah are strange children," she said. "Does your flesh-body not feel the *green?*"

"I don't understand."

"I suppose Null-bodies are better in that one way," Bec said, looking down at her hands. "Nulls allow my people to interface directly with Gremn and Crodah technology, while enhancing the capacity to exercise our primal force."

"What force?" she asked.

"The *green*, the power over the life-force of all green growing things. This gift was coveted by the Gremn, who longed to learn it for themselves, just as they stole from dragons the ability to change their form. But enough of talk! Now we must begin our journey. I will take you as far as I can, and then you will need to go on by yourself for a bit. It is fitting that we should start here, at the end of the world."

Hannah turned, and was startled by the sight of the mound—a high hill with rings of ruined walls from sunset-painted summit to the darkness gathering around its feet. The deeply shadowed pavement upon which they stood was strewn with what looked like rusted pieces of armor, and beyond this a kind of dock.

"Is it a canal?" she wondered, tracing the straight line of the water from east to west across a wide plain.

"It was. We will go north, along the road by the water's western edge. If we walk through the night we may come by morning into the inhabited regions of Tryst. If not, we will at least trade this sad place of battle for the Forest."

"And then what? I mean, this is all new to me."

"You also have a purpose, Hannah Aston," the Fomorian said. "No one comes to this place who is not supposed to be here."

"Then what are *you* doing here?"

"I will take you to Islith."

"*The* Islith? Like the one that's supposed to rise again?"

"Some of the Forest People may yet dwell there. They will not harm you, though you are here against the Ban."

"The Ban?" Hannah wondered. "I don't know anything about this place. Couldn't I just stay with you?"

"You will go to the Forest People, for you will require their help to reach Islith's sanctum. There you will learn your purpose. As for me, I must go on to Gilthaloneth. Though it is a journey that none of my kind have ever made, Bal-Ona will be there before long, and she will need my help."

With this, Bec turned to the left and set off for the canal. They passed quietly through the courtyard, like ghosts. Hannah noticed something puzzling on the pavement just before they struck the road by the water.

"Wait!" she called.

Bec halted and turned to look while Hannah bent to the ground. There at her feet lay another hunk of metal. At first glance it was nothing but rusting scrap, something that had lain there for years. Then she turned it over.

"It's an AR-15," she said, lifting it gingerly in her hands. Then her eyes marked something scratched into a flat surface below the sights. It was a name.

Nuta.

16
ABSCONDED

Why is it no one ever ends up where they're supposed to be?

White wings circled high above the prow of the Royal Mail Steamer *Olympic*. The traveler lay on his back, and with arms folded under his head he watched a flock of gulls drifting idly in a stream of air, turning their dizzy roundabout route overhead and screaming at the wind. Betrayed by trails of steam from four smokestacks, the path of the unseen wind was made visible. Taran considered the clockwise motion of the birds and the racing shreds of smoke. He wondered if there was some other unseen road that might be found, a road in time, a lost road that could bring Val home.

His father and Cedric DePons seemed to think so.

Taran was less optimistic.

From the deck beneath his body, the languid thudding of the engines was muted to a faint tremble. Louder and more arresting was the sound of waves sucking at the hull as the ship clove an eastward expedition of the Atlantic. Though the wind was chill, he had come here often during the past six days. He enjoyed the brisk air, the company of the gulls and of his thoughts, and the sounds of the sea. There was no confinement or clutter here—an arrangement far easier to endure than what waited below-decks, where stuffy aristocrats and their ladies skulked in smoke-filled chambers. DePons had assigned him some sort of minder, a woman who was introduced to him as Hest. He avoided her, and she seemed happy enough to leave him alone.

This was what he wanted.

Mimicking the bubbly ebullience of their chatty genteel counterparts, the seabirds wheeled endlessly and tirelessly over Taran's head. He imagined that he was winging the currents of the wind alongside them, and then laughed at himself. The gulls would appreciate his company no more than he his shipmates'. He couldn't blame them. Birds were truly noble creatures—lords of the sky. The people in the staterooms below were lords of commerce. The difference was, the realm of the birds was still pure, untrafficked by the bustling and bartering of mankind.

But if a man could fly! He remembered how at first the notion baffled him, and then excited him, and how he built gliders, and then a working airplane—the very first machine capable of controlled powered flight. That was the adventure he dreamed of. That was what began all this. The infernal machine! If he hadn't dragged Val into making the Flyer, she wouldn't have been in the barn; and if she wasn't in the barn—

229

If Val hadn't been in the barn the day he took flight, he wouldn't be traveling first-class on a steamer, crossing the Atlantic on an improbable quest to bring her back from wherever she'd got to. He sighed deeply, troubled once again by thoughts of destiny and purpose, thoughts placed in his head by a man he couldn't trust.

Prying his gaze away from the sky, Taran shut his eyes and considered once again the curious events that had brought him here. He wondered what would meet him when he came to Liverpool, and if DePons would finally confide in him the secrets that he and Father were keeping. He replayed his parting conversation with Father in his mind, but it was no use. He couldn't understand why they believed there was some way to find Val, where she'd gone, or what the stone had to do with it all. They told him almost nothing about the stone in particular.

The steamer's course shifted slightly. Taran stretched and rose. He went to the rail and stared at a heavy black line on the horizon. Every minute added a bit more thickness to it, the hopeful end of the vast blue-grey waste of sea. After six days they were finally nearing the end of the ocean passage, where a trip by ferry would bring him to his final destination. He massaged his temples, wearily recounting the ill effects of a plague of dreams—dreams so vivid and weird that their specter haunted him even in the light of day. He had never had such dreams before, but ever since he got on this boat they chased him through the watches of the night. Last night's terrors still gnawed at him, a memory of some other place peopled by creatures of fancy. Between the dreams, the disappearance, his life on the run, and his new mission, it was no wonder he was going mad. He just hoped it wasn't as noticeable to everyone else as it was to himself.

Taran knew he couldn't hide the appearance of his malady any more than a man who has been drinking, and that made him paranoid and reclusive. Every uniformed officer seemed to regard him suspiciously, eyeing him as if they were aware of his most recent profession. He got no better treatment from the steamer's more opulent inhabitants; but they were all useless sycophantic drones. In an uncomfortable way, they reminded him that he himself was a creature manifesting no outward virtues. He fought the idea of making some small business among them during the voyage, but the allure of theft had completely left him.

The allure of hobnobbing with the rich and famous, on the other hand, was something he never fancied at all. A helpless lot of pasty patricians, they were so ignorant of all matters not pertaining to themselves that they would have had little hope of survival were they stripped of their many servants and tenders. Listening to their conversation was like hearing the lowing of cattle; their boasting tongues framed a dialogue fairly supplemented by an array of facts that was plainly and practically useless. Nothing that arrested their attention would have turned even an infant's head. Like gas-filled dirigibles, they were all self-inflated, drifting along on the fringes of the energy created by the miserable laborers and industries that made them rich in the first place—

Taran sighed again, and shook his head to clear these thoughts. He had vowed long ago that he would never be a slave to progressivism or its figureheads. It was of no use, therefore, to indulge in a mental tirade. The voyage would soon be over, and then he would be free to pursue whatever plans had been made for him by his father.

With this thought surfaced still other reservations. He could almost feel the snare closing over his head. He didn't like *not* knowing what was before him, so used was he to his own kind of selfishness.

It was time for the evening meal. Taran braced himself, preparing for a quick foray below. He would try to hide among them as best he could. It was no use, he reminded himself, getting into any debates with the sorry saps that would soon be clamoring to the mess like so many beasts of the pasture. He had learned a sort of quiet manner early on: questions he seldom asked, for questions asked were seldom answered. He dare not speak, lest he betray the fact that his lifestyle didn't match the measure of his new wardrobe. He had been living *under a bridge,* for heaven's sake, like the troll in the story of the three goats. Even one stray glance might land him in a drawn-out conversation about croquet—or worse, the fashions of ladies gloves. The thought made him shiver with dread.

The stacks bellowed three times, signaling a community event. He scented food on the air, blown forward on the wind from aft. Taran made his way quickly to the A-deck open promenade, then rushed down the forward stair to the first class dining saloon, his feet clacking on polished floors. He reminded himself that the definition of extravagance consigned the rich to more than financial gains; equal to possessing money, the rich must also possess the qualities of their wealth: self-interest and self-service. Or, as they would posit it, *venerability and savviness.* The scent of perfume, rich balustrades, and gleaming oak paneling with paintings done in warm oil colors, all fixed in his mind the fact that he had entered an alien world. That being the case, he decided he would have been better off flying among the gulls, or pursued by the horrors of his nightmares.

The stair was wide, fanning out at the landing of each deck until it finally reached D-deck and the level of the dining room. A few other stragglers were making their way down. As he hurried to stake out a quiet corner, he wondered why he had not thought to downgrade his ticket. He ought to have known better than to stick it out with the well-to-do, unless this was also part of Father's plan. A serving man held up a mirror towards him in the landing of the stair's final turn, revealing to Taran's startled gaze a face lost in a rather untidy bundle of dark hair. The mirror had an unsettling effect. His heart leapt suddenly, though he couldn't understand why. It *was* just a mirror—

The feeling that there was something wrong intensified. Smoothing his locks back in a deft motion, he saw—or thought he saw—something else in the reflection: there were men standing just behind him, men dressed strangely in armored battle-gear. When he turned, however, he saw no one.

"Mister Taran Morvran?" a nasal voice dripped in his ear. Taran returned his gaze to the crewman, who had lowered the mirror and now extended his hand. His heart was thumping wildly now—he was certain that he had seen something behind him.

"Are you alright, Sir?"

The crewman had noticed his disorientation. Taran was suddenly impressed with the dread of drawing attention to himself. He shook his head and blinked, combing back his hair once again as he did to mask an abrupt wave of dizziness.

What had come over him?

"Sir?"

"I'm fine," he said.

Taran glanced down at the man's hand. There he saw a card—his own ticket for passage, which had been collected for inspection when he tried to board with the upper-class passengers. Taran took the document with a curt nod. He'd been hoping no one noticed the falsified address, his abandoned university apartment. His reason for travel was simply stated *touring Europe*. Father had taken care of the rest, including a passport.

"We're very sorry to have inconvenienced you in any way," the crewman chirped. "You see, it's so unusual for us to be carrying a one-way passenger *out* of New York. These days everyone wants to get *in* to America. And one-way passengers are usually third class."

"I know."

His head felt like it was floating above his body. He wiped his eyes while the drone continued to offer condolence.

"I think that must be why the officer on the first class gangway insisted, sir, that your ticket be inspected. I assure you, you are a valued guest of this ship and the Line."

"I had my doubts."

"No troubles then, Mr. Morvran?"

"No trouble at all. Good day."

The crewman tipped his hat and disappeared back up the stair, mirror tucked under his arm. Just in time. There was no one else in the stair, so Taran quickly turned his back to the stair-rail, closed his eyes, and held his breath. Behind his closed eyelids the world spun madly. The sensation continued for another few seconds before he was able to regain a sensate condition.

He opened his eyes.

Briefly, for no more than a moment, Taran knew that he was looking into some other place. There was a corridor, long and dim, wherein the walls were composed of dark glistening flesh. Warm pungent steam was drawn into his lungs. He saw a door ahead, a door like the one he imagined seeing the morning he had left his lair under the bridge in New York. He heard a single word, spoken in Val's whispered voice—

Avalon.

And then it was gone.

The air was sweet with the aroma of food, and the walls were richly paneled. He saw no door. There was no rational explanation at all for what he had seen, yet he was firmly convinced that he had not imagined or dreamed it. His nightmares were coming to life before his eyes.

He needed a cup of coffee. There would be no sleep tonight.

The few steps to the landing of D-Deck were a terrible journey, and he almost turned back. Taran was by now looking as much as he was feeling insane. Worse, he entered the reception room to find that the dining saloon—about one hundred feet in length—was nearly full.

Hest, his minder, was nowhere to be seen. A tall narrow brunette would have been easy to pick out in this crowd. Taran felt suddenly a great urgency for her company, and an unaccountable feeling of danger in the wide-open room. He couldn't understand this, since he hadn't spoken more than a few words to the girl their whole voyage, and he had not seen her at all for several days. He made a mental note to go and check on her before he retired, and this seemed to settle him for the moment. He pressed onward, and was led to a seat at a table that was already swelling with self-satisfied customers.

As he was led through graceful double doors to his torture, Taran did not take notice of the beautiful Jacobean alcoves; nor did he relish the comfort of the green-padded chair with arms that enfolded him almost lovingly. He didn't even linger over the items on the menu—the roast duckling, the salmon, or the sirloin. He tried his best to ignore the grunted greetings and less-than-convivial looks from those engaged in private conversation. His mind was full of the strangest thoughts that had ever come to trouble him—thoughts of ships under the ocean, of the name *Avalon,* and of Val being led through the darkness of a womb by men in armor.

He had the presence of mind to point to the smallest, most modest meal on the menu—chicken and a boiled potato with a cup of coffee. While he ate, his thoughts continued to wander. Here he was, on his way to search for Val Anna in another world than that which he had known.

If she was out there, he would find her. He felt certain that this was his purpose.

His thoughts were ever more strongly echoing what DePons had said to him the evening of Val Anna's disappearance, when he sat alone in the barn and searched for her in his soul. DePons had spoken then of purpose, and Taran dismissed it out-of-hand. Now that his nightmares were haunting his waking steps, he realized that he was ready to hear more.

"You look simply awful, child!"

The words broke through his thoughts like a gunshot. Taran was startled, and looked up to see the old woman beside him eyeing him as he shoveled a massive helping of scalding hot potatoes into his mouth. The food burned him, and he swallowed in loud and painful gulps, causing worse discomfort. Somehow he dropped his fork in the process. The dropped fork landed on his knife, which in turn dislodged a sliver of chicken from his plate, and this was launched airborne with more skill than honest intent could have managed. The missile landed in the tomato soup of the lofty drone seated across from him, splashing a small quantity on his lapel.

There was a long pause, during which many pairs of eyes darted to and fro, assessing the improbability of what they had all just witnessed. Taran took the opportunity to gulp a mouthful of coffee, which didn't quite go down. In fact, he ejected most of it across the table towards Chief Justice so-and-so's wife.

The table rumbled with applause.

"It would be better," the offended male drone announced with upturned nose, "if you were more careful with your *things*."

"Sorry," Taran mumbled, wiping his mouth. He nervously pulled at the uncomfortably high collar that poked at the bottom of his chin, and adjusted his cuffs.

There was more laughter. Handkerchiefs came out, and eyes were dabbed. Taran wanted to disappear. Then there was a voice beside him—the old woman who had been watching him from the moment he sat down.

"You look as if you'd been laying in the whole nest of those dreadful birds," she chided. "You're simply *covered* with ghastly flecks!"

"Those aren't droppings, Margery," said the elderly gentleman to her right. "Can't you see? They're flecks of white paint, from leaning up against the rails on the deck. Here, lad, why don't you let me brush you off?"

There were more chuckles coming from farther down the table now, as news of the dinnertime disruption spread. Taran sank lower in his seat as the old man slowly rose and came to stand behind him with a cloth table-napkin.

"My, but I stand corrected," the gentleman said in shocked tones.

Taran swept his shoulder with one hand, and it came away besmirched with gull's-droppings.

And again they laughed. The old man resumed his seat, beaming in pride at his own cleverness. Despite the fact that he was surrounded by people, Taran had never felt more alone in his life.

"Such finery he wears!" Margery stated. "It's hardly designed for the man who likes to lay on his back and watch the gulls, though."

Taran closed his eyes against the peal of laughter that followed. Pushing his chair back from the table, he nodded to those around him, and offered another apology to those across from him, before quitting the wilderness of isolation. He missed being able to blend in with the crowds of the city. He only wanted to get away, to disappear.

The man who had been watching him from the opposite side of the dining-saloon waited a minute before rising to follow him back to his cabin. Before slipping out into the reception room he paused to whisper a few words to the crewman who had met Taran on the stairs.

Taran ducked inside his cabin for a few moments to change his clothes and splash some water on his face. He stood in the doorway as he left to check up on Hest, and looking back inside he noticed that the lamp beside his bed was lit, and his travel documents were out on the nightstand. He had not left them that way.

Had someone been in his room?

He put his passport in the pocket of his pants and locked the door behind him, and then went to the neighboring stateroom. Hest had been holed up in there for days. He was a little hesitant to knock on her door, now that he suspected someone had been in his room. Had she been poking about his things? Taran decided it would be best not to make any accusations, and settled on asking her if she was okay, since she had remained incognito for so long. He knocked on the door.

No one answered.

While he waited, he listened for sounds from within. There were none. A tingling sensation began to trouble his belly, and an alarming sense of danger. He knocked again, and this time he definitely heard a noise. At first this calmed him a bit, but the longer he waited the more convinced he became that there was something wrong. He was considering going to find a crewman who could open the cabin, when suddenly there was a loud thud against the door. He backed up a step and looked around.

"Hest?" he called.

There was no reply.

His hand reached out for the door-latch, but it was locked. He peered once more up and down the corridor, and when he was sure no one else was around he stepped back a couple feet and kicked the left side of the door where the lock bit into the jamb. There was a loud crack, and the wood splintered around the frame. The door was ajar but unbroken—thanks to a trick he'd learned from the Big Man. Taran stepped inside and left the door open behind him because there were no lights within. The electric lights didn't work when he touched the switch, and the light from the corridor illuminated only a mess of sheets and clothing strewn across the floor. There was something else there—a hunched shape near his feet, hidden in shadows.

"Is that you?" he whispered.

His heart was pounding again, this time with fear. He was afraid that she was dead; but then he remembered the noises. It was time to light a match.

With trembling fingers he scraped a match against the striker. It was immediately snuffed out by a sudden rushing form that moved past him. Taran froze. He heard a sound like creaking leather, and heavy footfalls. He turned toward the open door, but at that very moment the door slammed shut.

"Who's there?" he said. Something moved in the shadows, but no one answered.

He looked back into the room, searching blindly. This was one of the staterooms that had access to a deck via a door on the outer hull. Heavy curtains were drawn tight, preventing the light of the setting sun from entering. Taran walked quietly to the other side of the room, hands outstretched, but paused after taking only a few steps. His toes touched something soft, laying on the floor. He decided to try another match.

He struck the match, and was relieved to see that there was only a bag on the floor before him. The whole room was ransacked, as if it had been turned upside down. There was no one there, and no one by the door. Maybe whoever had made the mess had sidestepped him, shutting the door as he made his getaway; but the warning sense of danger that troubled him in the corridor remained. Taran heard a sharp sound of creaking again, but he could see no one—only a shadow that moved swiftly from the corner of his vision.

A cold hand clapped a rag over his mouth. Breathing in sharply, he tasted almonds. The grip on his upper body was enormously strong, and in seconds he was beyond the thought of struggling. Before he succumbed to dizziness, in his last desperate attempt to move, he brought the withered match up towards his own face and saw with startled eyes that the hands that held him were claws.

Then the world faded into a dark blur.

17
THE TENNO OF NARA

The night was black, and gritty sand was everywhere: it sloshed through his sandals, chaffed in his tunic, collected around the openings of his nose and mouth, stung the corners of his eyes, and cemented itself to the sweat-glazed surface of his skin. He ground it like meal between his firmly clenched teeth, and felt it scratching in his parched throat when he swallowed.

Everywhere.

Since his arrival, he had not seen a sliver of the three moons that welcomed him here. Whatever conjunction he'd witnessed had concluded, or else was obscured by the dusty skies. Either way, the moons left him alone feeling no less certain that he had come very far away from his home. The nights were black and empty, and besides the endless grating sough of the sand and the wind there was no other sensation save one, and that one he could have done without. It was a grief like the sand, permeated everything—an enduring grief for Nunna.

The darkness framed a fitting counterpoint for his torment. He felt no relief when the slight amber hue on the eastern horizon before him betrayed the arrival of day. The fifth night of walking was over, and though he was chilled to the bone he knew he would be scorched before long. What a fool he'd been, running off into the desert without preparing himself first. He could have used leaves or grass to craft a simple hat to keep the sun off his bare head. Worse, he'd already lost his shirt when some animal dragged it off into the night. It probably still had the scent of apples on it, he guessed. As for the apples, they didn't last long. There'd been nothing at all to eat for almost two days. Kal-Nergal was counting the hours until he was completely spent. He didn't figure he had much time left.

He remembered when vengeance was a driving force strong enough to carry him through. He wrung his fingers and thought about Shu, and then his thoughts turned to each of those he'd left behind when they split up in CAC. What had become of the girl, Bal-Ona? How helpless she seemed to him at first, before she was immersed in the black water and dazzled everyone with her magical stone. He wondered if she was faring better than he, and if her power was also waning. Even now, the blurred images of words scrolled past his eyes. They were faint, though, and growing fainter. He no longer had the knowledge to read the words, though he wondered if that mattered anymore. The strength he was given had a purpose after all, but what did it mean that his strength was failing?

The miraculous transformation that had made him a fitting receptacle for the Source did not necessarily extend to his morale. He hardly wished to endure another day of torturous heat, sand, and sorrow, even if he was physically capable of doing so. Thus it was that he anticipated the approach of an hour darker than any he had ever faced before, one in which he made the decision to lay down and die.

As the wretched desert slowly became visible around him, he began to realize that his wandering thoughts had come close to betraying Nunna's sacrifice. What would dying accomplish? It wouldn't go far to prove he was the master of his fortunes. This was surely another lie of the Source, which scratched like the sand at the back of his mind, a silent but powerful influence over his thinking and actions. He fought the doubts sowed there with a valiant effort, and with a single thought.

Was this blighted journey not also according to purpose?

A blast of sandy wind clawed at his face, the tread of approaching dawn. The ground near at hand seemed to move, as the lighter dust was whipped along in the warm currents of air. As dangerous as it was to travel by night in this new world, he dreaded the prospects of travel by day, which was far more disorienting than the darkness. Stumbling about in a dehydrated daze in the blinding sunlight was so bad that he decided never to try it again. The only refuge was the stone spires, and he had learned to avoid these both day and night.

He first spotted them on his second day: looming fingers of red sandstone poking up out of the desert floor towards the pink sky. Some of the spires were quite tall. Occurring in patches of several dozen, they looked like a petrified forest, though on closer inspection he discovered they were really hollowed-out vents raised by some disturbance deep beneath the surface. He had explored these once, desiring a haven from the daytime wind and blowing sands; and in so doing, he also found the subterranean forces that raised them.

Fearsome creatures, monsters, crept in the cool shadowy places between the pillars. As far as he knew, they inhabited only the regions where the stone towers stood. He had glimpsed them only briefly, horrible horned serpents with great scaly wings. Their weird cries could be heard at night, sometimes from high above.

He winced at another slap of the wind. This time it was warmer, and the light shone brighter. It was time to stop and regain his bearings. The flying horse told him to head east, following the course of the river. He had not mentioned that the river would disappear completely from time to time, and that for long leagues he would walk with no clear idea of where the water had run off to. Along the way he had almost been lost twice, when dawn found him far off track and the light of day presented him with no landmark; for this abominable desert moved in the light of day, flowing like a reddish-brown sea blown along by the winds.

With a sigh of relief he spied the river, a sparkling line far to his left, dimly visible now as a slash across the blur of sand. He had drifted far in the dark, but not too far. Still, it would take him an hour to cover so much ground and regain the trail, and once he got there he had little to do but dig in and wait out the sun. The river offered no real refreshment, thanks to the endlessly blowing dust.

Nergal could see even from here that there was no green by the water—only bare twisted slabs of grey and brown stone laying in muddy flats, weathered by sand into fanciful shapes like the bones of giants. Hunger was now so powerful a force that he would have gladly eaten grass if there was any. He dared not bathe. The first day he tried it, desiring only to cool himself, but was forced to bury himself in the sand while he was still wet in order to escape the sun and the dust. Myriad fleas and other miniscule predators had found him there, forcing him from his den into the river, where he had burned badly from exposure. That had prompted his ill-fated exploration of the stone spires the next day, which in turn had encouraged a routine of nighttime walks and daytime burrows.

A long drink was all he could look forward to for now; but how far could he go before this would no longer sustain him? When would he simply give up and die?

And where was this city, anyway?

The sun was almost up now, casting everything on the horizon into sharp relief. There was a forest of stone spires just behind him, towards the west. Though he hadn't noticed them at all in the dark, he must have walked among the outer fringes. With the rising of the sun, the stone was almost blood-red in color, spotted here and there with black holes leading to their interior shafts. He shivered with dread, and turning his head a little towards his right, he saw plumes of sand rising high above the rushing ground-level blur with a customary morning gust of wind from the south. He suspected the desert sands gathered deeper there, for never had he spied a single stone spire in that direction.

Nergal turned, and was about to head north to recover his path; but he paused as something to the east caught his attention. What at first had seemed a distant hill now took the form of a regular dome, black against the orange globe of the sun. Something glittered upon its summit. To either side of this peculiar dome he espied leaning mounds and projections that might have been towers, all of them roughly the same height as the dome. Some of these also glinted with reflected light, or he would have thought they were only stony hills. There was a jagged horizon between the towers, lower than the dome, and though it was an irregular feature it did suggest, in places, a horizontal plane.

Like a wall.

His eyes bulged with the effort to make sense of what he could still only half-see in the murky atmosphere; but it was no mirage. There definitely was something like a city away there. It must be a very strange city, for he had never seen buildings of such height or arrangement. Nor could he imagine how people fared in such a wild place. Curiosity spun his mind into a new mode of thinking, one that was more favorable. He would not sleep today; nor would he hide from the sun. Survival now rested on reaching those structures in the distance.

"What if they're an uninhabited ruin?" asked the voice in his mind.

Nergal was shocked. The thought had not originated within himself, and the Source had been silent for so many days that he thought he was finally rid of it.

"I must try to get there, no matter what awaits me," he said aloud.

He began walking resolutely towards the eastern horizon. For a long while he heard nothing but the wind in the sand and the shuffling of his own feet. His mind wandered over his conversation with the winged beast beside the water that flowed out of the forest. When he'd asked about the city, he was told it was a long journey, and that he would reach some other place first.

The horse had said, *"Follow the water to the Periphery Colonies. You may reach them after a journey of three or four days. There you will find a boat to take you the rest of the way. If any of the Galanon comprehend your uncouth Outland Tongue, it will be the priests. Go to them, and when you reach the city ask for Orlim. He will know what to do with you."*

He'd been out in the wastes for five nights already, so this collection of rotting walls and towers must be the so-called periphery colonies. What kind of people would he find here—if anyone at all? How would they welcome him? He only knew that the forest was dangerous to him because of the animosity harbored there for oath-breakers who came against the Ban.

As if to confirm his fears, the Source said, *"You will not be welcome here."*

"Then I will take what's coming to me without surprise, at least," he said.

"You must survive. It would be better to use caution. Stay out of sight until nightfall, and then enter secretly. When you know what manner of folk dwell here you may then make a more rational plan."

His feet found the edge of a path, and farther ahead he saw the unmistakable course of a road paved with crushed stone. There was also a cluster of bright red banners fluttering high on staffs raised in a small thicket only a little distance away. The banners were covered in white slashes—strange characters or designs that spoke no meaning to his mind.

These were things that even the Source had no knowledge of.

"I'm done with making plans," he said, hiking towards the banners and the road. "I think it's time for a little adventure."

The mental voice made no reply.

The pale white walls rose high above the desert floor. No wall of this sort existed in his own world. Coming closer to the imposing fortifications, almost within reach of their shadow, Nergal could see what he knew upon first inspection of their silhouette on the horizon: they were utterly alien. Their construction was like nothing he knew in Canaan. There were almost no straight lines at all here. Sections of wall a mile or more in length acted as enormous insets and offsets, cragged and weathered, covered with incised scrawling designs and script, studded with banners and cranes, and blistered with windows of crystal. Towers appeared to be growing out of the ramparts, leaning this way or that, with outer bastions sloped smoothly and capped in man-high conical pillars. He knew in a glance that these were immeasurably stronger than any towers built by his own people. Whatever the walls were constructed of he couldn't say. It had the appearance of mudbrick and plaster, but nowhere was the material checked or cracked, as was common with mud. It was more like carven stone, but it shone with a smoothness that spoke of burnished ceramic instead.

Who had ever heard of such a thing?

The strangest sight was the gate itself. An arch opened up in the westward-facing wall, high and narrow, and flanked by bastions covered with scrolling embossed figures of entwined dragons, men, and trees. Nergal had seen few examples of true arches before, but the sight of this one would have stopped even one who was more familiar with their kinds. As an entrance to a city, it was admirable for sheer size, but it looked utterly ancient—so ancient that he doubted it would withstand much harassment. It looked, in fact, like it had never been touched in a hundred years; yet the wooden panels of the doors retained still some regal honor of a distant era, being adorned with large swirling vine-shapes and fanciful creatures executed by the hands of master craftsmen. Though they stood shut, there was a small postern hatch of man-height set into the left-hand door, and this hatch stood open. There were no guards visible, neither on the road nor on the walls above.

His eye went up and up. The towers in the wall were overshadowed by larger towers looming in the dusty air behind, and, of course, by the huge dome. Nergal saw houses within the walls that were built right against the fortifications, sporting balconies and small domed doorways that accessed the wall like a public road. Though they were covered with projecting posts and looked at first rather ominous, they were not evil places, and many were decorated with brightly dyed fabrics of many hues, glimmering with silver threads as the rising sun shone through them. But where were the people who made these things? How could there be no one coming or going on a road to such a large settlement? Was it abandoned?

There were no signs of bustle, or of activity of any kind for that matter. Most walled towns were plagued by feral dogs at least, but here he saw nothing stirring. There were no cooking fires, no trash-heaps, and no flocks. It was all so unusual that he almost dashed his hopes of finding anyone alive.

Then there was a noise, a scraping shuffle so close that he nearly jumped with surprise. Up from the ground beside him there rose a monstrous figure. Towering head and shoulders above him, it seemed to be a monster indeed, but Nergal quickly realized it was only a man dressed in a suit made from a patchwork of shell—hard shell, like that of a crustacean, in varying hues of grey, brown, and red, and bundled all about the neck and limbs with strips of fabric. The head was masked and fully covered. Another shape rose to its feet across the path, to his left, and another in the middle of the road just a stone's-throw away. Nergal hadn't seen them at all, camouflaged as they were in the colors and textures of the blowing sand and dust.

He should have been glad to see people, yet these tall strangers were a sorry sight. Though he felt no danger, he stood his ground with a frown on his face, clenching his fists in alarm at their sudden appearance and strange garb. Their masks were made from close-fitting strips of carapace, studded with a pair of shaded crystals over the eyes, and were fitted with projecting filters—a device that found familiarity with information the Source had stowed in his mind. He realized these people had learned to live with the dust and the desert by donning survival suits, a luxury he had survived without. This made him feel a little exuberant; but one thing still worried him.

They weren't *human.*

"Better wait until they speak before betraying your tongue," the Source warned.

The figure on his right raised one hand, thumb extended across the center of his open palm. Nergal raised his own hand in reply, but lowered it again quickly.

"Peace between Wood and Waste, stranger!" said a man's heavily muffled voice.

Nergal understood this language. Perhaps the Source was translating for him? He stared at the leader of the three, wondering how to make a reply.

"Why have you come to our gates?" the leader asked. "Are you a sorcerer?"

"They see your eyes," the Source said. *"You are different."*

"No," Nergal said.

"Have you come for trade and refreshment, then, or are you on *Gilat* business?"

Nergal looked him up and down, puzzled. "Are you of the *Galanon?*" he asked.

The man glanced briefly towards his two companions. Nergal could see that they now regarded him with suspicion. Were his words not understood?

This wasn't going well.

"You have come to the Tenno People of Nara, which is the principal colony on this side of the River Karn. I take it you are an unhappy stranger to the Wastes, dark-eyed one, for you carry neither gear nor suitable clothes, and your voice is as dry as a Musab widow's well."

"Do you come from the Forest?" asked the figure standing to the left of the path, opposite the leader. "What do you mean, asking if we are of House Galanon?"

So they could understand him, after all. Nergal was suddenly regretting his impulsiveness. He hated to admit it, but he should have listened to the Source.

"Are you a spy from the Southern Forest?" the man demanded.

The leader held out a hand, prompting the end of this line of conversation, and the two glanced towards the third figure standing farther behind them. Nergal's mind was racing. Unfortunately, he had made no forethought as to what he would actually say when he reached his destination. So, he told the truth.

"I am not from any place in this world," he said.

All three stood silently, watching him. He could not see their faces to know how they were taking the news. A wind blew hot sand like needles against his skin.

"I have come against the Ban from the world you call *Ertsetum*," Nergal continued. "I have been in the Wastes five nights, traveling away from a forest to the west, for I was not welcome there. I am starving. I seek only food and shelter, and safe passage to the city. I am looking for a man there—his name is *Orlim*."

"Orlim?" the leader asked.

"He of whom you speak is no mere man," said the other guard. "And you, you are either a sorcerer or a liar, and possibly both."

Nergal sighed heavily. This was going nowhere; but then he remembered something else that the winged horse said at the riverbank.

"May I speak to your priests?" he asked. "I wish to speak my case, and then proceed to the city."

"You need not journey to the city if it is Orlim you seek," said the leader. "He is here today, reviewing the town and joining us for *Gilat*. I doubt, however, that he will make time for the likes of you."

"The priests, then?"

The three conferred with only a mute glance.

The leader replied, "If you will come with me, I will bring you to our tribe's priest. If he finds you worthy, the priest may lead you before Orlim."

The guard to his left raised a hand in warning. "Don't be overconfident, stranger," he said. "We of Nara may be a peaceful tribe, but we are ever wary of spies from the south that wander the periphery—and of sorcerers. We met you in the open with no weapons, for you bear none yourself; but know that we are accustomed to the wiles of mages and their kinds. Any sign of devilry, and we will signal our hidden guards to kill you where you stand with magic of our own kind, with a fire that kills from a great distance. Do you understand?"

"I do."

"They have marksmen with guns," the Source said.

Nergal nodded. He figured that as long as he appeared subservient he would be allowed some limited freedom. His heart warned him, though, that he was about to get himself into trouble.

"Come along, then," the leader said. "Let's get out of the sand. If indeed you are a threat to our peace, as my friend seems to think, then you will have it out within our walls."

He turned, and Nergal followed him towards the small open door in the gate. He noticed that the other two guards took position on either side of him. If they bore weapons, these remained concealed. However, Nergal suspected these were warriors of a different sort, who did not require a blade to kill.

"I must warn you that our priest is not currently in the favor of Orlim," the leader said as they walked. "He will not risk his neck for reckless wanderers bearing fanciful stories of the Western Wood, least of all those who speak of the forbidden and fabled land of *Ertsetum*. You will want to think up better lies than these before you reach the priest's quarters. It is not even certain that you will be granted an audience, unless it is that so strange a tale on your tongue may be fit to entertain his Eminence."

"It is forbidden to even speak of Ertsetum?" Nergal asked.

"What do you think, that the Colonies are full of Zealots?" asked one of the guards behind him. "A sorcerer or spy from the Southern Forest would know that the priests have forbidden the teaching of the Old Tales upon pain of death. There will be no talk of prophesies, either."

Nergal's eyes widened. Priests who forbade the teaching of faith and prophecy? He had heard of nothing like it.

What was happening in the World of Origins?

His eyes could mark none of the *hidden guards* until they passed within the gate, entering a square stone chamber in the wall where about one hundred men were gathered. Other than their exceptionally massive build and fine features, these appeared no different than the kinds of people he'd always known. He puzzled over this awhile, watching them stand or sit around cooking-fires. The fires gave off no smoke at all, and burned from metal objects like large spiders. He guessed it was some kind of oil, but then the Source spoke into his mind.

"Their stoves use compressed gas. Can you smell it?"

He could. It smelled like eggs, like the Salt Sea of Canaan. There were ceramic pots on the little stoves, and in these there bubbled and frothed a dark liquid. It had a pungent spicy smell that made his parched mouth water.

"Coffee, stranger?" asked a man who approached his wardens. He stopped cold the moment he saw Nergal's eyes, and lowered the proffered cup of greeting.

"This one's going straight to the priest," the leader of the guard said stiffly.

"Yes, sir," the warrior replied, staring. There was a hush all around.

"I have the roster," the man continued, his eyes still glued to Nergal's own.

"Order your patrols, then," the captain said.

When it appeared that the warrior wouldn't immediately comply, the captain gave the man's foot a solid kick. Scalding hot coffee sloshed over the brim of his cup and onto his hand, and he lurched away with an oath and a few backwards glances. Nergal watched him go, and then the captain spoke quietly into his ear, saying, "Stand here a moment. I have to make sure someone takes my place on the watch. Don't speak to anyone."

When he was left alone, Nergal glanced around the chamber, studying the unfamiliar fashions and manners of the men of the guard. Loose leggings of varied colors they wore, and these were cinched tight where they met knee-length leather boots. Long shirts of heavier material, richly embroidered, hung below the waist; yet upon their shoulders, and over the top of the breast and back, they wore a thick thing like an abbreviated mantle, decorated with distinctive glittering baubles or spoil. A few also bore skull-caps and cloaks with gems and other signs of rank or nobility, and others wore a cuirass made from huge plates of shell, studded with spines natural to whatever monster had grown it.

Their weapons were long light rifles, stacked along the walls. He stared in wonder at this arsenal until his guide returned.

"You have *guns*?" he asked.

"You know of these weapons?"

"Of course."

"Then keep it a secret between you and me, and avert your gaze, quickly!"

Nergal's curiosity grew every second. His quick survey of the chamber also noted the presence of melee weapons, including swords made from the same stuff as the armor, and very long bows. The limbs of the warriors were clean and smooth, knotted with muscle. There was no sign of disease here. He also found it difficult to tell how old any of the men were, for their appearance carried both the character of age and the fairness of youth.

"Will you be sending him directly, Lothar?" asked one of the warriors.

"Use not my name before a stranger," the leader replied, removing his mask and cap. Nergal was surprised by the blond color of his short-cropped hair—a rarity among the people of his homelands. The mask removed, his head looked strangely small. It was a comical effect lent by the survival suit, huge and baggy.

"He may be a sorcerer," Lothar said, "and I am the only one here trained to deal with them. I will not be sending him with anyone else."

"The priest is in his quarters," said another. "Sure you don't want to bring him before *Amed* instead?"

"The Lord of the Tenno shall not be disturbed during Gilat," Lothar replied. "Unless, of course, the priest sends for him."

After his two companions had returned to their stations on the road, Lothar removed his survival suit. Beneath the bundled shell and fabric he wore a similar tunic and armor donned by his companions, though of far richer quality and colors. An attending officer among the guards took his suit, and then brought him a massive cuirass that covered him from waist to neck, tucking up right beneath his chin. The tones of the fabric, leather, and armor were all of blue, white, and gold, and the gleaming armor was etched in fanciful designs. Such regal bearing Nergal had never seen in the garment of a king, much less a warrior, and the sheer size of the man easily made him a rival of one like his old master. The weight of his armor alone must have been a hundred pounds. Dizzy with admiration, Nergal was startled by a firm hand on his shoulder. The attending officer was holding out a folded garment to him.

"Here," he said gruffly. "Put this on. You'll attract a little less attention."

Lothar nodded approval as Nergal held out a plain vest in dusty colors. It was a little loose and much lived-in, but he shrugged it on gratefully. When he was finished, Lothar rose and led him out of the gate into the streets, where his startled eyes encountered ever greater wonders.

They toured a narrow cobbled street that ran straight from the wall. The first thing Nergal noticed was that there was no dust. The bite of stinging sands and the burning sun were gone, as were the sounds of the wind. Now there was a noise of crowds, a market unlike any he'd ever seen, bustling with early traffic. He saw here mostly textiles—bright fabrics and pillows—though there were also shops selling strange mechanical equipment. The shop stalls occupied the bottom floors of massive buildings to either hand.

"Your dark eyes betray something," Lothar said while they walked. "You are surprised by us, and by the simple bustle of our markets."

"I saw no traffic on the road, and no one but soldiers in the gates," Nergal said.

"Traffic comes by boat to Nara. None come by the West Gate but foes and sorcerers from the Wastes, or so our ancient legends say."

"Legends?"

"In the course of the past three hundred years only a few have come from the west through the Wastes, and these were all spies."

They reached the end of the market street and came to an intersection of ways. Lothar waved him on to follow as he turned left; but Nergal was frozen in his tracks, staring across the intersection. He took two steps closer to the middle of the road, and halted, trying to make sense of what he was seeing.

What gave him pause was a strange and terrifying beast, a ten-foot tall creature like a bird with a curiously elongated neck. Its sides were covered in reddish-brown scales, and its body ended in a short leathery tail. Though it had wings, these appeared to be flightless, and were clad in feathers of golden brown hues, matching a scarce few that grew from a cap atop its head and down its back. The blue beak was that of a fruit or nut-eating bird, though magnified to enormous size. Its eyes looked back at him intelligently, and the head cocked to regard the warrior mounted on its back.

Lothar grabbed his arm, and tugged him urgently towards the left side of the intersection. Nergal glanced over his shoulder at the terror-bird, his heart quivering with excitement as he was led away with a firm grip.

"What was that thing?" he asked, trying to cover the wonder in his voice.

"What thing?" Lothar asked, turning aside briefly.

"That beast. What was it?"

His warden regarded him strangely. "You mean the *Rook*?"

"The Rook?"

"It is of a breed of *Guildcrest* Talons, which are sired in Gilthaloneth," he replied, steering Nergal away. "The Guildcrest are the best, almost good enough to stand claw-to-claw against a full-grown *Dwimmer Drake*, or so say our foemen in the Southern Forest. That is why they send spies to steal eggs and kill our breeders. You have an eye for Rooks, have you?"

Nergal heard the note of suspicion in his voice, and felt it in the cold grip of the hand on his shoulder. He felt ashamed, but not because of any ill-treatment. He was ashamed because he felt he deserved no better. After all, he was here because he had killed someone. What was there about him that was *not* suspicious?

"I don't know who you are, stranger, but you'd better not act so foolishly in the presence of the priest. As I said to you at the gate, we are a kindly people. I don't want to be ordered to kill you."

There were many people walking the streets by now, wonderfully beautiful people, and they all treated the warrior Lothar as if he was someone of importance, bowing their heads and stepping aside as the two of them passed. Everyone was dressed in similar fashion, which surprised Nergal mightily. What he had taken to be the garb of warriors was the fashion of choice, and there were few distinctions other than the decoration of skull-cap or mantle. Some of the women wore a frock, which was the most varied garment he saw. Nergal knew that *he* was the oddity here, and he was aware of more than one curious glance at his travel-stained tunic, ragged sandals, and at his wide black eyes.

More of the town was revealed as they walked farther in. There were more Rooks, and other creatures as well—mostly strangely distorted beasts of his own country, variously combining features of cattle and dogs and deer. Nothing else was even vaguely familiar. The street they were on was lined with tall structures of many stories, and those on the right-hand were definitely residences, having windows and doors on the lower floors. All the buildings were constructed of the same whitish material. The mudbrick walls he knew so well would not have stood up to the punishment that these withstood, framed as they were with windows and heavy door-jambs, and supporting tiered palaces and bridges to heights that he could only guess.

It all spoke of an occupation that lasted millennia, unchanged; and yet it was not a terribly grim and stuffy place. There were open spaces here and there between the buildings, where gardens sprouted and vines hung. Trees of many kinds he saw, and some along the road itself, casting cooling shadows over passers-by. Fountains rejoiced, and hoses brought water from hidden springs to green the grass where children played. Flowers scented the air delicately—flowers, and the fragrant spice he'd detected outside the walls. There were also many pleasant food-odors, all very fresh and invigorating.

His guide turned suddenly towards a door on the left side of the street. He paused at the entrance, which was guarded by nothing more than a veil of bright red fabric adorned with stylized figures of men and beasts. Nergal watched as the man drew aside this curtain and rang a small bell attached to a string just inside the threshold. They waited a few tense seconds, and then a voice called indistinctly from somewhere within.

"Warden of the Western Gate!" the guide shouted through the curtained door. "Dropping off a guest for you!"

With no warning, Lothar planted a hand firmly in the center of his back and shoved him through the door. Nergal tripped on the threshold, stumbling face-first into a chamber lit by a single flame.

18

DARK TERMINAL

A flame white and hot, towering like a boundless wall, slammed against her with the force of a hurricane. Shaken by its thrilling energy, Val was suddenly face-to-face with an unfolding frame of reference that exceeded mortal perception, an expansive universe that embraced her in a maelstrom of violent powers that shaped and sang and bent light itself into the forms of worlds and men.

However brief, this glimpse into the heart of the stones revealed to her their connection to the Dark Worlds. Gazing back at her was the destiny the dominion the stones would build;

and like the cord of a monstrous song, one desire thundered out across the void. That desire struck her like a blacksmith's hammer. She knew that it was not the desire of her friends, nor of herself, but of the stone; for she and the two stones she possessed had merged.

Yet her friends were gone. She was alone with something that contained all matter and energy within itself, and it was inside her while she was simultaneously inside of it.

The light and flame vanished swiftly to a cold darkness, leaving Val suddenly aware of herself, of her body straining against a crushing force. Her mouth opened, but no breath came—only a screaming pain in her chest. She felt the chair squeezing her, and realized that she was still suspended upside-down in the Viaduct Chamber. The sensations of cold and pressure intensified until she imagined she was lost in the depths of the sea. Then, with a great gasp, air finally entered her aching lungs, and with that breath her voice shouted the name of the Great City, the Last City.

"Gilthaloneth!"

There was a rushing noise, a crescendo of hollow thunder like a cresting wave, accompanied by a shaking that could not have been worse than the transition from life to death; and thereafter she perceived only deep silence. Her aching body lay upon a hard surface. Val's eyes flew open. What she saw then was a great disappointment.

Everything was black. She lay on her face, as if fallen from the navigational chair; but she knew she was no longer in Avalon. Pushing herself up to her knees, she wrapped her arms tightly around herself for warmth while peering into miserable darkness. She was someplace underground. The air was freezing, but her armored gear was well insulated, and in a short while the cold dissipated to a pleasant coolness. Though her courage was crumbling her breathing had calmed, and she was able to think clearly again.

What a wretched development! But for a faint blush of light on the stone floor, all was dark and bare and desolate. The light bloomed gradually more and more, dispelling the darkness; yet it gave her little cheer. Val noticed that the light moved when she did, and realized that it was coming from a device in the chest-plate of her outfit—from a small glowing lamp near her right shoulder. She looked down and saw its illumination shining out from her, activated by a micro-switch on the armor. Pressing the switch turned the light off, and she was immersed in darkness. Val pressed it again. The light wasn't very bright, having a reach of only twenty feet or so, but it was better than nothing.

At first, she had actually thought that the glow was emanating from the stone. Val remembered how it burned so brightly before disappearing into her hand. The stone was still inside her. Or was she inside of it? The understanding that seemed so clearly impressed into her mind just moments ago was gone, vanished. She only knew that she was in danger, and that the stones must be brought safely to their destination. The stone, for its part, responded to her anxious desire with a little more warmth. Was it alive? She could sense its presence, which was very unlike the presence of a person. It was more like a cat, sitting and watching, *waiting for something to happen.*

A sliding noise in the dark announced some movement above. A rain of pebbles fell from a great gaping hole in the ceiling, where twisted and rusting rods of iron protruded from a crumbling concrete slab.

"Hello?" she called upwards.

There was no reply. She had come here alone, and it was a frightening place to be alone. The break above looked like her point of entry, but she would have been mangled had she passed through those bars.

So, where was she?

She supposed she wasn't in Gilthaloneth. At least, she hoped not.

From where she knelt she surveyed her surroundings—a square room about twenty feet on a side, with a shattered doorway that was blackened by fire. Val relaxed a little, as danger seemed far away. Sadness rushed in to take its place. A strong sentiment of abandonment inundated her then, an oppressive loneliness borne to her grieving heart via the darkness, the heaviness of the air, and the smell. It didn't smell like Avalon, and for that she was actually a little grateful. Instead, it was a smell of desertion, like an old barn, and that was what brought her to focus so sharply on the horrible solitude of the place. A brief gust of air touched her face through the hole above, stirring the dust around her and bringing with it the bitter tang of wet concrete. Val rose to her feet, but too swiftly, and the fast motion made her head dizzy. It was then that she remembered something Shu said about the transitions.

"You might experience auditory and visual hallucinations. It's called Displacement Syndrome...the effects wear off with time."

The last trip through a Mirror left her incapacitated for a full week, and she had passed out within a day of her arrival. That meant the disorientation would grow stronger and stronger, and then—

She had better find a safe place, soon.

With no other idea of where she was going, she left the room through the broken doorway and passed into a dark subterranean hall. There were no other lights of any kind than the one she bore.

"How convenient," she thought aloud. "I'm a walking advertisement for anything dangerous."

She felt so very conspicuous, like she was being stalked.

Val shrugged off her mounting fears and continued until she saw a wall in the near distance. Getting to it involved crossing an area littered with broken wooden benches and metal cabinets. There were consoles and screens everywhere, and steel lockers with rusted combination locks imbedded in the doors. She also noted large ceramic planters with small trees and shrubs in them, mostly tumbled on their sides. Though they looked very real, the plants turned out to be artificial, like the silk flowers on Mother's hat. Some were partially melted, as if they had been briefly exposed to intense heat or flames.

Picking her way through this mess, she saw no sign of recent human passage; yet there was more than randomness in the configuration of fallen and jumbled debris. Slowly it became obvious that all this was dragged or pushed across the blasted concrete floor and assembled into a kind of barricade nearer the far wall. It was a fort built hastily from bits and pieces of junk. Whom had it defended? Against what foe was it raised? There wasn't so much as a ghost left to tell the story. Viewing all this in the somber glow cast from her slender figure, a small woman in the midst of all that ruin, she was beset once again by feelings of loneliness, and of intense sadness. Something dreadful had happened here.

Had the Gremn finally claimed their revenge?

Just short of the barricade, she came to a place where the concrete floor was sparsely tiled. A child's ragdoll lay before her feet, and bending down to take a closer look she saw that the tiles were stained black with what appeared to be dried blood. She stretched out her fingers to touch the doll, when suddenly she heard glass crunching underfoot.

Val straightened and turned. A few upended benches cast crazy shadows all around, but she saw no one. Was it possible she made the noise herself? Just to be sure, she hunted for the microswitch on top of her lamp. Her fingers fumbled for a moment, and finding the tiny raised blister she squeezed it. The wide chamber was cast suddenly into darkness. That was when she noticed the *other* light, emanating from somewhere beyond the heaps.

Passing as quietly as possible along the front of the barricade, she found a breach and passed through. To the left she found a kind of path between the heap and the wall, and this led towards the faint light she saw. Walking towards the light, Val's ears were alert for sounds of stray footsteps, but she heard only her own.

She continued along the path, passing many doors and fences bolted tight with padlocks, until at last the dim glow ahead became a light, and then the barricade ended where it joined a real wall opposite the one she'd followed. She stood at the bottom of a grand flight of marble steps. Gazing up from the bottom, she surveyed a world in grey twilight. It was like the light of a rainy day in winter. She shook off her melancholy and proceeded up the steps.

Halfway up she noticed that the illumination fell straight down from above, for the staircase was merely a shaft in the floor of the upper hall, surrounded by a low steel rail. This new upper room was greater than the one below—far greater, in fact, than any indoor space she had ever seen or imagined. Val paused when her head was a little higher than the level of the top step, and though she was apprehensive her eyes were glowing with astonishment. Where the steps ended, the marble continued, glittering green now in the bolder light. The space the light filled was simply magnificent. The nearest walls were hundreds of feet away. Directly overhead, an enormous clock was suspended from the ceiling. Its face was fading to black, and its hands were gone.

As she took in the wonders of the hall, she slowly recognized among several mixed periods of construction a few elements that were strangely familiar. The long arched vault of the ceiling, shaped like a great barrel lain on its side, was encased in an intricate webwork of steel. The vault itself, through which the cheerless light entered, had once been paneled with clear glass. Now the glass was accumulating into drifts and heaps upon the floor, revealing the dull grey sky above through a rusting grid of iron.

It looked like a train station.

Contrasting the abundance of metal and glass, a colonnade of huge stone columns—all cut in pink marble—ran down the sides of the hall from a high gate on one end to a low wider entry opposite. The effect of all the combined elements was a little disconcerting. The place was a Roman Cathedral that wanted to be a railroad bridge. It was a waiting room big enough for an emperor's palace.

And it was completely empty.

Everywhere there were signs of fire or outright battle. The pillars were blackened, and pocked with shallow depressions that must have been caused by rifle fire. There were more potted trees lining the central colonnade, but these were real, for they were all dead and leafless. The air was rank with a smell of mildew, and rainwater dripped from the broken ends of cables that dangled like the roots of trees from the steel webwork above. Loose yellowed pages of newspapers lined the walls, but they were all blank, their letters too faded to read. There were no rats or birds, nor any signs of life—only endless banks of machines of various sorts that lay tumbled here and there beneath the columns, and broken glass scattered like sand. Mist climbed in through the far door, making it impossible to see anything beyond.

Val cautiously ascended a few more steps, stopping again when she noticed the figure of a man. He stood very still a little way to the right of the stair, just beyond the surrounding handrail, and his back was towards her. She made her way to the very top step and saw to her relief that he was only a statue, almost like the one that stood in the main street of her hometown—the statue she saw the day the comet appeared.

The moment seemed to freeze, isolated from the rest of time, and she felt a strong urgency to go and look upon the statue. She also felt a hidden danger. Her eyes darted to and fro, searching among the many shadowy nooks beyond the columns; and so her gaze rested at last upon something that was truly worth seeing. Behind her was a sign, posted over the head of the stair. Downward arrows on either side of the inscription indicated the direction of the lower hall she had just exited. It read:

LONG ISLAND TRAMS

Looking up from this sign she saw a billboard raised above the level of the handrail:

DOWNSTAIRS FOR REGULUS TRANSIT
GATEWAYS

She suspected the word *tram* had something to do with trains, but *Regulus Transit Gateways* sounded downright suspicious. Regulus was the name of a stone Kabta mentioned.

Regulus was a stone that was lost in another world.

Val trembled to think of the implications. She forced herself to turn away from the signs, and rounding the handrail she made her way towards the statue. It was covered with so much verdigris that she was unsure if it was made of stone or some kind of metal. The mortal depicted was wearing a kind of business suit. He didn't wear a happy look; it seemed he was aware of his surroundings. An inscription on the pedestal announced his name and title.

ALEXANDER JOHNSTON CASSATT
PRESIDENT, PENNSYLVANIA RAILROAD COMPANY
1899–1906
*Whose foresight, courage, and ability achieved
the extension of the Pennsylvania Railroad
into New York City*

Below this text was another, longer, but in smaller letters.

IN MEMORIUM
*Presented to the Pennsylvania Gravrail Group,
Inauguration of the New Pennsylvania Station,
September 11, 2101,
By the generous gifts of Dr. Cedric DePons,
Regulus Transit Systems, FTI.*

Dr. DePons? How'd he end up memorialized on a statue dedicated a hundred years in the future of her future?

"I hope that wasn't my fault," she said to herself. "Maybe Shu was right, and we were all displaced."

At least she knew now where she was. In her own time, the Pennsylvania Railroad Company had been angling for a station in New York, but they ran into too many problems. Passengers making the trip to Manhattan had to catch a ferry from Exchange Place in Jersey City—she had made the trip with Taran and Dr. Morvran a few times. Whatever obstacles had prevented the construction of a direct line to the city had obviously been overcome.

She walked around the statue once, searching for another inscription, but there was none. Then she wondered, looking up at the statue's face, if the dereliction manifested in the station was localized here, or if the entire city was abandoned. The stern face looking back at her was pitted by corrosion, and this was answer enough for her heart. She was certain she had come here to witness the end of something.

There were no noises from outside, and only a lingering terror within. The sadness of the moment compelled her to reach out and touch the cold pedestal with her hand. There was no quickening vision, as she had almost hoped. There was, however, a bit of dark paper pasted to the top of the pedestal near the figure's left foot, camouflaged from sight until her hand brushed it in passing.

It wasn't much, being a palm-sized remnant from the bottom right-hand corner of a larger poster; yet this chance fragment she touched gingerly, for she saw small letters upon it. Gently she tugged it free of the statue and held it in her hands. She was initially disappointed, though, for there wasn't much to see—just a single line of text. It bore a date: 2/14/2109. *Valentine's Day, 2109.*

The rest of the line read, *"Printed by the HSA,"* whatever that was.

Then, sensing that she was meant to find it, and that it was the final key that would unlock the mystery of what happened here, she read the scrap again. The riddle of the disaster began to unravel.

She had displaced all those who depended on her for safe transit from Avalon.

Gaining force as a new understanding unfolded in her mind, Val's emotions almost brought her to her knees.

She was not only displaced, but displaced in another world, a reflection of her own.

The decay around her was filled with a ghostly presence; the specter of all the missing people of New York seemed suddenly to fill the shadowy margins of the hall—a jury keenly focused on the cause of their calamity.

The people of that world were gone.

Val felt the weight of their accusation like the weight of Nunna's dagger, still clamped cold against her right hip.

Something had gone terribly wrong.

She had trusted the Fomorian, who had praised her for being someone she was not. The Lady in White had told her to travel through the stone. Though she complied to the best of her abilities, it was obvious that she was unable to control the stone's power. Some further fracturing of time and space had occurred, and now she was farther away from her goal than ever before.

It was her fault.

She had failed everyone's trust only to land here.

Here, in a ruin, where Regulus slept.

What else could it mean, but that her attempts to lift the Ban had led to the disaster evidenced all around her? Now that she was here, she had become the inescapable cause of her own destruction! A sigh escaped her lips as she absently dropped the paper from her trembling fingers.

Her misery was interrupted by a wild, bestial scream.

Whatever had made the awful noise, it was nothing good. The scream repeated; a shriek that rose and fell, followed by a series of low roars that sounded a little like the cries of an elephant—a rather enormous and demented elephant. Feeling suddenly exposed, Val crouched and stared into the far end of the hall. There, among foggy mounds of accumulated ruin, something was moving. She saw first a shadow, long and black, that moved like a snake, and then a looping tendril that crept swiftly along the farthest expanse of floor.

Another scream broke the sad silence of the place. This time it lasted a shorter duration, and was ended with several more at a higher pitch. Val clapped her hands over her ears, terrified. A noise of tumbling metal and stone crashed from some other part of the building, and this time there were answering cries, several roaring and shrieking voices raised in dreadful chorus. Her mind raced in circles, so her feet made the first move.

She turned from the statue and ran, low to the ground, rounding the handrail and stairs and keeping a straight line to the left side of the hall. There, beyond the columns in rows, a dark inner sanctuary of the terminal lay in relative quiet. Meanwhile, more distant crashes and cries trumpeted through the far end of the vast room, masking the noises her boots made—a clattering and cracking over broken tiles and bits of glass. Her heart and gasping breath were louder in her ears.

She passed beneath the supporting columns and raced ahead into the dark hall beyond. Danger was closing in fast, and though her eyes could not see it coming she could feel the blind fear of approaching evil. That was when she first noticed a glimmer of blue out of the corner of her eye—just ahead, a darting figure ran. Val didn't slow her pace, but now her attention was turned towards a wall looming out of the darkness before her, and to an opening in the wall where the blue glimmer disappeared.

There was a teller's-window, and an open door.

The ceiling high above began raining hail-sized bits of stone, and a foul gusting wind had overtaken her. The air was heavy with the noisome stench of death. Tremors jolted through her legs. Val didn't pause to look, but focused on the doorway of a teller's booth. It was still a dozen yards away. She sprinted, and made the door just as something brushed her shoulder.

She was inside.

Darkness swallowed her, but she hadn't gone two more strides before her cumbersome boots caught the edge of a broken rim of interior drywall, sending her sprawling headlong. She hit the ground hard, sliding with a loud scraping sound and spinning sideways on the greasy concrete. A jolt went through her legs, and a table collapsed across her back. She was pinned to the ground.

The crash of her tumble echoed loudly around her ears, and in the moments that followed she lay very still, shivering with fear. For a little while there was no other sound but that of her own breathing; but she knew that the beasts were just outside, waiting for her to stir.

Val waited, calming herself, closing her eyes to shut out the deeper dark that pressed in on her terror-stricken mind. Unreasoning fears of monsters clamored up out of a childhood spent in the grip of waking dreams. Here was a real monster to hunt her—several of them. Whatever they were, they were not Gremn.

And they stank.

There was a slithering, cold, rasping noise in the direction of the door, just ten feet away. Val saw only smooth undulating shadows, but the scraping and crunching tread she perceived clearly enough. A snort of indrawn breath followed, and then silence. She waited a moment more, but the noises subsided. Her fear did not. Crushed and hopeless, and certain now that she had somehow brought destruction on Mankind for using the stones in Avalon's Viaduct Chamber, Val felt a tear slide down her cheek. The stone, still keenly alert, still waiting, chose that moment to speak hope into her despair, saying, *"All things happen according to purpose. There is only one outcome to all events. Even this is no coincidence."*

Strangely, she discovered that she was speaking these words aloud to herself, though it seemed they came to her from some other place. There was no answering sound from her pursuers. The quiet held her in fear of them for a little longer, and then she exhaled a long breath. She was calmed enough to take stock of her situation.

Val wriggled beneath the heavy steel table until she could get her arms beneath her body. Then, thanking the maker of the armored suit, she flexed her fingers and pushed upwards from the floor just a little bit. The table bumped something else nearby, and a heavy piece of equipment clattered loudly to the floor. Val paused, balancing the weight on her back. The doorway across the room stared at her ominously, but nothing was moving.

Giving it one more try, and with a greater sense of urgency this time, she raised the table and drew back her head and shoulders until she was free. Then, lowering its weight gently to the floor, she scooted backwards until she was pressed against a wall. There was nothing between her and the open door. To her left was a large metal cabinet, but it offered no protection.

Thus Val found herself crawling to her right along the wall. Blindly forwards she went, feeling with her hands. There was nothing she could see except a grey twilight coming through the door, away to her left. When her hand found a corner ahead, she raised herself to a crouching position, and there she paused, wondering what else she could do. It wasn't safe to leave yet; but she was afraid of waiting, for a sense of impending disaster haunted her, daring her to make a dash for it. A giddy feeling came over her, and she realized she was once again in the grip of Displacement Syndrome.

In that anxious moment, a hand clamped tightly over her mouth.

Something else was here!

Val turned like lightning and grasped with both hands. She didn't think about what she should do, for she couldn't see anything, and she was dizzy and sick; but then she heard a grunt, and felt hair and flesh in her fingers. There was a sound like a whimper, and then a choking voice.

"Please stop!"

She relaxed her grip, her heart tearing a pace in her chest like a racing rabbit. The figure pushed her away, and Val released her fingers from around a slender throat. More rustling noises came from beyond the door, and someone huddled against her side.

"Don't move!" the voice whispered. Val guessed it was a woman, by her gentle voice.

"It won't leave. It knows we're here. We'll have to use the elevator."

She felt the girl move away from her, towards their right, and heard a muffled creak. In another moment, a hand tapped her foot. She crawled forwards, reaching out with her hands, but the girl had disappeared. Val felt along the baseboard of the wall, exploring for the door she had heard, but there was nothing. Then a hand touched the top of her head, and grasping it tightly she felt her arm being pulled upwards through a hole in the wall. Its edges were smooth and regular, forming a rectangular space about three feet wide and two feet tall. It was a dumbwaiter. The opening was at waist-height. Val doubted she could fit inside, even if the other person wasn't crammed in there with her. She let go of the hand and stuck her face into the opening.

"I can't fit in here!" she said.

"It's deep," the whispering voice replied. "You can fit!"

"You go first, and send it back."

"No!" the girl replied. "If nothing turns up soon, they'll send in fire to flush you out. We have to escape together, or else we'll be tracked. Just let me turn around, and then get inside."

Val waited a moment while the girl resettled herself, and then she gripped the edges of the frame and thrust herself in hands-first. Her shoulders barely fit, and it was impossible to do more than wriggle. With her rear still outside, she bent and pushed with her boots, which scraped loudly on the floor and on the sill. There was a loud crash from the teller's-booth, and a sound of snuffling.

They both paused for a long minute, listening. Val, who was in quite an uncomfortable situation, bent in the middle with her legs dangling out of their compartment, tried to squirm a little farther in. A hand shoved against her side, and a warning finger tapped her forehead. She paused.

"I can't fit in here!" she whispered.

"Hush!" came the reply. "They'll hear you!"

"I don't care if they hear me," Val said, pushing her feet against the sill. Her outstretched hands found the far end of the box, which was open, exposed to a chain that clanked heavily in the girl's hands. After a little more shifting and settling they rested against one another and lay down. Val felt the box ascending as the girl worked the chain.

"We're going up?" she asked.

"We must. All below is dead."

"Who are you?"

"What do you mean, Val Anna?" the girl asked. "I heard you speak the code-words."

"Code words?"

"*All things happen according to purpose. There is only one outcome to all events. Even this is no coincidence.* Am I not the one you were supposed to meet here? There's no one else left who can lead you to Regulus."

"Regulus?"

"You sound really muddled. Why'd you attack me? That was some greeting for an old friend!"

"I thought you were one of them!"

"Really!" the girl huffed.

The clanking and creaking of the chain continued. Reaching for the front of her outfit, Val switched on her light. The glow was very dim, coming mostly from beneath her, but what she saw almost stopped her heart.

She was face-to-face with the last person she ever expected to see.

19

THE WOLVES OF LÍR

"We don't receive many guests."

Lolling face-down on his cot, Taran awakened from a drugged sleep. He knew this terrible voice that roused him from terrible dreams. It was the voice of the last person he'd ever expected to see. The problem was he couldn't see at all, for everything was dark and noisy, and the air stank of grease and burning coal.

"Colonel Naruna?" he mumbled, pushing himself up on his elbows.

He was certain of the voice, uniquely textured as it was, so he needn't have asked; and likewise his query received no answer. He reflected dully that he'd never been able to call Val's father *Mr. Naruna*. In fact, Val almost exclusively referred to him as *The Colonel* herself. Taran had met him a few times, and easily pictured in his mind a man strong and tall, often frowning, seldom speaking; yet the voice was his own, without mistake.

Never before had he greeted Taran as a guest.

Rolling over, he stuck out his legs so that he was sitting on the edge of the cot. While adjusting to an upright position, he glanced around the darkened cabin, observing with some foreboding that the speaker was nowhere in sight. He took a moment to rub his eyes and stretch, for his hands and legs were free; yet he was not. Away to his right, a yellow bulb swaying gently between cast iron boilers shed enough light to show him that he was locked in a cage, and that the cage was bolted to the floor in the middle of a strange room.

He saw no sign of Hest.

The room swam in a dizzy haze as he strained to see; yet it was more than the drug they'd given him. The floor was rolling and pitching. Amid a continuous thudding noise he discerned the scrape of shovels and the shouts of working men. The air was thick with dust and sweltering heat. By all these signs even a blind man could have guessed he was still on a boat. The plinking and chugging of pistons, more distinct now that he was fully awake, told Taran that he was aboard a different boat than the Olympic—a much smaller vessel.

His eyes were fixed now on the gloomy spaces before him, beyond the cage's door. There he saw a man, wrapped in shadows, seated on a stool. His shape was massive and muscular, and his eyes glimmered eerily in the twilight of the engine room.

Taran asked, "We're not on the Olympic, are we?"

"No," the voice answered from the darkness. "We're on the *Sylph*."

"The Sylph," Taran said groggily.

"The President's yacht."

"President McKinley's yacht?"

"Is there another President?"

"What are we doing on his yacht? Why am I here?"

"She's still a baby," the rough voice said. "Only three years old now. The captain's making better than 15 knots on calm days, but she was meant for coastal waters. It'll take us some time to get to your destination, so you'll have to be patient."

"Where are you taking me?"

"You're Art Morvran's kid, right?"

"I'm the son of Dr. Thaddeus Arthur Morvran."

"Then you already know where you're going."

The figure rose from the stool and walked leisurely towards the cage. Though he stood now right at the door, gripping the soot-blackened bars, Taran still could not see his face clearly. However, it seemed to him this man had the shape of the statue that stood sentry in the street of his hometown. He knew then for certain that it was really Naruna; and worries about what his father had said began to wrack his troubled mind.

He coughed on the dryness of his throat in the dusty air.

"Hope you'll excuse our rough greeting," Naruna said. "You really don't know why you're here?"

Taran shook his head.

"You were in danger. We got you off the Olympic as fast as we could. It was necessary to knock you out—made it easier to get you off the ship unseen."

"Who was I in danger of?"

Naruna did not answer, but looked away towards the boilers. Taran saw a patch of natural light appear somewhere beyond, and a stairway that ascended to an upper deck. A man was coming down the steps, and he was dressed in something relatively new in those times: a US Navy denim jumper. Taran had spied these grubby dress-down uniforms worn around the shipyards in New York, and shared the opinion of many that they were rather un-military in appearance.

"That'd be the lieutenant," Naruna said, returning his attention to the cage and its occupant.

"If you're trying to help me, why am I in this cage?"

"It's for your own protection. We're here to offer our support."

Taran watched as the lieutenant walked towards them between the boilers, where a few others dressed in similar fashion hustled coal into the hungry open mouths of the ironclad guts of the ship. Something like fear or fury began working on Taran, and he found it impossible to restrain himself any longer.

"You're here to offer me support?" he asked. "What do you think, that I'm stupid? Let me out of here!"

The officer stepped up to the cage door beside Naruna, who leveled glimmering eyes on Taran and said, "Why the flash-pan temper? I'll let you out when you're safe."

Taran heard the click of a key in a bolt, and the hinges of the cage door creaked. Naruna entered the small cell and faced him off only a foot away from the edge of his cot. He was attired in dark colors, outlandish in fashion. Most striking was a black and red leather vest with high shoulder guards, which fit snugly across his massive chest, exposing bare arms knotted with muscle. Seated quiescent and prim in his ill-suited finery, Taran felt like a gnat before the storm-god. A long uncomfortable moment passed as each regarded the other in strained silence. Though the light was dim, Colonel Naruna's scarred visage and patent scowl were quite visible.

He was face to face with the man whose daughter he'd lost.

After a moment, the colonel's scowl twitched to one side in something like a grin. It was not an unfriendly gesture, though it was savage and a little frightening, creasing his face into a thousand crags and scarred ridges.

"You have no reason to fear me," he said. "I'm not your enemy."

"Father said you had some words with him."

"Art and I never got along. You and Val—"

He paused, and then went on more cautiously.

"You are not to blame for what's happened to her. You know I've never been much of a father for her, being away so often. Part of the blame for her disappearance is definitely mine. Try to understand, it's nothing personal, you being in this cage."

Taran found this impossible to believe, but he knew better than to shoot his mouth off again. Albert Naruna was not one to trifle with. He would have to tread more carefully. There was a plot at work against him, and it needed finding out if he was going to survive.

He knew that Naruna was no stranger to plots. He'd seen action at manila Bay under the famed Commodore Dewey, for he was a Navy man in those days. It was more recently, when the assistant secretary of the Navy—now Vice President Theodore Roosevelt—commissioned Naruna and transferred him to the offices of Leonard Wood of the Army. There he was instrumental in raising and training the first all-volunteer cavalry, nicknamed the *Rough Riders*. That led the colonel to Cuba, through the terrible San Juan hills to risky meetings with General Garcia's pro-independence rebels, and ultimately to Santiago. After all the fighting was done, he had gone on to Puerto Rico, and to many other adventures. All this made him quite a hero in the old hometown.

Dr. Morvran had never spoken ill of the colonel, though he sometimes lamented Val's girlhood as fatherless. It was reported in the local papers that Naruna had managed to escape capture and death by a "superior wit and intelligence," but Taran never heard him once applaud Val's efforts at learning. He supposed it was because he was stiff and old-fashioned about women's roles. If the colonel had survived all this time by more than his brute strength, his cleverness was more instinctual than tactical, and his meanness was deeply rooted in his personality—even if now he claimed it wasn't to be taken personally.

Taran regarded the other man, the lieutenant, who lingered nearer the cage door.

"Did Cedric set this up?" he asked. The officer ignored him, and turned his eyes away towards the colonel.

"Cedric DePons?" Naruna asked.

"Yes. He's with the Army, so he ought to have known you were coming. I wonder why he didn't tell me."

The men looked at each other, silently conferring. Naruna said, "You think he set this up as some sort of transfer? No way, kid. He's got nothing to do with us, and we're not here with the Army or the Navy. We're here for you."

Taran wondered what was meant by this, since they were aboard a Navy vessel, but Naruna continued without giving him the opportunity to ask another question.

"You'll notice I don't wear a uniform anymore," he said. "I retired after the memorial service. I wondered why you didn't show."

Taran nodded, and left the implied question unanswered.

"Did you know your father sold the farm?"

"What?"

"Just last week. I won't ask you where he went—he probably didn't tell you anyway. He also sold that invention of yours, the flying machine."

Taran wasn't surprised to hear about the farm. It was a shock, of course, but he had already received some token of this by his father's own mouth. What did shock him was the fact that the flyer was gone. Worse, it was sold! He felt his heart leap up into his mouth, and struggled against a groan as he remembered the weeks and months that he had spent with Val laboring over that machine.

He'd named it after her.

"That machine was the cause of all this trouble," Naruna said, his voice reaching lower than usual into its natural grating tones.

Taran's eyes widened.

"You agree? Of course you do. Look at what's become of you in the past few months."

"If what you say is true," Taran said, "I do not doubt that my father had good reasons for whatever he has done."

"Right," Naruna said, waving his hand dismissively. "The lieutenant here wants to ask you a few questions, and then we'll reintroduce you to your friend."

"Who?"

"The woman, DePons' assistant. We're checking her story against yours, just to make sure she's not a danger to you or your mission."

"My mission?"

Naruna smiled again, and stuck out his chin a little.

"Yeah," he said, "your mission to retreat safely to a hiding place off the coast of Scotland, where you're supposed to learn more about your father's work and discover a way to find your friend—my daughter, Val Anna. *That* mission."

"I didn't even know it was a mission."

"The world's about to get a whole lot more complicated, kid."

Naruna then left the cage without another word, pausing only briefly to glance at the lieutenant as he stepped by.

"Shimeon bar-Kochba," the denim-clad man said, offering his hand. "Just call me Shim."

Taran stared at his hand hesitantly before taking it, whereupon he wondered a little at the man's limp and clammy grasp. He was smaller and shorter than Naruna, but stout at the waist and chest. He glanced around a moment, presumably for a chair, and finding a campstool at the other end of Taran's cot he pulled it around so that they could sit facing each other.

"I need to ask you a few simple questions," Shim said, placing his hands on his lap. "The answers to these questions can only be *Yes* or *No*. Do you understand?"

"Yes."

"That's good."

Taran noticed an accent beneath the man's words. Was he Middle Eastern?

"Do you know Dr. Cedric DePons?"

"Yes."

"Does he have red hair?"

"No."

"I want you to think about your first meeting with him, when you were very small. Can you remember that meeting?"

"Yes."

"He came to you more recently, on the evening of your friend's disappearance—the evening of the comet. Do you remember the man who came with him when he approached you in the barn?"

"No."

Taran wondered where all this was going. Then Shim asked another question.

"Do you know Dr. DePons' assistant, Hest?"

"Yes."

"Do you know where she is from?"

Taran paused a moment, because he wasn't sure. "No," he said.

"Do you know anything about the work she has done for DePons?"

"No."

"Do you know why she was set up to be your traveling companion?"

Again he hesitated. Hest was assigned to him as a kind of guide to his destination, but he was far from certain if that was her only purpose.

"No."

"Okay. I only have a few more questions."

Taran nodded.

"First, have you ever seen this symbol before?"

He offered Taran a scrap of wrinkled yellow tablet paper, upon which was scribbled a strange symbol like a rectangular frame enclosing a horizontal y-shape.

"No," he said with a shrug of his shoulders. He handed the paper back to Shimeon, who folded it meticulously and stuck it in a pocket of his uniform jacket.

"Have you ever heard of a man named Lír?"

Taran frowned. *Lair?* He certainly would've remembered a name like *that*.

"No."

"Are you aware of Dr. DePons' work, or of anything that he has conspired to do?"

"Didn't you already ask me that?"

"Please answer the question."

"No, I don't know about his work."

"Alright, then. Last question."

Shimeon leaned closer, uncomfortably so. Taran no longer heard the scrape of shovels or the thud of pistons. He only heard the stranger's voice.

"Do you know about the other stones?" he asked.

Taran's mind reeled. He knew what the man was asking, but he couldn't understand its significance. Nor could he hide from his face the fleeting jolt of surprise that he felt.

"No, I don't," he said, and quickly he added, "What stones do you mean?"

"That's enough for now," Shim said, standing suddenly. He walked to the door and held it while looking away towards the boilers. Taran turned and saw two figures approaching. One was Naruna, and the other—bound in iron cuffs and looking a little ruffled—was not Hest, but the Big Man's girlfriend.

Taran stared at Drusilla a moment in utter amazement, but to his credit he had the presence of mind to hold his tongue. Having so quickly ruined his attempt to cover his knowledge of the stone, he scrambled now to keep what pieces of the secrets he had left, if only in the hope that he had something to bargain with at the very end.

But *Drusilla?*

"Unbind her," Naruna commanded.

Shimeon arched his eyebrows.

"We're on a ship at sea. Where could she go if she escaped?"

Taran watched the exchange with great interest. These experienced soldiers seemed afraid of Drus, as if she was a threat. Shim only shrugged as he took the girl's slender wrists in one hand. With the other he retrieved a key from his coveralls and unlocked the cuffs. Drus rubbed her wrists in silence, ducking her head as if she expected to be struck.

"Get in," Naruna said in a warning voice.

When she stepped inside the cage, Shim shut the door and locked it with the same key. Then, without another word, the two men exited the engine room, leaving the captives alone in their rocking and vibrating prison.

For a long while, Drus wouldn't turn around and face him. Taran stared at her back. She wore a blue dress, quite expensive by the look of it. Her wild hair was a little bit wilder, and her arm sported a dark spot that could have been a bruise. Taran couldn't really tell, since it was so dark. Anyway, Drus was always bruised somewhere.

"What's going on?" he asked. He spoke to no one in particular, and she did not reply.

Hanging his head and sagging his shoulders, Taran finally let slip the mental and emotional bonds that had held him together since the day DePons had found his hiding place.

The day this girl had sold out her friends to lead Taran back to his father.

There was a creak from the campstool in front of him, and Taran raised his eyes. Once again he was in for an unpleasant shock, for it wasn't Drusilla who stared back at him, but Hest.

"Great," he said, holding his head in his hands. "I'm seeing things again."

"What have you seen, Taran Morvran?" she asked.

Her blue dress was the same, but everything else was changed. Her dark hair, falling in a long braid across her shoulder, was matched by eyes of lighter color. He held those eyes with his own, wondering. He'd never looked into a girl's face so long before, and would have been very embarrassed to try it only a few days ago. That was before he'd been kidnapped, and before a street urchin turned into someone else.

Or was he mistaken?

Was it because he'd just been thinking about the day he met his father that he *imagined* he saw Drusilla?

"What you lookin' at, Toady?" she asked in the rough-edged voice of the urchin.

"Hest?" he wondered.

"And Drus," she said, this time in the clipped tones of DePons' assistant.

"How is that possible? You don't look anything like Drusilla!"

"You'd be amazed by what a woman can do with some makeup."

"But you looked like Drus just a minute ago!" he said, exasperated.

"That's because I *am* Drusilla."

Taran sat up, keeping his eyes on her face. The strangeness of the situation focused him into a frenzy of conflicting doubts and fears. Long had he suspected he was going mad, but he was also certain this woman wasn't what she seemed—that she was hiding something from him.

"How can you change your appearance in the blink of an eye?" he asked.

"You've obviously been drugged," she replied.

"I feel fine."

"I'll explain what I can, but you need to remain calm."

"Start explaining, then!"

She rose to her feet and walked away to the bars of their cell. Taran watched her closely, looking for some sign, for some subtle shift or slip that might betray the secret of her deception. There was nothing unusual about her, though, and this only made him more suspicious.

"I didn't have time to warn you," she said, facing the outer room. "I was trapped, and they took me immediately overboard in a life raft. The whole thing was arranged. They must have had someone aboard Olympic the whole time, communicating our coordinates to this vessel. I'm guessing they took you later the same day."

"They gagged me in your stateroom," he said darkly. "I went looking for you when you didn't show for a couple of days."

"Your concern is flattering," she said.

"It wasn't exactly concern. I was just a little…frightened."

"Frightened of what?" she asked, turning slightly.

"Nothing." Then, setting his gaze on the floor, he shook his head and passed a hand through his unkempt hair.

"What is it?" she pressed.

"I just—I saw something, and it scared me."

She turned fully around to face him, leaning against the bars. "What was it you saw?"

"It didn't make any sense."

"Did it make less sense than a woman who can change her appearance in the blink of an eye?"

"Maybe," he said. "I saw something weird in the reflection of a mirror."

"Tell me what you saw in the mirror."

Taran closed his eyes and let the moment pass through his mind again. He remembered only a little of it, and the little he remembered still struck him as very good evidence of his descent into madness.

"I saw the inside of a tunnel of some kind. There were men behind me in the reflection, dressed in dark armored clothing."

"They appeared in the reflection?"

"Yeah," he said, nodding. "I mean, it was so real that I turned around. The guy holding the mirror must've thought I was a loon. The worst part was the *feeling*, though."

He looked up at her, and at that moment the feeling came upon him anew.

"It's like there's something *wrong*—something wrong with the whole world!"

Hest nodded. "I feel it too," she said, and looked away into the darkness.

A long moment passed. Taran glanced around the cell, studying it in detail for the first time since he awoke. His eyes were now sharpened to the dim light, and revealed to him how uncomfortable their stay aboard the ship would be. There was but one cot inside their cage, and no other amenities except a large chamber-pot in the corner opposite the door. With nothing else to fix his attention on, he returned his watchful eyes to the figure of the girl, standing tall and silent before him.

Taran was still apprehensive about this woman, and thought she was playing out some kind of plot with him. Maybe DePons was involved with this scheme, and maybe he wasn't. Either way, Taran was trapped.

"DePons feared this might happen," Hest said, breaking the silence. "The nets that were woven to find you have been drawing closer every day."

"Why were they looking for me? Is it because of what happened to Val?"

"You do not yet realize how important your confidence is to these men," she replied. "Nor do you realize how important it is for you to keep your confidence, and say as little as you possibly can—especially about your dreams."

"What's so important about these crazy daydreams?"

"They are glimpses of the places Val has gone."

Taran didn't wish to argue the point. In his desperation to make an explanation to himself for the dreams, he decided to let it be.

"Tell me," she asked, "have you seen her in any of these dreams? Was she in any danger? Did you see any of the stones?"

His glance was sharp and his tone bitter. "You and DePons and my father all say you're working hard to protect me while keeping me in the dark," he said. "Now that we're in this cage, I'd like some real answers, not more questions!"

"Even so, I hope you will learn to trust me," Hest said. "We're approaching land. We will come to the port of Aenfer in just a few more hours, and then we will go on with our plans."

"We're going on to our destination as if nothing's happened? They're just letting us *go*?"

"No," she replied. "Obviously, they will be watching our every move. Our part now is to act as if in agreement with Naruna."

"He's offered to help me," Taran said.

"You trust him?"

"No way."

"I ask, because I need to know. Did you make an agreement with this man, Taran Morvran?"

"Why would I? He's a mean old liar who thinks I'm responsible for losing his daughter."

She locked eyes with him. "The deal will be offered, and we will take it—but we shall use him for our own ends."

Taran regarded her curiously.

"These men are members of a private society operating under cover around the world," she said, lowering her voice so that he had to lean forward to hear her. "Vengeance for his lost daughter is not what drives the man you know as *Colonel Albert Naruna.* He is the puppet of a very dangerous international criminal, a man named *Lír.* We will play the part of willing captives, and we will survive for as long as we serve their needs."

"And how is this guy Lír connected to me?"

"His purpose, like yours, is to find Val Anna."

"Why's Val so important to him? And if these men are looking for her, why is my father opposed?"

Hest looked at him quietly, waiting.

"Is it because of *me?*" he asked. "Is it because I gave her that stone?"

"I was also given something to pass along to *you,* Taran Morvran. This was not the agreed place, nor the hour appointed by your father, but that can hardly be helped now."

Walking to the stool, she sat in it so that they were eye to eye. Then, hunching forwards so that their faces were inches apart, she spoke low, saying, "The circumstances require me to do this now, before fully securing your trust. You must forgive me in advance, but I am loath to hold onto a treasure which can be taken from me by force."

Taran looked on in confused wonder as she reached a hand to her bosom and withdrew from her dress something small clutched in her palm.

"What is it?" he wondered.

"Its name is Regulus, one of twelve stones identical to the one you once bore. There is now no safe guardian for it in this world. But, as it is not wholly in this world, and because you are already linked to Val Anna in some other place, I will risk all our hopes on this one chance."

She reached out and took his hand firmly in hers, cupping something round and hard between their palms. Taran felt it only for an instant before the pain hit. A fire burst under the skin of his hand and raced like lightning up his arm. He tried to let go, but Hest's grip was surprisingly strong, and though he struggled he could not get free of her grasp. His other hand grabbed his scorched forearm, and he felt flames between his fingers. Just when he thought he would pass out, wonder overcame his pain. In a bright tolling of bells, Hest's form wavered.

Val sat in her place.

In his weary months of hiding, Taran had heard men speak while under the influence of strange substances. He had heard the conviction in their voices as they described things that could not possibly exist. Now he understood something of their passion, for what he saw and heard next were completely impossible—yet they were.

Val's mouth moved; her forgotten voice echoed in his ears.

"Three are one now. Please, find me!"

A fresh shock of agony pierced him. Taran opened his mouth to cry out, but Val's hand was instantly over his mouth. The heat reached deeper into his flesh, coursing into his chest, but then slowly it began to subside. All the while he sat staring into her eyes. The smell of her hair was all around him, like a field of blooms.

Hest removed her hand from his mouth, allowing the other to linger in his. She turned his empty palm upwards. It was whole—nowhere maimed by the flames he'd touched. Taran looked from his hand to Hest's face. His heart sank.

"I did not think it would be so painful," she said. "At least we know now where Val is."

"Just who in Hades are you?" he asked in a growl.

Hest's eyes were lowered to their joined hands. "It must seem like deception to you," she said quietly. "How I wish I could reveal to you my true face, and then you would trust me."

"What do you mean?"

Her gentleness melted away at once. She removed her hand from his, and sat facing him with a cold stare.

"Does it still hurt?" she asked, a little disdainfully.

"It burns."

"You will recover," she said. "A shard of Regulus has passed through you."

"That stone went inside me?" he asked, wiggling his fingers.

"It has completed its journey, and is no longer here. That in itself is answer to many questions. What is more important to us is what you saw when the pain entered your arm."

"Tell me first what this *hope* was you risked my pain on."

Hest softened just a little. "It was the hope of finding Val Anna. DePons only said to me, 'Val Anna cannot come back the way she left.' He said that you must go to find her, and that Regulus will help. In your dreams you have glimpsed what Val Anna is doing in other worlds. Now Regulus has gone back to itself, and in so doing has passed through you into her. Thus you saw her, and heard her speak."

"And I thought I was crazy!" he exclaimed, staring at the palm of his hand. "Tell me you didn't just drug me in order to use some kind of *hocus-pocus* to locate Val!"

She leaned forwards again, silencing his hysterics with a mere glance.

"Three was the price of lifting the Ban," she whispered. "Thanks to you, we now know that Val Anna is in the World of Origins. All that is left for us is to retrace your grandfather's steps; yet this is but the first stage of a long journey you and I will make together, Taran Morvran. It begins at the Castle."

20
OLD THIRTY-TWO

Shoved through the door of the house, Nergal tripped across the low curb of the threshold and stopped just short of falling on his face. He looked around a spacious room. Except for the light of a single candle on a stand in the center, all within was dark, lending to the illusion that the building encompassed a larger space on the inside than its external dimensions described. The effect was disconcerting. Nergal stood a moment and watched the candle fluttering in a slight breeze, dripping wax into fanciful wing-like shapes. The breeze did not come from the doorway behind him.

What did come from the entrance was a distant sound of shouting, and briefly he turned his head to see what was happening. Lothar stood outside, his bulky shadow cast on the curtained partition. Something was happening in the street; but as it did not seem so important, Nergal returned his full attention to the room.

He didn't know why, but his heart was pounding. The smell of the spice was very strong here, though not unpleasant, and there was a plinking sound of bells or chimes. Then came a startling voice from the darkness.

"Well?" the speaker hailed.

The voice came from his right, where dimly now he saw another doorway leading to an inner room of the sanctum. Nergal detected the silhouette of a man standing against the grey twilight.

"Your Holiness," Nergal greeted, and remembering his manners he ducked his head.

As far back as he could remember, he'd always been afraid of priests. It wasn't just the smell of death that hung about them, or their filmy eyes. It was the heaviness that choked the atmosphere wherever they were present—the heaviness of the presence of the gods.

This man was very different from any of those. He did not stink—not from this distance—and he was richly clothed in a flowing mantle that chimed with the sound of tiny belled tassels. There was no sense of dread in his presence at all. This was so unlike everything he knew that all Nergal could manage in the silence following his greeting was another curt nod of his head.

"Speak, and stop wasting my time!" the man grumped. Even ill-disposed, his voice was less cruel than that of the priests of Hazor. He'd been whipped by those a number of times, chasing after Shubalu's contumacious schemes.

"I am called Kal-Nergal," he began.

"That is a strange name, if it is your *true* name."

"It is the only name I've ever had."

"Is that so?"

Nergal paused, considering. He had lost the ability to perceive the thoughts of others since his transit, and now he was frightened by a new and dismal prospect. Was this man able to know *his* thoughts? He decided to tell the truth, just in case.

"No, your Holiness, it is not so. I was once called *Kalbu*, until our priestess gave me this new name."

"A priestess? Women are not permitted to attain the rank of a priest of the New Council."

"I do not know how she should rank among your people."

"Ha! So you admit to being of the other brood," the priest said, stepping regally into the candlelight. "Well, don't expect me to tell you *my* name. It's not wise to share one's name with strangers from the Wastes—the haunt of sorcerers and hags."

As he came into the light of the flickering flame of the candelabra, the man's features emerged from shadow into sharp relief. Most striking was his nose, which was wide and flat, as was the front of his head. His eyes were wide-set under heavy wrinkled brows. The eyes were sharp and blue, like sapphires, and they did not blink when they stared back into Nergal's own.

"An unnatural-looking man, you are," he decided. "Though I suppose I'm not one to say so myself."

Nergal remained silent, studying the man's bat-like features. He had no facial hair of any kind—save for thin eyebrows—and his crown was completely bald.

"What's your business in Nara Colony, Kal-Nergal?"

"My journey began on the edge of a Forest," he said. "It was west from here. I met someone by the river who told me to follow the water to this place, and to speak to the priests. I was told the priests would hear me out."

"What matter would you have to speak before a priest of the Council?"

"It is difficult to say. I was treated roughly at the gate, where I first stated my case."

"What did you expect? They are warriors, and they have their uses. Listening to strangers is not one of their skills, but protection is; and they would not have let you in to see me if they thought you were an assassin—you're not, are you?"

"No, Sir."

"Then let's have a look at you before I send you back to the Wastes."

"You're sending me off? But you haven't heard my case!"

"What've you got to say that would interest me? It's my job to take note of nuisances before they're chased out. Now walk towards the light, and mind how you go. I was born into the Warriors' Guild, but paid the penalty fine and switched to the priesthood. I know that uncivilized Outlanders regulate nothing, thinking perhaps that they can do all things equally well; but if you're looking for trouble and thinking me to be a lamb, know that my service in the Army was long enough to hone me into an efficient killer."

Nergal wasn't much daunted by intimidation, but stepped cautiously into the bare stone chamber nonetheless. There was fear behind the man's warning, but also curiosity. Rather than dismissing him outright, the priest wanted to see him closer, and that seemed good enough for a start.

The walk to the candle was probably no more than fifty feet, but it seemed far. The floor was constructed from whitish stone, fitted here in a strange jigsaw pattern that generously expanded the visual plane. As he neared the candle Nergal admired its high stand of solid gold, figured in the likeness of fearsome winged serpents entwined in battle. He stopped beside the stand and turned towards the shape of the robed man.

"What happened to your eyes?" the priest asked, stepping closer.

"They were changed."

"You think speaking in riddles will placate me? What about your hair, then? You are no priest, yet you go around shaven? Even the Forest People would think your looks dishonest!"

"How so?"

"Well, you have a *devilish* look about you for starters, with your hide all scabbed and dry. Where in the Forest do you come from?"

"My journey began by a forest, but I was afraid to go inside."

The priest looked suspiciously at him through half-lidded eyes. "And where were you before the Forest?" he asked.

"I was in a far country," Nergal said, avoiding the simpler truth. "I came to these lands fleeing a war."

"War, hmm?" the priest asked. "That would mean you came from the south, for that is a land of ongoing conflicts; but you say you are from the west. Your story is impossible, as you well know, for to have come from the west you would have had to cross the Ceregor and pass through the perilous heart of the Forest Tryst."

Nergal understood nothing of the geography of the World of Origins. It would be so much simpler if he could just tell him how he got here. The priest spoke before he could frame an explanation in his mind.

"If you are from the western forest we call Tryst, you may well stand trial and die here in Nara. Seldom have we received your kind over the centuries, and only as prisoners or slaves. The people of Nara remember the Gilat-attacks of several years ago, attacks carried out by one of your tribe—a man named *Taran Morvran.*"

Nergal blinked. The name was somehow familiar, but he couldn't place it.

"I've never run into any by that name," he said.

"He is rumored to be a leader among them," the priest replied. "He escaped, but not before doing us serious harm. He had inside help. That means there are other spies among us."

"You think I am a spy?"

"You did say you were sent to bring word to the priests. Who sent you? Was it this priestess of yours?"

Nergal heard another change in the priest's tone. He returned the man's eager expression with one of surprise.

"Well?" he asked, waving his hands.

"Was it you I was sent to speak to?" Nergal asked. "Are you the one he was speaking about, when he said I would be heard by the priests? Was this arranged ahead of time?"

The priest looked scandalized. "What would possess you to suggest such a thing? Was it Lothar? Did he say anything to suggest that I, a priest, would arrange contacts among the ranks of our foes, *terrorists* from the Forest?"

"Terrorists?"

"What else do you think we should call you? We are forever warding off your unseen spies by increasing security around our borders. All our roads are slowed by the memory of your mischief. The seven excavation shafts closest to the River were damaged by the explosion the southern saboteurs set off last month. Hundreds disappear every year on the roads by the western forest. The list goes on and on!"

He leaned closer to Nergal, and lowered his voice.

"So tell me, who was it sent you? Lothar would not have brought you from the Western Gate if he did not suspect you to be some sort of courier. Were you sent to broker a trade of information; and if so, how am I to trust you?"

The priest was pressing him for information that he could not provide. The thought still struck him as highly probable that this man was playing both sides in his people's fight. It was no less probable that he would be in the priest's power if he did not quickly make some kind of intelligent reply. Nergal cleared his dry throat with a cough, and he tried to imagine in a few frantic moments what might pass as a civil exchange of terms between enemies in another world than his own. As hopeless as it all seemed, he was aware that his answer might color his favor fair for as long as he was stuck here. On the other hand, it could also get him killed. This was foremost on his mind when he finally made his reply.

"I was sent by the winged horse," he answered honestly. "His name is Aon. I parted ways with him by the western forest several days ago."

The priest grimaced horribly, baring his teeth.

"You know him?" Nergal asked.

"Do I know the winged demon? Of course I do! What was his message?"

"So this meeting was arranged," Nergal thought. Desperation grasped his mind, and against his better judgment, he put words into the horse's mouth—as strange a concept as that would have seemed just a week ago.

"He spoke a warning, but not just to you and your people. He says that strangers are arriving in these lands—strangers from far off."

"I don't know what kind of strangers you mean," the priest said. "We get all kinds here, as strange as you and some even worse. We're on the main throughway in the Wastes!"

"These strangers are not like any you have met before," Nergal replied, lifting his darkened eyes more confidently. He jutted his chin a little, certain that he had finally found what he wanted to say.

"They come from *Ertsetum*."

Nergal caught a glimpse of real surprise on the priest's face, but only in passing.

"It is forbidden to speak the name of the Dark Worlds here, Kal-Nergal!"

"What is your law to me? It is true, in any case."

"Tell me, how do your people expect me to believe this?"

He realized then that he had no proof at all. *"Now I've done it,"* Nergal thought. *"I'm back on the wrong track, just as Lothar warned."*

Now that he was on it, though, he felt it was easiest just to keep blundering along.

"I have urgent news for Orlim regarding the strangers," he said. "I don't expect you or anyone else to believe a word of it. There are no proofs that I can offer, but it will not be long before proofs become unnecessary. They are already here!"

The priest stared with an angry scowl.

The game was up.

"Preposterous fool! What would drive you to make such claims before a priest of the Council? Do you realize what trouble you've just caused yourself?"

Nergal shrugged. "I hadn't much hope to begin with. What does it matter now? Either you will believe me, or you won't. In the end, you will know the truth of what I say."

"A fool on a fool's errand! You wanted to be captured? Is that your scheme? If you were a spy from the Southern Forest I would at least have been able to grant you some kind of asylum pending your willingness to share information, but now you are headed for destruction. At least you could have concocted some sort of proof—"

He stopped almost in mid-word. For a moment Nergal was afraid the man's heart had also stopped, for he simply stood and stared at him in the candlelight, mouth slightly open. Then he heard what the priest also had heard. There was a noise of shouting in the street outside, and footsteps at the door.

"Your Holiness!" Lothar called, ducking his head past the curtain of the doorway. His eyes were wide with alarm.

"What's going on?" the priest asked.

"Excuse me, Eminence, but there are strange tidings here that demand your immediate attention!"

The priest looked from one man to the other, his thick neck shaking and his fists balled. "What is this?" he shouted. "More nonsense?"

"The diggers have found something!"

Nergal joined the commotion outside, guided by the priest's insistent shoving. Before he knew what was happening, he was immediately surrounded by a ring of four heavily-armored guardians. The priest, who looked very pale and fleshy in the light of day, stepped ahead of him, and Lothar the Warden of the Western Gate walked behind. All up and down the long street throngs of curious people were gathering. Besides the warriors of the gates, girt in their masks and armor, there were riders with gleaming shielded greaves and feathered beak-shaped helms, and a host that accumulated swiftly from every side-street and house. Others leaned out from balconies high overhead, gleaning news on the wind.

Walking towards them down the street from the north were two men, both of them clothed in strange blue uniforms that covered the whole body from booted feet to shoulders. The men and their clothes were soiled from digging, so Nergal guessed they were the diggers that Lothar spoke of—though as to the significance of digging, he was truly at a loss. Whatever it was about, the diggers were very excited, and their excitement was infectious.

"I told you, I did!" the elder of the two exclaimed, waving his hands emphatically at the onlookers as they came. "I told you Shaft Thirty-two had a few more surprises in store!"

"You've come from Thirty-two?" the priest called, looking grim.

The whole crowd hushed suddenly, listening closely. The old man nodded his head, combing his hand through the white tangles of his beard as he came to stand directly before the priest.

"Your Holiness, Teomaxos," he said with a bow. "I am William. It was my father that opened Thirty-two, and I dug the pit with him from the ground down. Now it's my job to close it. This here's Ryce."

He nodded aside to his younger companion, a thin man wearing a helmet that was rather too large for him, and goggles pushed up on his forehead. He didn't look especially comfortable in the center of the crowd, and kept casting his eyes around in a nervous manner while sucking his upper lip.

"We went down this morning to remove the last of the equipment before the backfilling operations begin," William said. "It's a big job, because the pit's deep."

"There are none deeper, and all know it," the priest said. "I give honor where honor is due, to you and to your father, for excavating the best technology our colony has gained from the Ancients. Without your efforts, and those of your League, we and our neighbors in Tara would long ago have ceased to be free and independent colonies of the periphery."

Nergal heard whispers all around him, and began to understand that there was something unusual about this business of excavation.

"You reached the level of the ancient grasslands some years ago," the priest continued, "the grasslands that were the home of our people during the Destroying Fire—"

"Long has it been whispered that we tapped the original foundations of Cipa itself," William said with a nod.

There were more whispers around them now.

"Well, whether you believe it or not, it's true!"

Many voices in the crowd began speaking at once. The priest held up his hands, and silence gradually resumed—but not before one loud voice shouted over the rest.

"Show us some *proof!*"

The priest looked like he was about to say something, but then he turned instead towards Nergal. As the man's wide-set eyes glanced sideways to catch his own, Nergal felt a shiver race up his spine. Taking advantage of the lull that followed, William continued.

"You all know that the League doesn't require us to have inspections or provide detailed records, so long as the shaft doesn't collapse," William said loudly, speaking to those around him. "We keep our secrets for the good of the colony! Far be it from me, however, to offer you good people no other proof than my good word—be it as good as my father's."

He paused a moment, basking in the crowd's attention.

"No one's ever been down to see the bottom of Old Thirty-two except for my father and me, and Ryce—and a coupla hundred Null-Navvies that do all the digging—but you've all seen the kind of stuff that comes out of the shaft. That stuff is what makes our town great!"

Heads nodded all around.

"And that's proof enough that I've hit the foundations; but now I've got something very peculiar on my hands, something that requires the examination of a priest. Now, I don't know what it is, but it seems to me it's something important. I found it this morning, after I insisted to Ryce we go down ourselves for a last look around."

Ryce looked suddenly brightened by the mention of his name, and Nergal realized that the man was an idiot. He was probably unable to speak.

The whole parade shuffled slowly down the street, the riders keeping those in front and those behind a good distance away from the priest and his entourage. Nergal, distracted once again by the amazing creatures called Talons, was commanded to follow closely behind the priest, whose name he discovered was *Teomaxos*. Nergal couldn't figure out why he was wanted, and Teomaxos wasn't in the mood for explanations.

"What kind of thing is it?" the priest asked. He had already asked the same question three or four times in as many minutes, but the diggers would not offer even a brief description.

William stumped along looking important and solemn. "There's nothing else like it, Lord Teomaxos," he replied. "I'm hoping it'll fetch a lot of business for the colony. That's why I sent word to Orlim and Colony Governor Amed directly. They will be expecting a report from you."

Teomaxos frowned.

"It's League policy, as you know," William said. "Anything we find that's still running and putting off heat requires an immediate investigation by a priest."

"It's still running after a thousand years?" Teomaxos asked, eyes widening.

"Orlim himself sent a reply via Old William's messenger," William said, a trifle loudly. "It bears his embossed crest and all!"

"Hush your voice!"

"He specifically requested you examine the findings in situ."

"Wait a minute," Teomaxos said. "You're saying it's still beneath the surface? Orlim wants me to go down that hole?"

"He insisted," the digger replied, taking a folded piece of yellow parchment from his breast pocket.

"It says, *'The priest Teomaxos is to make an investigation of the object in situ and report his findings to the Governor and myself in person at today's Gilat-festivities.'*"

Teomaxos tore the paper from the old man's hands and read it himself. He stopped in his tracks, and spun on Nergal.

"You are to bring along with you any strangers from the Wastes who met you here recently," he read, and fixing his eyes on Nergal he tilted his head inquiringly.

"The proof you required," Nergal said with a shrug.

Inwardly, he reasoned that someone else must have been alerted to his arrival. Maybe Bal-Ona or the others were here before him. Nergal cast his gaze around at the crowds of onlookers, but there were no familiar faces.

The priest turned in a rage, thrusting the parchment back into William's hands as he passed. The old workman lovingly folded the message and placed it in his pocket for safekeeping.

They continued past two or three more intersections, all the while continuing north. Nergal noticed they were followed now by many more people, perhaps several thousands. Was the whole town going to show up?

The road terminated at an enormous many-lobed structure stuccoed with pale-red daub. It was a looming blot on its surroundings, ominous in every aspect. There were no windows near the ground floor, and many guards stood at the entrance of a gate that was at least as large as that in the town wall. These guards wore rich leather outfits, but very little armor. Their weapons were strange boxy clubs that he recognized from a fading image in his mind.

More guns.

"These are hired men," William said, turning to Teomaxos. "It's necessary, you know, since the blasting last month."

"I am very familiar with the League's penchant for self-preservation," the priest replied sourly.

The guards stepped aside as William led the priest through the gate, and closed ranks again behind them. For a moment, Nergal was afraid that he would be forgotten; but then Teomaxos turned back to look at him, and waved to those who guarded him. He was shoved forwards towards the door, but the rest of the retinue was forbidden to pass—even Lothar. He continued alone with Teomaxos, William, and Ryce.

"You stick close to me," Teomaxos said quietly. "I don't know what Orlim wants with you, but I won't be answering to him if you disappear!"

Inside the entrance of the gate, William removed a small piece of equipment that hung from the wall by a nail. He turned a knob that projected from its side, summoning the power that awakened the lamp's light.

"Follow me," William said. "It's tricky in here. A fellow could get lost for days."

He turned quickly and set out at a swift pace. Nergal struggled to keep up as they went along narrow twisting corridors and wider interconnecting passages.

"Mostly storerooms for equipment and machines up here," their guide called over one shoulder. "When we find something really big, it's disassembled and boxed before being escorted out under guard to Tara and the markets. Too much interest in these items, if you ask me."

"That is a strange thing for a merchant to say," the priest remarked.

"You might think so, your Holiness, but what my father and I really were after were works of art and the like—not the weapons that Thirty-Two's become famous for."

"You think the thing you've found is a weapon?"

"Maybe."

They came suddenly to a large antechamber where there were rows of strange lights: metal wands that spat brilliant blue flames in tiny jets. When a knob was turned at the arched entry to this chamber, all the jets within turned orange, and the shadows of a wide hall were cast back in the spaces beyond.

302

Nergal looked in amaze at ordered piles of machinery—things that looked like they might be at home aboard the Gremn Auriga. Then he wondered why this surprised him. These were the ancient remains of the world that the Gremn and Crodah destroyed in fire, for which reason they were exiled.

"Null-Navvies were packed up and shipped out just yesterday," William said. "The League recirculated them to other holes hereabouts, wherever there's a need for bots."

Past wondrous machines for digging and drilling they went, following the torches along a widening passage. He was followed closely by his four guards, while the priest and the workmen walked ahead. At length they came to a cavernous space. It reminded Nergal sharply of the Underworld, where Morla's slaves had uncovered the Auriga. This was different, though. The darkness before them looked far deeper.

Something like a song erupted from Ryce's mouth, startling everyone except Ryce himself. The odd skinny man ambled ahead toward a massive jumble of steel armatures and bracing. Following at a slower pace, they listened while he continued in a light canting rhythm, taking up his position at a bank of levers and cranks. William went to join him, and together they pulled on cables and levers, pausing momentarily to take note of some peculiarity in their practiced methods. All their familiarity with the equipment and the surroundings only intensified the strangeness of the place.

It was very warm, and seemed to be growing warmer. Despite looking on with wide eyes, Nergal could not see very far into the empty space beyond the machine where William and Ryce were working. There was a sharp insistent clanging sound from above, and raising his eyes he saw giant skeletal arms of braced girders and beams, all extending into the darkness before them. Some of these suspended boxes on chains, lifts containing huge machines covered with augers and arms.

Teomaxos started out towards the workmen, and Nergal followed, noting that an empty cage was descending slowly from one of the cranes. As he went on, he was at first puzzled that the darkness ahead did not dissipate, until he realized that it was a huge empty pit, a bore-hole even deeper than the one that hid the buried Gremn ship beneath Hazor. He came to a halt beside Teomaxos at the edge. The shaft was monstrous, as wide as the dome above. There were lights running down along its smooth inner face at regular intervals, rows and rows of lights that faded into black nothingness below.

"Where is your lift?" Teomaxos asked, standing well away from the edge.

Ryce laughed suddenly, and pointed to the descending cage. Nergal began to suspect that something was afoot.

"That fool!" the priest shouted. "Orlim just wants to do me in, doesn't he?"

"Not to worry!" William said, smiling as he grabbed the frame of the cage and yanked it closer to the edge. "Old William will be joining you, your Holiness!"

"What about him?"

William looked at Ryce. "Why, he's going to work the crane," he said.

Nergal felt a tingling in the base of his stomach. The black water had cured him of his terror of high places, but it seemed to be coming back. Prompted by the priest, he stepped into the cage, which jiggled and fluttered a little with his jostling. It was suspended over the shaft by only a few slender chains. Teomaxos and William entered behind him, and William paused to regard him questioningly.

"Forgive a man his peculiarities, your Holiness," William said aside. "I saw how you had him under guard. You know how we diggers get a trifle paranoid about our work, with spies loose in the League, and now these saboteurs—"

"He's under guard, but Orlim's ordered him to accompany me."

"He's got a name?"

"He is Kal-Nergal," the priest answered. "Can we get on with this?"

William bobbed his head towards Nergal. "Got the strangest look about you as I've ever seen—those eyes and all," he said. "I don't suppose you're from around here?"

Nergal sensed hesitation, and fear.

"He's here because Orlim wants him for something," the priest said, "and because I can't let him out of my sight. Your secrets are safe. I will answer personally to the League for any violations to your charter that his presence may represent."

Nergal said nothing. He knew that Teomaxos would not have let him tag along if he really thought he was a spy. He couldn't guess what purpose he had in joining them, though, no more than he understood how Orlim knew about him.

"I hope you boys aren't afraid of heights," the digger said, giving a thumbs-up signal to Ryce. With a loud squeal, the cage jerked, scraping the rock ledge.

They descended.

Down they plunged, very rapidly, so fast that the levels of lights along the wall of the shaft sped by in a blur. Soon there was only the sound of a rushing wind, coming up from below. The air grew warmer, and closer.

After they had descended thus for about three minutes, the cage seemed to slow. Nergal's ears popped. Gradually, the lights that had accompanied their passage down to the bottom grew fewer and farther between, until at last there were only single gas jets burning here and there. The walls of the shaft were no longer smooth, and a rich earthy smell permeated the air. It was very wet, and a sound of rushing water grew louder. The cage touched down with a slight bump. The door opened, and they exited on broken rocky ground.

Teomaxos led, with William close behind him. Even Nergal, whose eyes were sensitive to darkness, found it nearly impossible to see until William rekindled his lamp. Their attention was immediately drawn to a large metal wall nearby. The sound of a waterfall came from this colossal retaining device, and some water as well, collecting in little pools all around. When the workman lifted his small lantern higher, they got a little better idea of the place.

"A natural pocket?" the priest asked, looking around.

"That's what the Guild inspectors called it," William replied. "This is why we had to shut down the works."

Nergal could see that it wasn't just the bottom of a blasted hole. Here and there were the ruins of walls and columns, and many things of wonderful construction in various stages of decomposition. The broken walls were made from pale white stone, and were covered with colored tiles, gleaming faintly in the lamplight. A similar tiled surface peeked through thin layers of mud and rock underfoot.

"Watch it," William said, and grasping his shoulder with a firm hand he pointed with the lantern towards the floor at Nergal's feet.

There, only half a step away, was a broken narrow hole ribbed with twisted rods of iron. *Reinforced Concrete*, he recalled—another term that had been stored in his mind, a word that had until now no meaning.

It was a manmade material.

A breeze blew up through the hole, cold and damp, and moaning eerily.

"The machinery broke through some kind of level there," William explained. "We don't know what else is down below, but we all oughta watch where we're going."

"Are these *tunnels*?" Teomaxos wondered, looking around.

The others looked up and followed the line of the walls from the side of the shaft where they stood on into the darkness. There was a clear indication of an overhang to either hand, and this indeed suggested the line of a tunnel.

"Now that you mention it," William said, squinting into the darkness, "I think you've gone and hit the nail on the head, your Holiness. But why would the Ancients have built a tunnel in Cipa with houses and all inside? Wasn't all this above ground at one time?"

"This is below the level of Cipa and the ancient plains," the priest replied, peering at the ruined walls and metal studs rising here and there from the rocky fill.

"These weren't houses. They were bunkers and connecting passageways spanning thousands of leagues between the twelve cities of the Ancients. Even among Guilders it remains a little known fact that Cipa, which became Tara and Nara, lay in the path of these passages."

"You don't say," William muttered. "Well, tunnel, cavern, or mausoleum, whatever it is, it threatens to collapse the whole pit—"

The others looked at him nervously.

"—but we'll get out of here long before that happens," he added hastily. "What we're looking for is just over there."

He pointed away, towards the far side of the excavations, where something glimmered softly. It was an unnatural gleam, not just a reflection of William's lamp.

"There are a few curiosities there, the likes of which I have seen only once before."

"I thought you said you didn't know what they were," the priest said.

"Go nearer, Holiness, and you will see. Just be careful. There's still a lot of heat coming off them."

They wandered carefully across the miry ruin, and when they came at last nearer the far wall William lofted his lamp a little higher. His eyes stared out at a few long low objects that lay still upon the rocky ground. He would go no farther. Teomaxos stepped forward, and Nergal went with him, drawn by curiosity. As they went, the priest spoke to him quietly.

"If you're not from the Forest, where are you from?" he asked.

"I am from Ertsetum."

"You think that's funny? I know you no longer fear me, because Orlim has asked for you. Well, what if I just leave you down here when I go, and tell Orlim you're a spy?"

"That won't work. He obviously knows me, and was expecting me."

"How does Orlim know you, and why didn't you tell me that he does?"

"He knows me," Nergal said, "but I don't know him. We've never met."

They stopped suddenly and stared ahead, for the light that had broken out from the ground a little distance away was awakened, multiplying the nearer they came. In the light they saw five cylinders on the ground in a coil of cables and broken bits of machinery. William came up behind them, walking slowly, and his voice trembled when he spoke. With every step, one of the pods glowed brighter.

"I have seen these before," William said from behind them. "It was long ago, when I was a boy and this shaft was just half the depth it is now. There was a probe cut to this level. My Dad brought up one of these in the sample."

"And what was it?" the priest asked.

"Well, the one we brought up stopped glowing after a few days. We opened it, but there were only bones inside—bones of a man dead at least a thousand years."

"It's a glowing *coffin*? Am I supposed to report to Orlim and Colony Governor Amed that you've discovered a glowing coffin?"

"I don't believe that's what it is, Eminence. What does your companion say about it? He looks mighty interested, he does."

Nergal was staring at the glowing pod with a look of wonder on his face.

"He knows nothing—"

"I know this is a stasis-tube," Nergal said.

The priest fixed his angry gaze upon him. William only looked confused.

"It's a *what*?" the digger asked.

"It's just some sort of projectile," Teomaxos said, bending down and wiping the surface with the edge of his robe. "This shaft has produced many like it. I wonder if it's glowing and throwing off heat because it's unstable."

"It's not a weapon. It's a stasis-tube."

"What do you know about it?" the priest snapped angrily.

Nergal advanced towards the artifact with cautious steps. He saw this was a pod of a different sort than the one in the center of Auriga's archive. This looked metallic, but was pale like ceramic. Its upper surface was as transparent as glass, yet all he could see inside was a white glimmering liquid. It wasn't black water. It was more like *light*. He dropped to his knees, feeling the edges with his fingers for some kind of latch or control. It was hot to touch, but tolerable.

"What are you doing?" Teomaxos demanded.

Nergal's heart began to hammer in his chest. From some recess of his mind, where it had lain dormant since he visited the grave at the Forest's edge, he was immersed in a memory of those he had left aboard the Auriga. He wondered where they'd gone when the Mirror opened. They had tried so hard to free him from the Source, all to teach him one thing.

He had a purpose.

Everything had a purpose.

"I think I know how to open it," he said, wondering at his own voice.

"Open it?" William asked.

Nergal looked at the pod, which was like an ossuary—like the boxes that held dead men's bones. He did not think it was a coffin, though. Surely there must be life here, where there was light?

He turned towards Teomaxos, and asked, "Do you believe that there is a purpose guiding everything?"

The priest seemed taken aback by the question. "I don't understand," he said.

"Do you believe in coincidence or blind luck?"

"What the devil does that have to do with this device?"

"Though it is no longer required, I believe I can provide you with more of the proof you wanted."

Teomaxos scowled. "You would try to use this thing to defend your honor before me?" he asked. "You have no idea what it is!"

"If I am right, will you listen to what I have to say?"

The priest said nothing in reply.

Dropping his hands to his sides, Nergal stopped fumbling with the pod and spoke the words that Nunna had taught him.

"Even this is no coincidence," he said.

The tube's surface slid back with a crack and a sharp hiss. Inside, the liquid dissipated into a white mist that clung to a reclining figure.

"A body!" the priest muttered, obviously impressed. Then, taking control once again, he asked, "This is proof of what? That people die?"

"It's not like the one I saw when I was a boy," William whispered, backing farther away and covering his face with a corner of his overalls as the mist evacuated the pod. "It's perfectly preserved—perfectly!"

Teomaxos and Nergal looked closer, and inside they saw the form of a person robed and hooded in white. Teomaxos knelt abruptly, leaning closer. Just as he was about to reach inside the pod, its light was extinguished, and a slender hand shot out and grasped Nergal's arm.

With a yell, William dropped the lamp and ran for the cage.

For a few moments they were in complete darkness, listening to William's cursing and yelling. He'd tripped in the dark, and was rolling on the ground somewhere nearby, agonizing over an injury. Neither Teomaxos nor Nergal moved to help him. Nergal felt the warmth of a hand on his forearm, and a breath upon his cheek. Someone turned towards him, and spoke.

"I dreamed of this," a voice said. The voice was deep and beautiful, and very familiar.

Behind them, William kindled and hoisted his lamp. He was finished with his yammering, having done no worse harm than scare and scrape himself, and now he was curious to see what would happen. From where he stood he raised the light.

Held by a very pale hand, Nergal's arm was released gently as the occupant of the stasis-tube rose and stepped out. The lamplight fell full upon a figure in spotless robes of radiant white, whose face was partially hidden by a low hood so that they could see only a heart-shaped chin sticking out. The sleeper turned towards him directly, and Nergal's inward eye was shocked to see a scene replaying in his mind—a scene from his old life. Once again he was kneeling before a pair of fair white feet, and he heard a stern yet lovely voice speaking to him.

"Rise, Kal-Nergal!"

He stood slowly while the priest and the digger looked on in wonder. The figure lifted slender arms and withdrew the hood. Nergal peered into her unveiled face, taking in the light of her wide and piercing eyes. In every other way she seemed now transfigured into a woman more wonderful and terrible than the maiden he once had known. Her long silver hair flashed like lightning, and she shone with a sudden light that made the mechanical torch in William's hand look like a candle against the brilliance of the day-star.

"Morla?"

She smiled.

21

THE RED DRAGON

The smile was all Val could see of her face. It was a smile that
said nothing was wrong in the world, projecting serenity in
defiance of the brooding darkness around them. It was a smile
that should not have been.

Their shadowed refuge was tucked sparingly beneath a
concrete stairwell, the cobwebby reverse of which ascended
above their heads from left to right. Illumination came by slivers
of amber sunlight breaching a crack in one shattered wall. Val
sat opposite that narrow fissure, her back propped against one
of the two rusting metal crates flanking the dumbwaiter shaft.

The shaft itself was closed now by a steel plate and a latch, precautions that seemed rather flimsy after the excitement on the main concourse.

Like a sheaf of harvested wheat, a clutch of mop-handles — each lacking its business-end—leaned in a corner where hasty hands had abandoned them. No mopping had been done for an awfully long time, by the looks of things. By the looks of things, there were very few people left to mop up after.

And she was still smiling. How could she smile?

How could she even be?

The girl sat a few feet away on her left, resting against the other crate, shrouded in shadows with only a slender beam of light touching her chin. The chin worked up and down vigorously. She was eating from a can, using her fingers to scoop a pink substance called SPAM into her mouth. Still smiling, she looked up from her meal and greeted Val's questioning gaze with a satisfied belch.

"Excuse me!" she said. "This stuff does terrible things to you. I don't blame you for abstaining. So, are you going to tell me what took you so long to get here?"

At a loss for words, Val looked across the room. The crack in the wall let in more cold air than light. It also let in strange sounds from the world outside—sounds of crumbling and crashing, and of distant cries. She had taken a long look through that crack when they first arrived, and all was a devastated wasteland of mounded metal as far as the eye could see. It was like stepping into Hell, and there were monsters out there. But who was this, her rescuer? Val hadn't found words to share with her since the dumbwaiter. What could she say to her now?

The girl slid forwards on her bottom until all her features became visible in the light. Val could not help but stare, could not bring herself to think of what it meant to be here with her. Something was very wrong.

She was sitting with Nunna.

Val had watched her die, yet here she was, looking very much alive—if also a little changed. The fact that she was speaking

English wasn't the only amendment to her character. She wore now a jumpsuit similar to her own, and her smallish head was covered with long silvery-blue hair. She looked a little older.

"You look like you've seen a ghost, Val."

"Maybe I have," Val replied.

"What do you mean by that?"

Val shook her head. "I don't know."

"You weren't prepared for what's out there?"

Val shook her head again.

"I understand. Still, it's amazing you made it here in one piece. How *did* you get into the city?"

Val didn't know how to answer.

"Did you bring any weapons with you? No? That's alright. I guess it doesn't matter. Our chances are about the same either way."

Val fell to studying the blue jumpsuit, filthy and patched, that clung tightly to Nunna's thin frame. It was ribbed here and there with reinforcements like her own, but lacked armor. Across her shoulder she had slung a bandolier to which were affixed many useful items—a watch, gloves, and a pair of fancy goggles with shaded lenses; but she hadn't so much as a stick to defend herself.

"You know, Val, you don't look half bad decked out in CM7s."

"CM7s?" Val wondered, looking down at her battle armor.

"Yeah," Nunna said. "They only outfitted me in this older model. The power-unit just died on me, though, so I was badly backlit when I ventured outside earlier today. I dumped the armor so I could run, but I guess they spotted me and followed me into the concourse downstairs."

"You go outside?"

"I have to. Supplies run out from time to time, and I can't carry much."

"Why not go somewhere else?"

"What? And leave the objective?"

"I mean, why not leave the city?"

"You hit your head or something?" Nunna asked. "You're not making sense. I'm still at my post, right where I'm supposed to be. I won't leave until you or Kabta give the order. Besides, Val, the whole world's messed up, and this is the last building standing for miles. Where else is there to go?"

"I guess I'm just tired," Val said. "I've been through a lot today."

Nunna glanced around the cell with a dull look. "Yeah," she said. Cleaning the can of SPAM with her finger, she placed it on the floor beside her.

"So, I guess you're here to tell me Kabta's left us on our own?"

"If he's still alive in this world, I think he must be hiding."

"If you don't know where he is, who sent you?"

Val hesitated, wondering how much longer she could pretend.

"It's complicated," she said.

"If *you're* here, something else must've gone wrong. What about DePons?"

"I don't know where he is."

Nunna scowled. "You know," she said, "sending me here with rookies was one thing, but yanking DePons and Shubalu out of harm's reach just when I needed them really says a lot about what the upper echelon thinks of the rest of us. They hooked me up with the HSA, but we lost track of the objective; and Kabta doesn't exactly come when he's called. If I could get back to the Foundation, I'd measure the size of a few backsides with my boots. Maybe I'd get the chance, if you'd tell me how you got here."

"There's no way back, Nunna."

"Sworn to secrecy, huh? Well, you were shipped somehow, and right here to the middle of it all. You got a rendezvous for pickup?"

Val shook her head. She feared saying more.

"Great," Nunna muttered. "Well, until you feel like telling me whatever it is you know or give me some instructions, I guess we're both stuck here."

Val nodded, and looked towards the light.

Nunna yawned and stretched. "The fact they sent you at all means they think I'm KIA," she said. "I suppose you have no way to get in touch with them?"

"No."

"Then they probably think you're dead, too."

Nunna was looking at her, and a sly girlish grin tugged at the corners of her mouth. A hush fell over them, and Val marveled how their conversation had turned so uncomfortably surreal. Over the silence a distant shrieking cry was raised, echoing at its highest pitch and wavering just a little before it was broken off. Other cries followed in chorus.

Something struck Val's arm. She flinched at the tiny pebble Nunna had thrown.

"They're smart," Nunna said, regarding her passively. "They're not just stupid animals. They hunt, staking out places near water, gathering stores of imperishables and guarding them. They've probably already figured out this hiding place."

"What do you think they are?" Val asked nervously.

"You've never seen one in person before today?"

"No."

"How is that possible? They've been here three years, and you're just discovering this?"

Val made no reply.

"Well then, I suppose there's something good about being locked up with Kabta. What can I tell you about them? They sleep a lot during the day. That makes them easy to avoid, if you can manage to keep away from the Watchers. The chief danger is at night."

She bent her gaze towards a bundle of rags in one corner.

"They killed all the others after dark. That's when they see you, no matter where you try to hide. So, we have to hide in places they wouldn't think to look—sewage tanks, graves, or even burning buildings. I don't know how many people are left. You're the first person I've seen in a few months. What I do know is we're outnumbered, and if we don't outsmart them, we're dead."

She looked up from the bundle and caught Val's fearful expression.

"We have to get to Regulus and shut it down," Val said.

"That's why they sent you? You came for Regulus?"

"Isn't that your objective?" Val wondered.

"You do realize what DePons was doing here, right?"

Val guessed, "He made the stone Regulus known to the United States, and then exploited it."

"And what do you think of that?"

Val looked at her curiously, but seeing that her question was genuine she said, "Whatever advantages DePons imagined he had achieved when the stone was secret were lost as soon as this station was built."

Nunna chuckled. "Regulus is such a pussy-cat!" she said, wiping her eyes. "It's submissive to anyone who comes along. You can go anywhere you please—and they hand it over to a governmental bureaucracy!"

"It's a mass-transit system," Val said quietly.

"What it is is suicide! It makes me wonder if the whole thing was arranged—like a weapon."

"I don't think it can be used like that," Val replied. "I think all this happened because the stone is calling others to itself."

Nunna rose to her feet. "You think Regulus caused the Decoherence itself, just to recohere itself with the dark stones? Maybe you're right. After all, you were right about everything else. I guess you feel vindicated."

"Why would I feel vindicated?" Val asked, looking up at her.

"Sorry. I suppose that's a really awful thing to say, isn't it? You didn't make this happen, you only predicted it; and no one listened."

"I don't remember," Val said, looking away.

"What? You don't remember being locked up for loony because you kept prophesying about the *Dark Worlds*?"

"Dark Worlds?"

"The Dark Worlds—the end of everything and the decoherence of the stones! You made such a stink about it, too."

Val frowned. "I'm here for Regulus," she said.

"Yeah, you said that."

"Can we get to Regulus?"

"Regulus Platform is deep down in the old tunnels. The Human Solvency Army couldn't hold back the things that came out of that place, and no one's ever made it very far in."

"So, it's impossible?"

"Yes, for a large force. Maybe if it was just the two of us we'd have a better chance."

The sickness was worsening. Val fought a growing nausea, and was anguishing over a new thought. If Regulus was accessible and all but guaranteed a way home, and if Regulus could be contacted before she collapsed under the strain of Displacement Syndrome—if that could be done, the choice still lay before her. Would she go home, or would she bring the stones into the World of Origins?

"Are you okay?" Nunna asked.

Val's strength seemed to be slipping away the longer she sat, so she stood up and adjusted the armor on her chest. It felt heavier than ever.

Nunna grinned roguishly while watching her. "If there's one thing I've learned over the past few years," she said, pulling a worn and folded paper from her belt, "it's that there's no such thing as coincidence. Luck is totally bogus! We're going to finish this operation, and I think I know just where to begin."

Opening the paper, she walked to where Val stood.

"You wandered into the main concourse from outside, right?" she asked.

"No. I came up from the lower halls."

"The lower concourse? How'd you come in from down there? Did you walk up a tunnel? They were all blocked as of a year ago."

"I only remember falling from a hole in the ceiling, and then I went up some stairs to the big hall where I met up with that monster. Everything before that is kind of foggy."

"You're not joking, are you?" Nunna asked, showing her the map she held. The blueprint showed only the main concourse, but it was enough.

"Those are the stairs," Val said. She thrust her finger at the map, tapping the central stair.

"Impossible! Nothing gets up or down those steps!"

"I did."

"You had your chameleon suit powered?"

Val looked at the complicated control console on her forearm. "I don't even know how to make this suit work," she said.

"Well, there's one for blind luck," Nunna muttered, turning the map over. "Look here, this side's a diagram of the lower concourse. I'm afraid it's just an architectural drawing, but I'd really like to know if you could point out the hole you said you came through."

Val stared at the page in the gloom. She saw very little that seemed familiar except the stairway.

"I remember there was a barricade there, at the bottom of the steps, which narrowed to less than half the width of the corridor." She held her hand on the page to demonstrate. "The barricade bulged a little over here, in the middle of the hall. Beyond it there was nothing but destruction."

She brought her finger backwards through the open concourse, and noticed a row of doors on a far wall. One of them led to a long tunnel with rooms along its way.

"I came out of one of these rooms, I think."

"Well," Nunna said quietly, folding the map. "That's proof enough for me."

"Proof?"

"Proof that you're not telling me half the story of how you got here, for one thing. There's no way into the tunnel above that room from the lower concourse except via the 32nd Street concourse. All the tunnel exits are blocked, and Old 32 was rerouted to the Regulus Platform when the transit was being constructed. It's a dead-end, unless you somehow used Regulus itself to get here."

She paused, looking at Val thoughtfully.

"Anyway, however you ended up here doesn't matter. It's like I said, there is no coincidence."

Val looked at her questioningly.

"The hole you said you came down? I just happen to know how it got there. There was a guy with us in the beginning—I don't remember his name now, maybe Bob—and Bob says to me that he got stuck on the wrong side of the collapse when we brought down the tunnels deeper in. How'd he get out?"

Val stammered, "I—"

"First he got totally lost," Nunna continued, barely missing a beat, "and then he was corralled into a train tunnel with nothing but horrors closing in fast. Bob had a bit of C-4, and just enough wit to realize he couldn't use it without vaporizing himself. He says to me that he stopped in one particular spot, just between the rails, because he kind of saw something unusual—now, whatever he thought he saw was so unusual that he'd stop and take note of it as he was about to be eaten by dragons and some-such, Bob never did say. He did say that the C-4 went off in his hands, though."

"C-4? Is that—?"

"Yeah, I know! The amazing thing is that instead of being blown to atoms Bob was immersed in a rushing light. He said it was like a whirlpool sucking him down through a hole in the floor. He assumed the explosion reacted somehow with the concrete to perform this miracle, but that's because Bob believed in fool's luck. So did I, at the time. No more, though. I've seen enough weird stuff in the past few years to understand that messing with Regulus made Swiss cheese of space-time all around this city, and maybe all around the world. However you got here, it seems to me that you and Bob fell through the same hole, and that's the hole we need to find."

They stood in silence a moment, Val digesting the breathless ramblings while Nunna paced the circuit of the maintenance closet. Val feared she was warming up for more when Nunna held up one finger and turned to face her.

"No one's been back since all that happened, and Bob didn't live long after the day of his big adventure; but you proved that the hole's still there. The tunnel he was in when he got trapped can't be accessed by any of the existing platforms in the lower concourse, or from outside, and that tunnel's the only one left that connects to Old 32."

"So we need to get to that hole?"

Nunna looked her up and down, shaking her head. "Feel like going back down there?" she asked.

Val shuddered at the thought of returning to the lower halls.

"Neither do I. So, let's go before we change our minds. Nightfall comes in another three hours, but they'll begin scoping us out in less time than that."

She nodded her head in deference to the croaking chorus of roars that had been going on outside.

"Notice how it's gotten a little louder? They do that until it's dark. I guess it's like a countdown for their little game."

"Game?"

Nunna knelt and pulled the heavy crate away from the wall where Val had been sitting, revealing a battered metal door.

"Think of it as blind-man's-bluff, with higher stakes," she said, opening the latch in the door. "Don't worry! I'm a New York girl. This is my town. I'll look after you until we get everything straightened out."

"Aren't you a little scared?" Val asked. Her own eyes were growing wider with fear as the monstrous roars grew louder.

"Don't know where you'd get that idea," Nunna replied, poking her head and shoulders through into the rooms beyond. Turning back once more she said, "Quiet now. The coast is clear, but it won't be for long. Stay in my shadow, and try to minimize your noise—unless you want to find out what happened to Bob."

The room behind the small door was a large water-closet full of flushing toilets in stalls. Val's first impression of such a novelty was that it was not as convenient as its function implied. Even after years of abandonment the place was still filthy, stinking much worse than the outhouses she grew up with. Then again, it had been used by many more people.

"They never were able to track us through here," Nunna said quietly, pausing at an outer door just ahead. "They'll figure out the dumbwaiter, though, when we don't come out of the room we ran to in the main concourse. This whole section of the building will be smashed before they give up the chase. Very cautious beasts, they are, though they have little to fear from you or me."

"Were any of them killed during the fighting?"

"Never managed to bring down a single one of them when I had a gun. The trouble is *seeing* them. It's like the CM7s—they blend in perfectly with their surroundings. Stay sharp now, and follow close."

Holding her breath, Val followed her out of the room and then down a maze of narrow halls choked with burned debris. In time they reached a flight of steps, but these ended abruptly on a wide broken landing standing like a cliff twenty feet above the floor of the main concourse. She marked the statue of Cassatt and the central stair to the lower terminal far off. Orange beams of sunlight slanted through high side windows, but nothing moved upon the green marble floor.

"How do we get down?" Val asked.

Nunna finally seemed to have run out of words. She pointed to their right. There the landing continued the width of the hall, eventually accessing an intact stairway that descended to the main floor below. In between the spot where they stood and this stair, however, there was another wider stair, and this one ascended to a series of tall doors—frowning eyes once paned with glass, now staring out on the desolation in mute witness of its terrors. The only way to the main concourse was to dare the path beneath those horrible doors.

They were like the doors in the Round Room of Auriga.

Walking slowly behind Nunna, Val could not help glancing up to her right, her eyes peering fearfully into the void behind the shattered glass and twisted metal frames. Nothing moved in the darkness, but it seemed an eternity before they reached the far side and descended. When at last they had gained the main floor, she stooped beside Nunna in the shadows of the columns. Terrible fear clouded her mind, the terror of a watchful presence. Neither of them spoke.

It was then they both realized the noisy cries had grown silent.

After a few minutes of patient waiting, Nunna tensed, grabbing her shoulder. Val was poised to run.

"What?" she whispered.

"Hush!" Nunna said in her ear. "Stay close and keep quiet! It might not have seen us yet!"

She set out without explanation, leading Val swiftly towards the center of the room. They walked stooping low, and soon passed half the distance to the steps. Every footfall brought a sharp click and the sound of grinding stone, and the noises echoed wildly. Val couldn't see whatever it was that made Nunna so tense, but she could feel the gloom deepening with every step she took. By the time they reached the low metal rail that rounded the back of the stairwell, they were both very near panic. Their passage slowed to a cautious goose-stepping, until crossing before the lone statue of Cassatt they paused again.

There was someone standing in the near shadows of the colonnade.

Nunna grabbed her shoulder again, tugging her towards the stairhead; but Val was drawn by the figure standing there. It was the shape of a man, and was dressed in what appeared to be a worn-out business suit. It didn't move, but stood and stared at them from the shadows.

Who could it be? Wasn't he aware of his danger?

She pulled free of Nunna's grasp.

"No!" Nunna whispered.

Val was confused. How could they leave this man alone in a dangerous place?

"Not what you think!" Nunna said.

Val allowed herself to be led away, but even as they reached the second step the figure ambled suddenly towards them, raising a noise as it came. Its manner of walking was a little odd, for it waddled quickly from side to side, like a toddler. They paused, and it paused also, leaning forwards as if to catch an elusive scent. Val felt Nunna's hand begin to tremble. Then they heard it speaking.

"*Mhhhhmmm?*" the low voiceless tone rose a little in pitch, then broke off sharply with the sound of a deeply indrawn breath through the nose.

"Don't move!" Nunna whispered.

The figure barked a harsh muffled coughing sound, "*Gesh!*"

Leaning towards them, it emerged from the shadows into the amber evening light. Nunna's hand froze to her arm, hurting her. Val looked on, and she understood at last that this was not a man at all.

"*Geshhhh!*" it said, and then began mumbling and warbling like an empty stomach.

The noises came from no mouth. There was no nose, either. There were no sensory organs or other features on the hairless head at all, save two charcoal colored lumps where the eyes should be and a few broken teeth protruding from the middle. Standing only fifty feet away, it showed signs of confusion, as if it could not exactly place their location.

Yet it knew they were near.

Leaning forwards again, it pointed its head back and forth. There was a bulging and twisting movement behind its slick skin, as if something wanted out, and the monster turned one way and the other every time its face squirmed. Watching it was torture. Val tried to study the rest of its features, and noted that the hands ended in clawed flaps instead of fingers. Its bare feet were stumpy, ending in two toe-like projections. It wore men's clothing, ragged and tousled.

Why?

What was it?

"Watcher!" Nunna whispered.

Then, as if summoned by a call that only it could hear, the monster shuffled quickly off into the shadows where it had been standing before they arrived. Straining to see, Val marked the furtive movements of something much larger gliding stealthily along the wall beyond the columns. The sound of a gurgling intake of breath, so low and gentle, was yet loud enough that they knew it for what it was: a warning growl.

Nunna pulled at her shoulder again, but Val was frozen by the sight of something less frightening than it was surprising. She saw clearly an ordinary man standing nearer the far end of the hall, facing her with a smile on his face. She knew that face.

It was *Nergal.*

"Come on!" Nunna hissed, and with both hands around Val's waist she pulled so hard that they almost tumbled down the steps. Val looked back over her shoulder, but by now she'd lost sight of him.

"What is it with you?" Nunna asked, tugging her away.

Val allowed herself to be led slowly down the steps. Into the upper hall, from every direction, the forms of the evil man-shaped creatures were slowly shuffling. Nergal had vanished.

Was he ever really there?

They descended quickly into the darkness. When they reached the bottom of the steps, Val whispered into Nunna's ear, asking, "What is a *Watcher?*"

"How can you not know about these things?" Nunna replied tersely. "You keep trying stuff like that and we'll both get killed!"

"Please, just tell me!"

But the fear of the warning growl made Nunna uncharacteristically silent. Walking quietly ahead along the barricade, she broke her demure only after several minutes, and only in whispered fragments.

"They're dangerous, but slow. We caught one a long time ago; couldn't figure it out. It escaped and led trouble back our way. That was when we lost most of those who had made it through the first year. The more imaginative among us thought these might be Regulus passengers, crossed over and messed up somehow when the system went bad. Others say they're demons or ghosts. They don't have eyes or ears or noses, but they can find you pretty easily, so we call them Watchers. They congregate in places where the big ones are lurking."

"And what do you call the big ones?"

"What do you think we call them? They're dragons."

They continued in silence after that, slowly and quietly, casting occasional glances backwards towards the steps, but there was no more indication that their passage was marked. They found the exit from the barricade open on their right, and there Nunna paused.

"This is as far as we ever got," she said.

As they looked out into subterranean night, black as pitch, a sudden light burst forth before them. Nunna staggered backwards so quickly she almost fell. Val shielded the light on the shoulder of her chest-plate.

"Sorry," she said. "I should've warned you before turning it on."

"Turn it off!" Nunna gasped.

Val scoped the darkness in the beam's bluish light, and stepped out boldly into the concourse. "It seems pointless to walk in the dark," she said. "Besides, I came through this way, and I wasn't attacked until I reached the upper hall. Maybe whatever's up there is only guarding its territory."

Nunna scurried to her feet and followed after her, crouching a little as the light swept the breadth of the room around them. There was no sign of danger. They walked this way until they had reached the far end of the area where there were doors in the wall. One of these was open, directly ahead.

"That's the one," Val said, pointing to the prints of her boots on the dusty cracked concrete. They both stopped for a closer look, for there were other prints in the dust, prints that followed her out in the direction of the barricade.

They were flat, dragging side to side.

"Could they be *guarding* it?" Val asked, turning slightly.

"Huh?" Nunna wondered, looking behind them.

"These beasts, could they be guarding Regulus? Or has Regulus called them to itself?"

"You keep asking questions that have no answers," Nunna replied. "I have no idea why these things are here. Maybe it has nothing to do with Regulus at all."

"You really believe that?"

Nunna glanced at her. "No," she confessed.

Val stepped through into the passage behind the door. Looking up this hall, she was sure the door at the very end was the one she had come through. It seemed so far—more than a hundred feet.

"That Watcher couldn't see us," Val remarked, "but he knew we were there."

"It'll tell the others. They'll come."

"They talk?"

"I don't know what kind of senses or speech they have. Light and noise attract them."

"Maybe something else, too."

"Maybe blood," Nunna said. "What could they want with us, but to kill us?"

"They kill? How? They looked pretty slow to me."

"They're massively strong, and they show up in droves to trample, claw, and tear. Some have mouths and teeth that can bite. They don't need eyes or ears to find us, I can tell you that."

Val was thinking about the stones she carried within her. She was sure that was it. The creatures were gathering because they sensed the stones.

"I think we'll make it," she said aloud.

"If you're wrong, it won't make much of a difference," Nunna replied.

"That's not like you, Nunna. What happened to *there's no coincidence?*"

"That applies to disasters as well as to good things, you know."

The room was as unremarkable as Val remembered. They stood gazing up through the hole in the ceiling, but Nunna hung back by the door. Val knew what she was thinking. It would be great if they could somehow block the passageway behind them. Then again, what lay ahead was probably worse.

"You have a rope or something?"

Nunna began to fumble her hands about her shoulder. "Use my bandolier," she said. "I haven't got more than a few feet of it, though."

She removed the goggles and gloves, and handed the belt over to Val, who took it hesitantly. She wasn't steady on her legs, and was remembering a fall from the loft of the Morvran barn. Dizziness swept her innards with the ebb and flow of displacement.

"You can stand on my shoulders and squeeze through first," she said to Nunna. "Then tie off that sash on a metal rod and lower it down to me."

"Are you crazy? I'm not going up there first!"

Glancing at her, Val saw that she was very nearly immobilized by fear.

"I can't stand on your shoulders, Nunna. This armor makes me too heavy."

"Then take it off. We *all* had armor once. It made no difference!"

Nunna was hyperventilating. Val empathized with her survivor-mentality. The trouble was, she needed Nunna's help if they were ever going to reach Regulus.

"Okay," she said. "Just calm down. I need you to boost me as soon as I'm ready."

"Right," Nunna replied, eyes bulging as she peered back into the hall.

Turning off her light, Val began to dismantle her suit piece by piece. It took her awhile, for it was the very first time she had ever taken it off. When she was done she stood shivering in a one-piece padded bodysuit almost identical to Nunna's. To Val it was little better than long underwear.

Looking on from the doorway, a hand cupped to one ear to listen, Nunna didn't move at all until Val finally tossed aside the last piece of armor.

"You're making too much noise!" she complained. Turning her head slightly she added, "You'll want to keep those boots. Put 'em back on and we're all set."

Val sat down on the cold cement floor to pull on her boots. They looked so incongruously large on her skinny legs that she smiled, even in spite of their danger, and she remembered the Arctics that Mrs. Morvran had offered to her in some other distant world. The smile faded into a memory of her last words to Taran.

"Hurry!" Nunna said, her whisper returning Val to the present. She reached over and unfastened the light from the cast-off chestplate. It clipped easily onto the neck of her jumpsuit, and could be rotated about eighty degrees in any direction. She turned it first towards the heap of cast-off armor. For a moment she pondered the possibility of flinging the stuff up through the crack in the ceiling; but when she pointed the beam upwards, she realized it was impossible. The opening was too narrow. She had to leave it all behind.

All but one thing: the knife.

She couldn't really have forgotten it, for it had become a constant weight on her leg. She tightened it firmly in the sheath fixed to her thigh, where it had been the whole time since she left the substations. She didn't imagine it would be of much use, but she certainly wouldn't leave it here.

Nunna glanced aside, and seeing the knife she looked up into Val's eyes.

"Not of much use, I know," she remarked. "I'm ready to go."

"It's about time."

Nunna came and knelt beside her. Val took the bandolier and looped it over her right shoulder.

"Get ready," Nunna said, snugging her gloves and pulling the goggles down over her eyes.

Val set one foot gently on her left shoulder. Nunna settled her arms against the floor and gave the count.

"On my mark. One, two, *three!*"

Nunna stood, bearing her weight with only a slight grunt, and Val lifted her right foot up to the girl's other shoulder while reaching upwards with both arms. She was able to grasp one of the stout rods that hung from the hole like rungs, and lifting her slight weight gently—she had been a first-rate tree climber—she thrust out her hand to the next visible rod, lifting her feet from Nunna's shoulders as she did.

The hole was quite a bit deeper than she imagined, though. With her back braced against the jagged concrete and her feet on twisted metal to either side, she looked down. Nunna looked up, her jaw set and teeth clenched. Val was about to ask if she was alright when she heard the sound they both had been dreading. There were footsteps in the passage, many footsteps, and the soft muffled noises of Watchers.

"Don't leave me!" Nunna said, raising her hands to Val.

Val shifted herself until she was able to reach her arms down through the hole, but the distance was just too far. The bandolier slid from her shoulder, but she caught it in her hands just as Nunna took the other end in hers and wrapped a short length around her knuckles. It was then they heard a crash above the noise of many shuffling feet. Something was battering the narrow doorway to the hall from the lower concourse. A sharp gurgling roar vibrated the walls.

"Hang on!" Val shouted.

Regaining some of her bantering manner, Nunna yelled back, "What else do you think I was going to do, Stupid? Just pull me up!"

Val pulled hard. Nunna was off the floor, but her fingers only brushed the edge of the hole. Val tugged harder, fighting sickness and a ringing sound in her ears. She closed her eyes, straining in desperation, and doubled forwards until her top half was almost out the hole.

Then she paused.

The room had gone silent. The creak of the cloth belt was the only sound they could hear. Val opened her eyes, and Nunna stared down at what was happening below her feet. In the pool of light cast by Val's headlamp, they saw that the room was full of Watchers. All stood sheepishly huddled, looking around with sightless eyes, making no noise. A smell of sulfur rose from them like a choking cloud. The bandolier creaked again, and several of the monsters shuffled madly. Nunna began to slip.

"Nunna," Val said calmly. "I'm going to pull, but you're going to have to let go one hand and grab hold of something."

Nunna looked up into the light, her face framed in long blue locks, her eyes glimmering with fire behind the lenses of her goggles.

"Pull!" she cried.

With one last desperate effort, Val pulled upwards with a shout. Nunna gained a handhold, and Val yanked her up so that they were squeezed face-to face in the hole. At the very same instant the room below erupted with a crash and a roar. Everything below was a whirlwind of smashing and breaking.

Whatever had come, it was pulverizing the Watchers with wild abandon.

There was no time for thought. Gathering herself, Nunna squirmed around until she was climbing the uneven surface just behind Val. The concrete fissure rocked and bucked with the force of an explosion, threatening collapse. Hearts racing, they climbed, and no sooner had they flopped out into a dark tunnel than the hole spouted flames behind them, melting the soles of their boots as they scrambled backwards. More flames followed, dissipating slowly, flickering on the gravelly pavement around the perimeter of the hole. They crawled just a little farther and lay down side by side between metal rails.

"Holy Saint George!" Nunna huffed, panting.

Val trained her light on the edge of the hole. "Whatever that thing is," she said, "it's not giving up."

She pointed, and dimly in the smoke they saw a clawed appendage reaching up through the opening. It looked like a two-fingered hand at first, though it might have been a tail. The flesh was ruddy and scaled, and the claws looked like they might have been made of metal. Smacking down on the concrete only a few feet away, the talons scraped around blindly. Val and Nunna lay back and watched, frozen with wonder and terror at the sight.

"You've seen this thing before?" Val asked.

Nunna shook her head, a little breathless still.

"Let's get back a bit."

They scuttled backwards on hands and feet. The tail slapped the floor of the tunnel for another few moments, and then lunged with sudden ferocity. They rolled to either side just as it slashed the ground between them, scattering fragments of rock as it thrashed about, searching. Then, even as they rose and made their way to the far wall, it retreated, striking sparks from the steel rods as it was quickly withdrawn through the hole.

Then the floor of the tunnel thudded.

"It's trying to break through," Val said. "You think he can break through ten feet of concrete?"

A hellish cry rose through the pit. With a mighty thump, the floor cracked. Val traced a long fissure that spread quickly, reaching up both sides of the tunnel. Dust trickled down around them, and a horrible sound of snarling, like an enormous lion, erupted up from the depths along with another spouting flame.

"You've not seen what they did to the city," Nunna remarked quietly, slipping her goggles up to her forehead. "He'll be through that in no time. You know where you're going from here?"

"I told you, I only remember waking up at the bottom of that hole."

More bumping from below, and the cracks widened. They stood, knees bent and ready to run, but something held them. Val felt as though she had lost the desire to move, and the longer they stayed in one place, the worse it became. From the darkness to her right there came subtle noises. Val turned, and in so doing brought the beam of light into a new passage, and new fears.

The forms of several Watchers appeared, standing only about a hundred feet away. More arrived as the seconds passed, and soon there were hundreds standing just on the edge of Val's light. The Watchers were definitely alerted to the noisy intrusion, but none were moving closer.

"How far away are we from that tunnel—the tunnel that connects to 32nd Street?" Val asked.

The creature in the room below roared again, and they brought up their hands in an involuntary gesture, covering their ears.

"I have no idea. It should be to our right, no more than a thousand feet."

Val set out at a run, straight into the crowd of Watchers.

"Wait!" Nunna shouted, sprinting up behind her. "The knife!"

Val hadn't even thought of using the blade, but unsheathed it anyway because its weight on her leg made it difficult to run. In her hand it felt no lighter. She hadn't even registered a plan with her body as to what she was going to do when she plunged into the mass of hideous creatures. It hardly mattered, for even as they closed the last fifty feet to the waiting Watchers she could hear the sounds of a collapse behind them and a bellowing shriek. Then, like the subway cars that had clattered along this tunnel for long years before its arrival, the monster screamed as it rose up into the tunnel, howling a ghastly shearing noise.

Whatever the Watchers thought of all this, they certainly took enough interest in self-preservation to shuffle out of the way, parting before their charge like the receding waters of a tide.

Running along the tunnel, for awhile they saw nothing more than railroad ties and the backs of fleeing Watchers. They arrived at the platform, just ahead on the left. Stairs descended at one end. Nunna helped her as she struggled to climb up out of the railway, and they ran together for the steps as the Watchers continued their journey farther down the tunnel.

They leapt down the stairway to a junction passage, long and dark. Pressing their backs against the far wall for a moment to breath, they both looked up towards the platform. Nothing followed. The air in this new passage was still, though charged with a warning fear.

Val sheathed her blade. "What is this place?" she asked, directing her light up and down the hall.

"We're close! Old 32 is nearby. Just follow the signs."

Nunna pointed to a green sign set into the wall behind them.

"32ⁿᵈ Street," Val read. "To the left, then; but what's this passage to the right? Couldn't we have gotten here from the lower concourse?"

"That way's sealed from the other side," Nunna said, moving on at a slow jog. "That's what trapped Bob down here. Funny, if he hadn't been trapped—hadn't blown that hole in the tunnel—we never would've met here."

Val jogged beside her, noting the stern set of her jaw. The fire was back in her eyes.

They followed the passage, gritty stone and glass crunching loudly underfoot. This corridor was very narrow, less than ten feet wide, and they doubted the monster could gain entry.

That didn't exclude the possibility that it would simply burst through some other tunnel and head them off.

Something slid suddenly out of the path of the light before them, several curious somethings—creatures like large segmented insects. Val recalled seeing these things before. She'd seen them aboard Auriga, when Kabta discovered that Magan had taken the Gremn-stone that powered the ship. It seemed he thought they were somehow significant. What had he called them? It began with an *M*. She couldn't remember. If most of the knowledge she had gained by the black water was gone, her own recent memories were also fading fast. Was this, too, a result of displacement?

"Down here," Nunna said, turning down a side-passage ahead of her.

It was another stair, but this one went to a lower tunnel. Val followed, peering ahead in the light of her beam. There wasn't anything to see but a platform below. Reaching it, they looked around a bit before climbing down onto the tracks. They hadn't heard anything from their pursuer since they'd left the previous tunnel, but its dread still hung heavily on them, slowing them to caution.

"The tunnels aren't connected," Nunna said, catching Val's backwards glances. "The one we were in is a level above this. He's probably hunting around the platform back there—lost our scent, I'd guess."

"I hope you're right."

"It does seem too easy. Just don't get distracted, and keep your ears open."

Nunna led her to the left, and the tunnel sloped gently downward into the dark. They hadn't gone more than half a mile before they ran into a stopped subway car. It looked very different from the drawings Dr. Morvran once showed her. Her curiosity piqued a little—not least because of the obvious puzzle this car represented.

"Through here," Nunna said, pulling herself up onto a kind of back step. There was a door in the rear of the car, and she tugged it open. No sooner had she done so than she tumbled off the step and scooted backwards, waving her hands in the air. A fluttering of bats echoed around them for a few seconds, chattering noisily as Nunna laughed.

Far behind them, a dull crash echoed through the tunnel.

They both turned their heads, but heard nothing else. Nunna hastily climbed back onto the step, and Val followed.

Shining her light inside the car, Val saw scattered bones in a wreckage of seats and metal bars. Sniffing the air in an experimental way, she was surprised to note nothing more unpleasant than a smell of mildew.

"There are no signs of fire," Nunna observed. "I wonder how these died."

"Well, come on," Val said, stumbling forwards. "Whatever did this is long gone, or we'd know about it by now."

They headed quickly for the forward exit. A few sprawling skeletal forms made morbid hurdles, one blocking the aisle completely so that they had to climb over a mound of mummified flesh and clothing. The man's face was well-preserved. He looked calm, eyes staring ahead as if he was just taking a nap on the floor.

"Maybe it was a gas leak or something," Nunna suggested as they stepped through the exit. "It happened fast, whatever it was."

Val said nothing, and avoided looking at the bodies as they neared the exit. The broken doors on the port side of the car were open, but too close to the wall of the tunnel, so they climbed out the smashed forward portal and stepped down onto the tracks. There was a platform about a hundred feet away. It was unlike anything Val had ever seen.

Since the dreadful day Regulus had brought these horrors into the heart of the stones, no one had yet returned to the platform that bore its name. It was nearly immaculate, even cozy. Before she could bring herself to explore its wonders, though, Val turned back to the puzzle of the tube-car.

"Those monsters," she said, looking at the stopped car. "They couldn't have all come through these tunnels. Where did they enter this world?"

Nunna shook her head, dazed by the sight of new paint ahead, by the gaudy signs announcing special rates for transfers. There was music playing softly from a storefront situated in the rear of the platform. The items on display didn't even look dusty.

"I wasn't here when it happened," Nunna said.

"Were you ever here?" Val asked, turning off her light.

"No. I was in the HSA office on the main concourse when the lights went out, trying to find out how I could bypass our own security to accomplish my mission. Blast DePons! He could've done it himself, and we could've gotten him out afterwards; but he decided to try and save face instead by sending in a team to steal the stone back from the government."

"Looks like Regulus took matters into its own hands."

"You mean it brought all these monsters?"

"Well?"

"Maybe. When the trains stopped in almost all the tubes, I knew it had nothing to do with a power outage. The cars are independently powered."

"So they were in the tunnels first."

"Yeah; but you're right. They couldn't have gotten everywhere in the world through one tube-car and tunnel. You know, at the time all this was happening, I volunteered my team to come down here, thinking this was my only chance to get to Regulus. On my way through the main concourse we met a crush of people head-on. They weren't upset about the power outage—people were screaming and making no sense at all."

They continued walking towards the platform as she spoke.

"When people in the streets outside asked what was going on, we told them it was a suspected terrorist attack. Nothing from these tunnels ever passed through the lower concourse on its way to the surface, but within the hour Martial Law was declared throughout the city. Days later, we lost contact with the outside world."

"The stone brought them, and deposited them where it would."

"That theory doesn't seem a little strange to you? It's an inanimate object, Val. It can't think or make decisions."

Val felt suddenly queasy. Standing in the train tunnel and talking about the stone wasn't getting them any closer to it. She could feel their danger increasing like the approach of a train along the tracks.

"You've never seen it before," Val said, heading for the platform. "When you do, maybe you'll understand."

"Or maybe I won't."

Val kept walking, and Nunna followed her, lolling a bit. While they walked, Val slowly wrestled with her own suggestion that this stone had intentionally and strategically attacked its keepers.

What *was* Regulus?

"Too bad you got locked up," Nunna said, interrupting her thoughts. "I always knew you weren't crazy."

"What would have changed if I wasn't detained in this world?" Val asked.

"Well, you and Shubalu could have gone on that op to take Regulus through the Mirror and find the other stones. Then this whole mess would never have happened."

"Really?" Val wondered. "But the worlds weren't aligned. Kabta said we have to wait for them to come to us instead."

Nunna was quiet. Val wondered if she had finally figuring out that she was bluffing.

"There's electric power here," Nunna noted, suddenly pointing to the lights.

"Yes."

"The stones double as power sources, right? We'll find Regulus here somewhere, and then we'll see what we can do."

"We'll find it somewhere, indeed," Val thought. Looking up at the platform, she scoped a marketplace hundreds of feet wide, and very long, with dozens of brightly lit shops. In the near

distance there was a kind of plaza where benches were arranged around two slowly rotating fountains. Between the dancing columns of water they saw moving stairs going up and down in perpetual motion. Nothing else moved in the terminal, and there were no bodies laying about as there were in the train car. Classical music played softly from speakers recessed in the storefronts, and the sound of splashing water came to them on a sweet air scrubbed by ventilators.

It was eerie, and the feeling of approaching danger only intensified.

Nunna stepped ahead of her and reached the edge of the platform first. She pulled herself up, and surveying the terminal she said, "Where to begin looking is the question. Let's take those escalators. If there's an upper level, we'll find the offices there."

She paused to wait for Val. When they stood side by side on the platform, Val cringed and looked back over her shoulder towards the dark train car in the tunnel.

"Did you hear something?" Nunna asked, suddenly alert.

"No. I have a terrible headache, is all."

"You don't look so good, now that I can see you. Your eyes are all dark, and your skin's pale. Have you eaten anything at all in the past twenty-four hours?"

"No," she confessed.

"Well, this is a place to find food—lots of imperishables, I bet. As soon as we yank the stone free of DePons' device, we'll come back here and make a feast."

She eyed the storefronts with eager eyes. Val took a moment to follow her gaze, and was awed by the oddments of a world she knew was far in the future of her own. Though she was very hungry, she also knew there was no point in making plans beyond the capture of the stone.

"Didn't you say those monsters hoarded foodstuff in order to lure and trap the unwary?" she asked.

"Come on," Nunna called. "Trust me a little! This place is untouched."

She hadn't taken two steps before stopping in her tracks. Turning back, she saw Val looking into the train tunnel again.

"This time I did hear something," Val muttered.

"So did I."

They waited a little while, listening to a sound of scraping. The tube-car jostled, and then was lost to sight. Something black obscured the tunnel, a sliding shapeless fear that wrapped darkness around itself.

They ran.

The escalators drew nearer, but there was no noise yet of pursuit. Glancing back, they saw the lights on the edge of the platform flicker and go out. The music was silenced.

"It's very presence has an effect on the power of the stone," Val thought.

This wasn't good.

They reached the mechanical Jacob's-ladder even as the platform lights died around them, and then the moving steps rolled to a stop. They jogged quickly up. Val heard a sliding scrape in the darkness, and hurried her pace. Though it must have spotted them by now, the monster made no challenge, allowing them to reach the upper room safely.

Nunna paused at the top, her eyes whirling this way and that around a huge round chamber with tall arches spaced every fifty feet or so along its sides. Under each arch there was a great wooden door. The doors were all flanked by flashy booths advertising prices for transits.

"$120,000.00?" Val wondered quietly, reading from a posted sign featuring transit to, of all places, Siberia.

The value of traveling anyplace, anywhere, in the blink of an eye, was obviously quite high. Regulus Transit was all about greed. The evidence was in the opulence all around them. Every surface gleamed as if it was polished only yesterday. The floor was marble. A mighty crystal chandelier lit the room with regal elegance.

No sooner had they gotten a good look at the place than the chandelier went dark.

Nunna grasped Val's hand and pulled her away from the top of the escalator.

"Why is it not attacking?" Val wondered quietly as they approached the far wall.

"It has us trapped," Nunna replied. "They don't always take us the way it tried to take you in the main concourse. Sometimes people just disappear."

"Let's disappear, then. Try one of these doors."

"If it can squeeze through that train car, it can fit through a door!"

Val had to see what was behind the arched doors, though, and as they were near one she pushed lightly. A loud snap sounded in her ears, and the chamber within was revealed in a ghostly glow of red lights surrounding a complicated cone-shaped device in the center—an arrangement hauntingly similar to the Learning Station aboard Auriga, she thought. Arranged in concentric circles around this central cone were rows of seats.

"Looks like a planetarium," Nunna whispered. "I've never seen inside a transit room."

"It's too big a place to hide," Val said, nudging her away. "Let's look for a smaller door."

The air around them was suddenly warm. They stepped beside the archway, backs flat to the wall, and peered into the inky darkness around them. There were no sounds of scraping or sliding—no noises at all.

"He could be nearby," Nunna said in a very low whisper. "Stand still."

"They don't need to see or hear us to find us. Something else is drawing them after me."

The two listened for a telltale sound, trembling hand in hand in what had become a dragon's lair. Val's mind suddenly retrieved an errant memory, an unwelcome but vivid remnant of her childhood dream-world. She remembered this fear of the red dragon. She knew it well enough to give it a name.

"*Glede,*" she said.

341

Though spoken nearly at a whisper, the name trembled in the air around them. The effect was electrifying. Her right arm burned with icy fire. Val felt them awakening within her flesh. Would the other stones help her to locate Regulus? Would they preserve her from this creature, a fairy-tale dragon?

Val's hand gripped Nunna's tighter, and her free hand brushed the heavy scabbard strapped to her thigh. Fighting was no use. She felt the handle of the long Mesopotamian blade and remembered something else—something spoken to her by the creature named Brisen, the woman in white.

"You safeguard the past and future of all our worlds by what you protect. If you perish, then the stone's purpose shall never be fulfilled."

She thought of the transmission Kabta had shown her, and marveled how everything fit together just so, as if according to a Greater Purpose. Surely she was meant to survive this?

"It is a perilous road, and a difficult choice. It is the Lost Road, where all of you are joined in purpose. Even while you are apart, you are still trapped within the destiny of the stone. You dream its dreams, as you have always done."

"I know where to go," Val said suddenly.

"You do?" Nunna asked.

"It's like a dream. I see a red panel in the wall away there, on the other side of the room. I remember it somehow. I know that Regulus is at the end of a hall on the other side of that door."

"I don't see it," Nunna said.

Val lifted the hand that held Nunna's, pointing. Just as she did, the light of the panel flickered, then resumed, and then flickered again.

"It's already there. Now what do we do?"

"It beckons," Val replied, clenching a fist to her chest.

"Beckons?"

"I think it means to speak to us."

"I take back what I said back there in the tunnel," Nunna said. "You *are* crazy!"

They crept silently around the room. No matter how quiet they were, Val knew they were observed. They reached the panel without incident, but the room's lights were still out, and that was enough to tell them they weren't alone.

Val found the edges of a door beside the panel, and trying the handle she discovered what she already had guessed. It was locked tight. The red glowing interface offered no clue as to how to gain entry, but Val knew she only had to touch it and the door would open. She knew this because the stones were guiding her, leading her to Regulus.

She paused, responding to some other force. From beside her, a familiar voice spoke in the darkness.

"You know his name?" it asked.

On the other side of her, Nunna asked, "Who's there?"

"You called him by name," the voice replied. "Isn't that odd?"

It was a man's voice, heavily accented. It was a voice she knew, but which had never spoken English before in her hearing. After a few more moments, a figure dressed in something like a medieval costume stepped into the dim red light of the panel, and Val had the answer.

"Nergal!"

"Val Anna," he replied, staring back at her. "You left us upstairs. Sorry if we frightened you."

"Us?"

"*Us, yes,*" another voice said.

This was a voice deep and bold; and if it was a bit hoarse and wispy, it wasn't all unfriendly. The tone did not mitigate its other qualities, however. Val felt Nunna's hand squeezing hers in a spasm of terror, and she shared some of that fear herself, knowing what it was that made the voice. Her mind denied her the credit of that knowledge, because it came from the deep memory of her dreams.

The horned and scaled side of a massive arm passed noiselessly by in the gloom, and then an enormous eye appeared not far from her own, an eye that glowed softly with a sick greenish light.

Trying not to sound breathless, Val asked, "What are you?"

"Glede is the name you called, and Glede I am, Val Anna Naruna."

Val and Nunna held their backs to the door now, looking at a beaked maw on a head that was much larger than a horses'. Just beside the head, Nergal's small form stood fearlessly in the dark. However brave she tried to appear, Val was trembling.

"How do you know me?" she asked.

"You and I have met before."

He was right. They *had* met before, in a forest.

"But that was only in a dream," she whispered.

The face withdrew into the shadows. The eye disappeared.

"We chased you because we wanted to help you," Nergal said to her. "Those Watchers would have flattened you if we hadn't shown up."

The dragon's gurgling breath echoed in the deeper darkness of the room.

"You aren't here because you were displaced?" she asked.

"We came because he's going to help me stop you from making the same mistake twice. We're here to save you, Val."

"Save me from what?"

"Don't listen to them!" Nunna whispered into her ear.

Her voice was cut off abruptly by a loud growl that shook the floor.

"And who is this?" the dragon asked. *"Nunna, she called you on the platform below. It seems I have read that name in a stone in the grass near the boundary of my realm. Well met, Nunna!"*

"Don't worry," Nergal said, stepping closer to Val. "Just go and claim the stone. We'll take care of the rest."

"You want us to take it?"

"You must take Regulus away from this place. Take it to the World of Origins, where you were heading before you came to this Dark World. Take it there and use it to stop the Council from making war."

"How do you know about the World of Origins?"

"What's that?" Nunna asked.

"We just came from there," Nergal said. "We will return there when you recohere the stones."

"It's another place, Nunna," Val answered aside. "This world is inside the stones. We can go anywhere inside the stones."

"*You* have them? Here? *You're* the one who got Kabta's message!"

"The stones will travel through her to a place called Gilthaloneth," Nergal explained. "You may go there with her, Nunna, if you wish."

His eyes rested on her in a familiar way. Nunna grimaced.

"And what then?" Val asked, leaning closer to him. "If you go back with these dragons in tow, you will bring death to all in the World of Origins!"

"When you leave," Nergal said, "all that was displaced here will be sorted out. There is no choice, Val Anna. We will be going to the World of Origins with you. You'll need our help with the Council."

"To do what?"

"To stop the war. We've already arranged it. Glede will take his people to a faraway place when our work with the Council is done."

"How likely is that?" Val asked. "It's more likely that the factions will unite to fight you! The war will be reignited, and you'll be destroyed!"

"*A fine threat!*" Glede's voice thundered. "*A fine threat, but hardly the thing a warrior should say after taking off her armor!*"

"I don't need your help!" Val shouted.

"*I recall Taran Morvran said the same thing.*"

A grim silence filled the darkness where they stood.

"*Ah,*" the dragon said, its voice deepening to a gurgling sigh. "*Don't you wonder how I know of your companion?*"

"No," Val said, turning abruptly to the lighted panel.

"*It was in the colony of Nara. I saw him there, and offered to help him. Don't you want to know how he came to be there?*"

"No," she repeated.

"*Fleeing those who believed him to be responsible for your disappearance, he was captured. You have brought him many sorrows.*"

"No!"

Reaching her hand violently towards the panel, Val held back her anger a moment and glanced upwards. The memory of ceiling-mounted artillery resurfaced, but she saw no indication of hidden guns.

"Too bad," she said to herself. "They might have made this meeting more interesting."

She slapped the panel hard, and the door slid open. Lights turned on in the narrow corridor beyond, and at the very end there was a small chamber—a room flooded with white light.

Nergal said, "I'll see you again, Val Anna."

Val stepped into the hall, but paused briefly, pulled back by the power of the dragon's will. Turning to peer over her shoulder, she saw in the dark behind them a pair of green eyes glaring, lit by a light of their own. The air grew still, and so silent that she felt afresh the terror of the beast.

Glede said, *"What stone is the Stone of Foundation? Find it, and the factions will find an end to their quarrel."*

The dragon's eyes blinked once, and were extinguished. Nergal bowed stiffly before turning and walking away into the darkness.

"Are they gone?" Nunna asked, walking beside her. "What do we do now?"

Val clenched her fists. "We get the stone like we planned," she said.

Nunna noted her dark mood with a sideways glance. "Who's this guy Taran?" she asked.

"He's someone I hurt very badly."

"Just because you disappeared? I hardly think that counts as hurting someone."

"I've caused everyone sorrow," Val replied, hanging her head. "It's because of my previous transit that Regulus awakened and turned against you."

"If you hadn't come here with the other stones, maybe none of this would have happened. But I think it would have. Besides, you were cleared for the door lock."

Val turned questioning eyes on her.

"You were cleared for the door lock because of the Val Anna who was already here. That wasn't just a coincidence. If you think about it, nothing you've done is coincidental. You showed up and saved my hide in an impossible way. I would have died here if you hadn't come. Even if a lot of other people died, your arrival here saved at least one, and I'm grateful."

"I guess I am, too," Val replied. In truth she wasn't very encouraged, for even if this Nunna lived, somewhere else Nunna had died.

"There is a destiny in the stones," she said. "Despite this, we have to make choices about what to do with them. Some choices were really bad, like when DePons decided to use Regulus as a transit system. What I've learned here is that all choices have consequences."

"So you think all this was somehow caused by a choice you made?" Nunna asked. "It's like a nuclear war out there!"

Val raised her eyes to the bright room ahead. "Wherever I go, people get hurt," she said. "That's why I can never go home."

They entered a room so radiant with white light that both of them stopped to cover their eyes. The air was fresh, filled with a sound like tinkling bells and a strain of far-off music. The horrible fear of Glede began to lift from them in that music; but Val was sullen. She allowed the pause to think about the dragon's words.

"It seems I have read that name in a stone in the grass near the boundary of my realm."

"That's it?" Nunna asked, pointing.

They faced a ceiling-mounted needle surrounded by a ring of consoles on railings. The blue-black molten thing drifting in the air below the projecting needle was clearly not what Nunna expected.

"If the light inside you is darkness, how deep is that darkness," Val said.

"What's that about?" Nunna asked.

"Regulus dreams, even as I have dreamed," she replied. "Its dreams are deadly to us, and have filled this dark world with terror. It was divided from its pair, and wounded deeply. I wonder if its anger can be extinguished."

They stared at Regulus' gently undulating form. A small static discharge sparked upwards along its surface. Val reached out her hand as she had done with the panel. She experienced a mild shock from the field that suspended the stone, and then, for a few seconds, a crystal disk lay in the palm of her hand, gleaming and vibrating a faint ringing tone. The two stood shoulder to shoulder, mute with wonder, listening to the music of Regulus and marveling at the delicately etched lines in its glassy surface. Looping curves and radii they saw there, tracing impossibly complex patterns with infinite connections; and in its heart glimmered a tiny galaxy of stars.

Then came the pain, an alarm, and a blazing light.

The sensation of burning in her arm was so intense that she cried out, but this time it lasted only a tiny fraction of the time she'd experienced it aboard Avalon. The noise was far more painful—a metallic honking blast that repeated once every few seconds. Then the lights went out. A blank wall of darkness sat around her, brooding deep in the dreams of the stone. A voice buzzed in her ear, but it was impossible to hear anything over the alarm.

They were already in transit.

There was no ghostly sensation of floating or falling, yet Val knew they were no longer in the transit station. Deep darkness leaned over her from every direction. It was impalpable, impenetrable, and utterly lonely, until she heard a sound—a chugging noise like pistons in a large engine. This was accompanied by a regular metallic creaking. The ground moved gently, swaying side to side, up and down. It was like a ship.

Then there was a break in the wall of darkness, and looking down she saw a light that came from her hands, one of which rested in the grasp of a stranger. While she looked on, a brilliant blue flame wreathed her fingers, leaping across the hand of the hidden figure before her. The fire was only mildly painful to Val, but the hand that held hers gripped reflexively in spasms of agony. The light flared brighter, revealing more.

She was face to face with Taran Morvran.

Taran looked at her with the same incredulity that she felt. Immediately she felt herself slipping away from him, and she panicked. Focusing her mind on him, she was aware of the presence of another mind, a Gremn mind, but she could see no one else. There was only herself and Taran, and Regulus; and whereas before she felt only an echo of Regulus' song inside her, now that song bloomed entire. Whatever had happened, she knew that Taran had given her something in their brief moment together. It was like their moment in the loft of the barn. Something powerful had passed from him into her by their touch. All this she realized without any kind of complicated logic. It was as if the stone revealed it to her, as indeed it had.

The darkness was returning, and Taran was fading; but she knew it was really herself who disappeared, leaving him again.

This was a place inside of Regulus.

Regulus was inside of her, yet she was inside the stones.

Taran was there, too, but Regulus was leaving him. The pain of parting was great. He opened his mouth in torment as if to scream. Val's heart was crushed, longing to take away his pain. All she could do was place her free hand over his mouth. Then, gazing into his eyes, she spoke words that came to her from the heart of the stones.

"Three are one now. Please, find me!"

Then, staggering backwards, she fell.

Balmy gusts of air touched her face. The air was different, and all was very quiet, for Regulus' song had ended. Val opened her eyes to see Nunna looking down at her, and then they were both aware of another change. They were in a place far grander than Regulus Station. It was so big, in fact, that it was more like being outside than inside. Grass was beneath her, and small star-shaped flowers nodded around the place where she lay. Val gazed up at a structure, vast and rather open at the sides, being dome-shaped with supporting bastions and columns arranged in a circular pattern around a huge grassy plain.

"Where are we?" Nunna asked. "Is it a mountaintop?"

Val pushed herself up onto her elbows. Before them, in the center of the field, there was a low pedestal beside a strange stone seat. The dome above was all of white alabaster, thousands of feet high, and a sound of distant bells floated in the air. Clouds drifted on the edges of the field. Squinting her eyes against a rising light on the horizon, she understood that the transit she initiated in Avalon was only now being completed.

This was Gilthaloneth.

Then the nausea struck, much worse than before. Val held her head as dizziness gripped her body, a sickness with such gravity that it forced her to lay back on the grass. Nunna moved to kneel beside her, but the girl's attention was fixed on something that stood at a little distance from them. A shadowy figure was moving their way.

"A Watcher?" Nunna wondered. She knelt beside Val as the shadow strode forth to meet them. Before she lost consciousness, Val opened blurred eyes once more to see a man on a horse, and faintly her ears heard a deep and kindly voice calling her name.

"Val Anna!" it exclaimed. "You return to us in the hour of our need!"

"Who are you?" she muttered.

"It is Orlim. Your return was long awaited, my Lady!"

"Lady?" Val said softly to herself, her sight and other senses fleeting before a wind out of some forgotten place. Memories from her dream world came to visit her. She saw a familiar face.

"Nergal again?" she wondered. "He's already in the Colonies?"

Then she slept.

22
BOOK OF INVASIONS

A strong cross-breeze struck the wings, rocking the flyer violently on its wheeled sled. If this kept up much longer, Taran wouldn't be flying today. His stomach was in knots. Every minute that passed cost him fuel. As the clock inched closer to an abort, he tried to stay sharp.

The moment came. The gusts receded to a steady breeze—gentle, but still unpredictable. Poised for action, he moved by instinct. In his right hand he'd been gripping a wing-warping control staff; his left he now raised to wave to Val in the loft. He couldn't see her past the upper wing, but she must've gotten the signal because the flyer lurched forwards along the rails. In seconds he was fifty feet off the ground. The catapult cable unwound evenly, and already he could see the tops of the trees.

That's when everything started to go wrong.

A mighty gust knocked him sideways, so hard the flyer almost inverted. The heavy cable was pulling well enough, but its weight and the angle of the aircraft were working against one another. He was like a box-kite, sliding sideways out of the sky. He was heading right for the tree line.

With only moments left to save himself, Taran released the tow and pulled hard on the right-hand control staff. The cable slithered away to the ground below, and his thrust was cut so sharply that the flyer became a parachute. If he was lucky, he might nose into the breeze on the left-turn, enough maybe to lift its front end and ease him up over the trees. It was not to be. Gusting only moments ago, the wind now betrayed him, holding its breath as he held his own. It was at this crucial moment that the engine sputtered to a halt. He was out of petrol.

Clinging to the control staffs, Taran stared helplessly at a tangle of branches straight ahead. In that moment, time seemed to stop. He could see every detail of the forest canopy; every leaf stood out sharply, as if he was looking at a photograph. When the right wingtip struck a branch, though, the entire machine swung around and broke up with incredible ferocity, its thin wooden limbs splintering like glass. The restraints snapped, and Taran was granted a brief and terrifying free-flight of his own. Flung end-over-end, a glorious sensation filled him, and sunlight dappled by the trees swirled around him. He swam briefly in the light before falling to the stony ground.

In a tangle of thorny raspberries he lay, and there was nothing more but pain, pain like a vice gripping every bone in his body. He could not move, but lay still, listening to his own labored breathing. At first there was no other sound to hear but his breath and the wind, but slowly he became aware of a steady rumbling and rattling. Fear gripped him. He commanded his arms to grip the earth and pull him back towards the field, back to the barn and to Val; but his body was broken. With his last strength, he lifted his eyes to rest upon a narrow splintered piece of the fuselage laying nearby. It was a fragment of the runner that supported the canard, painted white, which bore in golden letters a name written by his own hand.

Val Anna.

The rattling noise increased. A rocking motion aroused him, and he awoke.

"Welcome back," Hest said, gazing down into his face.

They were still in the carriage. Taran sat up quickly, embarrassed that he'd been leaning against her while he nodded off.

"Still fevered?" she asked in a sharp tone.

"Yeah."

"You will recover."

He didn't bother asking how *she* felt. Hest looked like nothing fazed her. His own memory of the voyage was somewhat muddled now. He still suspected Hest of drugging him in the engine room, and the effects of the experience hadn't yet worn off. Rubbing his stubbly face, he listened to another gust of the island's strong winds rattling the cab. It was a chill air for the end of summer. The sun shining through the heavy curtains of the carriage was dimmed by the shadows of trees that danced and waved.

"Are we almost there?" he asked.

Hest stared forward. Seated across from them, Colonel Albert Naruna nodded silently.

"Good," Taran replied. "I could eat a horse."

"The Morvran estate has a richer larder than that," Naruna growled, folding his arms. "Just you remember why you're here."

"I'm here to discover what's happened to Val—as if that's any different than the reason I was coming here in the first place."

"There is a difference," the colonel said. "There's the matter we discussed."

"What if I don't find the things you asked for?"

"I thought you wanted to help your father."

Hest continued to stare ahead into the dim interior of the carriage, as much a help in his hour of need as a bit of luggage. The coach lumbered across a rut. Taran bumped his head on the low interior as the driver plowed ahead through the fen, jostling them all in a back and forth motion—a movement that was making him sick. He hadn't gotten his land-legs yet.

"This road was forged by deer or something?"

Naruna lifted the curtain a little and peered out the window. "That's the stream. We've arrived."

"Master Morvran!" the driver called from his perch.

"I am still here!" Taran grunted.

"We're coming to the place. Just 'round this hill and up through the wood."

Taran parted the curtains on the carriage door, and he gazed out at a strange new country of shabby wooded hills and misty moors. The island was not very large, but from here it seemed boundless. There was no sign of any town or village. In fact, all other habitation was limited to the sad patch of hovels by the quays where they'd landed.

"What's this island called, again?" he asked.

"It is known locally as *Aenfer*," Naruna said, "the Lone Island."

"Sounds charming."

The scent of pines drifted in through the window, and the songs of birds. Taran pulled the curtain away a little more as the road wound along a rocky ledge overlooking a deep comb of wooded hinterlands. On his left, an earth bank climbed into a wilderness of pines and thick undergrowth. Taran stuck his whole head out of the window for a better look, and his eyes started at a wonder.

The castle lay directly ahead, sprawling atop a mound of green grass, a position that commanded a view of the surrounding wood and the moor in the valley below. It was not like the illustrations he had seen of German castles, built in tiers with lofty buttressed spires. Instead, he looked on a series of squat and blocky square turrets caged by massive walls, a fortress established for lasting strength. Frowning at the top of the hill, the cluster of grey and dun stone buildings was truly a beast of a house—both magnificent and terribly forbidding.

The embankment to their left gradually leveled out, at which point the road veered sharply towards the foot of a wide green terrace running to the fort's cyclopean foundations. There was a bump as they left the muddy track for a cobbled lane. This approached the walls indirectly by skirting the fringes of the terraced lawn. Taran noted banks of flowers along winding paths in the woods on the other side of the road, and a stately spring-fed fountain that foamed and flashed. It was not at all what he expected.

The cab jerked to a sudden halt, and the driver scurried down to open his door.

"This is the place?" Taran asked, stepping stiffly out.

"Morvran Castle," the driver replied, tipping his hat and closing the door in one swift gesture.

Taran tucked in his much-rumpled shirt while the cabby hurriedly went around the other side of the carriage to open the door for Hest. The colonel stuck his head out the window.

"Forty-eight hours," he said. "Remember, if you don't find what I asked for in two days, our deal is off."

"I think I can remember that," Taran replied gruffly.

"We'll be watching. And *you*—" He now addressed Hest, who had just stepped to Taran's side.

"No tricks!" he said.

She looked on idly, without expression.

The driver climbed up into his seat. "Good luck!" he said, speaking in a voice that sounded a little loud and very nervous. Then, with many a snap of the reigns, he navigated a roundabout in front of the castle at top speed.

Taran watched as the dust raised in the cab's passage was blown away on a chilling breeze. Almost as soon as the carriage was out of sight, a cloud covered the afternoon sun. A light pat of cold water on his cheek roused him. The sky was only just beginning to darken with clouds, but the rain ran ahead of it on the wind.

"There's no one here to meet us," he said. "Aren't we expected?"

"We're a day late," Hest said, walking towards the front gate of the castle. She seemed even more formal and forlorn than usual.

Together they ascended a wide stone stair that led up to the gate. It was not the kind of gate customary to Victorian period European castles, which one could normally approach on level ground. This was quite a bit smaller and rectangular, like the entrance of a common house. The stairs that led up to it were steep, and the door that faced them at the top was painted a deep crimson color.

They stood on the threshold. Taran glanced up at windows that glowered like the slits of eyes upon them, but he ignored the threatening appearance of the place and focused on the curious emblems that barred their passage. In the center of the door was a plain device the size of a man's hand, wrought of iron: a triangle within a circle stamped with the initials *FTI*. He was still studying this mark when the right-hand door swung inward into darkness. Taran stepped back from the portal, alarmed. Slowly, an elderly bonneted woman peeped out, her eyes wide with wonder.

"Hello there!" Taran said, trying to look cheerful. The best he could muster on such short notice was a wide grin with darting eyes—the look of a hunted man. The woman looked back with an expression no less shocking than his own, and then turned to examine Hest, whose eyes alone among them remained impassive.

"Who are you?" the woman asked in a quavering voice.

"My name is Taran Morvran. She's Hest. We're expected."

Taran heard the surprise in his own voice, and cursed himself.

"*Taran* is it?" the maid said, and her jaw dropped open. "Yes, I can see it now!"

"Ma'am?"

The door slammed shut.

Taran shivered as the rain continued to fall. Beside him, Hest was as still as stone, staring ahead at the door in grave silence. Water ran from her long braid in a steady stream.

"I guess the castle doesn't get many visitors?" he asked.

"No," Hest replied.

The door nudged open again after a long and uncomfortable wait, and more heads peered out at them. There were seven, four women and three men, all in advanced stages of aging, and all with the look of scared cats when a bad-tempered dog is around. They pushed at one another to allow a better view, and muttered in low voices. The sky turned black, and the rain fell in sheets. Taran guessed that some decision about the authenticity of the strangers was being made, and practiced undue patience despite their circumstances. He was startled when the door finally opened wide, and stepped back as a tall man with snow-white hair pushed to the front and approached to inspect him. The others stood behind, wondering silently at their guest, sizing him up as for a fight.

"Taran Morvran?" the man asked with a grin. He clapped his hands on dingy overalls before reaching out to grasp Taran's shoulders.

"Why, he's the very image of old Master Fain!"

His voice carried an accent full of rustic charm. Taran would have felt better, had the storm not then broken fully over them.

"We were expected!" he shouted over a sudden peal of thunder.

The old man pulled him inside, suddenly aware of the pouring rain. "Come in, young Master!" he said. "Come in Hest. I can see there is a tale to tell here; and you must forgive our astonishment. It is as though many years have fallen away from our old eyes. If only you knew!"

The door shut behind them and the old man set off at a fast pace, forcing him to keep up as they moved brusquely along a narrow passage. The first impression Taran had of the interior was that it was quite dark. The stone walls were very nearly black, and scarred by a long story of passing ages. It no longer seemed so forbidding. Indeed, Taran felt at once as if he had come to a safe haven, if there was any such place left in the world. He almost forgot that he was still a prisoner—a prisoner to his deal with Colonel Naruna, and with a man named Lír.

Hest stalked the passage just behind him, and behind her the serving people walked at a respectful distance. The chief servant turned his head so that Taran could see his smile.

"I am called Giles," he said. "Welcome to Castle Morvran! We've been waiting for you."

"I'm sorry we're late," Taran said. "We were delayed."

"I'm sure you'll tell us all about your *exciting* voyage," the old man said with a hint of hidden meaning. "Well, what do you think of the place? I guess it's not so grand as one of your American plantations."

There were many doors opening on either side of them now. Taran had no idea of the layout of medieval castles, so he looked everywhere with a fixed expression of startled awe.

"Plantations?" he mouthed stupidly, his eyes exploring the dark.

Giles turned, and the curiosity sparkling in his eyes seemed to ruffle his wild eyebrows. "Oh, are they not the kind of houses where men of renown dwell, in America?"

Taran wondered from what distilled source these folk gleaned news of all else outside their walls. Or was the comment meant—as he sensed—to be a kind of joke? When they reached a junction and proceeded down another even narrower hall, Taran had to confess his wonderment.

"Father never told me anything about this place," he said. "I'm a little surprised."

"He waited so long to share this secret with you," Giles replied tersely. "Your grandsires were born here over countless generations. The first was a man named Connor Morvran—"

"When did my father leave?" Taran interrupted.

"Young Thaddeus departed when he was a boy, and I have not seen him since."

"But Mr. DePons has been here?"

Giles stiffened a little, and slowed as he approached a chamber at the hall's end. The air was smoky here, and thick with the smell of a wood-fire.

"Your grandfather was Mr. DePons' apprentice," he said, turning.

"Don't you mean—the other way around?"

"No, young Master," he said, standing so that he blocked the passage. "DePons it was who taught Fain Morvran the sciences. Cedric has been around for quite a bit longer than your grandfather."

Taran's puzzled look won him no explanation, but he was certain Giles was wrong.

"And she's been here, too?" he asked, nodding towards Hest. She stood idly, seemingly disinterested in all their talk.

Giles smiled at him. "Of course. Her purpose is to guide you safely, so that your family's legacy may continue."

"My family's legacy?"

"This was the place where the *tinker* awoke in your grandfather, with DePons' help," Giles said, gently touching the stone wall beside him. "Here before him for many generations the Morvrans put away other pursuits for the crafting of things that don't yet exist—or maybe some that do, but no one knows about them yet. Fain made a real breakthrough, though, and here in Old Morvran his secret work has lain dormant all these years. Mr. DePons sent us a message that you would come and get things back on course. I assume your father gave you careful instructions."

He didn't have a moment to answer before Giles clapped his shoulder, startling him. "Here's the man, fresh from the boat, and we haven't even offered him tea or a blanket! Some staff we are! You are home at last, young Master. Take a seat in the kitchen while I fetch you something warm to drink."

Taran didn't move. He caught the elderly man's eyes, framed in the head of wispy white hair, and the look he saw there chilled him. Despite his friendly manner, those eyes were troubled by doubt, and fear.

"I thought Father was coming," Taran said.

Hest stepped forward suddenly, and gave him a sharp look. Her eyes were wide with a silent warning.

Giles nodded sadly. Standing before the entrance of a low arch in the wall, he lifted his hand from Taran's shoulder and waved the smoky air around in front of his face.

"The plan has changed, then?" he asked. "I feared it was so. There's another surprise waiting for you in the kitchen, Taran, and I want you to know that it's not one to our liking."

Without a word of explanation, Giles led the way down through the arch, around a tight corner, and down a narrow stair. At the bottom they entered a place that was warm and bright. Taran noted every feature of the room and its vaulted ceiling in a glance. It was an ancient kitchen, complete with a stone hearth that could have admitted the entire trunk of a tree. A fire burned there, and sitting on a stool beside it was a man. Taran knew him at once, and stopped in his tracks.

"Jon!"

Jonathan Morvran stood. In all his looks and manners he was much different than Taran, taking after his maternal grandfathers. He was a full head and shoulders taller, and though they shared the deep brown eyes of their father, Jon's were wider and a little wild. His sensible clothes and expression were sharply contrasted by a mane of long black hair, which he wore braided.

"Brother!" Jon said, beaming. "I see you've arrived safely. I was worried. I haven't seen you for months!"

"What are you doing here, Jon?"

"I might ask the same of you."

Taran noted something in his brother's manner, heard something strange in his tone that unnerved him. Jon approached and wrapped him in a fierce embrace, thumping his back for good measure. Then, thrusting him at arm's length, he inspected Taran from head to foot.

Both said in unison, *"God, how you've changed!"*

"The clothes?" Taran wondered, straightening the tousled and much-worn collar of his shirt. "Father made me buy them."

"Looks like you've been living in them, too! I suppose Father sent you here to begin the work that would bring her home."

Taran looked at him curiously. "That's right," he said.

"Well, isn't that a coincidence? I was sent to help you!"

They stared at each other in silence for a moment. The blood drained from Taran's face. He knew it was a lie, and already he had begun to guess Jon's part in this. He wasn't given much time to think about it, though.

"Come, Taran, take a seat!" Jon said, gesturing towards the stool. "We have some catching-up to do!"

When Taran did not immediately comply, Jonathan pulled a second stool from an adjoining table. Setting this beside the other, he immediately plopped down and unbound his braided hair, composing its length over one shoulder. It was so vainly foppish a gesture that Taran wondered if he was serious.

Giles and one of the other servants looked on. Only, they tried not to look as though they were looking on, and busied themselves about a pantry off the main room where they began taking out bits for a supper. Hest held her ground, but didn't say a word. Her eyes were fixed on Jonathan, watching every move.

Taran stood beside her. "Jonathan," he said, speaking the name as if he had not heard it before.

"Yes?"

"I didn't expect to see you here."

"You mean you didn't expect to see me ever again," Jon said, grinning rigidly. "You did not expect many things, I am

361

sure; but that does not prevent many things from happening, does it, Brother?"

Taran nodded.

"Then come and sit with me."

Taran obeyed. He slouched, staring into the low flames of the cooking fire. A cauldron of water boiled there, suspended by a hook. Taran saw the sleeves of a man's shirt inside—laundry.

"Giles makes a mean stew," Jon said, smirking as he gazed at the cauldron. "You're probably hungry after your *bumpity-bump* ride down our rabbit-track of a road. I hope you like lamb, though that bit of laundry there is probably just as tasty."

Taran said nothing. The fire was low but the hearth had been burning long, so it generated an enormous amount of heat. Though drenched from the rain he was sitting close enough to feel uncomfortable, and because he ached from head to foot he put on a rather dismal face and glowered.

"How can you be so glum?" Jon asked. "This is truly amazing!"

Taran blinked. "What is?" he asked, folding his hands on his lap.

"What's amazing? You sit in a place that you never would have dreamed existed. Here, on the far side of an ocean, is a castle older than Rome that bears our name! Morvran, *the Raven!*"

"It can't be older than Rome, Jon. You never did take to histories. I wouldn't have thought you'd be interested in any of this."

The sounds from the pantry stopped suddenly. The mood had grown strangely tense, and Taran wondered what was happening.

"I began to take interest about the time of your unfortunate accident," Jon fired back. "Why do you suppose Father never told us about this place, Taran?"

"Father's not coming," he replied. "Otherwise he could answer you himself. Why are you here, Jon?"

"I told you, I was sent."

"Father didn't tell me you'd be here."

"I know. Isn't it great! What a surprise!"

Taran heard a little genuine joy in his brother's voice, but it did nothing to quell the sensation that he sat very near a danger greater than the fire.

"I hear you fell on some hard times recently," Jon said, taking a more conciliatory tone. "I want you to know, Taran, I stand behind you. It must've been horrible, losing her that way."

"I didn't lose her!"

"What's done is done, Brother. No matter how she was misplaced, she's got to be found. I suppose that's what we're here to do, you and I."

"And Hest."

"Hest?"

Taran looked back towards the stairway, but Hest was gone. Jon leaned closer to him.

"I hear you did some questionable things in the city. You don't have to worry about any of that, Taran. I think we all understand. I've done some things myself—things I'm not proud of. It's just a part of growing up."

Taran felt a touch on his shoulder. An elderly woman in a bonnet had appeared from the pantry with a kettle and a tray of biscuits, and Giles stood by with cups of something hot.

"Tea?" Taran wondered.

"Coffee," Giles said. "Brought by Master Jonathan."

"I thought it more homelike," Jon said, taking a cup.

The offering was set down on the hearth before them, and a wool blanket was laid over Taran's shoulders. Then the maid left. Giles lingered only a moment more before he also retreated to the pantry. Taran heard a door close from within, and he knew that they were alone.

"It's awful stuff," Jonathan said with a grimace. "It's not easy to roast coffee in a pan."

"Tastes fine to me," Taran replied, quaffing a gulp of the strong bitter brew.

"Well, put on that brave face when Giles offers you supper, and you'll be alright," he said with a conspiratorial grin. "We'll find ourselves something more palatable in the cellars later on. There's a whole lot of stuff down there besides fine vintage, too. I've found much to keep me busy for the past few days, but I need your help. I mean, you'll need my help, just to get oriented."

Taran was frowning. The coffee was bitter indeed, but given his present mood the shock was welcome.

"You know Grandfather Fain liked to build things?" Jon asked.

"Yes."

"Do you know there is a bit of a mystery about his disappearance?"

"Disappearance? Father said he died here after setting him up with the University in America."

"Do you know *how?*"

"No."

"Well," he said, "I have learned Grandfather Fain was lost in one of his experiments!"

"Lost? You're saying he's still alive?"

"It happened somewhere in Britain, though I'm not sure where exactly. There is a lab below the castle, stocked with all his notes and journals. We could figure out the location—"

"What does that have to do with finding Val Anna?"

"Did Father tell you nothing?"

"He was secretive."

"Really? Well, finding Val requires us to find out what happened to Fain, first."

"I don't understand."

"I'll show you, tonight!" Jonathan said, grinning madly. It was the same mischievous grin that Taran remembered from their childhood.

"The last time you smiled like that, Jon, Father punished us both."

"Father isn't here now," Jon replied.

"What's kept him?" Taran asked. He already knew the answer, though.

"He's run up against some legal problems, Taran. I think it had something to do with your recent activities. It's like I said, though—I don't blame you. These things happen. We can make it right again."

Taran felt suddenly very dizzy. It wasn't the coffee. He could no longer refrain from bringing up the obvious question.

"Why are you really here, Jonathan?"

Jon put down his coffee cup and stared at Taran. His hands were on his knees, and his face was a grinning mask of light and shadows painted by the firelight.

"Jon, I know you're working for Colonel Naruna."

"What do you mean?" Jonathan asked, still smiling.

Taran placed his cup on the hearth beside his brother's.

"You can't lie to me, Jon. You know exactly what I mean. You went to him the very day I flew the glider, the day Val vanished. You think Mother couldn't figure out the meaning of your note?"

"You think I joined the Army? Taran—"

"You're working for him, Brother, and all I want to know is *why*. Why would you side with a menacing fool who's plotted with a group of international criminals to destroy your own family—all for some weapon that Father was building with DePons? Did he blackmail you into an agreement the way he's trying to blackmail me?"

Jon looked away into the fire, his face contorting with passion.

"Jon, he's already taken the farm, the university position, and the credibility of our family name. Even you are not beyond his ire. Did you think when you agreed to make sure I do what I'm told that he would spare even you?"

Jon shook his head. "You have no idea, do you Taran? You have no idea what's really going on here. What's at stake is so much bigger than all that!"

Taran was about to reply when a small door by the fireplace bumped open. Giles stumbled in wearing over his tall figure a black leather fisherman's cape. Rainwater fairly cascaded from him onto the floor as he shut the door and began to shrug off his overshoes. He bore a load of rather soggy kindling under both arms.

"Well, young Masters, I've fetched some wood for the supper-fire. Taran, your room is prepared, and the bed turned-out. It will be cold weather tonight; but never fear. Old Morvran keeps out the fiercest wind!"

Taran and Jon stared at each other.

"Tonight," Jon said. "I'll come for you tonight, okay?"

"Okay," Taran replied warily.

Jonathan arose and left. Giles watched him go, and then walked after him to the stair, leaning forwards to check that he had really left.

"Giles?" Taran asked.

"I can see that you two have got to the heart of the matter quickly enough," he replied, turning back towards the kitchen. "Supper will be put on soon. Perhaps you'd like to rest a bit first?"

"I'm feeling fine, thanks."

"But, your long journey—"

"Really, I couldn't sleep—"

"I think it would be good for you," Giles insisted. "I'd like to take you to your room right now, just to see if everything's satisfactory."

Taran saw a nervous twitch in the man's eyes.

"I'll go with you, then," he said, rising.

Wrapping the blanket around his shoulders like a cloak, Taran followed as Giles entered the pantry. They passed by shelves of foodstuff and hanging baskets of vegetables, and then proceeded through a small door in the back. Beyond the door there was a very narrow passage. It was like a little alley behind the walls, where lords of ancient times hid the traffic of their servants and spies. All was dark within, lit only by a candle that Giles procured from a ledge outside the pantry.

"There are many hidden passages in Old Morvran," Giles said quietly. "I haven't found all those rumored to exist, but this one will bring us back to the front hall."

After a quick turn to the left, they stepped out of a low arch beneath a stairwell and entered a grand corridor. Walking the dim passage, Taran wondered what Giles had to say to him that was so important. He wondered where his father and Dr. DePons were, and he wondered what had become of Hest. All his mind was already in a muddle before this adventure began, and now he was thrown into total confusion.

"I'm sure you must be curious," Giles remarked. He truly realized he was understating the obvious, for he turned and smiled as he spoke.

Taran had nothing to say in reply.

"I have lived here almost my whole life," Giles continued. "I was a boy when your grandfather took me in. Never did I have any other family than those who lived and worked behind these walls. We are few enough nowadays, but once we were many. The riddle of it is that all of us came here from so many places, yet all of us with the same need for companionship. It's almost as if we were called here—called by something, or by some purpose. Take a look at that, now!"

They had just crossed a threshold. Where the corridor ended there was a wide and lofty chamber with high windows on the left wall. The wind's-eyes let in both wind and rain, but that wasn't where the authenticity of the place ended. The entire chamber was kept as an exact model of a medieval reception hall. There were shields and tapestries on the walls, and richly carved wooden tables and benches. Halberds and broadswords hung in racks among axes and maces, all assembled with attention to period and spotlessly clean.

Giles stood a long moment, allowing Taran the opportunity to look around. When he started off again, Taran lingered a second more, struck dumb with amaze at all the details wrapped up in the still and darkened room.

"Much of the castle is uninhabited," Giles said as they marched through the drafty space. "The cells branching off from this room are unused. At one time, they lodged visitors and scholars who came here to study."

"Historians?"

"Most recently, yes; but I was thinking farther back in time. This place hasn't changed for over a thousand years, lad. The earliest guests were men of the cloth seeking solitude—or maybe something else."

Again, Taran caught the suggestion of a hinted meaning to Giles' words.

"I was told that Grandfather Fain was a scholar of antiquities before he became a tinker," Taran said.

"That is true. The upper hall of the keep is full of those objects he brought back from pagan lands, as the Old Master was so fond of gathering on his journeys."

"He went to the east?"

"Many a time, and always he returned with new items, and new tales. Those were happier days. I decided after he passed on that the upper rooms ought to be kept as he left them."

"You know how he died?"

Giles glanced briefly at him, eyes wide in the candlelight.

"I did not say that he died, young Master. I only said that he *passed on.*"

"But surely he is not still alive?"

"I did not see him die," Giles replied. "I can't answer your question."

While Taran digested this, they ducked under a low threshold at the other end of the reception hall and entered another narrow passage.

"Giles," he said, "is there something you wanted to tell me?"

"Up ahead there is a very old room, even older than the one we just passed through. It was the Old Keep of the castle—its very heart. There is something there I need to show you."

"You could have told me plainly," Taran muttered in relief. "In the kitchen, I thought something was wrong."

Giles glanced at him again, and nodded.

"Many things are wrong, and much more seems to be going wrong every day. It is very fortunate you came to us in time."

The Old Keep was a deep pillared hall, stretching its broad rectangular length before them. The sound of rain hammering on slates came from somewhere up above. Taran stood on the threshold and let his jaw wag as he looked up into the far reaches of a black void. He couldn't see the wooden beams of the ceiling. The only break in the fathomless dark came through a stout pair of paned windows on the long left-hand wall. The bluish evening light that poured in through these presented a ghostly forest of heavy columns, descending from unseen vaults, which rested their square chiseled feet upon a floor decorated with dull stone tessellations in repeating geometric patterns.

"The Old Keep," Giles said. "The glass windows were added twenty years ago. Your father spoke of returning about that time, for he had thought of making this place into a college."

"He wanted to come back and live here?"

"Your mother persuaded him to stay in America," Giles said. "Now, look over there, in the center."

There were no tables or other furnishings in the place where Giles was pointing, just a circular raised surface around which a low brass rail had been constructed. He stepped closer, and saw that the thing was obviously arranged for display. Inside the enclosure there was a great black piece of polished stone almost thirty feet across. It had the look of a very ancient thing, and upon it were strange signs, long wedge-shaped strokes, and a variety of symbols. Lit sideways by the moon, these mysteries were sharpened so intensely that they seemed to stand up from the dark surface.

Walking up to the stone wheel, Taran asked, "What is it?"

"It is called *The Book of Invasions*," Giles answered. He turned his candle from side to side over the rail so that more of the rich carving of the piece was revealed.

Taran asked, "It's a book?"

"The Old Master brought it back from Babylonia, from an excavation there. He seemed to think it was very important."

"Why?" Taran asked.

"What would you say if I was to tell you this stone bears, among many other details, the name of Morvran and your family's ancient crest?"

Taran stared at the rock, noting rows of cuneiform wedges incised around a few odd tangles of lines. There were many unfamiliar symbols arranged around the outer edge, but one he knew well. He'd seen it before, in the stone he'd given to Val.

"There is probably a translation of this in one of his journals," Giles said, catching his eager expression.

"You will have to show me those books," Taran replied. "I wish Father was here. And what about DePons? Is everybody going to disappear except me?"

Giles' mouth was puckered in a grim frown.

"I was dead to the world until they found me," Taran continued, "and now, after warning me not to fear the threats of our enemies, they're gone. I'm beginning to think this was all a big mistake, Giles."

"If you wanted direction, there is something else I would like to show you before we go to your room. It is a treasure your grandfather cherished above all else."

"Very well," Taran replied wearily. "Let's see it."

He led Taran along the right-hand wall to a massive fireplace, its coals dead and black on a grate that hadn't been lit for years. On the mantle above the cold hearth there was a sack. A curious thing it was, very long, and bound at one end with a length of cord. Threadbare and covered with cobwebs, it seemed no one had disturbed it for centuries. Setting his candle aside, Giles reached out his hand towards the artifact; but at the last moment he drew back as if he had touched something hot.

"Begging your pardon again, young Master, but I am forgetting something that I need to ask of you before I release this to your keeping."

"What is it?"

"If I am not mistaken, the circumstances of your arrival resulted from a deviation from the original plan. And if this is so, you've probably run into Naruna already."

Taran frowned. "How'd you know about that?" he asked. "Were you talking to Hest?"

"No, and if I had she wouldn't have given me as plain an answer as you just did. That's because she knows I am more than just a stupid old man who takes care of the place while the family is away. No one here is what they seem, least of all *you*."

Taran stared.

"You have already used it?" Giles asked.

"Used what?"

"Something that was supposed to wait until your father and DePons arrived, a great secret that would unlock memories and prove your worthiness to hold this relic."

"What kind of memories?" Taran wondered.

"You're truly puzzled by all this, are you?"

Taran's despairing look was answer enough.

"It's not easy to explain," Giles said, planting his hands on his hips. "You were asked to come here to find a way for someone to come back—someone who's left."

"Yes."

"That is where it begins, lad; but not where it ends. Fain opened the door, and we were trapped here—trapped all our lives."

"Trapped?"

"Called and trapped, yes. He couldn't send us back. This friend of yours, though, she has begun something, and now she needs your help. Fain's door is the only way."

"Wait, I don't understand what you're talking about! What do you mean you're trapped here?"

Giles inhaled deeply through his hawkish nose. "Taran Morvran," he said, "You are your father's son, and he can't help us now. He stands in your place, in America, answering for things that you are accused of. You must go in his place."

Taran was about to speak, but Giles held up a hand.

"Some of us have invested a lot in the work of exploring the *Dark Worlds*. Don't ask me what it's about. I can't explain it to you in words. You will discover it soon enough. If you want answers for your questions, and if you want to see your friend again, all you need to do is tell me the name of the one that binds the three."

"You mean *Regulus*?"

Giles lifted his gaze and clapped his hands once. "Regulus, like the star," he said, and removed the bag from the mantle with a flourish.

"Like a compass to the seafarer, Regulus points the way to the other stones," he said. "This item, however, wields a power wholly different."

He weighed the bag in his hands, as if making a decision.

"What is it?" Taran asked.

"It is something you must return to the place your fathers came from," he said. "It is yours now, Taran. Your young hands will feel its history, perhaps. Mine feel nothing, for long labors have toughened them; yet that is nothing compared to the stuff that made the men who were among the first to carry *this*."

Taran adjusted the blanket across his shoulders as Giles handed to him the bag. It was as long as the length of his leg, but its light weight felt well-balanced in his hands. Beneath the ancient leather there was a hard surface. A musty smell lingered in the air as the dust was stirred. Taran caught a whiff of something else, something utterly unearthly, and a tingling sensation ran all through his arms. Time seemed to stand still. It was as though he held time itself in his hands.

"Well, aren't you going to open it?" Giles wondered, breaking the spell.

Taran kept his eyes on the old man as he tore the rotten cord away from the mouth of the sack. He put in his hand and pulled out the contoured handle of some kind of tool, wrapped in lambskin. Fumbling with the wrapping, he revealed a pale weathered wooden scabbard, gently curved, inset with delicate gold veins in the shape of vines. From its mouth stretched a hilt of fanciful shape, and a pommel of solid gold.

"A sword?" Taran asked, his voice catching in his throat. "I've never held one before. I've seen a Claymore, hanging in the home of a gentleman in New York—"

"Never mind what it looks like!" Giles said. "This is no ordinary weapon of war. The Earth has not seen the like of this thing. It is a seal of authority, the crest of a Great House of long ago. If it belongs to you, you also belong to it. Let's have it out, then, and see its edge by the light of the flame."

Taran tugged the old scabbard out from the leather bag and unclasped a dry-rotted thong at the sword's hilt. The wood was infirm at the mouth of the sheath, and he wondered how the blade could have survived so long untouched. Surely the edge was no longer useable. He pulled hard at the length, supposing the rust would prevent him from doing more. His arm jerked back, however, and in one swift motion a full foot of the blade's long edge was free.

It was like nothing he'd ever seen.

Slowly he drew more of the length out, studying the grace of its complex curving lines. The basic shape was of a cavalry sword, but there was much more to it than that. This was forged in the manner of Japanese blades. The metal—if metal it was, seemed strangely light and flexible; and though the decorative tracery of vines and letters on the blade glittered with gold, much of the rest gleamed oddly, with a faint blue translucence.

"That's not steel," Giles said.

"What is it, then?" Taran asked, running a finger along the curving edge.

"It is a type of ceramic. Your grandfather examined the composition a little, but feared to attempt any extensive testing on it, lest he destroy the inscriptions."

"Inscriptions?"

Taran examined the blade closer, removing more from the sheath. As he did so, he noted that there ran along its length a flowing script, more beautiful than any written language he'd ever studied.

"How did this come to our family?" Taran asked.

"The tale is that your long-fathers were descended from a young chieftain who bore this blade almost fifteen-hundred years ago. He was named Morvran, and was descended from Morvrans."

Taran chuckled. "Modern or ancient, I'm not used to handling weapons! Being that it's so rare an object, maybe we should keep it here, for safety."

Giles gave him a curious smile.

"What is it?" Taran asked. Yet he thought he knew what the man was smiling about. It was this strange giddy feeling in his stomach. He was suddenly confused by memories that didn't seem to fit in his experience—memories that were not his own, of a forest and a white horse.

"You feel that you have held this sword before," Giles said, jabbing a bony finger at him.

"It is familiar, I must confess. How strange is that?"

"It is a memory of the future. But beware! As a very wise woman once said to me, *a memory of something that has not yet happened may yet be changed.*"

Giles picked up the candle and began shuffling away towards the doorway and to his room. Taran looked after him a moment before following. He knew then there would be very little sleep tonight. Hopefully, whatever he got would be a sleep without the torment of dreams.

23

THE NEW WORLD

Walking a little behind her, Val noted Mother's dress, worn and soiled now as if stained by long travels. Mother said nothing, but tugged her hand playfully as they made their way down the street. The markets were crowded, but not with shoppers. Everyone was gathering to watch the comet. Voices were rising, people were pointing and shouting, and all seemed poised suddenly on the brink of hysteria. The light around them bloomed, and Val looked up. Earth and sky paused as the world fell silent. Her hand slipped free, and her mother turned; but

Val had eyes only for the comet. It was so huge! Surely it was bigger than before.

Before? Had all of this already happened?

Tearing her eyes away from the figure of impending doom hanging above, Val faced the woman leading her. It wasn't her mother.

It was Nunna.

"Where is my mother?" Val asked.

Even as she spoke, her view of the street and the crowds dilated, and then faded into mist. Yet the comet remained, hovering in the sky like a warning angel.

Nunna said, "Only we are here, with *him.*"

She pointed upwards at the comet without moving her eyes.

"This is a dream?"

She nodded. "I can make them. I can share them. I can see farther this way—almost as far as you have seen. *He* also sees, though now I suppose all he can do about it is wait for someone to awaken him."

Shielding her eyes with one hand, Val gazed at the comet and asked, "Who is he?"

"He is Aerfen, the Sky Power, the one whom the Empress protects."

Val shivered at the flat tone her voice took. "I don't understand," she said. "This isn't what Brisen said would happen."

"Thank you for bringing me here, Val Anna. You rescued me from a Dark World and awakened me to a new beginning. I sense that this place holds the answers to our dreams."

The girl stepped backwards and quickly vanished into the mists of the barren dreamscape. Val walked a few paces to follow, but stumbled over an obstacle in her path. The mist lifted a little then, enough to see that she was standing on a grassy surface. A long low heap of stones lay at her feet.

"Is it a grave?" she asked.

Peering closer, she examined one flat rock atop the rest. Upon this was scratched a single word in strange characters.

Though she did not comprehend the script, the meaning was translated to her mind. It was a name.

Nunna.

She awoke.

Whispers and girlish giggles filled the darkened room where she lay, raining down on her from somewhere above. Val listened awhile, idling in the soreness of her limbs. She rested upon a soft couch. How long had she slept, and who had placed her here? The memory of her transit returned then to wash her in cold grief. A sigh of such melancholy escaped her lips that it immediately silenced the small voices she'd heard. Then, with a sound of scampering feet and the pulling of heavy drapes, the darkness was thrown back before the piercing blaze of a rising sun.

The sun turned the room into a glaring furnace of light, and she couldn't see much around her at first. The noise her visitors made informed her they were descending steps on the run, and shielding her eyes a little she saw the spiral staircase opposite the place where she lay. Three small figures, laughing lightly, turned from the bottom step and fled across the room to a doorway. Val caught only a glimpse of petite shapes in white gowns, and then, with the sound of a door shutting, they were gone. She was alone with the dawn.

The room revealed itself slowly to her bleary eyes, and she studied each of its curious attributes with attention to detail, for this was no ordinary lodging. The chamber was an open octagonal tower of two stories, measuring perhaps fifty feet across and twice as high to the domed ceiling. The second story was a carved wooden balcony that wrapped around the interior, accessed by the spiral stair she saw earlier. Supported by gracefully fluted stone columns, the balcony gave access to pairs of tall windows, one pair in each wall. The walls below had no windows, but bore grand bookshelves instead. There must have been thousands of volumes here, she thought. It was like a library; yet there were many notes of comfort.

A richly paneled privacy screen and table stood beside her couch. The couch was deep and wide, and artfully designed, its upholstered high side being fashioned in the shape of a goose with backwards-arching neck. Its wooden beams were inset with carved ivory and colored stone. Luxurious weavings of embroidered silk covered her. Pushing these aside, Val discovered that someone had bathed and dressed her while she was sleeping.

"Should I call it a short white dress, or a very long shirt?" she wondered quietly, looking down on her costume. She cast her gaze around, looking for something else to wear, but the only thing she saw was even less enticing. There upon the table, cleaned and neatly folded, her CM7 bodysuit was ready and waiting. She frowned darkly at it.

"I guess I'll call this a summer dress," she said, swinging her legs over the edge of the couch. Her bare feet touched the cool floor, tiled with squares of greenish brown hues. She stretched and yawned, breathing an atmosphere saturated with complex odors. The air was warm, and the golden drapes in the windows above sparkled in gentle undulations with breezes blowing in from the world outside. Rising cautiously, she shuffled towards the bottom of the stairs. All the other wonders around her could wait until she had a look out of the upper windows at the World of Origins.

Could such a room as this exist anywhere else?

The windows arrested her gaze as soon as she reached the top of the steps. There were two on each of the eight walls, high thick-paned eyes framed in richly carved white alabaster. Those to her right, the south, were shaded; but before her a view was open to the east and the rising sun. The landscape unfolding before her was a world much bleaker than any other.

Sunrise lit the landscape below in shades of sullen red and ochre. It was like Canaan, though on a much grander scale. All was desert for a thousand miles—nothing but jagged red stone spires and dunes.

"It is a woebegone sight, is it not?"

The gentle womanly voice came from beside her, so soothing that she could hardly be startled. There was only one who spoke with such a voice.

Morla sat upon a high-backed wooden chair beside the window. Val's mind was bursting with questions, but she stood a moment to take in the sight of the beautiful seer. Morla wore a knee-length white dress that gleamed with silver threads throughout, and a veil covered the lower part of her face. White leather slippers and a matching vest completed her raiment, while dark brown eyes and silver hair, both radiantly shining, confirmed beyond doubt her identity.

"You are finally awake." The calm of her voice quavered with a note of concern. "Welcome to Gilthaloneth. It is the principle stronghold of this world, and the last."

"How long was I asleep?" Val asked, walking to her side.

Seeming suddenly wan, Morla turned her face towards the desert. "The sun rises quickly," she answered, "but time is counted the same here as it is in Ertsetum. You have been asleep for three full weeks since your arrival."

"Three weeks! That's even worse than the first transition!"

"You were greeted by Orlim. You told him Nergal was in the colonies. He left at once, and finding us there he retrieved us."

"Orlim?"

"You recognize the name?"

"I've heard it before. What are the colonies? Was Nergal really there?"

Morla closed her eyes and bowed her head slightly. "I knew there would be difficulties with your memory," she said. "I am hoping you will recall more when I take you to the Council. Considering Nunna's current state of mind, however, I wonder if either of you shall ever be made whole again."

"What do you mean, Morla?"

"The displacement was very strong."

"And Nunna isn't well?"

"All things considered, she is in better health than you. Then again, she did not come here bearing the price of return against the Ban in her flesh."

The anxiety in her voice was clearer now. Val considered this quietly. She didn't feel particularly ill at the moment—the waves of dizziness were wearing off, and though she was stiff, it was probably because she'd been abed almost a month. Her arm especially was tender to touch, but there was no other symptom to betray the presence of foreign objects in her body.

"Why was the displacement worse this time?" she asked. "Was it because I picked up Regulus along the way?"

"It isn't because of any of the stones you have gathered. It is because of those that remain in the darkness. The inhabitants of the Dark Worlds are tormented because of the shattered fragments that yet lay hidden among them. They are transformed into living deaths by a gradual acceleration of displacement."

"So I'm like the *Watchers*?"

"Yes," Morla answered without hesitation. "But not for the same reason. You are the balance in which the dark stones weigh against those that were rejoined in you. The fragments call to one another, like the fragments of your memory, and you must bear their struggle in pain."

"And hopefully with no worse transformations," Val said quietly. "Will Nunna also suffer these changes? She doesn't even remember Hazor."

"She was never there," Morla said, looking out over the desert.

"What do you mean?"

"It isn't that she does not remember Hazor; it is that we do not remember her."

"Morla?"

"The Nunna we knew was one of many. She is a person made by others, in the image of a person."

Val tried desperately, but vainly, to understand. "What person could make a person?" she asked. "You're not speaking about natural birth, are you?"

"The Ancients made them first. Then the Gremn made them when they could not find enough Crodah vessels to operate their Combat Units and ships. The girl you knew—"

"You're saying that Nunna is some kind of cookie-cutter monster made by the Gremn?"

Morla turned sharply. "She is much more than that! She has a real Gift—one that is preserved in more than just her physical makeup. And the Gift has transferred to every one of her copies."

"Her *copies*?"

"We've called them Null-Navvies ever since the Gremn-Crodah conflict, because they were numbered in the Null Navigational Construct. They were necessary to carry out the Plan, but their purpose is not for war. Many of them may not even be aware of the Plan or their purpose."

"You're saying there are many Nunnas, and that they are unnatural creations of people fit to serve someone's plan?"

Morla nodded. "Yes."

"I don't know how that's possible. Whose plan was this, and why were they sent into the Dark Worlds?"

"The plan was yours. They were sent out to retrieve the stones, but they failed."

The two stared at one another a long moment before Morla continued.

"There is so much about this business of the Viaducts that is hard to unravel," she said. "We have been worlds apart, and we are all from different times and places; yet here we are in the place where it all began, speaking a language that is strange to the land of my birth. The Plan is unfolding, but according to another's will I think."

Val was stunned to silence. She hadn't paused to consider that Morla was now fluent in everyday English. It threw her for a moment, but she recovered quickly enough to ask another question.

"The Nunna we knew, the girl at Hazor, she was killed, right?"

381

"It must have been a shock when you found her alive," Morla said.

"Actually, she found me. She seemed to expect me there, though I had no more knowledge of that world than what was preserved in a fragmented Gremn message."

"They are alike, then," Morla replied. "Yet they are all entirely different people."

Val puzzled this for a moment, and then she said, "But there aren't copies of *everyone* in the Dark Worlds, even though we appear in every one of them."

"No. Nunna is a construct, but we are all one and the same. Did you not discover this on your journey? The stones were divided, and the world and its people shared this fate. Each time a division occurred, a new frame of reference emerged from the course of time. Now it is impossible to tell a shattered image from the original, and that is why we were given the *mirrors*."

"You mean the mirror-devices?"

"No," Morla replied. "These force the stones to look back along their frame of reference to the previous division, and thus to another timeline. I am speaking of something else entirely."

She removed her veil so that Val could see her face. She was beautiful, but somehow changed.

"We are mirrors to each other," she said. "You look at me and see through the division to the one who waits for the stones to be rejoined. However, in some others the division is all that remains, until they are so distorted that their original forms are lost—even to themselves."

"The Watchers."

"They are what remains when displacement has run its course."

"How much time have I got before becoming one of these?"

"Such a question cannot be answered," Morla replied. "It may be that you are in no more danger than the rest of us, though certainly no less. Do not worry about such things, Val

Anna. You must learn to see beyond time, beyond the sequence of events."

"See beyond time?"

Morla rose. "Much loss and sorrow you will suffer until you learn that all times are present in the stones. Now, let us make ready, for the Council has issued a directive. You were summoned to appear as soon as you are fit to stand before them."

Far from comforted by the seer's words, Val followed her down the stairs to the privacy screen near her couch. Beside the wall there was a wooden chest.

"Your washroom and toilet are beyond the door beside the stair," Morla said, pointing. "Inside this chest you will find a gown fit for your rank. Wash and dress quickly. Here is the key to your tower."

She produced a bronze skeleton key. Val took it, examining it curiously.

"Dress quickly. You will find the manner of these clothes familiar, for you once wore such things."

Morla bustled off by way of a stout pair of wooden doors. They shut loudly behind her, and a series of bars and bolts snapped in place automatically. Val looked at the key, and wondered why she felt like she was being hidden away.

She washed in a sink with hot and cold running water, and even took the time to pass an ivory comb through her perpetually messy hair. The toilet and shower were both similar to those aboard the substations, but there was an array of strange little machines by the sink whose employment remained a mystery. She ignored them, and turned her attention to the clothing left to her inside the chest.

The lid opened with a loud creak, revealing a sea of red fabric. Val would have been happy with a plain dress, maybe in light yellow or blue. Instead she found herself delicately handling splendorous imperial silk. She pulled out the skirt first, and saw beneath it a lacy corset embellished in front with an embroidered flower. After placing these side by side upon her couch she looked in the trunk for the rest of the dress, but there was nothing else. Puzzled, she examined the corset closer and discovered that it was trussed up the back with a gaudy ribbon, and was clearly meant to be worn as an outer-garment. Lacking straps to hold itself up, it was truly a lady's dress—but there weren't even any sleeves. She pulled it on grudgingly, surprised that she felt more uncomfortable now than she was the first time she wore pants.

There was a mirror in the back of the privacy screen, and when she was done Val stepped before it and peered sheepishly at her reflection. The crimson beauty staring back at her was hardly the girl she expected to see; yet the feeling she had worn this kind of dress before grew stronger, just as Morla predicted.

"We are mirrors to each other?" she wondered.

The mirror did not reply. It was just a mirror, like the one in the Morvran's washroom.

She tucked the key into a hidden pocket sewn into the seam of her corset and made her way to the doors. The large latch on the left-hand door was easily turned, smoothly releasing the bolts and sliding back the locking bars. She opened the massive door and stepped into the street outside.

Val felt as though she had stepped out into the street of a quaint Mediterranean town. Here were private shaded nooks and little alleyways, window-boxes planted with herbs and spice, and a few people passing with baskets full of ordinary market-goods. Looking north, to the right from the doorway, she noticed a sharp eastward turn in the road where it found the edge of a cliff. There were no buildings near the precipice, just a few trees lining the switchback road guarded by her tower.

Morla was standing in the street, beckoning her with a wave of her hand. Val hesitated, blinking in the bright sunshine. The buildings lining the street shared very close quarters, just like the houses and businesses lining the Main Street of her old hometown. As crammed as they were, the nearest came no closer than fifty yards from the base of her tower, as if affording it special privacy, and those closest were ornamented the more lavishly. All the buildings were tall, however, and though she knew the tower stood upon the ridge of a mountaintop her view was blocked in every direction except north.

Val gazed back at the interior of her sanctum with awkward fear, smoothing imaginary wrinkles in her dress with pale trembling hands.

"Come," Morla said. "Your attire is fitting."

Val closed the door behind her, and hearing the bolts slide into position she felt suddenly exposed. It was as if she'd just left the only place of safety in a hostile land.

"It's not to my liking," she mumbled, meaning the dress.

"Clothing more comfortable to ordinary tastes will be waiting for you when we return. I have already requested a tunic, leggings, and a cloak."

Val frowned, trying to imagine herself dressed in a tunic.

"That is a garb that will hide you from wary eyes, should you feel the need to walk outside your chambers."

"But these are meant to grab everyone's attention. Why?"

"We strive now to make a lasting impression. This is an important meeting we are attending."

Then, nodding towards a slight bulge at her side, she added, "You decided to bear a weapon?"

It was the dagger. There was a small pouch on the inside of the belt, and it was big enough to hide away a few small belongings gleaned from her old clothes; but there was no proper place or fitting to hang a blade. Val had wondered if it was noticeable.

"It's always been with me, Morla, ever since Nunna dropped it."

"Isn't it strange," Morla asked, "how some things return unlooked-for after so long an absence?"

Val frowned.

"At least you look the part, Val Anna."

"What part?"

"You are a part of the story of this world and its people, to begin with. I will help you reorient yourself as we travel the Over-City."

Morla turned to the left, where the road wound gently uphill between houses.

"It all seems so ordinary," Val commented as they set out.

"The Over-City is mostly like this. The Under-City is another matter entirely. I hear it is very deep, and dark, with bustling passages navigated by motorized flying carriages. I have never been there before to see it with my own eyes."

"Where are we going now?"

"We go now to the Council. I have tried to make clear to Orlim that you are not well, and that the Council should not tire you with many questions. Your health and wellbeing are of greater concern even than the matter of the Ban."

Val held a hand to her side, trying not to look pained. "Speaking of my health," she said, "could you slow it down a bit?"

Morla nodded, pausing so that Val could lean against an ivy-draped wall. They went on at a slower pace, halting from time to time under shaded awnings along the straight cobbled road.

Though earlier she had noticed narrow alleys on the right descending by stairs to a lower tier of the city, the buildings on either side soon joined together to form an unbroken wall. The street was darker here, and only a little farther on it came to a high-walled circular court. Here Val saw a marvel: three grand Combat Units stood guard in a green grassy sward fifty yards around, each beside a tunnel that exited the circular space. The walls that defined the area were brightly frescoed, bearing images of trees and animals, and were capped by a dome of colorful crystal panels. Braced within a framework of silver worked into the shapes of branches and delicate leafy vines, the panels let in a dazzling display of light to reflect off the hard metallic shells of the Combat Units.

Gazing up at the combat unit standing beside the nearest archway, Val realized these squat models were *Kerub*, whose stout legs met at a sleekly contoured pilot's chamber bristling with weapons. As they watched, each PCU rose up to full height in a kind of salute. It was then Val noticed they were too large to access the arch and use the roadway. They were permanent fixtures here.

Without a word, Morla led her past the guards into a passageway across the green. There were no more buildings here, only a wall on either hand, and the walls were so high and the way so narrow that they could no longer see much of the sky. After awhile the passage wound one way and the other, gradually climbing a steep slope. Val saw apartments to the right, some with open drapes. She tried her best not to peer within, but sometimes she couldn't help herself. In one particular instance she paused as a small girl ran up to the doorway of a house and looked out. Val surprised such an expression of startled wonder on the child's face that she thought she must be scared, but then she grinned widely and ran away.

"There are few children," Morla said, urging her onwards. "Very few have been born, I am told."

"Is there some sickness which prevents them from having children?" Val asked.

"It is the stress of war, I think. The people are attuned to news of new conflicts away south, and the fighting has spread. You bring them hope of a different sort of news. Now that you are here, they know something has changed."

"I bring word of the collaboration of Gremn and Crodah, but little else."

"You misunderstand me," Morla answered. "A thousand years ago you and I dwelt here in a time of peace. We were both lost in the War, and now we have returned. Your presence here is very unsettling to some, and a great miracle to others."

Val thought silently for a moment. "It's like Arthur and Merlin," she said.

"Marluin?" Morla wondered. She stopped and turned to face her.

"Marluin?" Val asked. "I do remember the name from somewhere. What does it mean?"

"It means much to the future," Morla replied cryptically. She turned again and started up the road.

Following on stiff legs, Val said, "You and I were here long ago, but where have you been since we last parted?"

"When I left Hazor, I ended up here—a thousand years in the past. I was here the whole time since then, stowed against my will in a stasis tube."

"I didn't know Gremn tubes could keep a person alive for so long."

"They certainly could; but it wasn't a Gremn device you ordered me into all those years ago."

"Me?"

"I can't blame you now," Morla said. "Neither of us knows what you were thinking, but it saved my life, and it also preserved me so that I can assist you here."

"We were all together before the war?" Val asked. "I don't remember it."

"It hasn't happened yet, for you. Now we are coming together again, returning against the Ban. That is why we must stand before the Council."

"The Council's meeting to enforce the Ban?"

"It meets for you. We will come to the gates of the High Place soon."

At that moment, the pale ivory colored stone of the walls opened into a wider passage, and their height diminished. Grass covered the tops of the stonework, and above the gutter-road there rose one gigantic foot of a metal tower, angling gracefully upwards into a sapphire sky. Val looked up at the monstrous beam of glimmering steel curving like the buttress of the walls of heaven itself, and farther above she saw the edge of a dome. Beyond this, wings of glittering silver sparkled among the stars of mid-morning. A gust of wind, heavily scented with a spicy smell, blew over her and flattened her dress. Though the air was warm she shivered. The colossal High Place would have been visible from her windows, if only she'd had a chance to look to the south. She was glad Morla had the foresight to leave the drapes closed on that side of the tower.

"It's alright," Morla said, noting her anxiety. "It's just a little farther."

"What is this place, Morla?"

"It is the sacred heart of this world," she replied, taking Val's hand. "You installed me as Priestess here, long ago. Now the Council has granted me a provisional pardon, pending the outcome of our summons. Its look is cold, for it has long been without a *Bringer of Dawn*."

"You make it sound like the markets of the Musab, Morla," said a voice behind them. "It isn't all that bad, is it?"

"Orlim," Morla said, relaxing her grip on Val's hand.

Stirred by that deep brassy voice, Val felt a landslide inside her brain. She turned and looked upon a sight no less startling than the High Place itself. Standing behind them in the road was a horse and rider, but the two were joined where the horse's neck and head should have been.

He was a centaur.

"You forbear the burden of the veil, Morla?" the creature asked with a frown. "Or do you imagine, perhaps, that the beauty of your face will melt the hearts of those wicked old men of the Council?"

"Now that she is here, I will allow the Empress to command me in such matters."

"As well you should," he replied, stepping closer.

Val swayed on her feet, and found herself absorbed in the study of his hooves. They were almost too much to gaze on by themselves. The rest of the creature was dappled white and grey, except for the human portions. He wore gleaming black armor and a red tunic that covered his front, and in his hand was a great black spear, stout and shining like polished metal. His hair, like his body, was white, bound high atop his head with a crimson band braided with feathers. It was a curious thing, she noted in some detached corner of her mind, that she did not cry out or faint on the spot.

He looked somehow familiar.

"I have foreseen your swift recovery, dear friend," the centaur said, turning towards Val.

Val paled and stepped back a pace.

"You are surprised at the sight of me?" he asked, his frown deepening.

"Yes, sir!"

"*Sir?*"

Val turned towards Morla, who said, "Exalted Ladies should never confer to their servants as equals."

Orlim looked at Morla. "So, her memory is lost?"

"I've never seen anything like you before," Val said, staring.

Morla closed her eyes and nodded her head silently.

"Well, that poses a problem," he said. "The Council was *most* displeased at the mere mention of the possibility."

They both stood and stared back at her. Val blushed.

"Well, let's not keep them waiting too long," Orlim said, stepping past her. Val absently scooted to one side, fearful of touching him; yet he smelled nice, not at all horsey. It was a fragrance she knew.

"It smells like Nunna," she whispered.

Morla was close enough to hear her—or else she had heard her thoughts.

"You sense it?" she wondered quietly as the two fell in behind the centaur.

"He also was made by people?" Val guessed.

"There are no others like him; and as long as the crypts beneath this mountain remain sealed, there never will be."

The three walked on in silence until the widening way climbed to the level of a high terrace. Here the walls on either hand receded to meet ground covered in soft springy turf. The mighty steel bastion to their left was mirrored by another standing hundreds of feet away, and still another. They seemed to encompass a circular space, vast in size, high on the summit of the hill.

Looking to her right, Val could now see that the road they were on was also part of a terrace, a step cloven deep into the hillside beneath the summit. Below, the land fell away into steep treeless slopes and cliffs. The tops of towers appeared lower down, and other walls and structures that were built on lower terraces. Beyond, long miles away, she descried green fields and a wide bluish-black lake like polished glass. Farther still there lay the endless red wasteland. The wind that came up to them from below carried more than the scent of spice; an acrid fume was also detectable, the smell of ancient stone, and an occasional whiff of sulfur.

Just ahead, Orlim came to an intersection. A wider way, its stepped and sloping path worn from passage, met the road they were traveling at a perpendicular angle as it ran up towards the High Place. Val followed the centaur as he turned upon this straight way, straining to ignore the fiery pains in her legs and back. Morla, who had taken her hand again, was now partially supporting her. Orlim kept their pace slow. They did not proceed much farther before passing the first of the many mighty pillars lining the way, and then Val looked up.

There was a wall of crystal ahead, framed with saplings and flowers unfolding in gleaming veins of silver and gold. A gate of ivory opened in these costly windows, carved in relief to depict scenes of hunters and a forest full of magical creatures. She hardly noticed the gate for the warriors who stood before it. Two ranks of men were assembled there, one on either side, and they were arrayed in such armor and draped in such finery that they looked more fantasy than fearsome; yet their faces were scarred, and though each bowed his head in respect as she passed, Val sensed their tension. These were men skilled in many weapons, hardened by long years of war. Guarding such a door as this was obviously a matter of great honor to them.

One of the guards ran ahead to warn the Council of their arrival. They were signaled to wait, and while they waited Val took note of a series of three blue circular emblems above the gateway. The one to the left contained the symbol of a stylized sword, and the one to the right a shield. The one in the center puzzled her mightily. There was something striking there that Val didn't expect to see.

Fishing in a pouch in her belt, she removed one of her personal treasures stowed there—Taran's silver dollar, retrieved from the clothing she'd worn on her very first transit. She gazed upon the emblem of the eagle on the coin, its claws clutching an olive branch and a quiver of arrows. Then, raising her hand towards the central symbol above the gate, she placed the two side by side in her field of view.

"What is that?" Orlim asked, leaning over her slightly.

Val trembled at the nearness of him. "It is an emblem of power in my world," she said.

"So it has ever been," Morla observed. "It is the first thing I remember of this place from my visions, long before I ever came here."

"But how can that be? It's the eagle! It's exactly the same!"

Orlim reached towards her hand, bending over at the waist so that he was close to her head. One of his long tapered ears touched her own. He took the coin delicately in his great fingers, and he snorted surprise.

"No," he said. "This says *one do-lar*, but there's something different on the crest above, written in ancient and indecipherable words."

Val squinted at the stone seal and read the Latin uncials inscribed on a banner in the eagle's beak.

E PLURIBUS UNUM

She snatched the coin from his hand and tucked it back in her belt.

"From many, one," she translated. "It means that there were many people and nations who banded together and became one tribe. It is a motto of my people."

"One tribe?" he asked, squinting at the emblem. "You're sure?"

"Why wouldn't I be? It's Latin. Everyone knows *Latin*."

"Is that so?" he asked, ears twitching. "All I know is that this eagle adorns the crest of a Great House of the Galanon, House Gaerith, whose lord was exiled from Gilthaloneth. He joined the Crodah in Ertsetum under the Ban, leaving behind a son who has lived these thousand years in hiding. Maybe the symbol on your medallion was brought with him into the Dark Worlds, for there is no other place under heaven where the tribes will become one. Look there."

Orlim pointed up towards the three circular symbols.

"These three Great Houses of the four were forced to depart under the Ban for crimes against the Council and against Syrscian. This is their gate, the Exile's Gate, the only passage to the High Place for those committed to the Wastelands of Ertsetum and Iskartum."

"Who are the Exiles?"

"House Crodah, House Gaerith, and House Gremn," he replied, pointing to each of the three seals in turn. "These of the four Great Houses were deemed more or less responsible for the destruction of our realm."

"Crodah and Gremn I know," Val said, "but what became of the people of House Gaerith?"

"Who knows? Dead or vanished, not one of them has been seen since the exile of their lord. It is believed they all perished in the Destroying Fire."

"And what of the Fourth House?" Val wondered. "They were not exiled?"

At that moment, the guard returned.

"Ladies, Master Orlim, if you will follow me."

They were beckoned towards the doors, through which they passed side by side. As soon as they'd crossed the threshold a clear high trumpet-blast sounded from within. Val almost jumped, never having heard such a noise; but the novelty wore off in an instant. Ahead there were many thousands assembled, a sea of colorful silk that stood about the edges of a flat grassy space that must have spanned miles. Far off in the center was an odd rock formation. She recognized this as the location of her arrival.

Above, an airy skydome of translucent pink alabaster floated high. Birds flitted across its expansive surface, and as she looked closer she discerned a pattern etched there, the shape of an enormous intaglio of a dozen signs and figures. Val was not given time to study them, however, for the mumbling of the masses stopped immediately after the sound of the trumpet, and then the voice of a herald cried out from the chamber before them. His words rang out across the mountaintop.

"The Council welcomes Our Lady, Val Anna!
Empress of Syrscian and the Dark World Ertsetum!"

Their guide backed away five paces and knelt. There was a deep percussion, a single drum-beat, and every person within the High Place slowly dropped to one knee. A hush followed, and then a second drum-beat.

"Follow me, Lady," Orlim commanded.

Leading the way, he strode out onto the lawn and made for the rocky altar in the center. Val looked at her feet and listened to the swish-swishing noises of her dress as she walked. Her heart was pounding, for she could feel the eyes of all those strange people upon her.

Morla was walking quietly on the other side of Orlim. Val wished she would walk beside her, but there was a certain rigidity to the unfolding spectacle, a rhythm of roles and parts that must be played out for ceremony's sake. They were very slowly nearing the center and its strange jumble of rocks—it would take another ten minutes to reach it at this rate—and Val was already thinking how much she wanted to leave.

Bells interrupted these thoughts, beautiful silver bells, ringing from some lofty place. Val slowed her steps, and Orlim stopped. The multitudes were no longer facing her. Their attention was fixed now on the eastern side of the airy Temple, just ahead, and there Val saw a wonder. Revealed between the low wall of crystal and the pillars of the mighty skydome, shimmering in a wine-hued sunrise, a new world was rising.

Beyond the gathered masses, beyond the green grassy bald and the far fenestrated pillars whose windows looked east, there flashed into view, still ascending, a mound of purple above the edge of the horizon—a wavy hill awash in the light of the sun. Before this had fully risen, another smaller world, grey and mottled, appeared just before it, literally materializing out of nowhere.

Within moments of the grey moon's advent there flared a brilliant light, and before the other two a blue world appeared. From the moment this world burst into existence, Val sensed its hold on her. She knew it intimately.

It was the Earth.

Somehow she kept walking.

In the span of a few more breathless minutes, they reached the stony center of the court. The rock formation was much larger viewed from close at hand than it had seemed, and now Val could see it was shaped like a great chair facing the rising worlds. The seat was at least ten feet above the ground, and the back rose higher. Val stood between Morla and Orlim upon the northern side, where a low parapet accessible by a step offered a more modest vantage. They stood until the bells stopped ringing, and then the crowds rose. The noise of their garments was like a waterfall.

"I bring you the Protector of the Stone," Orlim announced. "The day has come for the fulfillment of what was written in the Book of Invasions."

His voice echoed loudly across the entire chamber.

Far away to the right, there was movement. A couple people were walking towards them from the crowds, and as the lead figure drew nearer Val saw that he was a very curious creature indeed. His shaven head, the wide set of his eyes, and his bat-like nose caused her to think of *Quasimodo.*

"The *Pope of Fools?*" she wondered.

"Any louder and they will all hear you, My Lady," Orlim warned in a hushed voice.

Val pressed a hand to her mouth and studied the figure as he strode closer, his long white mantle flashing with cut gems and tinkling belled tassels. He stopped at a distance of about fifty feet, close enough for her to see that her original estimation was close to the mark, for right behind him stalked the hunchback's *Frollo.*

"Nergal!" she whispered. "So he came back, did he?"

Morla stepped around Orlim to stand beside her. "He stays with the priest," she said quietly, "and I stay here with you. That is my burden."

"Your burden?"

"Our long acquaintance makes us accomplices in the Council's thinking."

Before she could explain, the priest spoke.

"Orlim, last of the Dragon Slayers," he began. "The Council receives your exiled guests. It is with deep affection that we greet the Empress upon her fortunate return to these lands, her arrival having been verified by a spectacle no less splendorous than her appearance, coming as she has in the very hour of the conjunction which the ancient records state last passed on the date of her departure. Welcome, friends of old!"

Strangely, his tone reflected none of the joy his words conveyed. The speaker paused about a hundred feet away, gesturing grandly towards the worlds on the eastern horizon. Nergal stood beside him with a dark glowering pout on his face. The look in his sorcerous black-within-black eyes confused her. It was not the mood Val had left him in, in New York.

"Orlim will now present her with the articles of her office," the speaker continued. "She laid them down when she departed, long ago, and our Councilors past bade him keep these tokens and to guard them all these centuries against the day of her return."

Val was looking around for some kind of sound amplification device, but could see nothing. The acoustics of the chamber were far superior to anything she had experienced, or else there was some clever technology at work here. Before she knew what was happening, Orlim lifted something from the stone step beside them, and standing before her he positioned a light half-circlet of entwined golden serpents before her face.

"You return in our time of need," he said gravely. "You who protect the sacred stones, we look to your wise government to preserve us again, as once it did."

With these lofty words he slid the diadem on eyeglass-style, so that it rested over her ears. As the circlet settled upon her brow, she caught the flashing gleam of a blue gem that hung down between her eyes.

"And there is this also," he said, raising a blue pendant on a crimson ribbon. "It was a gift from your mother."

"My mother?" Val wondered, staring goggle-eyed at the flashing oval crystal.

Orlim gently lowered the pendant over her bowed head. The metal fasting was cold upon her chest. There was no applause from the Council, only a rumbling of low voices. Val was stirred with emotion and confusion, and turned her head this way and that, adjusting to the feel of the crown. She wondered if she looked anything like a queen, because she certainly didn't feel like one. In her bewilderment she turned to the centaur, and the awful creature was smiling at her. Then, in a swiftly passing moment, she experienced a strong sensation of déjà-vu.

She knew she had dreamed of this before. Now the dream was coming true.

The entire assembly waited until hushed silence resumed. Nergal whispered something in the priest's ear.

"The Empress herself carries the artifact?" *Quasimodo* asked.

Distracted from her examination of the pendant, Val looked at Orlim and nodded.

"She bears three, Priest," the centaur replied.

The vast chamber echoed with the sounds of many voices, all of them speaking at once. Val discerned some considerable doubt in those voices.

"How am I going to convince them I have *any* stones?" she whispered to Morla. She hardly needed to whisper, the crowd made so much noise.

"What do you mean?" Morla asked.

"I can't very well make them come out of me the same way they've gone in! And besides, don't you think they'd better remain secret?"

Into the midst of this confusion there rose a loud voice, the voice of the priest, who said, "I am Teomaxos of the Tenno! Hear the voice of the Council!"

The assembled reacted with subdued silence.

The speaker continued in gentler tones, saying, "The Empress will forgive a brief speech of introduction. I was summoned by this Council, as was she. It is an honor to have been selected from among the many priests of the colonies to preside over this interrogation."

"Interrogation?" Val wondered. Her voice was lifted high, to every corner of the Temple.

"I have come this way to the Great City, through many leagues of the Wastes on a road plagued by raiders of the Forest Tribes, in answer to the summons of Orlim and our lost Priestess—Morla, long-departed, and now returned."

He bowed. There was some applause, but Morla frowned deeply, and Val caught a flash of uncharacteristic anger from her. Something prompted her to inflame it.

"I don't trust him," she said to Morla, "not if he's with Nergal. Nergal was with the dragon in New York."

Morla's head turned, but her eyes wore more than surprise. She paled, matching the color of her hair.

The applause ended. "I am learned somewhat in the lore of the stones," Teomaxos continued. "I will be able to answer the Council's questions regarding your Ladyship's situation if you will first answer some of my own."

"He's my *attorney?*" Val asked, turning to Morla.

"Nergal was with a *dragon?*" Morla wondered.

"My wish is that my courteous words here may help to restore our beloved Empress' memory without increasing the strain of her transport under the Ban, and that in so doing the Council will be resolved to permit her lasting refuge here with any or all of her companions, and will restore to her the scepter of government over these lands."

More mumbling and muttering arose over this, and some shouting, too. One voice rose above the others, coming from afar, saying, *"It is the forbidden prophecy! The blood of those who died under the harsh law of this Council cries out for vengeance, Teomaxos!"*

Teomaxos was not moved. Val now knew what kind of person he was. She also understood that he was the only person capable of speaking on behalf of all the Gremn and Crodah who had sacrificed themselves to send her here. In other words, all the exiles were now at his mercy.

Her eyes met Nergal's. Just what was he up to?

With a clearing of his throat, Teomaxos of Nara turned towards the assembled masses and began a recital of the deep history he knew.

"Given in the Book of Invasions, recorded by my father's fathers of old, we know that in the Beginning the four races were one, and that they dwelt together in peace with the Ancients, the first children of the light, servants to the power of their Creator in the vast and bountiful realms of Syrscian. The four races quickly learned the ways of the wide world, and of the heavenly bodies above, and taught by the Ancient Ones they excelled in the crafting of song and tale, for then there was no want or need of anything. All the toils of the people were rewarded with rich bounty, and all worked to ease the burdens of others. Children were many and healthy, and no one grew weary of life in the ever-even of the moons, locked fast in the Life of the Light, which does not diminish with the passage of time."

A chorus of thousands of voices answered the litany, saying, *"Thus the first age."*

Val glanced at Morla, and watched her lips repeat the catechism as if she had done so many times before.

"Then came the Shadow," the priest said. This time his pause went unanswered.

"An evil entered into the hearts of the Ancients. Dark and twisted demons arose among them, and pupils were taken. Bent and broken, these became the first sorcerers. Their purpose was to upset the balance of authority, to claim all power under heaven as their own, and to do this they sought the favor of others by promise and by gifts. Their works slowly spread, darkening the world and dimming its first light. The master of these renegades was an Ancient so powerful that he was bound with time itself, and cast out into the worlds to gnaw upon his anger in the torment of exile. He is the Destroyer of life, the bringer of darkness."

"Thus the second age," sounded the refrain.

Teomaxos continued, saying, "At this time darkness was eclipsed and light reborn, but the strife of the sorcerers cut too deep. The wounds they made in the world threatened resources. War was born. While one rose up to enslave his neighbor, another was slain in the night by his brother's hand. The woes of the land increased, and a mighty maker in the house of light was loosed upon Syrscian to fulfill his hidden and timely role. From the beginning he was known of only among the Ancients as one of the *Dyn Hysbys*—wise spirits, clothed in the frame of the children of the light. These *Wise Folk*, as they are called, were sent to seek out the children, to warn them of the power that threatened their peace; but the children were not yet wary, and they failed to understand the danger posed by the appearance of the Destroyer's minions. These came upon us cleverly, enticing untested souls to join in war; and so war followed war. In Kutha dwell the true bringers of the Wastes, the sorcerers and demons, and all who have busied themselves these ages plotting our miserable end. In the tower of sorcerers, in Ost-Thargul that once was light, the polluted darkness of all the Dark Worlds resides."

The assembled stood in lasting silence. Val sensed a great tension in the crowds, gathering force as the priest readied himself for the recitation of words already known to all except her.

"We are a people divided, who should not be divided. We were given one to rule over us, who was taken from us. We were entrusted with one stone, which was divided into the twelve. The twelve contain all the worlds, but all the worlds cannot contain our sorrows and strife. Gremn and Crodah were exiled, never to return until the twelve are restored. Thus the Empress spoke with her own tongue one thousand years ago, and thus some have used lies to make her words seem like prophecy. The grief of those lies and the waste of lives taken in the hopes of our sovereign's promised return necessitate careful consideration of the costs of her accession, and a tribunal review of the misuse of her powers in the past."

Morla clenched her fists. *"How can they hold you responsible for what others have done in your name?"* she whispered.

Val could not respond, for her heart was too full. Her eyes were brimming. She bit her tongue so that she did not cry out, but could not help the contortion of her face as she wrestled with the horror and the woe of what was being spoken by this priest. Every eye was turned upon her, and in that very moment a shadow obscured the moons in the eastern sky. But the shadow taking shape from the words of Teomaxos obscured only Val's sight. Only she could see it, though it wrapped heavily around her. It was a shadow she knew, which had come to her at Hazor on its day of ruin; yet this was not the least of the ill tidings its presence brought now to trouble her.

There was no speech with the Destroyer, yet Val felt his mind touch hers in no uncertain way, thrusting meaning to the front of her confused thoughts, stirring memories. She knew that she was somehow linked to this monster, just as the priest had said, and the certainty amplified in her heart a growing dread.

Teomaxos' voice broke suddenly through the mire of the shadow, saying, "Upon our dear Lady's orders, the Vault was opened and the Crypt's seal broken. Gilthaloneth's treasures, technologies hidden deep by the Ancients since the worlds began, lay in her hands. With clear yet secret orders, weapons were removed from the Crypt, and given to one by the name of Ard Morvran, master of House Crodah. These weapons ended the Gremn-Crodah conflict, and in so doing turned all of Galaneth into a desert."

"Thus the third age," they all said.

The shadow dispersed suddenly, and her heart burst within her.

"My God!" she cried. "What are they accusing me of? How I wish Kabta were here!"

The peculiar acoustics of the mighty chamber carried her words to every ear. The Council remained hushed as the echoes of her outburst travelled across the hilltop.

"That's done it," Orlim muttered in the ensuing silence. "We'll have to think of another way out of this. It's not enough that they've recognized your basic sovereignty, Lady, for the power remains with the Galanese majority. Even among the minority of Lesser Houses, any evidence of collaboration with Kabta of House Gremn will push us back into the dark."

"It would be best to refrain from mentioning ties to any other enemies of the Council in their presence," Morla whispered.

Teomaxos stood the while with his hands apart and his head bowed—a posture of respect; but his ears were opened. He raised his head just enough to look upon Val, and when he saw how distressed she'd become at his words he ducked and backed away several steps. Val caught his silent pleasure at her discomfort, however. Lower and lower her heart sank. Morla took her arm gently, but there was no comfort in her touch.

"One thousand years ago," Morla said in a whisper, "these people were decimated by the War of Destroying Fire. You are the one who began it. It was you. *You destroyed Paradise.*"

"The Empress requires a moment to accept the burden the Council places upon her," Orlim announced. "She doesn't recall any of these events, for by transit between the worlds the stone has begun a change in her."

"You say she brings the Holy Jewel," Teomaxos said, "but this has not yet been established."

"What...what does he want from me?" Val stammered. "What kind of game are they playing?"

"She bears the stones in her flesh," Orlim replied sternly, speaking over her voice. "Our word will suffice!"

"Can you confirm it?" Teomaxos asked. "I'm not asking you to, but it would help."

"The Empress would not have been able to cross against the Ban without them."

"Unless she came by some forbidden way," Teomaxos said.

"Enough!" Orlim shouted. His voice shook the air like thunder, and silence descended on the gathering like a smothering hand.

"I have passed two thousand turns of the year in Syrscian," the centaur said. "That is long before your families ever came into the priesthood; yet in all that time I have not witnessed such open hostility in the Council. For now, her honest words will have to be enough to satisfy the Empress' claims. Know you nothing of honor?"

Teomaxos looked like he was about to say something, but Orlim held up a hand to stop him, and said, "There was once trust between us—a trust that will yet be reestablished when the Ban is lifted and the Gremn and Crodah are returned. I look forward to the reformation of all four Great Houses, as they were of old. These events have begun to unfold today in your presence, though maybe not with your blessings."

Loud shouts arose. Val saw a movement from the gate, far behind them now, and turned to note the presence of many warriors entering the green. They rushed forward through the narrow entrance, forming a barrier between the crowds and her only escape from the High Place. When he saw the soldiers in the Temple, Teomaxos turned fearfully and gave hand-signals to several attendants who hung back at the edge of the crowd. These men immediately and urgently began to exhort the multitudes to silence.

"I request permission to remove my friends from this place so that you may conclude your assembly without further uproar," Orlim said.

"Granted," Teomaxos replied. "Take your warriors with you."

The priest turned and stalked back towards the tumultuous masses. Nergal stood a moment longer, keeping Val's gaze, and then he also took his leave.

Orlim looked after them. Then, turning to Val he said, "He will regret that request when it comes time to making his war with the Fourth House."

He didn't look happy, but his frown wasn't for her. Val nodded.

"I was supposed to ask about lifting the Ban," she said. "It's very important."

"That is truly a matter worth discussing," Orlim replied, "but I fear the time for the great event is a long way off yet."

"What do you mean?"

"Let's go, Lady. You need your rest."

As they neared the gate and the soldiers gathered in a defensive ring around them, Orlim spoke again, saying, "There are things My Lady must know. We are currently engaged in open war with the Forest People, and the outlook is not good. You have come to bring the exiles home, you say, but I ask, who among the exiles would desire to leave the Dark Worlds for a world at war?"

"What can I do for them, then?" Val wondered. "There are so many relying on me."

"You must make this a welcome place for them. Your wise counsel is needed to quell the murderous threats breathed by the priests, or we may *all* end up exiles."

"But I know nothing of war!"

"You are involved in this conflict from the beginning, as am I. The walls of your tower will not long hide you from the poisons and daggers of would-be assassins, fanatics on both sides who believe the only way to end all this is to slay you."

Val paled.

"Your personal safety is a priority. Elements of the Council are becoming a threat. Though for now they have no real power outside the governance of the city, this may soon change. For the time being, I am their might in warfare, and they would not dare strike out against you directly so long as you are in my protection."

Val nodded. *He uses his loyalty as leverage over me,* she thought as they exited by the Gate of Exiles.

"Even so," he continued, "you should both remain in your lodgings until summoned by my own messengers. I will fill you in on the details of our situation, and of anything else you must know, at your convenience."

"She needs rest before a briefing," Morla insisted.

Val heard a hint of the old Morla in the tone of voice she used. It was the way she used to speak to Nurkabta: agitated and with a suggestion of covert intention.

Orlim looked back, his face oddly expressionless.

"What's this really about?" he pried. "Is this another one of your secrets, Morla, the kind you always tried to keep to yourself until you realized they were no longer so secret? Does it have anything to do with the *Null-User* the Empress retrieved from the Dark World?"

The two exchanged silent stares.

"What's that over there?" Val interrupted, hoping to dispel the rising tension. She stopped and pointed ahead to a statue standing alone beside the road where it intersected with the narrower way leading back to her tower.

"It's a statue," Orlim replied, expressing puzzlement in his voice.

"It looks familiar," she said.

This seemed to interest both Orlim and Morla. They walked together towards the decrepit stone, the monument of a man standing on a small mound.

"He looks like a warrior," Morla said. "He wears armor."

"This piece was placed here about the time you left, Lady," Orlim muttered. "With all due respect, I never could figure why you commissioned this ugly calamitous thing."

"I did?"

Amidst the clinging vines and patched moss, Val was lost in wonder. She experienced a peculiar double-vision, and saw again the statue in the train station—and then the memorial where her mother stopped to pray.

"It is a memorial of the war," Orlim said. "That is what the inscription reads."

"It is in English?" Val wondered, looking at the words.

"It is our common speech you see written here. What is Eng-lish?"

But Val was absorbed in the inscription.

CEDRIC DEPONS, LORD OF HOUSE GAERITH

Purveyor of Wisdom was he, who read the seal and opened the crypt.
*"Those who would take credit for the rain
should not complain when they are blamed for the drought."*

"DePons!" she exclaimed.

"The mysterious Lord of House Gaerith," Orlim said. "You remember him?"

She paused, wondering if her memories of DePons were memories of events past or future. "I know some things about him," she replied. "Why is he called *Purveyor*, though? That's just a fancy word for *source*."

Morla took her hand. Val felt a warning squeeze.

"He was a source of trouble, and nothing more," Orlim answered bitterly. "A thousand years after the events that won DePons his ticket to exile, his son now takes up the family legacy for generating conflict—"

"Lord Orlim!"

At the cry of his name, all three looked down the climbing road towards the sound of the youthful voice. A boy appeared. He came sprinting, and his eyes were wide with more than just the exertion of his ascent.

"Islith!" the youth cried. "Islith's core is reactivated!"

Morla's hand squeezed tighter. Orlim stepped forward to meet him.

"How long ago?" he asked.

"No more than a few hours. A Null-User must have awakened in the Hive! We wouldn't have noticed at all if you hadn't posted someone on that old prompter!"

"A thousand years I've waited," he said, turning his head aside, "and now all this comes back to us in a moment?"

Morla did not answer. Val felt her hand trembling, and wondered what it was all about. Of course she had heard of Islith, from Kabta. It was a city in the World of Origins.

"No ordinary *Null-User* could have managed this," Orlim said. "Only a Fomorian can activate Islith's core."

"A Fomorian!" Val exclaimed.

Could it be that Bec made it here, too?

Morla definitely caught this afterthought, and turned a questioning frown on her.

"Who're they?" the messenger wondered, eyeing the two women.

"It is as I briefed you this morning," Orlim replied sternly. "Your Empress stands before you, and beside her the High Priestess of old."

The boy paled, and trembling with terror he began to kneel.

"Wait," Val said, reaching out her hand. "It's not necessary!"

He hesitated, and glanced up briefly into her face before looking to Orlim.

"You will be trained in protocol when the time has come," Orlim interrupted.

Val wondered whom he was speaking to—to herself, or to the boy.

"Rise," Orlim commanded. "Go back and tell them they must keep tracking the signal—and speak no word of what the Watchers see to anyone else outside our syndicate."

Val stiffened.

"What task should I set them?" the messenger asked, his voice low and uncertain.

"Our next priority is to hunt down Lord Bregon. We will need the help of Lothar, his captain, who is serving his sentence as Warden of the West Gate at Nara."

Orlim's ears twitched, and looking up suddenly he stretched his long hand against his brow to peer into the sky. Following his gaze, the others caught a fleeting shadow against the sun. Then there was nothing.

"What is it?" Morla asked.

"A bird, I guess. It's just, it reminded me of—"

He shook his head.

"Tomorrow, then," Morla said, tugging Val toward the descending track.

"I have waited too long for tomorrow to come," he replied with a shake of his head, and taking the main road he made for the lower city at a trot with the messenger running after him. When they had passed out of sight, Morla turned to Val.

"You are not accustomed to court intrigues. Be wary of him, Val."

"Who?"

"Orlim led his people for centuries, and later became the chieftain of the Dragon Slayers, your royal bodyguard. They are all dead but him, slain in the War of Destroying Fire—slain defending *you*. His kindness towards you feels strained. I think it's because you've changed. He will try to use you to make a strong move against the Council. He also has plans for me. Those plans, like Nurkabta's, are very ancient."

"Can I not trust him?"

"Orlim helped reaffirm your title, but he has a long way to go before the tribes and houses are united under your government. Though his intentions are good, he will not soon let go of the power granted by his time-honored position. The last thousand years have made him a figure of legend, a king in all but title."

The path before them sank steadily beneath the upper tier of the hill. When they reached the circular chamber with its guardian Combat Units, Val noticed that the murals she at first thought were of animals were actually of humans with animal features. There were bird-people, cat-people, and even deer-people, and these were accompanied by a host of fauns and other creatures familiar to mythology. The characters were posed in a forest setting that wrapped around the interior of the chamber, engaged in an assortment of ordinary activities such as carrying water, planting, and harvesting. The realism in their execution and the brightness of the paints astonished her. As her wandering eyes took in the many details, they lingered last upon the form of a red-haired girl with wings who stretched out her arms towards the creatures around her as if welcoming them into an embrace. Rays shone down on this figure from above. Gazing upwards to the cap of the dome over her head, Val saw the silver emblem of a pegasus.

"The seal of the Fourth House," Morla said, following her gaze.

Val glanced once more at the winged girl before she was ready to move on. While they walked to the level of the noble houses on the long winding street to her tower, her thoughts returned to the murals.

"Morla," she wondered, "Why does the Council hate the people of the Forest?"

"Because the Forest People are different," Morla answered, smiling slightly. The smile faded quickly, though.

"What became of the people of the Fourth House?"

"It is a sorrowful tale," Morla replied. "Long ago, the Council initiated hostilities with the Forest Tribes by destroying the Sacred Trees they protect."

"The Council started it? Why?"

"The trees are Fomorian sleepers, the spirits of the people of Bec's tribe."

Val was surprised by her use of the name.

"Yes," Morla said, reading her reaction, "I speak of Ard Morvran's *pet*. Loosed from her Null-body, Bec is the most powerful being ever to walk beneath the sun and the three moons. She is the last princess of her tribe, the literal embodiment of the Forests of this world. The Council will learn of her, but we must find her first. Things will become very interesting if she comes looking for you here."

"Why would she do that?"

"According to the outlawed prophecy, the prophecy the Forest Tribes protect by guarding the Sacred Trees, the Empress will return to lead all the tribes in peace to a new beginning. Despite Orlim's open support for the prophecy, it is apparent that not everyone is in favor of a new beginning—especially not the nobles and priests in the Council. They will use every means in their power to prevent you from taking authority from them for fear that you would give it to the former Great Houses. And Bec, if she discovered you were here, would cross the burning Wastes to make sure this prophecy comes to pass."

They stopped outside the double door of her tower. Val felt better physically, but she was secretly longing for some time alone to ponder all she had discovered. Morla clearly understood, but lingered by the doors awhile in silent thought.

"There is one more burden I must lay upon you today," she said at length, her voice low and edged with tension. "The Forest has groaned for your appearance for a thousand years. It groans with a voice that words cannot express. If the Forest

Tribes discovered that you are here, and that the Council was holding you prisoner for war crimes, we would have quite a battle on our hands. Before that happens, you must remember who you are."

"Remember who I am?"

"Hear what I must now convey to you, speaking as a true friend speaks to a friend."

Morla took her hands, and speaking in a whisper she said, "As the Forest People tell it, the last daughter of the Ancients—the daughter of a woman named Brisen—was born into a human body in exile."

"Brisen?"

"This was necessary, so they say, in order to accomplish two things: first, to inform the Crodah of the Ancients, and second to give the girl a human heart—an understanding of love from the perspective of a lesser child, which the Ancients do not naturally cultivate. More than this, no one can guess; but you will know it when the time comes, for *you were that child.*"

Val stood stunned and quiet, her lips parting just once to permit the escape of a breath forced out by the pounding of her heart.

"My mother?" she whispered.

"The pendant upon your breast is the sign of Brisen's house," Morla said, letting go of her hand. "Maybe it will help you remember who you are. The Forest People hold the secret to unlocking the rest of your memories. Do not think of them as memories of things that have not yet happened. All time is present, Val Anna."

"I don't know if I understand what you're saying," Val said. "What should I do?"

"The question is, what will the stones do?" Morla asked. "They have reunited us, if nothing else. It is as you said, *from many will come one.*"

Val stood silent for another moment, her eyes downcast. She removed the diadem from her forehead and massaged her temples, but there was no relief from the sudden surging headache. When she looked up, Morla had gone.

Entering her dwelling alone, she found a mound of strange fruit in a bowl and a pitcher on the table by her couch. Besides these there was also a tidy bundle of clothing set on the floor, folded and tied with silk ribbons, together with a pair of thigh-high leather boots with chaps and leggings. A small cut rose lay across the folded clothes, and upon her couch lay a child's painting on a scrap of canvas, labeled *Fann*. Taking a seat, Val set down the diadem on the table and lifted the offered rose and portrait. The painting was of a group of three smiling girls standing around a tall red-haired woman in a gown. Val guessed that these were the three who awakened her in the morning. All were curiously embellished with long ears and foxtails. Silliness aside, it was a touching gift, and it comforted her.

She sat and stared at it a long while.

"I wish Taran was here," she said.

24
LABORATORY OF THE REFORMATION

*Island Aenfer,
A.D. 1901*

In a long fire-lit room Taran sat alone. His sleep, brief and troubled, was interrupted by dinner. Contrary to Jon's predictions, it was chicken—not lamb—and very tasty chicken at that. After he'd finished off an accompanying platter of bread and cheese, Giles pushed a stoneware cup into his hands. Taran sniffed the liquid inside. Limp bits of green floated around the murky brew.

"I don't like tea," he complained.

"Try it," the caretaker insisted.

He left the room. Taran sipped, and a pleasant mint flavor, sweetened with honey, burst on his tongue. By the time Giles returned, his arms loaded with books and loose sheets of paper, Taran had finished half the cup.

"This is tea?" he asked brightly.

"It's a recipe old Fain brought back with him from the Middle East. I thought you could do with some light refreshment before perusing *these*."

Giles dropped the books onto the dusty surface of the table where Taran sat.

"Fain's journals," he announced.

Taran eyed the books with a sinking feeling. "Grandfather's diaries?" he asked, pulling his suspenders up over an un-tucked and very wrinkled shirt.

Giles picked up his empty plate, nodding towards the sheathed sword that lay on the table. "Aside from that blade," he said, "these papers are all that is left. I fancy you'll find something of interest tucked away there."

"Why? Because they tell what happened to him?"

"I don't know," Giles said. "I haven't read them. Fain seemed to understand that you would come by one day, and said that I was to ask you to read through this when you arrived."

"How long ago did he ask you to do this?"

"It was more than fifteen years ago."

"About the time he disappeared," Taran said. "But I was only a child then."

"I expect you'll figure it out, young Master, just like you did in the hall with the sword."

He left, shutting the door behind him.

Taran cast his eyes around the dimly lit chamber. The dressed stone walls wore a coating of yellow plaster, and were paneled to waist-height with dark-stained oak. Tall thick-paned windows in the wall behind him, opposite the door, let in a terrible draft. The fire that burned in the hearth danced happily in the gusts that wandered the length and breadth of the room. Though his clothes had dried, hung before the fire while he dozed, the air chilled him.

He sat at a long table in the center, graced by only one high-backed chair. The table stood between the fire and the couch where he slept. Taran wondered at first why the couch was so far from the only source of heat, but then he noticed the smoke that gathered at the hearth-end of the room. It hung lazily in great tendrils, despite the breeze. He stared at it, his thoughts sluggishly mimicking the same slow lethargy of the grey-white wisps. Shapes he imagined there, shapes of faces that changed moment-by-moment.

Like Hest's face had changed on the boat.

He pulled one of the books from the pile and held it before him. Just as he was about to open it, his attention was distracted by a sudden hush outside. The rain had stopped. Leaning around the back of the chair, he gazed at the moon that appeared from behind drifting mountains of clouds. The trees outside the rattling windows were visible as jostling dark masses, giants that shoved one another for a place in an unbroken line surrounding the estate. From this second story he could also see the undulating hills of forested land, grey under the night sky. It was a very lonely sight.

Taran pried his attention away from the windows and looked down at the book in his hands, a huge and ponderous tome of the kind that children find threatening. Right now it looked about as inviting as an ice-bath. He might find answers to some of the questions he had been asking since Val Anna disappeared, but a strange apathy hung over him.

"Well, aren't you going to read it?"

Taran jerked upright, startled. Hest stood in the doorway opposite, a candle in her hand. She was dressed in a nightgown, and looked rather ghostly standing there.

"You could have knocked," he said, speaking more sharply than he intended.

"I did. Are you going to read it or not? They'll be back in just forty hours. We need to have a plan in place by then."

"A plan to help Father escape from America? What hope is there for that?"

"None. I was speaking of a plan to use what we learned from Regulus to find Val before they do."

"Regulus, huh?" Taran wondered, eyeing the cover of the book in front of him. It was entitled, *Laboratory of the Reformation, Vol. 1*, and like the other, it was bound in leather and completely hand written. The letters were formed by strong and steady strokes, the mark of a man who was confident and sure—the writing of Fain Morvran. He opened to the first page, and read the title of the first chapter aloud.

"*The Human Solvency Army and Foundation Technologies.* What in the world is this?"

"It is the record of Cedric DePons' work, written by your grandfather," Hest said. She stepped into the room and closed the door, sliding the bolt and locking it behind her.

"How do you know?" he asked. "Have you read this before?"

"No."

"I knew he was in the Army, but what's *Human Solvency?*"

She walked around the table and stood beside him, setting the candle down in his half-empty cup of tea. Taran watched as she then lifted the volume in her hands and opened it to a ribbon of silk left as a bookmark.

"Wait," he said, taking the book from her. "I'll read it, okay?"

Hest looked on with a smirk that Taran ignored. He started reading aloud in a low voice, puzzling often over Fain's loopy handwriting.

> *Lír is extremely paranoid and reclusive. None of his inner circle makes contact with him for more than a few moments at a time. It seems he is also afraid of a peculiar virus. Concerning his history little is known outside of what DePons has reported to me directly, which I have recorded here.*

He looked up, brow bunched and frowning.

"Keep reading," she insisted.

Lír is a direct descendant of the founder of the Great Corporations. He is a master of all spoken and written forms of language, and was a genius engineer, a senior Guild Member. He was outspoken against the aggressors who inspired the war until his own family was slaughtered in the Battle of Cipa. It was then his meticulous plans for revenge were drawn. He became a monster, dedicating his remaining life to the destruction of all who may have had a role in bringing about his sorrow—

Taran broke off and sighed deeply, taking his head in both hands.

"What's wrong?" Hest asked.

"This is all rubbish!" he exclaimed. "It'll take *years* for me to sort out the history of this guy *Lír*, and Naruna will be coming back for us soon!"

"We'll be gone long before then, I hope," Hest said.

"Where are we going? What happened to finding a way to use Naruna against his boss? Isn't that why I'm reading this?"

"I have already contacted agents within our organization who will be dealing with that objective. All we have to do is find out where Fain is."

"Fain? What about Val?"

"Find Fain and we will find her."

"That doesn't make sense to me," Taran objected. "Just because they've both gone missing doesn't mean they both ended up in the same place. And Fain disappeared fifteen years ago!"

"His disappearance and Val Anna's are related nonetheless."

"How?"

"They both involved the work that DePons began here with Fain."

"And the research they were conducting on the stone?" Taran guessed. "Well then, wouldn't we do better exploring the cellar for clues?"

"This is a written record," she said, pointing at the page. "We'll find more here than in the laboratory."

"I don't know. Didn't you used to come here to work in the lab with DePons?"

Hest's gaze was somber. "Read some more. I'm sure Fain must have put it in better words than I ever could."

Taran stared at her, fancying he saw in her face a flicker of something familiar. Was it Drusilla he saw there, somewhere in the lines around her eyes? He turned his attention back to the page, and began reading where he'd left off.

> *Lír it was who drew forth the Aries from its resting place, countermanding the brothers' express wishes to cover all traces of their activities. He also constructed Apsu, an undersea habitat located off the Welsh coast. It was for this reason our ancestors moved to the Isle of Aenfer, which is situated a safe distance to the north, yet remains close enough to Lír to keep watch over all he does.*

"This *Apsu* place sounds weird," Taran commented. "What's an undersea habitat? Is it something like a grotto—a sea-cave?"

"Technologically fantastic, isn't it?" Hest said.

"Fain makes it sound like this was accomplished a very long time ago, when my family first moved to the island; but my family has been here since the Middle Ages."

"The Byzantine Period, actually."

"So, Fain was just fantasizing?"

"Or Lír is really, really old."

"I think Grandfather must've been totally insane," Taran said, examining the page before him with new curiosity. "Listen to this: *Apsu served as Lír's strategic command post while he drew his plan of attack against Avalon. It may seem ironic that Lír was captured before he could carry out the plan, and that this inevitably resulted in his being trapped inside Avalon at the bottom of the sea when the great fortress fell from the sky. Ironies aside, nothing is apparent where he is involved. All this may have been planned in advance, though it is hard to imagine why Lír would allow himself to be captured. DePons tells me that he was instrumental in the Gremn attack, having won their trust in an exchange during one of his transits.*

He looked at her another long minute, quietly digesting the words on the page.

"If this isn't just silly fiction," Taran said, "it must be some kind of code-speak. Is that it?"

"Must be," she replied. Her eyes said she knew more than she would admit.

"Hest, why won't you tell me?"

"Dr. DePons has always been secretive about his work. He shares very little of it even with me. If you're trying to insinuate that I have inside knowledge of the events chronicled on that page, remember that they supposedly occurred a very long time ago."

"Then how could DePons have been there—on a fortress flying in the sky? And what's this got to do with where Fain went, anyway?"

"You're asking me as if I have the answers. The book is the key, Taran."

Taran leaned forward in the chair and began flipping through the volume at random, scanning for anything else that might give him a clue to deciphering the mystery. He paused at a page where only two short lines were inscribed.

Lír is still an aggressive player in the struggle to acquire Regulus. Many of our agents have died since this work began.

He spoke the words aloud in a stern, accusatory tone of voice, and then lifted his eyes towards Hest. Something between anger and despair smoldered away within him, and she must've seen it, for she stepped back a pace.

"Well, at least this part makes sense," he said. "Don't you think so, Hest? You were the one who first mentioned the name *Regulus* to me, and here Fain links it directly to Lír."

He stabbed the page with his finger.

"A man on the boat asked me about *other stones*. Is that what all this is about? These criminals know that father and DePons were working with a group to create an experimental weapon on this island—a weapon that was somehow linked to the stone I gave to Val—and now that she's gone they're chasing down others like it?"

"I believe you are very near to understanding the situation," she said, lowering her eyes.

"Fain discovered a use for this stone? Did it kill him?"

"It did not kill him. He disappeared, as did Val Anna. However, unlike Val Anna's disappearance, Fain's was not facilitated by Regulus or any other stone."

"So, these stones transport you to other places, except Fain found out how to do it without a stone—and got lost."

"You are correct," she said. "And we must also discover Fain's secret."

"Without getting lost?"

"Fain isn't lost," she said, looking back into his face. "We know exactly where he is, and Val Anna, too."

Taran couldn't help smiling despite his fury. "Then what in the world are we doing here?" he asked, trying to keep his voice calm.

"We know where they are," Hest replied, "but not how to get there."

"This wouldn't have anything to do with Giles' talk of *Dark Worlds*, would it?"

"I wouldn't know," she said, nodding towards the book. "We'll find out together."

Anger was getting the better of him. Taran averted his eyes from the book, glancing towards the door, and he noticed for the first time that she had locked it. Hest looked up, meeting his gaze. A lock of her long brown hair fell over one eye, and again Taran sensed a shifting of her facial features.

"You imagine deception of me," she said, "and that is one thing I will not tolerate from you!"

Her voice struck a wounded note, and her sudden sadness melted his anger.

"I'm sorry," he said. "I just feel like Father is setting me up for something nasty."

"There was a reason that he decided not to tell you about any of this. He and DePons knew, of course, yet neither of them felt it was their duty to explain anything to you. Instead they chose me for this task. And now you don't trust me."

He bore up under the strain of silence for only a few heartbeats before apologizing again. "I'm sorry," he said. "It's not that I don't trust you. It's just that I don't believe a stone can whisk you away to some other place that no one can get to. There has to be a logical explanation."

Hest smiled suddenly, throwing him into confusion. Taran wasn't used to seeing that smile. It made him nervous.

"You're giving up?" she asked. "You're not going to look for her anymore?"

"That's not what I meant!" he exclaimed.

"Then why are you pouting and slouching, looking for any way out?"

"I'm not giving up. I'm just not as crazy as you."

"This is the way you were in those days I used to come to the bridge. You weren't always like that, though."

"What?"

"I wondered what I would do when the order came to move out," Hest continued, rambling uncharacteristically. "I reported my concerns—the fact that you were depressed, disheveled, and hiding from the world. It all makes sense now. You really are a *lazy mop-headed toad*."

Taran slouched in the chair, looking down at his hands. "You *were* Drus, then," he said.

"It was a disguise better than the one you're wearing now," she replied sharply.

"What do you mean?"

"You want to know the truth, huh? The truth about me?"

He nodded. The doleful pale light creeping into his face was replaced suddenly with a blush of surprise when Hest leaned forwards and clutched the arm of the chair, staring into his face from only a few inches away.

"You look a little nervous, Taran Morvran!"

He nodded. A bead of perspiration trickled down his side, causing him to wince.

"You scare me," he confessed.

"Is it the *trick* by which I change my appearance? Is that what frightens you? What if I told you there never was a Drusilla? Your friend the Big Man saw me hanging around the street corner, and he asked me to run errands for him. He did this because another agent of the HSA suggested it to him."

"So, you just put on an act?"

"I can make myself look like her. You want to see?"

"No, really—"

"But I want to show you!"

Before he could insist, Hest turned away. Her nightgown seemed to shimmer briefly. Though he supposed it could have been the flickering candlelight, he could not account for the fact that she seemed to shrink suddenly, holding the nightgown around her like a loose robe; and when she turned around again, she was completely changed. There before him stood Drusilla—Drusilla, whose straight narrow nose, sloped forehead, tiny accusing eyes, and grimy features were unmistakably unique. Her hair, though, remained in the long braid that Hest always wore.

"How's that, Toady?" she asked in her rough voice, as mean and sassy as ever he remembered.

Taran thought he might pass out. His hands were numb. "How is it possible?" he mumbled. "That's not makeup!"

"No," she said, turning around. When she looked back, she was Hest again—Hest, tall and gentle of features.

They stared at each other a few moments in silence.

"I have no idea how you did that," he said.

"I wouldn't have shown just anyone," she said, looking suddenly tired. "That takes a lot out of me."

His eyes strayed to the hand that gripped the arm of his chair. It looked like an ordinary hand.

"Go ahead," she said. "Touch it. It's just like yours."

He pressed the back of her hand with the tips of his fingers. It was warm and soft, trembling slightly. He released a deep breath, chilled by all the curious events of this strange evening.

"Still think I drugged you?" she asked.

"I have to know, are you Drus, or are you Hest?"

"Which do you like better?" she asked.

He blushed crimson to his ears.

"You know," she said, smiling coyly and lifting her hand from his chair. "That's why I like you. You're so easily surprised! You know what your father said to me when he and Dr. DePons first chose me for *Operation Reformation*? He said you could handle all this—that the Morvran blood in your veins was somehow special. I must admit, however, I wondered if there wasn't something wrong with you. You're acting like such a *kitten*."

"Operation Reformation?"

She looked aside at him, and some of her sternness returned. "It is a research project of an international technological consortium named FTI. And since you wanted to know, I can tell you the Human Solvency Army is a privately contracted group working with paramilitaries. These paramilitaries serve the interests of Foundation Technologies International, which places your safety very high on its list of operational objectives."

"Me? I don't even know who they are!"

"They know all about you," Hest said, retrieving her candle from his teacup. "I am an agent of the HSA. You are my mission."

"Your mission?"

"I am to guide and protect Taran Morvran on his journey, and to assist him in any way I can—even at the expense of my life."

Her expression had returned to rigid and formal, adding weight to her words. Taran was terribly confused all the same. So quickly had she swung from one personality to the other, it was hard to perceive who Hest really was.

"I don't understand this," he said. "You're my *bodyguard?*"

"You don't think much of me, do you?" she asked.

He looked up at her tall slender frame, a girl in a nightgown, and wondered.

"It is my mission to protect you. It is my purpose for being."

"To protect me? From what?"

"The stones only synch with certain people," she answered, holding the candle before her. "No one's sure how they work. It has something to do with a thing called the Viaduct."

"Viaduct? Isn't that just an old word for bridge?"

"Whatever it is, it has to do with those stones, and it is the reason Fain disappeared. Naruna and Lír want you just as much as they want the stones, because you are able to synchronize with them—just like Val Anna."

"That's an odd coincidence, don't you think?"

"We proved it with Regulus, on the boat."

Taran drummed his fingers on the table and shifted his gaze to the fire. It needed more fuel.

"He's coming," she said, turning and walking briskly to the door. "I need to leave."

"Who's coming?" Taran asked.

"Your brother. I warn you, keep the sword a secret from him, and tell him nothing about Regulus."

"Why's the sword so important?"

"How should I know?" she asked. "Didn't Giles give it to you? Ask him."

"I think he's hiding something. He's less close-mouthed than Father and that ninny DePons, but nothing he said makes sense."

"Poor boy. Don't let your brother keep you up too late. I will be coming back for you early in the morning. We have lots of reading to do."

Unlocking the bolt, she slipped out into the hall. Then, pausing on the threshold, she favored him with one last parting glance.

"And by the way," she said, "Dr. DePons is my father."

He sat a long time, staring at the closed door. The night's curious encounter had left him completely drained. A wet log on the fire snapped suddenly, raining bright sparks across the stone hearth. The sparks reminded him of his scattered wits, of his scattered friends and family. So much had changed since Val disappeared. He had met so many new people, and spread strange troubles among them like a flame on the wind.

Rising, he took the sword in his hands. The only thought he had was to hide it beneath his mattress. When this was accomplished he stretched his tired limbs and yawned.

"Giles said that we were all called here," he said to himself. "What could have called us, though? Well, Grandfather Fain, you crazy old man, I don't know what became of you in the end, but I'm supposed to succeed where you failed. Let's see what else you had to say about all this."

He sat again and pushed away the first book. Opening the second, a torn edge of yellowing paper fell out, landing in his lap. Picking it up gingerly in his fingers, Taran read the fragmented note.

—has arranged more meetings with Gremn agents. We'll need their help with this new and unpleasant development. My son is involved in the project, but he's more interested in preserving the future of this world than in Reformation. He will never come here. The only chance lies in Taran, then. If he should ever become involved, it will be under DePons' guidance. If he wants to open the door, DePons will have to tell him

everything about the Britain Location, for Thaddeus has sworn to me that he will not.

Meanwhile, I've translated more of the cave inscription from the Welsh coast. It mentions something called the Ironfish. I have only one thought as to what that may refer to, and it does not bode well. Time for the past may already be running out, and every day it gains on the present. The time draws near. I have begun taking risks that I would never have tried in the earlier years of this work. I think I am closer to stabilizing the aperture, but there's only one way to find out for certain.

The power source is hidden deep beneath the dark tower, so the cave and its mirror should be reasonably safe for transit. Finding Arberth itself, should it disappear again—

He had a feeling this scrap was very important. Taran looked to the open book before him from which it had fallen. There was only a short passage inscribed in the middle of the page he had turned to. He tucked the note in his pocket and began to read, and slowly he felt that something inside him was changing. He wondered if he did not begin to understand something of this fantasy after all—

And he didn't like it one bit.

Though no one now remembers it, of her was writ in ancient times of our own world a history that occurred in another:

"Morvran, who had convened the Assembly for her, she promoted and made greatest among them, conferring upon him the leadership of the army, the command of the Assembly, the raising of weapons to signal the encounter, the mustering of the combat-troops—the

*overall command of the whole battle force. And she set
him upon a throne.*

*"'I have made you greatest in the Council! I have
installed in you the authority to rule over all! You
shall be the greatest, for you are my only lover! Your
commands shall always prevail over all the spirits of
the underworld!'*

*"Then she gave him the Stone of Destinies and made
him clasp it to his breast; and she said, 'Your utterance
shall never be altered! Your word shall be law!'*

*"When he was promoted and had received the
Sky-Power, and had decreed the doom of the gods of
the Dark Worlds, he said, 'What issues forth from my
mouth shall quench fire! My accumulated venom shall
paralyze the powerful!'*

*"Then she assembled his army, gathering battle units
against the gods."*

*The Book of Invasions, ll.146-162
Babylon, c.1900 B.C.*

"Sky Power?" he wondered, turning the page. "What
nonsense!"

What was written on the obverse was far more disturbing
than the poem, however.

*It was to Colonel Albert Naruna that the child came, to
a miserable warrior seeking retribution among exiles. It
seems he was chosen by Lír to be her foster father. How
came Lír to know when she would arrive? Though
appearing to us as a child, she is the woman who ruled
the World of Origins, the one who gave the Fire of the
Ancients to Ard Morvran.*

The child was brought by police to an orphanage in Manhattan last summer. She was very small, and her mind was blank. She was reported to call out strange names in her sleep, chiefly Orlim, Morla, and Nunna, but had no memories of a life lived elsewhere. That is because she has not yet done those things for which she was exiled under the Ban. Wherever she has come from, only the Ancients know.

Though warned of the girl's mental aberrations, the daughter of the missionary who ran the place adopted her, and she gave to her the love of a mother. This woman, Talia, was married the previous year by Albert Naruna. They chose not to tell the little one she was adopted. Talia Naruna was so alike in facial features and hair coloration to the child that few would have guessed the truth.

The family is moving to New Jersey, to the house beside my old estate there in the country. DePons arranged the whole thing, working, as always, invisibly. My son has been informed, and is willing that Taran should become the little girl's friend. It is best that they share as much time together as possible, so that their bond ensures our survival. Apart from being her teacher, however, Thaddeus refuses to become involved in Operation Reformation.

The stone must pass on to the girl eventually; but what will she do with us when she remembers who she really is? Will she be grateful or vengeful?

Taran turned the page, and to his amaze he faced a complete description of his life. The account was almost day-by-day, with bits of his written assignments and sketches pasted in, and recorded recommendations sent to his father regarding the level of his interactions with Val Anna. Near the end of the volume he came upon another loose scrap, this one bearing a child's drawing. It was a sketch of two stick figures beside a forest, one labeled *Taran*, and the other labeled *Me*. This paper he removed with trembling fingers, and folding it gently he tucked it into his pocket with the note written by Fain.

Then he shut the book hard, sending a cloud of dust up into the air. With no clear idea why he chose to believe anything written on the pages, he picked up the whole volume and walked it to the fireplace, tossing it into the deepest and hottest part of the flames. His heart racing, he spoke angrily into the smoky air.

"You can't plan and scheme the lives of others," he said. "I'm making my own choices from now on, Fain!"

25

ARIES' GRAVE

South Wales,
A.D. 498

"What's our situation?"

Hun shrugged. Tugging the strap of his rifle and pulling his cap lower over his forehead, he glanced up and down the long empty stretch of beach where they stood.

"It's a beach," he suggested.

Kabta gave him a frown before walking off on his own. About twenty yards away, Hanuta watched the exchange with interest. Hun and the others were acting strange. Even Kabta was uneasy. She knew what it was about, for she was feeling the effects herself.

The problem was, the long-lived Gremn really didn't do well at adapting to quickly changing situations. The *Plan* was so vast, so carefully maintained over millennia, that abrupt unexpected deviations caused something akin to human anxiety—only more bewildering. She wished Shu was here.

"Where are you, Brother?" she asked.

The music of waves crashing on the pebbly shingle was the only reply.

Though their transit was smooth, they hadn't exactly ended up where they expected. It was a beach, but not in the World of Origins. Hanuta traced the coastline northeast to southwest with her eyes, taking in landmarks and approximating distances. It was nearing dusk, and it would do them no good stumbling along in the dark without having a look around first. That was why Kabta sent scouts up to the cliffs. To the southeast, her right, the craggy heights drew themselves into a tableland where they might find some shelter from prying eyes come morning. There was no one else around, but she couldn't shake the feeling they were being watched.

Kabta stepped up beside her. The camouflaged armor of his CM9 gleamed bluish in the sunlight.

"*Nuta,*" he said, "Keep your eyes open. No one goes farther ahead until Breaker returns."

He waved his hand towards the cliffs.

"Uncle, are you distracted?"

He smiled, squinting towards the setting sun. "You are surprisingly perceptive for a pink-haired girl," he said.

However his tone may have sweetened the words, she winced. Among the warriors, *girl* was a pejorative. He was just teasing of course, for though Hanuta was a young girl by Gremn standards, she had spent much of the last three and a half thousand years training for combat.

"My hair is my personality," she snapped.

"Warriors with personality don't last long."

"Get over it, Uncle. You're just jealous females can wear hair."

"Maybe I am," he said, patting her head affectionately. "That doesn't mean I'd dye it pink!"

"You're worried about Shu?" she guessed.

She followed his darting glances up and down the beach. Hun and Abdaya stood some distance away. Behind them, sitting on a boulder and wearing an uncharacteristically dejected look on her face, Nephtys brooded deep in secret thoughts. Kabta's eyes narrowed at the sight of her, and Hanuta noted the quickening of his reflexes. He struggled to tighten the hold he kept on his shape.

"He'll be fine," he said. "I don't worry too much about your brother. He's probably better off than we are."

"How would you know that, Uncle?"

She saw a warning in his eyes. Among the Gremn there were only a few looks that read through the human expressions, and this was one of them. It was something primal, something feral, resonating fear.

"I know it because any other location he could have ended up in is safer than this place."

There was a noise of rocks falling. Hanuta instantly dropped to her knee and raised her weapon towards the cliffs, but Kabta's hand pushed down on the barrel before her eye even marked the tell-tale glint of sunlight on the scouts' armor.

"They're back," he said.

Breaker lay on his back at the bottom of a wash of scree. Malkin slid down a little more elegantly, holding up his rifle as he scooted forwards on his rear.

"We're all suffering a little from displacement," Kabta remarked.

"Nah," Hanuta said, rising. "Breaker was always the clumsy one!"

"Poor clumsy Gremn," Hun joked as he strode towards them across the beach.

Quiet, grey-eyed Abdaya followed at Attila's heals. Unlike the rest, he wore no armor at all, just combat-fatigues and a harness with pouches for his instruments. Ab was a technical asset of the UAD, the Foundation's *United Aerospace Division*. He'd served Magan faithfully for a long time, even until the years preceding Magan's betrayal of her father, Nurkabta. No one ever figured out what kind of arrangement this loner made with Kabta, or why Kabta took him into his inner circle. A suspicious creature he was, but Hanuta quietly admired him for putting up with Attila. He made no response to Hun's stupid remark, his mouth closing almost as soon as it opened. He had learned when to hold his tongue around the warriors.

They waited as Malkin led Breaker towards them at a jog. Malkin was a longtime friend of Kabta's, a valuable agent on the African continent. His influence had slowly produced favorable conditions for the secret manufacture of advanced weapons, and all the energy and material resources they had used to access Avalon. His knowledge was vast, but he said little. Upon his bare upper arms he bore blue tattoos of ancient origins, and his face was scowling. His manner was likewise gruff.

The Nubian's tall lanky frame was equal in height to that of his more massive companion, even excluding the helmet. Despite his size, Breaker was almost as young as herself. He was the most cheerful Gremn Hanuta had ever met, and also quite intelligent, despite the teasing of his relentless rival.

"Probably they didn't see anything," Hun said. "That Breaker couldn't find his way out of a bag, even with those specs on his head. Poor Abdaya's probably had it up to his eyes with that guy as his technical assistant, huh Ab?"

Abdaya said nothing; but Hun's comments were spoken loud enough to be overheard, just as the scouts came to a halt. They offered a salute to Kabta, but no reply to Hun.

"Nothing's out there," Breaker reported.

"What'd I tell you?" Hun asked.

Breaker's blocky head swiveled to regard him with a subtly aggressive expression. Hun reached out and playfully patted the dust off his armored back, but Breaker smacked his hands away.

"Am I wearing your body armor, Attila?" he asked.

"No. Why?"

"Well, I don't know, but, it just feels a little bit snug, especially around the arms and chest—"

Hun swung around quickly, his hands raised in fists. Malkin pushed him away, standing between the two with eyes glaring.

"Let's find a place to rest," Kabta said wearily.

"Don't need any rest," Malkin grumbled in a deep, sonorous voice, his eyes still flickering back and forth. "The sun will set in another hour. We should keep moving through the night, figure out where we are. It's dangerous for us to sit still for so long."

His gaze strayed towards Nephtys, still perched on her rock by the water's edge. Everyone else turned towards her.

"I wasn't making a suggestion," Kabta replied. "Displacement is a dangerous thing to ignore. We're all unsteady on our feet, holding our forms under stress, and we have very little water with us. Water is what we need to beat this, so until we find a good supply there's little else we can do."

"You make it sound like we're up against something new, like we don't know how to take care of ourselves," Hun complained.

"Maybe he said it for *her* benefit, Dummy," Breaker mumbled, nodding towards Nephtys. The sea air blew her fair hair up around her face, but she was otherwise as still as the stone upon which she sat.

"No, you heard right," Kabta replied. "We are up against a new challenge, Attila. None of us has been in a place that holds more possibilities, and few have faced greater obstacles. We need water, Breaker, and we need to make camp. Have you seen nothing of a river or lake from up there?"

"There's something like a river, far to the east," Breaker said, and hastily he added, "Malkin saw it, too."

"Low rocky hills to the south," Malkin added. "Maybe we'd find a spring up there, but it's greener to the east. It seemed like water."

"And no sign of the others?" Nuta asked hopefully.

"None," Breaker replied.

Kabta turned away from them abruptly, and began walking towards Nephtys.

"Come on," Malkin said, heading back to the cliffs. The rest exchanged glances before following him.

Breaker hung back until Hanuta was near enough to hear his whisper. "She's been like that the whole time we were away, Nuta?" he asked.

Hanuta glanced back down the beach towards Kabta, who was now leading Nephtys by the hand. It was so strange a sight that she almost did a double-take, but grabbed Breaker's shoulder and shoved him after the others instead.

"Leave her alone," she said. "I think something must've happened to her."

"Something happened to make the *Ice Queen* sulk? I thought old Level-Head was in charge of keeping an eye on *our* mental stability. I mean, quirky behavior isn't exactly one of her characteristics."

"She's not a warrior."

"So? She's been in the field with our warriors plenty of times."

"That's not what I meant. Look, the whole scheme is shot full of holes, and we're all finding it difficult to deal with the changes—especially the *older ones*."

"So, now she's afraid or something?"

"Maybe. Malkin got meaner, Hun got dumber, and Uncle's gone flaky. It affects us all in different ways."

"And what about me?" he asked, nudging her side. "You think maybe this mess is making me clumsier?"

She said nothing.

"Anyway, the sight of him dragging her along like that just gives me the creeps."

Hanuta looked back over her shoulder once more as they approached the bottom of the cliff. Nephtys had kicked off her shoes. Her suit was rumpled and torn, but she walked with greater confidence now.

"I think we just need direction. We all felt better when Uncle had a plan."

"You're right about that, Nuta; but I'm not entirely certain this side-trip was unexpected."

"What do you mean?"

"I overheard them when we first arrived. Nephtys knows where we are. So does Kabta—and Malkin, too. That's why they're acting so jittery."

"What is it about this place?" she asked.

"Don't know," he replied. "Guess we'll find out."

Breaker and Hanuta started the ascent behind the others, and Kabta helped Nephtys along behind them. It was an arduous climb, and they were all feeling the effects of displacement. Dizziness and nausea Hanuta could tolerate, but the sudden lapses in focus nearly sent her sprawling backwards on more than one occasion. She was relieved when, at a ledge about halfway up, Kabta pushed ahead and called for a halt. At a large boulder standing by the mouth of a rock shelf they rested. It was a nook that was partially hidden from the beach below.

Nephtys arrived last of all. The others quietly ignored her as she leaned against the boulder. Hanuta observed her out of the corner of her eye, and was mildly distressed to notice that she was bleeding from her feet.

"Gather round for a minute," Kabta said. "Now that we're out of the open, there are a few things you all should know."

The group fell in without a word, with Abdaya hovering close to Nephtys. He appeared to be keeping watch over the trail to the beach. Hunkering on their heels, the rest sat around Kabta like fawning schoolchildren ready for a game. This too, Hanuta observed, was a sign of the tensions they felt.

"We're in Cambria," Kabta announced.

"You mean Wales?" Hun asked, looking at Malkin.

"The shoreline stretches east here," Malkin replied. "We are far south."

Abdaya peered out around the edge of the boulder towards the water.

"Talk about coming full-circle!" Hun said, looking around fearfully. "This is where Nebo bought it!"

"Nebo, Kato, and Zeker," Malkin intoned. "They all died here, along with many others."

"What's here?" Hanuta asked, glancing aside at Breaker.

Malkin turned to them and said, "Not too far, just a few miles away in the shallow waters, lies Apsu."

"Apsu?"

"Lír's nest."

"Rotten luck!" Hun griped.

"It's hardly a coincidence," Kabta said. "I want you all to go on informed of the danger, but also be aware of the opportunity."

"What opportunity?" Breaker wondered. "The opportunity to get killed?"

"It's not so easy to kill a warrior," Kabta replied. "But they could do that, and they have. However, I was speaking of something else entirely."

"Collaboration may be necessary for our survival," Nephtys said quietly.

They all turned their heads and stared at her, but she offered no explanation.

"You won't find peace with Lír's people," Malkin said sourly. Turning to Kabta, he asked, "When they recovered him from his watery grave, did he offer you a hand of friendship?"

"We must be more ready with our tongues than with our weapons here," he answered. "You will follow this general order if you wish to survive. They already know we're here."

"You're right about that," Malkin muttered, looking up towards the top of the slope.

"Now that that's cleared up," Kabta said, "let's get moving again. The sun rises and the sun sets. Whether or not we perish on this road, we're here for a purpose."

"And what purpose is that?" Breaker asked.

"Why, to climb to the top of this hill while it's still light," he replied with a grin.

Without another word, Kabta started back up the ascending path. The others rose hesitantly. Hanuta found herself trembling slightly, for she had heard of all that passed in this terrible place, the *Apsu*. A hand slipped around her arm, and tall Nephtys stood by her side.

"You're hurt?" she asked, looking down at Nephtys' feet.

"Only a little," she replied groggily.

"Why not make it better?" Breaker asked, sidling up to them.

"I'm conserving energy."

"But it's only a few little cuts. You should just walk around in Gremn-shape for awhile until it heals."

"That's against protocol," she said.

"I don't think Kabta—"

"Kabta suggested the same things," she said. "Let's just get moving, shall we?"

But no one moved.

"What's that sound?" Hanuta asked, turning abruptly.

The sun was setting, and a chill wind blew up from the water. Hanuta looked back to where Abdaya stood by the edge of the boulder, his eyes fixed on the sea. Farther up the slope the others had also turned, and soon they were all able to hear the odd vibrating hum that echoed over the water and through the hills.

Hanuta gently pulled her arm free of Nephtys' grip and leaped lightly up the bare rock slope until she stood above the level of the boulder. Looking out to sea she saw a strange sight. A large shining object was surfacing a few miles away, and above it the sky was roiling with sudden clouds, like a cauldron of stew.

"Aries is rising," Malkin said.

"Really, *really* rotten luck!" Hun shouted.

No one could hear him over a deafening burst of squealing noise, followed by a massive sustained boom that set the ground trembling beneath their feet. The water of the sea danced in sharp pinnacles, and it began to steam. Far in the distance, there was no definite shape to the smooth mass of metal that had breached the surface. Whatever it was, it was enormous.

"Ab!" Kabta shouted.

The noise had subsided a little. Abdaya stepped out beside the boulder, holding up a small instrument like a cell phone towards the sea. A display set into the face of the tool was alive with scrolling data. He shouted something, but the horrible noise rose again to a higher pitch, throwing his words back in his face. The wind gusted suddenly to hurricane force, and the sky lit up with a burst of brilliant orange, reflecting off of the ship's sloping back. Forked lightning danced across the shining hull. They all cringed when the harmonics struck them—a thunder of ringing and wavy tolling noises.

Then, with a flash, the object in the water disappeared. Everyone stood and watched, still as stones, as a dark shadow approached the cliffs. A wave hundreds of feet high was heading for them with a dull roar.

"Grab hold of something!" Kabta shouted.

Hanuta hadn't a moment to do more than swivel her gun behind her and grab hold of the nearest large rock she could find. Just a heartbeat later, everything went black. She was pressed to the ground with tremendous force.

Stones crashed off her back and sides. Darkness and cold pierced every inch of her, despite her armored suit. Twice she felt her grip weakening, and twice struggled to hold on as the tremendous force of water blasted the rocks around her to bits.

Then, just when she thought the worst had passed and the pressure began to lift from her shoulders, a powerful current pulled her backwards with merciless fury, tearing her away from the cliffs. Her mouth opened involuntarily as her back struck something hard—the great boulder they had stooped beside only minutes ago. Her lungs burned as her last screaming breath left with a convulsive shiver.

The sky was black when Hanuta opened her eyes. The moon was up, and the stars were twinkling. She was on her back, upside-down on the hillside, water streaming from her mouth. Her side hurt.

"Thought we'd never find you," Malkin said, standing over her. He'd been gently kicking her side with his boot.

Hanuta coughed. A salty crust on her face crumbled away.

"The rest of us were washed out almost half a mile," he said. "We had to ditch our guns, and most of our armor."

"Got mine," she mumbled, hefting her rifle with one hand.

"That's good. You're so small. You're lucky the boulder held you back."

"Luck—nothing to do with it!"

"Listen," he said, "You and me both know, Kabta keeps you close because you are a danger to him."

"I can fight," she huffed.

Malkin dropped a water bottle near her head. She took the bottle and gulped down a long draught, noting that he had only his jumpsuit, boots, and utility belt with him. The bottle was empty when she handed it back.

"I guess you deserve consideration," he said. "I suppose a woman can fight. I also wonder what would happen if you were to lose a fight. Do you think Kabta has never thought of these things? Do you think he has not evaluated the cost of losing you in battle? That is why I say, he keeps you close because you are a danger to him. Never forget it!"

"Is that why you're here?" she wondered, her voice husky. "You came to tell me that I should have stayed in hiding because Kabta is in greater danger while his niece is out rambling, just begging to get kidnapped or killed?"

"I am here because we drew straws to search this area, and I lost."

He began walking away, up the path they were climbing when the wave had come.

"Wait!" she called, sitting up.

Malkin paused. "We made camp a few miles northeast of here," he said, his eyes shining in the moonlight. "We climbed a valley with a natural stair. He was pretty upset when we couldn't find you. You're all he's got left, the only weakness in his bony hide."

Hanuta's mind was still too muddled to put up much of an argument. She had been through it plenty of times before with Malkin.

"Could you stow it for later?" she asked, standing on aching legs.

"I am only waiting for you," he said, gesturing with his hand. "You take too long."

"Were you just in the same tsunami I was in? Give me a minute!"

"Being Gremn has its advantages! A Crodah would have been killed by a tsunami of such force!"

"This knowledge does little to ease my pain, Malkin."

She stumbled up the path after him. They were walking along beneath a higher shelf in the hilltop, trying to keep out of the glare of the moon.

"Mind explaining what happened to us?" she asked.

For almost a minute he did not answer. She was surprised when he finally replied, saying, "Aries lost its frame of reference, and vanished."

"What's *Aries?*"

"The ship—a ship we brought to Ertsetum when we came. Lír used it to build Apsu. Did Kabta tell you nothing about it?"

"You and Kabta knew this was going to happen?"

"It is a frame of reference before ours."

"This is the past?"

He looked at her curiously. "Of course not," he said. "This is happening now."

Hanuta knew from his tone that she would get no more out of him, so she followed quietly as they walked on into the night.

Gremn or not, Hanuta was tired. The air felt cold against her wet clothing. The pain in her feet and legs increased. Did the others ever feel so weak? All they had to do was change their shape, and all their hurts would begin to heal. Once more she wished that Shu was here. He was the only one who understood her.

It was a long hour later before Malkin stopped. "We should have come upon the watchman by now," he said quietly.

"Who was left on watch?"

"Hun."

"We may've walked right past him," she replied. "Maybe he fell asleep."

He shook his head. "Hun does not need to sleep so often."

"Well, he's stupid. Maybe he's up there breaking wind and trying to light it."

"He's not as stupid as you think. Besides, Gremn can't break wind."

"Either way, I was giving him the benefit of the doubt—"

"Hush now. I hear voices!"

They paused to listen, but Hanuta heard nothing.

"You sure?"

"Ahead, by that great shadow."

He pointed towards the right, uphill and some distance ahead of them. Hanuta saw a bulky shape rising from the top of the hill.

"It's a rock-wall. That's where we made our camp."

"Then let's go."

"It's not the voices of our men!" he growled, catching her shoulder with his hand.

She listened carefully, and heard an angry shout. It sounded like Kabta.

"Fighting?" she asked.

"Arguing. Let's creep closer and see if we can get a look at what's going on—"

"Come up here!" a loud voice shouted.

Hanuta ducked, but there was nowhere to hide. A powerful lamp washed the entire cliff-face around them in pale white light.

"I can see you! You're surrounded!"

Malkin looked up towards the source of the light, and he saw a single man standing at the top of the slope. His silhouette was black against the darker black of the sky, and in his hands was a boxy flashlight.

"You're lying!" he shouted. "There's only one of you, and we have a gun!"

The shadow whistled, a piercing high-pitched sound. Another light came up from below them, this one mounted on a rifle.

"Two of us, against two of you," the voice said. "Put that rifle in the air, young lady, and the both of you come on up! You won't be harmed."

"Who are you?" Malkin demanded.

The lamp dimmed, and swung upwards. Hanuta had never seen the face of the man standing there, but Malkin immediately recognized him.

"*Shimeon!*" he said.

"Good to see you too, Malkin."

Malkin allowed himself to be led up the slope, and Hanuta followed. When they reached an overhanging cliff, Shimeon turned on his lamp and set it on the ground, revealing five rather sullen faces. The prisoners were all seated with their backs to the cliff. Kabta was in the center, and except for Hanuta, none of them were armed.

Her own rifle was slung over the shoulder of the one named Shimeon.

"I see we're all together again," Kabta said, nodding in her direction. None of her other companions paid her any notice, though the five armed captors standing in a semicircle facing them looked surprised enough.

It's because I'm a girl, she thought.

Then she noticed Nephtys. She sat a little apart from the rest, without a guard, and she looked even more disheveled than before.

The men who'd captured them were obviously warriors, though oddly dressed for ballistic warfare. All wore simple leather tunics and soft leather slippers, rustic attire for the early medieval period in Europe. Their heads were hairless, a manner common to most Gremn males when holding a human form. The rifles she saw in their hands were clearly very ancient, strapped together with hide and patched with welds. Hanuta was mesmerized by their appearance.

"Who're these guys?" she asked, taking a seat on the ground between Kabta and Malkin.

The man who captured her and Malkin answered, saying, "We're companions of Lír. I'm Shimeon. Call me Shim, if you like."

"Hiko," said the man to his left. He raised his hand in a strange gesture, closing all but his index and middle fingers, which he held up together in salute by his forehead.

"Artakshasu," said the warrior on Shimeon's right. "That's *Artax*, for short. The two youngsters are Tlaloc and Chaac. Don't even try to guess who's who."

At the mention of their names, the two remaining warriors—just boys in age—moved closer to the light.

"They're identical twins?" Hanuta asked.

"Designed that way," Shim said. "Sorry, they don't speak the common speech yet. They were raised in one of our more distant facilities."

"Raising armies for Lír?" Hun wondered.

"Replenishing our dwindling numbers," Shim replied. "Our failure seems inevitable, however. The virus has crippled us. Even with the technology we've recovered from the old colonial capital, we cannot isolate the pathogen or treat the symptoms of the disease. I tell you, if the war between these last two factions continues, none of us will be left to rule over the Crodah!"

He chuckled, slapping his thigh. No one else was amused.

"We were just discussing the likelihood of an alliance," Kabta said aside to Malkin. His eyes strayed towards Nephtys.

"And I was just *loudly* discussing the likelihood that we'll end up dead!" Hun added.

"This time," Malkin said, "I will agree with Attila."

Shimeon nodded, resuming his grave manner. "I can see how you'd come to that conclusion," he said. "Too many have died in this place, and vengeance is a powerful motivator. However, since he's gone to the trouble of making a rare appearance on our doorstep, I'd like to hear Lord Kabta's explanation, in a friendly manner, without threat of force."

"The idea of collaboration has been on the table before," Artax added, "but to hear it from both Lady Nephtys and Kabta is truly an event which demands all due respect."

"If this meeting is to be conducted in a friendly manner, then how 'bout you put away your guns?" Breaker asked.

There was another long silence. Eyes moved back and forth on both sides as each calculated the risks of what was being suggested.

Shim crouched down opposite Malkin to catch his unhappy glare.

"For what good it might do," he said, "I need Kabta's promise first that you will *all* agree to a council. You see, this one and me, we have some unfinished business."

Malkin said nothing, but his anger seethed. He began to hyperventilate.

"Mostly, it's Malkin's business. He should know that I'm actually at a disadvantage this time, and that it would not be honorable to upset the delicate workings of his master's diplomacy with a vengeful outburst."

"I forbid it!" Kabta announced. "We will all obey the laws of council, but you must put away your weapons first."

Shimeon locked eyes with Malkin another few moments, and then un-slung Hanuta's weapon, tossing it to her. She caught it neatly in her hands. Malkin turned towards her at once, gripping the barrel of the gun with uncontrolled passion. His muscled arm twitched. The transformation of his face was only passing, but she shivered as the Gremn Malkin revealed to her his true form—huge, blood-red, with teeth bared in fury.

A clatter of rifles was raised all around them.

"No, Malkin!" she urged, pleading with her eyes. "Kabta says no!"

For a few moments, the whole gathering was poised on the edge of battle. The tension was abated, however, at the sound of a click as Hanuta ejected the rifle's clip. Staring at the clip on the ground, Malkin pushed the barrel away with a grunt, resuming the features of a marine of the UAMC. He lowered his face in submission.

As soon as Malkin was still, Shimeon nodded to his companions. Each lowered his rifle, ejecting the clip onto the ground as Hanuta had done.

"That was close," Shimeon said. "I'm glad you trusted us, girl. These rounds are explosive, a spicy little ballistic we use for defending the home-front. I wouldn't have wanted to see so many fine warriors reduced to quivering shreds over one man's bad temper—especially on a night of such tremendous losses."

"*Nuta,*" Kabta said, gesturing to her. "My niece will guard the weapons with Nephtys."

She rose, and walking away from the group she leaned her rifle against a sloping stone beyond the circle of light from the lamps, just beside the place where Nephtys sat. Nephtys didn't look up as Hanuta approached.

Shimeon's group followed her, each placing their rifle alongside her own. The clips were left where they lay upon the ground. This ritual observed, the five returned to the cliff. Kabta arranged his warriors in a semicircle so that Shimeon's sat facing his own.

Hanuta stood by, watching the rifles. This was her duty, according to the customs that Kabta taught her long ago.

"What would they have done if we weren't here?" she wondered quietly to Nephtys. "A negotiation of this sort cannot be guaranteed without a woman to guard the weapons."

"They would've killed each other," Nephtys replied glumly. "That's what you warriors were trained to do."

"Lord Kabta," Shimeon began. "Before we were interrupted, you were telling Hiko that your people have come here from another frame of reference than our own."

"That is correct."

"This is very interesting."

"I can see how it would interest you."

"Your arrival here at a moment like this, upon the very instant that Aries was lost—it is quite puzzling. I wonder, was it something we did that brought you to us, or something you did which caused Aries to be lost? Either way, it seems a very peculiar chance, does it not?"

"I leave nothing to chance."

"Neither do we, which makes our decision here more meaningful, don't you think?"

"Just what are we doing working with them?" Malkin growled, staring down one of the small twins.

"Aries was lost, and Lír was aboard," Shimeon said.

"What does that matter to us?" Hun asked.

"It's not what happened before," Kabta replied.

"How very interesting indeed," Shimeon said, leaning forward. "I think it's safe to say that you are not the man you were, Lord Kabta."

"No. We are from another fractured Earth than this."

A thoughtful silence resumed. Hanuta looked on with wondering eyes, and slowly she understood.

"We're in the past, but it's not a past that has happened before," Nephtys said to her.

"Which past really happened?" she wondered.

Nephtys' whispered answer chilled her.

447

"It doesn't matter. As the stones are recohered, everything we gain, and everything we lose, will all be one."

"There were two stones aboard," Shimeon said. "Revealing this to you places us in jeopardy, you realize. It is possible, now that these two are lost, that Kabta will use the stones in his possession to master all that is left of the Gremn in Ertsetum."

Hun chuckled. "If he did, there must be very few Gremn left with Lír!"

"You're looking at all of us," Shimeon said.

"You're lying!" Malkin yelled. His eyes remained fixed on the ground, his fingers flexing, cracking rocks like twigs.

"What was all that about replenishing your forces?" Hun asked.

"I tell you the truth, as these others here will testify, that we are all that remain. We were to guard the Apsu while the others went away."

"And where were they going?" Hun asked.

"We were about to move against your interests elsewhere. Leave it at that."

"We will," Kabta said, lifting his hand to silence a whispered argument that had begun between Abdaya and Breaker.

"You have something to say, Abdaya?"

"Is there a tunnel to the Apsu near here?" Abdaya asked.

Gremn in both groups eyed him curiously.

"Yes, there is," Shimeon replied.

"And the stone that was aboard the ship," he inquired, "was it *Lumnu?*"

"Our friend was among you a long time," Kabta explained, hearing the grumblings of Lír's men.

"Yes," Shimeon said. "It was Lumnu, the *Witch of Mars.*"

Breaker tensed suddenly. "But that stone was left on—"

"Yes," Shim said. "It was on Iskartum, our world of exile. It was retrieved on an ill-fated trip that also brought back something less useful."

"The virus," Kabta guessed.

Hiko cleared his throat. "It's newly mutated form has slowly wiped out half our numbers," he said. "If you have any knowledge of the virus, Lord Kabta, though it is from your own frame of reference, it might prove helpful to us all."

Shimeon deferred to him with a wave. "Hiko is our only medic," he explained.

"I'm afraid all the news I have is grim," Kabta said. "However, as you realize, it may not come to pass here as it has on our side."

Hiko nodded.

"Obviously, we survived contamination," Kabta began, "but the Gremn are truly fewer in number as a result of the outbreak. Among the survivors, genetic damage was done, leaving some unable to change their shape. I can only hope that there was some reprieve on Iskartum—"

"The virus totally destroyed our populations on Iskartum," Hiko said. "At least, that's how it was with us. We took Lumnu and a few other small items. We didn't plan on returning, even while we still could."

The quiet in his voice worked through the dark circle of Gremn.

Kabta was visibly shaken. "We're all that's left?" he asked.

"And a little more than two hundred just set out with Lír into oblivion," Shim said. "We're it, chums."

"In our frame of reference Aries was irreparably damaged," Kabta said, "but not lost."

The stares of Kabta's companions changed, Hanuta thought.

"May I ask for the details of this trip to the home world?" Kabta asked.

"There is little to say," Artax replied. "It wasn't the virus that killed them, but the vaccine they created. Its compounds were found embedded in all the organic remains that my team could recover. It seemed innocuous at first glance, but combined through a complicated process with the toxins secreted by infected tissue, these compounds were lethal to survivors of the infection itself."

"You went with them?" Kabta asked.

"Yes. I led the team that made the expedition. We studied the virus there, in its native environment."

"So, why'd you bring it back?" Hun asked.

"It wasn't intentional, if that's what you're getting at," Hiko defended. "We took every precaution. Besides, if we hadn't gone back, we may have tried to make a vaccine ourselves, with the same results."

"The chances of that are—"

"Enough, Attila," Kabta said. "We are trying to make common ground here. We should begin with the things most relevant to our situation."

"Yes, let's get back to the matter of the stones," Shimeon said. "There was a second with us besides *Lumnu*. It was *Agru*, which is also called Aries. Both were aboard the vessel Aries when it vanished. We also know that Auriga housed *Narkabtu*, the Chariot, and rumors have it that *Qashtu* and *Regulus* also abide somewhere in Ertsetum. Do you have one of these stones in your keeping?"

"We do not possess any stone," Kabta replied.

"What happened to them?" Artax asked in a surprised voice.

"The stones were entrusted to a girl."

"A Crodah girl?" Shimeon wondered, a bit of anger showing at last.

"No. I gave them to the Empress of Syrscian."

Every pair of eyes was fastened on him.

"It was my mission," he confessed, "long before any of you were selected to come to Ertsetum."

"What are you talking about?" Malkin asked angrily.

"My brother and I did not come here to pursue the Crodah. That was Lír's game of vengeance. No, we came here to prepare for her arrival, for it was whispered in Gilthaloneth before the Ban that the Empress had chosen to join the Crodah in their exile. We had no idea when she would arrive, and we found her only recently. We knew that she has power over the stones, and whoever is allied with her has the stones at their disposal."

"This was our mission?" Shimeon asked. "You would swear it to me?"

"I, Kabta, Lord of House Gremn, swear to you that it is so."

Kabta stood and bowed, and then he sat down again.

"Well," Shimeon said after a long pause, "I wish I had a card left to play. That's one little secret worth knowing, Kabta, and I dare say it's created enough common ground for us all to stand on; but how will you use it?"

"You were not completely honest with even your own people, let alone with us," Artax said.

"What does it mean?" Hun asked. "How does this change anything?"

"It means that all the in-fighting between the Gremn was a waste of lives and resources," Kabta replied. "I am largely to blame for this."

Again his eyes went to the place where Nephtys sat.

"Lír and his thirst for vengeance were the tools my brother and I used to gather our armies. Then I had a change of heart, and they didn't."

Shimeon shook his head. "I gotta say, this is one hard pill to swallow."

"Why did you not tell us?" Malkin asked in a mumble.

"I was sworn on oath by Orlim. I was warned that she must remain hidden until such time as she could be sent back. Thus I am now free to speak of these things. My purpose was to facilitate her return at all costs. Our cooperation would secure us a permanent seat in the New Council, and all the Gremn would be restored to the World of Origins."

"And you believed he could do all that?" Shim wondered.

"Orlim was her most trusted advisor."

"Regardless, I suppose this girl, the Empress, has gone back to the World of Origins," Hiko said. "That half of your mission was a success."

"The only problem is she took the stones," Artax added.

"She left via Avalon's Mirror before the ship was destroyed," Kabta said.

"You awakened the Fomorian?" Shim asked with a grin.

"She was most displeased. Even if we could regain access to Avalon's Viaduct Chamber in this frame of reference with Bec's help, there is no longer anything we could use to fix a Location in the World of Origins. Unless she comes back herself, and I hope that she does not, we are stranded in the Dark Worlds."

He looked hard at Shimeon.

"You look at me like I know something," Shim said. "This is a world where Auriga vanished into thin air and Narkabtu was lost to us—rejoined to its other iterations, perhaps. You know something about that, Kabta?"

"I do. I know that at least two stones are recohered, and one of them is Narkabtu. This happened aboard Auriga. It's Mirror was destroyed."

"Auriga's Mirror is kaput, and Avalon's and Aries' are inaccessible," Breaker said, counting on his fingers. "Of course, the Mirrors are all useless without stones."

"Well!" Shimeon exclaimed, slapping his thigh again. "Then I guess we're really up a creek. We're stranded here until we can retrieve Lír!"

No one spoke for a long moment. Hun broke the silence at last with the question that needed asking.

"You mean to tell us there's actually a way to get *to* Lír?"

"And to the stones aboard Aries," he said cheerfully.

"How is this possible?" Kabta asked.

"We rescued Lír only a few years ago from Avalon's sunken shell," Shim replied. "Took us a long time to construct suitable submersibles, and now he's lost again, along with access codes needed to get back inside Apsu. We've got it down to a kind of science, though, trying to locate the good General. He wears a special transponder, just in case he decides to get lost again, though we placed it inside him while he was still in stasis so he wouldn't know."

"You're saying Aries is somewhere here, in this frame of reference?" Kabta asked.

"Artax confirmed that before we left. We know exactly where Aries is. Her axial shielding fluctuated when warming up the Mirror—a variable the technicals were never able to eliminate after an accident that crippled our MMPPS—but she was at rest. Obviously, without rebuilding her propulsion system, the ship could only slip spatially—"

"Like an olive seed between slick fingers!" Breaker exclaimed. "Just like the Auriga!"

"Well, where is it?" Kabta asked.

"Approximately half a mile under the seafloor," Shimeon replied.

Malkin smiled grimly. "And Lír's buried inside that ship?" he wondered.

"It seems to me that we have a reason to try and rescue him," Kabta said.

"The real question," Shimeon said, "is *can* this be done? I can locate the ship for you. I'll even bring you to the Apsu, though it's all locked up now that the master's away. Beyond that, all I've got is some ancient mining equipment; but it won't help us excavate something as big as Aries."

"Aries cannot be freed from its grave," Kabta answered with a shake of his head. "It's simply too massive. Even if we could rebuild the MMPPS and expose most of the ship's surface-shielding, it would be suicide to attempt transit in such an environment."

"So, what can we do?" Hun asked.

"Well, I believe we can circumvent the issue of Lír's access codes to the Apsu. It's not like Avalon. I created the interface, so I think I could figure it out. Once inside, I can get us to Aries safely enough using your mining equipment."

"It's what Lír took from Avalon," Hiko said. "It was in poor condition, but salvageable."

"Then we'll try it. If we can create a stable access tunnel, I think we could punch through the hull. The rest would be up to you, Shim, and your willing companions."

Shimeon nodded. "There are about two hundred trapped aboard Aries," he said. "None of them would be too happy to see you—no more than that Fomorian, anyway."

Malkin laughed suddenly. "So, we're going to trust them to retrieve Lumnu and Agru from their master and bring them to us? This is pointless! And what would we do with these stones? There are no more Mirrors!"

"I'm thinking they'll probably just decide to leave their stones in the ship and send up their two hundred friends to capture us," Breaker said.

"That wouldn't be necessary," Kabta said, "because we're going down into Aries to meet them, and to retrieve the stones from Lír."

"You're serious?" Hun asked.

"I know something about Aries that Shimeon has not mentioned. There is a treasure stowed there that Lír never had the ability to use—not a stone, but definitely something we can utilize to our advantage, if we trust each other."

"But if there are no Mirrors," Breaker asked, "what's the point of rescuing these stones at all?"

Shimeon and Kabta looked at each other for a long moment before Kabta answered.

"We need to bring the stones out of this Dark World with us," he said. "We don't need a Mirror. There's another place of transit we can use, one that opens only in the World of Origins."

"And where is this?" Breaker asked cautiously.

"You've ever heard of the Dragon's Mound?"

"That place?" Malkin seethed, eyes narrowed in anger.

"It is a door made by the Ancients for their own use, which existed before the stone or the Empress. It is very dangerous, but it is all we have left."

"I have been told of this place," Shimeon said, "but only Lír knows where it is."

"We'll say that I also know its location," Kabta replied, "and this should be enough to assure the safety of all those in my care."

"Fair enough for me," Shim mumbled, "I wonder if all this was part of your plan from the beginning."

"If you mean that I expected to be captured by Lír's men, then no. All I needed was to infiltrate Apsu without bloodshed; but I suppose this wouldn't have been possible any other way."

He stood again, and raising his voice he addressed them all.

"I propose a joint venture to rescue Lír and retrieve those stones in his possession. We will take them to the World of Origins, together with all who would come willingly, and there we must protect the Empress from those who seek to acquire these things for evil purpose."

Tlaloc and Chaac were getting a translation from Hiko. When it seemed they also understood, everyone looked at Kabta with incredulous eyes. Shimeon was the first to stand.

"I don't think this is something I can decide for everyone in my group," he said. "And I believe the same applies to yours, Lord Kabta. So, who will stand with us and take on this task? Who will put away the memory of their losses in a war that has gone on long enough, and embrace a new calling, *one that will bring us home together?*"

This last he aimed at Malkin.

One by one, the gathering stood. Some more slowly than others, but still they rose. Last of all, Malkin lifted his tall lanky frame and fixed his eyes on Kabta. His fists were still clenched, but he stood with resolve.

"Good," Shimeon said.

"It's not over until it's over," Breaker remarked. "We need to save Lír, trust these guys not to turn on us, and then make transit to the lands we were all banished from by a Viaduct older than all the rest, just so we can protect the Empress who got us exiled in the first place. I don't expect all of us in this circle will survive, even if we don't turn on each other."

There was silent agreement all around. The council was ended.

The Gremn walked long into the night. Hanuta had overseen the distribution of weapons, but kept the clips in a bandolier around her shoulders. Nephtys walked beside her, looking a little brighter but still silent. Hanuta kept to the rear of the formation, hoping the older Gremn would open her heart to her and speak of her fears. Instead, they were joined by Shimeon, who wandered far back from Kabta's side to walk nearer the women. He caught Nuta's eye, and gestured for her to come closer.

She kept a tight grip on her bandolier, fearing some trick. Shimeon waited to speak until she was close enough to hear his whispered voice. Nephtys hung back, just out of earshot.

"Your father was a very close friend of mine. We go way back, to the World of Origins."

"Maybe Shu is already there," Hanuta said, hoping to end the conversation before it began.

Shimeon didn't seem to take the hint. "That would make me feel better," he replied. "I've fretted over your brother's wellbeing from time to time."

"Shu can take care of himself."

"Only because I taught him how," he replied.

Hanuta could not hide her agitation. Shimeon continued, unabashed.

"He told you about me, right? I once worked for your uncle, before I went to Lír. I helped raise Shu—taught him the edge of the sword after Hazor fell. I know him better than anyone, even better than Kabta. Many years ago he fought by my side, trammeling the cataphracts of Rome."

He paused, wistfully detached.

"I've heard," Hanuta said, softening. "Shu mentioned you after Kabta reunited us, but was forbidden to speak of you soon afterwards."

"You were a long time apart before being reunited?"

"Father had sent me away from Hazor to live in a secret place, because I am a girl. I was raised among humans as a human."

"That was wise of him. He always was a sharp one, Nurkabta."

"Uncle came for me many years later, and Shu was with him. They explained everything, and told me that Father died in the fight to prevent Magan from taking the stone named Narkabtu."

"Is that what they told you?" Shim wondered, his eyes twinkling.

Hanuta wondered what had so keenly sparked his interest. "Why all these questions about my family?" she asked.

"What can I say? You have an interesting family." Then, nodding towards Nephtys, he asked, "How is she?"

"Why don't you ask her?"

Shim arched his eyebrows slightly, putting on an offended look.

"She won't talk to me," Hanuta supplied. "She's been this way since our transit."

"I suppose she's just worried about DePons."

"Cedric?" she asked, startled.

"Yeah, kind of how you're worried about your two brothers, except she and Cedric—"

"*Two* brothers? But I have only one brother."

"Really? But Nurkabta's human wife bore twin boys before you; and I can tell you, twins are—"

"It's not possible!" Hanuta replied angrily. "Uncle would have told me."

"It makes sense that he never told you," Shimeon said, lowering his voice. "Just like he never cut your brother *Ibni* out of that PCU and explained it to him, either, because he was afraid that if he did, young Horus might just try to avenge your father's *murder.*"

457

26
THE PCU

Shu clung to the greasy stone step with trembling fingers. He cursed the dark and the fatigue in his limbs, and when he was through he took a deep breath and pulled himself halfway up. Shaking with exertion, he was glad there was no such sign of weakness in the rock.

Slowly he brought up his other arm, searching with battered fingertips for another crack in the stones. His breath was coming in gasps now. By time he managed to find a solid hold, he decided to risk it all on one last pull, and tugging hard with his shoulders he drew himself up.

The step held.

Up went his hip and right leg, and still he was okay. The next step was drier, easier to grasp. Clawing like a rat stuck in a barrel, he mantled a little landing above the fifth step and there collapsed, panting. According to his chronometer an entire day had passed since his arrival. That wasn't too long a period to go without proper sleep or food, considering his unique physiology, but the displacement was taking its toll on him. He was weary, hungry, and he was alone. All he had going for him was that he lived, but for how much longer was only a guess.

"Darksome place," he said, still panting.

There was no light but the one rescued from his CM9 armored suit, the bulk of which was left behind to facilitate his escape from the lower caves. The river helped remove the most important bits of gear he had on him, including his rifle. Still, he knew he shouldn't complain. He'd survived Avalon and the NDB, not to mention a plunge feet-first through darkness into a deep icy river. Being right about the displacement was cold comfort, indeed.

He sat up on the step, propping his back against a wall. The stairs were narrow, so the opposite wall was just beyond the reach of his boots. The ceiling of the winding stone passage was natural, unshaped by tools, and dripping with wet green mold.

"Still smells better than Avalon," he muttered.

He needed a rest. Closing his eyes, he allowed his mind to travel back to the Viaduct Chamber in Avalon. The details were blurred, leaving him only with the distinct memory of the moment the PCU arrived and everyone else disappeared. The transit that followed was a confusion of rushing lights and a vortex filled with the ringing of bells. The dip in an icy underground river was truly an appropriate finish to the whole experience, he decided.

A sharp clatter of stones alerted him. Looking to his right, Shu surveyed the wide crevasse that had opened where he was walking earlier. The distance was about twenty feet from one side of the collapse to the other. Flicking his lights to a higher setting, he took a long look around. The constructed wall to his back was something new, for lower down the passage was merely chiseled out of solid bedrock. He'd stumbled upon this tunnel after climbing up out of the water. At first the discovery of an exit made him excited. That was before the stairs broke under his feet.

He tossed a large stone into the black mouth of the chasm, but couldn't hear it strike the bottom. It was time to move on. He cautiously stood and stretched, preparing to resume his journey step by anxious step. His suit's power cell was keeping him warm, but he had no way of knowing if it was still intact after being banged around in the river. Once again his mind began to speculate the amount of time he had left.

At that very moment the first shafts of sunlight touched his face.

He stood at the end of the passage and looked into a large natural chamber, roughly cylindrical in shape with a gently domed ceiling. The ceiling was broken at its apex, and through this aperture sunlight streamed, revealing a puzzling scene.

"Was it a mining camp?" he wondered.

The chamber contained a jumble of broken walls, decrepit and leaning, strewn liberally with limestone blocks heaped here and there in low hills. It was difficult to judge the distance across from one side to the other, for there was nothing of familiar size he could use to gain perspective. The room looked huge. He was about to walk out and explore, but decided to spy out more of the place first before leaving the cover of the small passageway.

Something wasn't right.

Looking towards the far wall, he noticed a winding stair carved into the cave's walls, and an ancient-looking wooden gantry dangling down into the crumbling hole in the roof. Beams of a winch swung by fraying ropes, creaking away the idle lament of abandonment. Whoever made this place was long gone. Loneliness had moved in to stay, and a feeling of dread. Something must've happened here—something bad.

Across the way from where he stood, just to the right of the winding stair, Shu spied another archway. This passage was much larger than the one he'd traversed. A long wooden cart with broken wheels lay on its side in the tunnel's mouth, testament to his suspicions that he was wandering a mine. But where were the miners? The ruin didn't seem like the results of an earthquake—the walls were disassembled, not toppled, and bits of broken beams were scattered everywhere. It was more like the results of an explosion.

Swiveling his head towards the winding steps, his attention was suddenly focused on a soft pad-padding noise he heard up there. Then there was a scraping sound, followed by more padding and scuffling. He ducked back into the darker shadows of the passage and searched with his eyes.

Then he saw it—a shadowy figure, large and squat, going on two legs. He wasn't certain it was a man, for though it walked and was wrapped in rags, it made strange furtive gestures, darting with its neck this way and that in short jerky motions. It was very far away, so though the light was strong, it wasn't enough to more clearly define its shape. As he watched in fascination, Shu realized that he was afraid of the creature, and the fear puzzled him. It wasn't a fear of meeting an enemy, a fear he'd often encountered and had learned to overcome. It was a strange terror of evil he felt, a nightmare chill that spread across his chest like an icy claw.

The creature stood between him and his freedom.

He watched for a few more minutes, mesmerized and repulsed, trying to decide his next step. Chuckling to himself despite his fears, Shu realized there'd been no greater deliberation before him in facing Roman legions than this one unknown creature.

"What's happening to me?" he wondered aloud. "The sight of a starving man in rags has transformed me into a little child!"

His words momentarily boosted his morale, but the suspicion that he was dealing with someone or something unnatural only increased moment by moment. He needed to get a good look at it. If it really turned out to be nothing more than a wandering vagabond, he might have a chance to exchange words with him—maybe find out where he was.

He stooped to pick up a stone. It would be easy to throw something to catch the stranger's attention, or so he thought, and this would lure it down into the chamber. In the worst case, if it was a dangerous man, he would have to be ready to fight hand-to-hand—no trouble for a trained warrior. He bent his arm to throw the stone as far as he could, but then the trembling sensation returned to his belly, and with it, insistently, urgently, a quiet doubt.

Movement in the near distance—a shadow glimpsed in the corner of his eye—paralyzed him in the act of throwing. Another large white being was standing in the tall archway across from him. Shu stared into the dark, and using the newcomer as a reference for height he was able to guess the distance to the far side at about four hundred feet. It was very far, farther than he originally guessed, but even at that distance he could see there was something strange about the person standing there. It bobbed oddly, up and down, and its top-end looked too big. Unless it was wearing a large hood, the head was grossly misshapen. A faint echoing noise of its movements came to him from afar, punctuated with a gasping and sucking noise, and a long growl.

"Mhhhhmmm?"

Shu trembled inwardly, and crouching he placed his hands flat on the ground. His eyes stared, trying to see more, but the distance was too great. His ears picked up a long rising and falling hum, and a snorting noise followed by something like a barking cough.

"Gesh! Gesh!"

It was loud, and this suggested something rather unpleasant—that the creature was in the company of more of its own kind. Shu took some small comfort in the fact that there could not be any more coming up the passage behind him, for the stairs had collapsed.

The white creature leaned and wobbled now, ambling back and forth as well as bobbing up and down. When it fell over suddenly Shu almost cried out, but the creature hopped back up again with a jerk. Shu gripped the rock with greater tension than when he was climbing the steps. He drew in his breath and held it. Nothing had so distressed him before, not since he saw his father transform into a Gremn monster before his eyes in the Auriga at Hazor.

It began wobbling his way.

There was a clear line of sight across the middle of the chamber, so he was able to mark its passage from the far tunnel to the middle of the room. It paused there, at the foot of a mound of rubble laying directly beneath the opening high above, and in the better light Shu was able to see that its head was no more than a slushy wrinkled bag. As disturbing a sight as this was, it was also eerily familiar.

There was no mouth, nor any other distinguishing feature that he could make out from this distance. He didn't care to get a closer look, but his chance of a close encounter was increasing with every passing moment. He wracked his mind a few more moments before he remembered where he'd seen this thing before.

DePons had briefed them on a few FTI experiments gone wrong. He had shown them photographs of distorted mutant-children born to humans who were accidentally exposed to plasma propulsion systems during the construction of the substations, monstrosities the doctor had referred to as "Watchers" because they were a primary indication of the dreaded displacement syndrome. He'd also explained that this was something that happened to large populations during the war in the World of Origins, a terrible result of using the stones as a power source.

The creature hobbling in the dim hall was a *Watcher*.

"Have I come to the World of Origins, then?" he wondered.

As far as he could tell by its clumsy movements, the Watcher was going to be easy to avoid. Shu began to feel a little better, until he remembered something else DePons had said. Apparently, physical contact with Watchers resulted in transmission of their condition. Though it could not be explained pathologically, the Watchers' condition was like the progression of a disease. If they so much as touched him, he could become one himself.

The Watcher began moving again, picking a direct course to the tunnel in which he stood. Shu thought up a plan that involved avoiding contact at all costs. When the Watcher came to within fifty feet or so, he would run out past it, and make his way towards the high mound of debris in the center of the room. There he could pick a clear path towards the foot of the winding stair, currently hidden from view. He hadn't forgotten about the creature climbing the stair, but decided it would be best to tackle that obstacle when he came to it.

The Watcher drew closer. Just as Shu was about to make his move, the creature stopped. Shu could see the head bulging rhythmically as it turned its front one way and the other. It wore what looked like a skirt, torn and dirty, and the rest of its features also suggested a female form. It had once been human. He wondered if it was suffering much. While the Watcher stood and waited, Shu had no doubt that it was considering him with equal curiosity.

The stillness of that moment was shattered, as suddenly the Watcher launched several very loud choking cries, like the yelping of a distressed dog. With a sickening realization of his predicament, he saw another figure hobbling out of the distant tunnel, and another.

Within seconds there were hundreds of them.

The situation was deteriorating quickly. Shu's distress was mirrored in the movements of the new welcome committee. Their jerky progress across the room was alarming, no less than the fact that they were all moving in his direction. There was no use retreating down the tunnel. He would have to go out and meet them.

He stepped out from his cover.

The Watcher nearest him, which had signaled all the others, now stepped back a couple of paces. It was making more odd noises, humming and barking softly to itself. He stepped a little closer, and it stepped back again. Maybe this was going to be easier than he thought.

With his hands up, he progressed slowly towards the new arrivals, but he hadn't gone far before his heart began to hammer in his chest. A strong smell of sulfur struck him. His resolve faded quickly, experiencing these horrors up close; and now the rest were raising a racket, uttering weird cries, and surging violently forwards. It didn't look to him like curiosity. His hands dropped back to his sides. His plan was changing.

Without a second thought, he sprinted towards the center of the room. The ground was uneven, but he had little trouble keeping a steady pace as he dashed swiftly by the first. In her face he glimpsed two small lumps of black for eyes, covered by a thin membrane of pale skin. Dark vesicles pulsed in her flesh, and rotting teeth stuck out of the front of her bag-shaped head. Arms hanging limp at her sides, her swollen hands—like balloons, dangling uselessly—twitched in anticipation. He could see nothing of her feet beneath the sagging skin of her legs, but she was still capable of movement. His escape was turning into a game of tag with uncertain consequences.

His feet carried him swiftly past the first Watcher towards the middle of the room, right to the center of the onrushing mob. They were now growling fiercely, threatening to press in and stampede him. Gremn or no, he wouldn't recover very quickly from being trampled, and in the meantime he would be in their power. This thought drove him faster than he'd ever run before.

He made it to the mound of debris, a hill of stone blocks and wooden beams. The sun shone directly upon him, warming him, and everything around him was lost suddenly in darkness while his eyes adjusted to the light. He heard them coming now from all directions, even behind him. Looking towards the foot of the winding stair he was moved to despair, for a whole cavalcade was tumbling down the steps from the domed opening far above. He was completely surrounded. There was no way out.

Shu clenched his fists and held out his arms, forcing himself to breath more easily. Where was he? Why had the stones sent him here? Had the others all been routed directly to Gilthaloneth? Only one thing was sure. He faced his end alone, with the prospect of becoming one of these monsters himself.

Standing on the mound, ringed round within a sea of shadowy terrors, he fought the childish fears inside him. Briefly he wondered why it was he sensed evil in these creatures. They were victims—the unfortunate results of the Gremn-Crodah war. Lowing like cattle, moaning and coughing, they stumbled intently towards the hill and began to climb up towards him. It was slow progress, though, and he saw many injure themselves in the onslaught. Blood flowed freely from their baggy limbs, and was caked on their bulging heads. Soon they would be close enough to touch him, and there was nothing around that could be used as a weapon but small stones. He braced himself for the fight, clenching his fists, eyeing the bag-heads, wondering if they had anything like a skull in the pulsating mess that mounded up between their shoulders.

The cave echoed suddenly with a shuddering boom, coming up from some lower region. He could feel the vibration through his feet, and so did the Watchers. They paused and grew silent. The scene was hushed. Shu locked his eyes on the closest, only twenty feet away; and so it was he did not mark the arrival of the thing that captured their attention until its noise demanded his.

The air was filled with a loud thudding. Away towards the sides of the cave, large blocks fell from above. Another sound of crashing stone came from the direction of the larger arched tunnel, however, and there at last Shu turned his gaze. Looking back from the darkness was a pair of gleaming green eyes, familiar eyes. The eyes glowed with a light of their own, like headlamps, and as they advanced he heard a screeching sound like the noise of metal on stone. A low faint vibrating hum filled the air, and a scratchy wail that threw all the Watchers into a frenzy.

"I can't believe it!" he said quietly to himself.

A flat face on a bird-like head emerged before a pair of long jointed arms, pushing with three-fingered hands at the mouth of the tunnel to squeeze itself through. When the PCU had fully emerged, it stood unsteadily in the light that fell from above. The mobbing creatures responded as soon as it was clear of the tunnel.

They swarmed, several stumbling right past Shu across the top of the mound. He was all too glad to be ignored for the time being, yet found himself unwilling to turn and run for the winding stair. The clash that was about to happen before him was something he had to see with his own eyes.

The Seraph reacted as if it was surprised to see the terrible things heading its way, raising both arms before it. The host from the stairs joined all the rest in one huge press of bodies. They made their way towards the tunnel's mouth, responding to the new danger as if they were somehow able to combat it with nothing more than their wretched flesh. Shu knew what was coming. He could not look away.

The bulging apparatus on the mechanical giant's right arm gleamed with light for a moment before the fire came, pouring forth in fury from the entire front of the combat unit. The Watchers launched themselves headlong into a furnace, raising a hellish cry. The silence afterwards was punctuated only by the sounds of burning that accompanied the gout of flames. Waves of heat and a sickly odor of scorched flesh made Shu dizzy. The PCU lowered its arms and stood in a crackling sea of blackened twisted shapes, sweeping them out of its path with a wave of its arm, sending bits of the monsters flying towards opposite walls of the cavern; and still the remaining Watchers came. The right arm was raised; an energy weapon was loosed in shorter bursts, each with deadly accuracy. A few stragglers, creeping forwards with broken limbs over the charred remains of the rest, were picked off with single shots.

It was over.

The room filled with a choking haze, and through the smoke the green eyes blazed. It was looking directly at him. Gazing back eye-to-eye from the top of the mound, Shu was lost in fear and admiration.

At first, he had no doubt this was the same PCU that attacked them aboard Avalon—the one recovered from Auriga. The whole unit looked pretty beaten up, and there were patches where the skin was eaten away revealing a reddish subsurface beneath. Its eyes glowed a brilliant flashing green.

It was regenerating itself.

He knew it was useless to run, because there was more than fire and beam weapons at the Seraph's disposal. A rocket from its arsenal would be enough to take out the stairs that were his only road to freedom. It was better to wait and see what the pilot would do. After all, the situation had changed. They were no longer in Avalon. Shu suspected they weren't anywhere on Earth.

"Why have you been following me, Seraph?" he asked.

The eyes shone brighter.

"I am at your mercy. Will you not dismount?"

There was no reply.

"Well, then," Shu said. "Be you one of Lír's or of some other renegades, you've done me a favor by destroying those Watchers. I intend to escape this place by the stairs along the far wall."

He pointed to the winding stair.

"Will you try to stop me, or will you continue to pursue me?"

The PCU let out a squeal of noise, followed by static. Shu wondered if there wasn't some damage that prevented communication. In that case, why did the pilot not dismount and speak to him directly?

He shrugged, and turning leapt from the top of the mound, jogging through the cool dark towards the foot of the winding stair. He reached it in less time than it took him to figure out that the PCU wasn't immediately following him, but he wouldn't stop to ponder his good fortune. Going at an easy pace, he ascended the steps. They were very wide and deep, deep enough to grant passage to the assault armor if the pilot decided to follow. Glancing back, he could no longer see it. He continued on his way.

Nearer the top, Shu began to search out the path by which the dwellers of the mine made their way in and out. There were worm-holes all over in the rocks around him, all naturally formed by acids dissolving the soft limestone, and by one of these he saw a strange sign—a hieroglyph, painted in yellow. It was the eye of Horus.

Standing by the glyph, Shu looked up. Twenty feet or so from the dangling wooden gantry by the lip of the cave's mouth, he noticed a collapsed archway that once framed a tunnel. Though narrow and choked with loose stone, the route appeared to be open. He climbed up and made his way through the damaged passage towards the other side, bright with daylight. At the end of the tunnel he could see mountains and sky.

He paused a moment.

There might be more Watchers on the other side of that hole, he reasoned. For doubts that were still forming in his brain, he waited. It wasn't long before he heard a crashing noise on the steps behind, and saw the shadow of the Seraph darken the way before him.

They sat on the rocky shelf facing one another. Rather, Shu sat while the PCU squatted. The pilot had said nothing. Shu wondered if it wasn't more than damage to the machine. Perhaps the pilot himself was injured.

"The sun's setting," he said. "It'll be cold. We're on a mountain."

Of course, the pilot could have seen this for himself. Shu was speaking only to alleviate his own anxiety. He surveyed the wild country around them. They were about a thousand feet up a steep slope that was open to the north. The tree line was another several thousand feet above the mouth of the cavern, but they had a nice view of all the north, west, and east because of a sheer drop in front of the tunnel. A rough road, no more than a narrow trail of bare reddish stone, descended east from their little camp. There was no sign of the troublesome Watchers lurking about, and that was good. Shu needed a rest. He thought it a fine time to pry some information out of his silent companion.

"I think we're in the World of Origins," he said, "but I'm not sure. I hardly know anything about it. Do you?"

A plume of metallic quills sprang up from the back of the combat unit's head, rather like the frill of a cockatoo. Encouraged by this expressive response, Shu said, "If you'd just dismount, we could discuss this face-to-face, as Gremn should."

"Gremn?" the PCU said. The voice was sharp and hollow, but faint. The PCU lifted one of its large hands, the length of Shu's body, and looked at it as if pondering a deep mystery. It then placed the hand on its angular chest, to the circular hatch that sealed in the pilot, and gripped this tenaciously a few moments before lowering the hand again to the ground.

"Trapped inside," the pilot said. The utterance was mechanical, grating, carrying none of the music of a true voice.

"You can't dismount?" Shu wondered.

"Don't know how." The quills drooped. *"Don't lose hope, she said. Don't lose hope!"*

It looked out across the rolling green foothills of the mountain lands, its voice tapering to a static hiss.

"Why did you attack us on Avalon?" Shu asked.

The PCU looked at him. *"Attack?"* it asked.

"You weren't attacking?"

"Trying to tell it," it said. The voice broke into a kind of squealing pitch for a few moments, as if the pilot was groaning in frustration.

"Trying to tell it. Trying to tell it in my words, but can't!"

"Trying to tell us? What were you trying to tell us?"

"In our words, Shubalu son of Nurkabta!"

The use of his personal name stirred deep memories of the past, and then something else more recent—the holographic video he'd watched in Avalon's CAC. Hadn't Kabta said this pilot was known to them? Shu's heart beat quickly as the truth slowly dawned on him.

"*Atta Ibni-Addu, sharri Hazor?*" he asked in the language of his youth. "Are you Ibni Addu, king of Hazor?"

"*Anaku,*" the PCU answered. "*I am Abdi-Tirshi, whose royal name was Ibni-Addu, king of Hazor.*"

"Tirshi, huh?" Shu pondered. "No wonder you went with Ibni instead."

"*Tirshi is the birth-name given me by the priests of our people, in the language of our people.*"

"You are able to communicate in English, though. How did that happen?"

"*The Source teaches me.*"

"The Source? But its terminal was destroyed!"

The PCU shook its head. "*I know the way to the Source.*"

"How is that possible?"

"*The Source is not on Auriga or in the comet. It is a quantum system, located here.*"

"But it won't tell you how to get out?"

"*The Source says to report to Islith Manufacturing Facility for repairs.*"

"That figures!"

"*Didn't attack,*" Ibni said, lifting the PCU's hands in gesture of surrender.

"Well, you sure frightened us. You destroyed our undersea labs, and then came in through that hatch on Avalon punching and swinging."

"*Don't like to be alone.*"

"I know what you mean."

"*Friends, son of Nurkabta?*"

Shu sat pensively a few moments. The pilot's personality was showing more clearly the longer he communicated with him. He could almost discern the boy's true voice through the flat toneless drone. It was a voice he never thought he would hear again, lost even to his deep memory.

"*Ana muhhi sharri raktsaku,*" Shu replied. "I trust the king."

"*La sharri,*" Ibni replied. "*Not a king.*"

"Not even so long as you have one loyal subject left?" Shu asked.

Ibni was looking out across the mountains. "*Namutu,*" he said. "*Wastelands.*"

"Yeah," Shu said, rising to his feet and stretching. "The sun will set sometime soon, I think. We should get down into that forest if we want better cover. Man, could I use a cigarette!"

"*Fire?*" Ibni asked.

Shu chuckled. "No, it's a poisonous piece of rolled parchment that people put in their mouth and smoke. Gremn have no trouble with the poison, but to humans its toxicity is lethal. Hey, speaking of humans and toxicity, how are you alive inside that thing?

"*Don't understand.*"

"Those Combat Units are designed only for Gremn. Anyone not treated in the black water wouldn't last long inside a Seraph unit, but it's kept you alive for centuries!"

"*How long?*"

"The Source didn't tell you? It's been about 3,500 years."

The PCU shrugged, and then stood to its full height.

"Do you even know what that means?" Shu asked. Then, quietly he said, "I suppose there's no other explanation."

Ibni did not respond. He was looking down into the valley.

"I'm sure glad we ran into each other. You scared me half to death, but I guess I should thank you for saving my life."

"*Friends, son of Nurkabta.*"

"Call me Shu."

"*Fire?*" Ibni asked again, pointing the PCU's hand towards the forest below.

Shu looked, and this time he saw the long bluish trail of smoke creeping around a deep valley far below. Walking the descending path a short distance for a better view, he saw a larger area of burning trees, a sizeable conflagration happily consuming several miles of the hillside to the east. The prevailing wind was blowing the smoke downhill.

"That's no ordinary forest fire," he said. "Was that what drew them out of their hole in the ground? I doubt those things you toasted in the cave would be capable of making fire in any other way than they did for you, but this one sure looks deliberate. See how it curves around the north and east sides of that one spot, ringing it in?"

The PCU nodded. *"Nurkabta taught you well,"* he said.

"It *is* a good battle formation," Shu said thoughtfully. "But Nurkabta wasn't my teacher."

As if in answer to these thoughts, the sound of a battle-horn rang in the air, a rallying song sent up to the mountain's highest peaks. Mighty was the horn that uttered the cry, and mighty the warrior who sent forth its voice. Shu's heart resonated with the tone like an accompanying bell, transporting him to days long ago in a distant land.

"There is only one who sounds the trumpet like this!" he exclaimed. "It is the charge of my friend Shimeon bar-Kochba I hear!"

27
NERGAL'S CHOICE

The song she hummed was like a dirge, Morla mused as she looked on the scene from the doorway. Little voices picked up the wordless tune, but ended in a fit of giggles. Their backs to the door, Morla's three girls perched around Nunna on the edge of her bed and pulled ivory combs through her long blue tresses. Nunna continued the song a few measures, humming softly. It wasn't the kind of song Morla expected her to take to. Then again, this was hardly the girl she knew, the one brought to her tied in a sack, kicking and screaming.

"Yet she is unique," Morla thought, *"as unique as her purpose. Each one of them is matchless, irreplaceable, and I shall never forget it."*

The humming stopped.

"You've been standing there so long," Nunna said, keeping her back turned to the door. "We were waiting for you to return."

The three children scurried quickly from the bed, uncertainty in their faces, and clutching their tails behind their backs they faced Morla and bowed their heads.

Morla entered slowly and closed the door to the street behind her. "I was with the Empress," she said. "We were summoned by the Council."

"Didn't go so well, did it?" Nunna wondered. She turned, and it was then Morla noticed she wore a different manner of clothing than what was ordered for her. She was dressed now in the garb of a warrior.

"Who provided that uniform?" she asked.

"I don't like dresses," Nunna replied.

"This uniform is of a very ancient kind, and was worn by only the elite among warriors in our colonies."

"Are there no females who fight here?"

"There are. You *will* stand out in a crowd, however, and for other reasons than your attire."

"It's my hair?"

"Verily," Morla replied.

"But Lady Morla," the tallest of the three girls said, "yours is *white.*"

Morla smiled, and the girls seemed to relax. She wondered how long it would take them to realize they were no longer slaves.

"Blue hair coloring has very special significance among our people, Fann," she said, addressing the speaker.

"There aren't any blue-haired people in the Forest Tribes," the smallest said, her tiny voice lisping.

"Our hair is red!" the third added, her long ears lifting with exuberance.

Morla held her arms open, and the two youngsters ran to greet her. Fann remained by Nunna.

"I trust your new companions haven't been too much of a bother," Morla said, allowing them to hang on her. They nuzzled her slender arms, smiling all the while.

"They've been nothing but a pleasure," Nunna replied in a distant voice.

"I just thought it appropriate, sharing one place. You have all been through such trials."

"There's plenty of room," Nunna said. "Really, it's alright."

Morla looked down at her two hangers-on. "Faylinn, Finn," she said, "Go with your big sister now. She will begin with the fifth lesson of writing the letters."

Fann protested over their triumphant shouts.

"Oh, Morla!" she exclaimed with a pout. "Can't I stay here with Nunna instead?"

"I will be checking their work when you are finished. Nunna and I need to talk."

"*Fine,*" Fann sulked. She exited with her two wards in tow.

"We're learning to write!" Finn exclaimed. "I will write about Nunna's blue hair!"

They left by a small side-door leading to the rooms upstairs. Little Finn closed the door gently behind her, winking furtively at Nunna through the crack. Morla's eyes lingered on the doorway.

"They were tortured," Nunna said.

"Life in the caravan of a Musab trader is a living nightmare, but they were fortunate, being required only to sing and entertain. They spoke to you about their experiences?"

"No."

In the silence that followed, Nunna sighed deeply, and drawing up her feet onto the bed she pulled close her knees, wrapping her arms tightly around them. Morla glanced around the small room, examining the four walls with a critical eye, wondering if Orlim had put a spying device in here to listen in on them. The bed was against the left-hand wall, and there were no curtains or hangings anywhere, just as she had ordered. There was a privacy screen and a toilet, a washing basin and soaps, all in the manner of an inn one might find in the lower city; but this was no inn-room. It was bare of adornment, perhaps, but furnished richly with a bed and adjoining table, several upholstered chairs, and a low couch with its own supper-board. The board bore a half-empty flagon of watery beer and a silver tray with rinds of fruit and crumbs of bread—the remains of common fare, but of prime quality. All was brought from the stores of the noble houses, and Nunna had eaten everything set before her. Morla decided this was a good sign. Null-bodies required nutritional food and fluids just like everyone else's.

She walked past the bed and lingered by the window, standing so that she could lean out a little to see the High Place on her left. Morla had chosen to house Nunna here in a private villa that was accessible only from the uppermost tier of the city, but south of the High Place, opposite the Empress' tower on the northernmost spur. Only the girls and Orlim knew where she was hidden away, though Morla knew the room would not stay secret for long. She turned her attention back to its occupant, and to the chess-set on the table by the bed.

"Would you like to play?" Morla asked, remembering their games at Hazor.

Nunna shook her head. "I can't stand chess."

"I see you ate well. You must be feeling better."

"Are you joking?" She turned her head to meet Morla's gaze. "*You* try living on SPAM for three years! Of course I ate!"

Her face was tucked back into her knees.

"I guess I owe you something more than these creature comforts, then," Morla said. "You may ask me anything you wish to know."

"Why do you keep me here in this room?" Nunna asked.

"You may leave at any time. Do you wish to leave?"

"You don't want me to."

"You are not my prisoner. It's just that your appearance will cause unrest in the city. That is why you and the children were counseled to remain here."

"You're afraid of what they might say to me if they found me wandering the streets."

That she secretly feared outsiders would alert Nunna to the facts of her heritage was not a thing Morla wished to discuss. She would have to guard her mind closely from now on.

"Are all of the people here strange, like that horsey-man?" Nunna asked, lifting her head.

"No," Morla replied. "He is one of a kind. The people here are of four distinct races, originally of one, and there are also many scattered tribes that claim descent from the Great Houses; but they are all just people. None would seem so obviously different to you as Orlim, except maybe the Forest People."

"The foxtails are cute," Nunna reflected, allowing a faint smile.

"In the city, people buy them from the Musab, who raid villages on the borders of the forests. They are exploited by the nobles as slaves or pets. These three were gifted to me by the Colony Governor of Nara, who confiscated them from a Musab merchant who had cheated him."

"Fann says this is called *Gilthaloneth.*"

Morla nodded. "That is the name of this place."

Nunna lifted her face towards the window. "Gilthaloneth!" she said. "I think it's a beautiful name."

"Then why are you sad?"

"Because so many other things here are not beautiful," she replied.

Morla felt her senses sharpen suddenly. The girl was crafty, subtly tapping her thoughts with emotional cues. She would not long hide from her the significance of her presence here.

"I miss people," Nunna said. "I miss plain old boring people, in their rumpled business suits and skirts, going to and fro in the world. I miss them complaining about their jobs, honking their horns in traffic, wandering aimlessly in the Park on a sunny day before the dragons came. I think I could have happily lived my whole life without ever meeting a *centaur.*"

Morla's eyes narrowed. "You must have known many people, good and bad, before your world went dark. It is not always easy to tell what people are like by examining their appearance."

"I guess not."

"Was that why the Foundation sought you out, Nunna? Because you had unusual talents, talents that could be used to establish the identity of people who are able to look like whoever they want?"

Nunna turned startled eyes on her.

"Do you remember me from that other place?"

Nunna shifted her attention to the rectangular window on the far wall. It was almost sunset, and the desert appeared simultaneously farther away and sharper, as if viewed through a concave lens. The girl's eyes were at the window, but her mind was gathered like a shadow all around Morla, peering and leaning in at hidden portals not so easily shaded from a *Null-User's* gifted sight.

"I think you look like someone I knew there," she answered. "Are you the one who was with Kabta, the one in the message he sent to us?"

"Yes, and no."

"I think I understand now," she said. "It's because of that stone. It's because of Regulus."

"Yes."

Nunna studied her face with a frown. "It's just like it is with Val. You're different, but you're definitely Morla."

"How can you know for certain?"

"You would know what I can do, if you were really her."

"And you know that I know what you are capable of."

"Then say it!" Nunna pressed.

"You can sometimes hear what other people are thinking. You can peer into a person's heart and perceive the light or darkness that hides there."

Nunna lowered her eyes.

In the silence that followed, Morla walked to the street entrance and pushed aside the heavy wooden door. It grated on its hinge in an ominous way.

"She was like an angel in the darkness," Nunna said suddenly.

Morla turned curious eyes upon her. "You mean Val Anna?"

"There's something about her that shines like a beacon. It was like I had never seen or heard anything until she showed up, and then I began to think about stuff I've never thought of before—things like my purpose for existing."

Like Nunna at Hazor, Morla thought.

"What is she, Morla? And what am I?"

Lingering by the door, Morla looked back towards the girl sitting on the bed. Events were unfolding swiftly now, and danger was near. She would not easily keep Nunna's trust if she did not reveal more, and sooner than she was ready to do so.

"It is Val Anna's part to reveal this to you, when you meet again," she said.

The door creaked once more as Morla pushed it closed behind her. Turning left, she stood face-to-face with Nergal.

The shadow of his presence had encroached on her mind all the while she spoke to Nunna, but it was still a shock to see him. She stood and met his gaze for a second, and then stepped around him to enter the street. He kept pace beside her as she walked, staring at her face with undisguised curiosity.

"That's not very polite," Morla said.

"For long you have hidden your face and your intentions. Why have you kept the secret of this *Null-User* from the Council?"

"What do you know about it, Kal-Nergal?"

He chuckled to himself. "Morla, you have not changed a bit!"

"And you?" she asked.

"Truthfully, yes. I know now that I was wrong about many things. I hope you can forgive me all the ranting I did back then."

"Is that what this is about? You came to apologize for your behavior aboard the Auriga?"

"No. You know it's not so, so why do you ask?"

"Because I like to hear you say the truth."

"The truth is, I know about Nunna."

"She is not the girl you met at Hazor, Kal-Nergal."

"She isn't," he said, nodding. "Yet they all look alike, these *Null-Users*."

"Their primary purpose may also be identical. I think you've become a part of that purpose."

He looked surprised.

"As if you had not already thought about it," Morla continued, slowing her pace.

It was sunset. They arrived at a widening of the way, where in a circular space between the walls a copse of trees was situated in a sloping lawn. No one else was around. Stone benches were arranged beneath the trees, and there were small yellow and green birds hopping around them, piping loudly and flitting to and from the lowest branches. Morla stopped beneath one old and rather tattered moss-gatherer, and she idled a moment in the golden light that filtered sideways through its long narrow leaves.

"You know that it was her purpose to free you from the Source, Nergal."

"Yes, I know that."

"Because there are other Null-Users, this purpose did not end with her death. It did not end with your freedom, either. It continues to work out a role through you, even here."

She turned to look him squarely in the face.

"Kal-Nergal, you must make a choice about what you will do with the Source!"

His dark eyes shifted to the left and right, an almost imperceptible movement.

"In this world, Nergal, the purposes of those who have lived long in darkness will be worked out under the noonday sun. Nothing shall remain secret, for there are Powers here, and they will not let us rest!"

"I have no secrets to hide from you," he said, pouting. "You know me better than any living being."

"I know that you have a seed of love in your heart, and that it will break your heart to hold this in one hand and the Source in the other. The Source is an agent of the darkness that threatens to consume the World of Origins. It will use any means to achieve this end—even the Council."

After a thoughtful silence, he said, "The Council makes no difference. This is a dark world, like all the others."

"Why would you say such a thing?"

"The Source says it—and something else, Morla. You're so worried about what the Council would do with this *Null-User* you've found, but there's greater trouble brewing right under your nose."

"And you are its chief agent."

"Me?" he wondered, his voice betraying true disbelief.

"You are thinking about a plot of the Council," she said, "but the Source itself is our greatest danger. I learned about it before Val put me in stasis, a thousand years ago. I know that the Source is a quantum system resident in Kutha's fortress, and that it has been seeking a form in which it might dwell among men. A component of the Source's programming, long divided from that entity's native form, was incorporated into the Computer Core of Auriga, and also into the comet. That same intelligence introduced itself to me, through Nunna, as the Teacher."

"You're instructing *me* about this?" he asked with a laugh. "My, you've learned much since we parted!"

"You seem ignorant of the possibility that the Source may complete itself in your flesh."

His smile vanished.

"I warn you, Nergal, that if the light within you is darkness, then this world is where it will totally consume you. A war is coming, like none we have ever seen or imagined. It will bring about the destruction and rebirth of this world. Friends will be divided from friends. You must make your choice between the Source and the rest of us who are gathered here."

For a minute he seemed to think deeply about what she said. Then he asked a question.

"Have you thought about the meaning of Nunna's sacrifice, Morla?"

"Whatever are you getting at, Nergal?"

"Too bad there's not a sacrifice big enough to reverse the course of all the evil of these days. If the Council or Orlim moves against you, as one or the other most certainly shall, and if they take Nunna and the Empress captive, I bet there's someone in this city who imagines she can stand between these powers and her friends—like Nunna did."

"Why does everyone think I want to keep secrets?" she asked in a choked voice.

He raised his hands in an apologetic gesture. "If the secret's about Nunna," he said, "then maybe it would have been a secret worth keeping; but it's out now."

"You told them where she is?"

"They've only guessed she's somewhere in the city, but they've been following you to this place."

"Why were you sent here?"

"Islith has just awakened," he said. "I'm sure you already know."

"What does that have to do with Nunna?"

"Come on, Morla. When Islith awoke, its connection to the *Null-Users* once controlled by the Gremn was reestablished. Teomaxos already knew Nunna was somewhere in the city. They have plans for her. After today's botched meeting, they quickly decided to send men up from the Under-City to get her, whatever that means."

Morla paled.

"As it was explained to me," he continued, "the awakening of one of these cities can only be accomplished by something called a *Null User Neocortical Node Actuator*—a *Nunna*. Our Nunna was the Null of Auriga—the soul of the ship, the mate of the Source to which I am also merged. Nurkabta brought her into the city from the ship below. But she never knew who she was—"

"She died to help you realize who she was, and to give you a purpose."

This silenced him a moment.

"The Council plans on taking her by force?" she asked.

"I've only come to tell you what they've got planned for the *Null-Users*, Morla. Can you imagine armies of Nunnas in PCUs, all of them capable of peering into their opponents' minds while fighting without regard for self-preservation? And if they're linked to the other ancient technologies buried in these lands—"

"I will send messengers. They will move her quickly, maybe even to the Under-City. Of course, we'll leave altogether if we have to."

"I won't lead the Council to her, Morla."

Morla paused.

"You misunderstand me if you think I would betray you," he said.

"Then tell me, what will they do if they take her?"

"The cloning facilities at Islith are now activated, and Teomaxos says that's where they're heading next."

"They are fools, then," she said, anger making her gentle voice hard-edged. "The Fomorian who has activated Islith would destroy them all before they even reached the Forest."

"They have plans for the Fomorian, too."

"Teomaxos confided to you this whole plan?"

"No—he doesn't trust me, either. I only know the Council's objective is to capture Islith and its cloning facility, and the rest is a guess. It's obvious they need your Nunna to access Islith's computer core. And there's one more thing. They're planning something here as well, a massive sweep of the entire city. They will seize all the slaves within Gilthaloneth, specifically people of the Forest Tribes, and will use them as hostages."

He allowed her a moment to grasp what he was saying.

"I wouldn't stick around if I were you, Morla. Don't count on Orlim to come to your rescue, either. The Council has planned a diversion for him. However, I think there is still time for you to get away."

"Nergal, you have to stop them!"

"There's nothing more I can do here," he replied, shaking his head.

"There is a choice you must make—a choice to relinquish control of the Source."

"And how will my choice about the Source stop them from taking Nunna? The Council only needs me because Teomaxos is somehow aware of my link to the Source and the Nunnas. If I give up that link, I will be of no more use to you."

Morla regarded him with an icy glare. "And what do you think will happen to you when Teomaxos discovers the link is weakening? Have you thought about that, Nergal?"

Morla stepped past him, intending to walk away. He grabbed her wrist. There was a slight shock as he touched her skin. Their eyes did not meet.

"You knew?" he asked.

"I also have the ability to see hidden things," she said in a whisper.

His grip on her wrist tightened, and then relaxed. He released her gently. They stood shoulder to shoulder awhile, each facing opposite directions.

"Kal-Nergal!" she whispered.

He turned his head slightly.

"I still remember the boy whose ball landed inside the temple compound."

A long moment passed in silence, and he brushed past her on his way.

The walk to the High Place was long, and on his way he got lost. Part of him desired nothing more than to return to the desert, so maybe losing himself was intentional. Nergal found himself looking up and down a swiftly darkening alleyway. No homes or shops lined the road, and he hadn't passed anyone for several minutes. Then, to his right, he saw the head of a stairway at an arch in the wall.

"Now where do I go?" he muttered.

The ways of the imperial capital were vast indeed—as byzantine as its intrigues. Basically, there were tiered circles incised into the mountain's face below the High Place, and these were connected by stepped passages. Some were shortcuts, and others stretched for leagues through fairly empty country. Teomaxos had warned him about wandering off.

Did he care what Teomaxos thought?

Nergal cursed. He hated the old priest and his secret meetings with Forest spies. The whole Council was poised to move against his friends, and a terrible war was brewing that would end all life for hundreds of miles. He was powerless to do anything to stop it, and he didn't intend to stick around to see how things turned out.

The steps on his right went down to the lower circles of the city. They would take him out to the lake, and then to the river in the desert, and ultimately to isolation. He needn't bother anyone ever again. Before he had a chance to act on this plan, though, he was startled by a noise behind him. Turning around, he saw that the passage behind was already as dark as night. There was something moving in the darkness.

"Hello?" he called.

Straining his sharpened vision for all it was worth, he caught a glimpse of a large shape, coiling like a serpent ready to strike. An unreasonable fear gripped him, but he dared not run. He knew what was waiting for him there.

"It's you, isn't it?" he asked.

Eyes lit green in the darkness.

"You're going to get me into trouble," he said. "Someone will see you!"

"I can hide easily in the daylight," Glede answered. "The day makes me look like stone."

"You told me yesterday that we would not meet again until you discovered a way to help my friends."

"Timing is crucial to all things," Glede said. "There is something you needed to see, I think, before choosing your road. Besides, weren't you just about to leave all your troubles and your friends behind?"

There was a sliding noise, and Nergal looked down to see a clawed red-gold tail coiling around his waist, pulling him towards the darkness.

"Hey!" he cried. "What's this?"

"Do not be afraid," Glede said softly, his mockery of gentleness more terrible to hear than his rage. "You know that I cannot possibly harm you!"

"Yeah, well maybe I don't want to be touched!"

The tail dropped away. Nergal watched it slither back into the shadowy turn of the road, and walked boldly after it. He stopped when he could no longer see his way. Standing very still, he felt a tickling sensation on his cheeks. The air stank of rotting meat.

"First the kiss of a dragon," Glede intoned. "And now these words: *Pulvis et Umbra.*"

At first, Nergal wondered what the dragon meant. Then a sickening sensation stirred in his belly, and he lurched sideways, stumbling to his knees. Gasping, he turned around and looked towards the dim light beyond the passage. Everything he saw there was blurred and ghostly.

"What's happening?" he choked through clenched teeth.

"You feel it slipping away?" Glede asked.

"What's slipping away?"

"Look there, and see!"

Nergal shook his head. Breathing was slowly becoming easier, but he felt too sick to stand. He looked towards a shape rising from the ground behind him—a black shadow in the twilight.

"It's me?" he asked.

The figure standing and watching him was his twin in every aspect, down to the clothing it wore.

"What is it?"

Glede made a purring noise. "It is the manifestation of that which the Gremn call *Black Water.*"

"That's the Black Water?"

"You felt it leave you, did you not?"

"I can barely breathe!"

"Yet it was already growing weaker," the dragon said. "You could feel it every day. You said you can no longer hear the Source."

Nergal was weary of meeting with this dragon. It was a wily creature, and he knew he was being tricked. Still, seeing how the beast was able to manipulate the cause of all his woes suddenly perked his interest.

"I was hoping it would fade away forever," he said. "The power to dismiss its hold over my mind is not my own."

"I know a way to make it last—to make it stronger every day!"

"You can make the effects of the Black Water permanent?" Nergal wondered. "Why would I want that?"

"*You,*" Glede called to the twin. "Tell me what is happening now at Islith in the Forest Tryst."

Nergal stared at his shadow, and drew back in terror when he heard it speak.

"*The city has been awakened by a Fomorian infiltrator. There is a woman with her. The Forest People are assisting them.*"

It was a perfect semblance of his own voice, though very flat and lifeless.

"And in the Council?" Glede asked.

"*A decision has been reached,*" the shadow replied. "*They will delay any action against the Empress herself until the Great Houses have all had a chance to convene with Senior Members. They do this in order to gather their strength, as for war, believing they might use her as a figurehead when the time comes to move their forces west. This plan will commence with an attack on the city by pretended Forest Tribe saboteurs, Council nobles in disguise, whose goal it is to bring an end to the Fourth House forever. The impetus generated by this event will enable the Council to confiscate hostages from the city's slave population,*" *and will force Orlim to muster before he is ready, facilitating the capture of the Nunna."*

"Very interesting, is it not?" Glede asked, noting the astonished look on his face. "Remember the surge of power you experienced when it first came into you? Remember the feeling of intellect sharpened and triple-forged? Remember the visions, and the knowledge? If you want to save your friends, you could not do it without such knowledge as the Source can provide. There are no coincidences! Use what is yours to stop the Council!"

Nergal nodded weakly. "You're right," he said. "If only I could control it, I would be able to stay one step ahead of those who draw their designs against us."

As soon as he was done speaking, his shadow dissolved into a shapeless cloud of swirling particles and rushed upon him, wrapping around his face as if to drown him. He fought, wiping with his hands and beating his own face; but it was no good. In the end it was back inside him, and he could feel it stirring in his belly like an uneasy meal.

"Come with me tonight to a place where I will make you whole!" Glede said.

Nergal groaned. "I don't know about this!"

"Do you wish to remain here, then, where you will always be treated as an outsider? Even the friends you wish to save do not trust you."

"Where will you take me?"

"To a mound in the Forest Tryst, where there is a secret gate in a cave. It is a place only dragons know."

"Where does this gate lead?"

"It leads to your world, Kal-Nergal."

"Where would we go in my world?"

"To a city called *New York*. Then we will return to stop the Council."

Nergal paused thoughtfully, making his choice.

"What's the catch?"

"I only ask one thing of you."

The dragon's eyes blazed.

"I can only use this gate if a human will make transit with me. If you will take me with you, I promise to grant you whatever you wish on the other side."

Nergal stood, feeling like himself again. He turned to regard the writhing shadow in the darkness. "Why do you want to go to this city in the Earth?" he asked.

"To fulfill *my* purpose," Glede said.

"You won't tell me what that is?"

"It involves the Empress and her quest to recohere the stones."

Nergal frowned. "But Val's here, in Gilthaloneth."

"Because we're going to guide her here," the dragon replied.

"I see. And how will we accomplish this?"

"With the help of a mighty gift!"

The shadowy hand that reached towards him was as large as a horse. Nergal stepped back, startled, but saw that something was clenched in the closed fist. The hand turned and opened, revealing a beautiful round jewel, a stone disk small enough to fit comfortably in his own palm.

"A stone!" he cried, reaching out to take it.

Glede quickly closed his mighty claws tight.

"This stone is yours. It was made for you, and bears your secret name, *Kalbu.*"

Nergal stiffened at the use of his slave-name.

Glede said, "Come with me to the Earth, even if for a short time. I ask only this in payment for the stone, which will restore your connection to the Source, and more. Soon you will be able to control the Source—to use its power to do anything you desire, even to save your friends."

"The Council won't be able to stop me?"

"You will be far beyond their reach."

"Just so long as I get back before the Council makes its move," he said. "Will the journey take long?"

"We will return even before the hour of our departure. You will ride upon the wings of the storm!"

28

THE FALL OF AVALON

Kanno Ard Morvran stood outside the locked hatch of the CAC in Avalon. There were no sounds from within, of course, for the pressure-seal was engaged. He stared at the hatch, counting his heartbeats and his rapid breaths, wishing he could go back a few minutes in time to prevent what was probably the biggest screw-up of his life.

Cedric DePons. How could I have forgotten?

His eyes went up to that patch on the wall he had come to hate.

ISLITH RISES AGAIN

Today Avalon would fall, and it was a long time coming. Ard had been brooding on this day for a year, since the moment he'd captured Lír hiding out among the crew and put him in stasis. Bec had warned him that Lír would not have allowed himself to be captured. There must have been a reason for it. The Gremn had discovered them, had found a way to infiltrate their defenses, and now they would have their revenge. That was probably inevitable, Ard reasoned. However, he would not permit this traitor to capture Bec so easily.

Cedric DePons.

Thinking back, Ard could still remember how DePons' first messages reached him in the terrible days of the War. His communications with the lord of House Gaerith were informative and helpful, paving the way to some brilliant victories for the Crodah. He never suspected the information was coming from the Empress herself—not until she summoned him to Gilthaloneth. That was where Ard first met him, and together they sent the atomics to a prearranged location where the Gremn showed up in massive numbers to capture them, all according to plan. A daring young partisan of the Crodah had come up with this plan. His honesty convinced the Empress of his intentions to end the war quickly. She backed that plan without hesitation. She said she believed in him.

As he stood staring at the sign above the door, he recalled the thrill of leaking information of his plan to Gremn agents, coaxing them into capturing the atomics and transporting them to Avalon where he would later recapture and deploy—but not without help. The lives of his closest friends were sacrificed in the fight to infiltrate Islith, where he rescued the only Fomorian capable of commandeering Avalon and retargeting the atomics.

Too bad the plan didn't work out.

When the smoke cleared and the innocent victims were tallied, Ard's only consolation was that DePons was blamed for producing the weapons in the first place; and being branded a traitor, the lord of Gaerith was exiled for his part in the wasting of Galaneth. So was Ard. About the only thing he got for his efforts was Bec.

Staring at the door of CAC, Ard realized this was the most selfish thought he'd ever had. The vision of Bec laying helpless on the Command Deck, head lolling and eyes blank, awakened a cold determination in him, releasing him from both his hesitation and the pain in his joints. He dusted off his jacket and checked the clip in his pistol, thinking through the next few moments. It wouldn't turn out well. There was no way to win this battle, not with his crew unconscious on the floor and a madman to deal with; but he had to try.

So much for ending the war quickly.

Slapping the hand-plate beside the hatch, he dropped to a crouching position and aimed straight ahead just as the doors opened. Nothing moved in the darkened room. Checking his left and right, Ard moved fast, wincing as his knees let out a couple of painful popping noises.

Bodies were strewn here and there, some painfully contorted. He spotted Bec far off to his left by her station. His eyes lingered on her form for a moment too long. When they shifted back to the Command Center he saw DePons stepping out from behind the ring of consoles; but his LTL pistol was holstered, and his hands were raised in the air.

"I knew you wouldn't run far," DePons said, "not with your Fomorian sprawled on the deck like that."

Ard kept his pistol leveled at the man's chest. He could not miss from this range.

"They are coming, Kanno Morvran," he said, lowering his hands. "Whether you or I fall here, they have retaken this fortress. That places us both at a disadvantage, I think."

"The odds are fine with me," Ard growled.

He pulled the trigger, several times. It'd been a long time since he'd shot at a living thing, but it seemed the warrior in him was still alive. He struck his target center-chest, but something was wrong. A spray of tiny shards ricocheted away from DePons, imbedding themselves in the consoles and ceiling.

Morvran flinched and stepped back, grabbing his shoulder. A small trickle of blood was dripping through his uniform jacket. DePons stood still, facing him with a grim expression.

"You're shielded?" Ard asked, lowering the pistol.

DePons unbuttoned his collar, revealing the edge of a metallic jumpsuit beneath his uniform. "It's FPS technology," he stated.

"CM6 *FPS* didn't accompany us out of the World of Origins," The Commander said, gingerly probing his wound. "It was forbidden!"

"I developed this unit myself. It's an improvement on the original."

"Did Lír lend you the resources to do that?"

"I'm not here on his behalf."

"You gave this ship back to him!"

"Let me clarify," DePons said. "I'm not here to side with them *or* with you, Kanno Morvran."

"Then you're here for some kind of personal vengeance?"

"No. I'm just setting the pieces up for the next logical move."

Ard grimaced, holding his upper arm to keep pressure on the wound. It was just grazed, but it stung. He wondered if there wasn't a bit of metal lodged in there, sizzling away. Or was it that older wound—the deep one he'd earned fighting a nest of Dwimmer Drakes in the High Grass far south of the Karn?

"That's just how I remember you," DePons said. "You're older, but you haven't changed a bit. The day you came to meet her in the city, you were sporting a bandage on that arm."

The Dwimmers for sure, he thought.

"Yeah, I'm older," Morvran said. "What about you? You look exactly the same."

"You know the reason for that," DePons replied. "But my, you *were* an interesting fellow back then. The two of you had the Gremn running in circles," he waved a hand towards Bec where she lay. "I assure you, even those of the Galanese High

Council who hated you most were quite impressed by the stunts you pulled. Too bad your final exploit went awry."

"Not even Bec knew of the secondary protocol. After we captured the fortress, Avalon reasserted itself independently for thirteen minutes, and all we could do is stand and watch as atomics were retargeted and deployed on every colony in the region of Galaneth. They'd planned it all along!"

"You blame the Gremn for the Destroying Fire?"

"Who is not to blame? You were the one who opened the ancient crypt beneath Gilthaloneth and awakened the technologies that have slept there for millennia!"

"I only awaked the Great Change," DePons said with a nod. "Others besides me will one day move it farther along; but I intend to be around to see its last grand act."

They stared at each other across the room. There was a distant rumble, and the sounds of automatic weapons firing.

"They're coming," Morvran said.

"We'd both better leave before they get here. I've quite overstepped my bounds, and will not be trusted by Lír in any case when the others awaken him."

"What have you come here for?"

"There are two things I need from you, Kanno. One was given to you by Marluin for safe keeping."

Ard stiffened.

"I'm speaking, of course, of the stone named *Regulus*," DePons said, striding slowly up the stairs from the Command Center. "I know you're carrying it on you, just as Marluin requested. The time has come for me to take it to its next Location."

"You expect me to just hand it over?"

"I could take it from you."

"Why? Where would you take it?"

"It was not the only one given to you. Regulus is needed elsewhere. You may keep the other."

"If you think you can take it, go ahead and try!"

DePons smiled. "That's not the way to handle Regulus. It must be freely given. Therefore I will offer you the unprecedented gift of an *explanation*."

Distant echoes of shouting voices carried along the passageways behind.

"Its journey from this place must remain secret," he said, "but its origins are not unknown to you. You know what lies in the deep archives beneath the crypts of Gilthaloneth, Kanno Morvran, and few others do. You have looked upon the secret heart of the Ancients. No other human has done so."

"I never understood Marluin's plan," Ard said.

"It is a task that would seem madness to you," DePons replied, stepping closer, "and it is the price of my return. Primarily, I'm here to make sure this war between the Gremn and Crodah ends in the Dark Worlds. Secondly, there is the matter of uniting the Great Houses so that they may fulfill their purpose. This begins with Regulus, and with the gathering of the other Dark Stones."

"And who dreamed up this foolish quest?"

"The Empress, of course. She called it *Operation Reformation*."

Morvran's heart skipped. His eyes were startled wide.

"You see it now? All your trials and victories were scripted long in advance. *Reformation* is the end of all wars, Kanno Morvran—a longer end, perhaps, than your brief human life could envision, but an ending nonetheless."

"Even the Empress couldn't prevent this war from reaching its natural conclusion," Ard said.

Pulling his jacket open over the injury on his shoulder, he removed the small pouch from an inner pocket and held it in the palm of his hand.

"What I saw in the Under-City was a world beyond human understanding."

"Your understanding is not necessary for the plan to be carried out. I only ask for your cooperation."

"You may be a toy of the Ancients, DePons, but you're a bigger dreamer than I ever was if you think that world will ever come into being without even greater bloodshed."

"You are a warrior, Kanno. For you, fighting is living."

"You should speak! Look what you've done to my Command Deck. All these people might have evacuated safely. Now they'll be captured by the Gremn. Do you have any idea what they'll do to them?"

"They'll use them the same as you have, to wage their war."

"*Lír* wages war. I'm trying to stop him!"

"As you've no doubt guessed, this was also a part of the plan."

Morvran held out the pouch towards DePons, and said, "I don't like the fact that you've been working with them, but I have to trust you."

DePons gave him a curious look.

"The idiots of our Colonial Council have forgotten what life was like before the War," Morvran continued. "Before long we'll be fighting each other out here, *and* the Gremn; and then what will become of us?"

"You're trying to make a deal?"

"No," he replied. "I'm not that stupid. I know that collaboration with you is the only thing that will keep us alive, now that the Gremn have found us. I'll take part in the Empress' foolish plot, so long as I get to keep *Qashtu.*"

He tossed the pouch. DePons snatched it from the air and hid it away in his jacket.

"The success of my mission will result in Qashtu's recoherence with the other stones," he said. "You and I will also be affected."

"I won't be alive to see such things, DePons."

"You'd better stay alive, Kanno Morvran. The plan depends on it."

"Yeah? And how are you getting out of here? Hitching a ride with your new friends?"

"No. I won't be using Regulus, either. I've made other arrangements, and you'd better do the same. The Gremn won't have control of Avalon very long. This Convoy Hub is on its way to the bottom of the ocean."

"Is that what you were up to at my station?"

DePons glanced back over one shoulder. "When Avalon awakens shortly, it will already be too late. There's no one will raise her up from where I'm sending her."

"And what happens to Bec?"

"That's the second thing I wanted to ask. I need you to leave her here."

"Impossible! Take the stone, for all I care, but she comes with me!"

"Someone else has need of her—someone who will come back here one day. She is the only one who can utilize the Viaduct Chamber of Avalon."

"Do you know how many of my friends died to free her?"

"Leaving her here will save many others, including those who will return directly to the World of Origins via Avalon."

More weapons fire rattled down the corridor behind them, and several sharp explosions—grenades. The fighting was closer now. They could hear the harsh primal screams of Gremn warriors. The sound sent a chill up Ard Morvran's spine.

Walking past him towards the hatch, DePons said, "If you want to be a part of Reformation, leave her now."

"You're a man of many complexities, DePons," Ard said, watching him go.

DePons turned briefly. "I'm a man of many *consequences*," he said. "Millions died because of the part I've played in all this. I have a large debt to work off. I will make sure nothing happens to your Fomorian. As for the rest of these, however, I promise nothing. If you want to continue living, I suggest you find your way to a drop-ship before this section of the corridor is overrun."

He left.

Ard crossed the deck slowly, heading for the hatch. Listening to the sharp percussion of distant rifles and screams, a cacophony that matched the rhythm of his own heartbeat, he turned to regard his crew. They looked so peaceful laying there, unaware that the man who returned their empty stares, the man who was their friend, was now going to leave them behind for the monsters rampaging down the corridor.

More sacrifices.

Jak, Dan, Wolf, Loy, and all the others—they wouldn't understand if he explained it to them. They hadn't glimpsed the world he'd seen beneath Gilthaloneth.

Would Bec understand?

Last of all his eyes lingered on her. It was too much for him. He balled his hands into fists and pounded the gray wall by the threshold. It was a most dissatisfying blow, like hitting a sponge. He tried again, and made some of the red juice run out of the living tissue of the ship.

"*None* of us will prevent this war from completing its natural course," he said, looking across CAC. "The resolution of consequences for the decisions of those long dead is not for us to take upon ourselves. That's what the Ancient said to me. Forgive me, my friends, for trying. May Lír deal mercifully with you. I hope you will forgive me when we meet again!"

It took him a minute before he could wrench himself away from the hatch, and then he stumbled along in DePons' trail. He had entered CAC intent on killing the traitor and freeing his crew. Now he was the traitor. His soul was aflame with remorse, yet a seed of anger stirred in his heart—anger for the Empress. She knew exactly how this would turn out.

Jogging down the corridor, Morvran's mind ran through the evacuation procedures. There were only a few fallback positions in the ventilation ducts that he could access from here. He would take the first one he came to. His knees were complaining too much to take the second; his back would complain later for taking the first—if there was a later.

He found the rust-colored panel on his left at floor level, tucked between two massive support-columns. This particular ventilation shaft was long, but it was a straight shot to the room behind the storage area, a secret dock for three EEVs. The duct was large enough for a man to fit inside and turn about, but the Gremn would have to change shape to follow him. He wrenched the grate free and ducked inside, but when he turned to pull it back over the opening a huge claw slashed his hand. A terrible scream erupted outside, and he cowered backwards on all fours, staring at a pair of horned legs sheathed in glistening blood-hued carapace.

Lír!

He tumbled backwards, turning as fast as his body could. Forty sols on this world couldn't have slowed his response, nor any pain in his shredded hand or wounded arm. It had cost the lives of five men to capture the mighty general of House Gremn, and if not for Bec he would have been the sixth.

There was no other way to go, so he squirmed and thrust his body around, moving forwards in a pathetic worming manner while the noise of thrashing and banging behind him grew louder. Ard knew that Lír followed, and it sounded like he was widening the passage a little as he came. His heart was pounding, and he breathed like a man running a race. He was almost there, and he would have little time to prep the tiny drop-ship.

If Avalon cooperated.

As if in answer to his thoughts, the ship-wide intercom squealed:

"Avalon Delta to all personnel!" a voice cried. *"If anyone can hear me, the ship has been taken. We've been boarded and are completely overrun. CAC crew is presumed KIA. Anyone left alive must abandon ship! I repeat, this is Avalon Delta to any—"*

The transmission cut off abruptly.

"Avalon Delta!" Morvran hissed. "Black Hades!"

He stopped. There were no more sounds of pursuit, which told him that Lír had also heard and understood the com. Under *Avalon Delta* protocol, Avalon's AI was granted full control of the ship. With the Fomorian out of commission, DePons must have switched control of Avalon back to the AI, and it was anyone's guess as to what would happen next.

He started moving forwards again, and realized that he was almost at the end of the shaft. There was a light ahead.

The far end of the duct wasn't covered by any grate. He tumbled out indecorously into a storeroom and rolled onto his back, wincing with pain. His hand was a mess, and his shoulder ached fiercely. There was definitely shrapnel in there, he decided. As for the hand, he dared not examine it even if he could see it in the dim bioluminescence of the closet. What little he glimpsed revealed exposed bone and scraps of meat. It bled surprisingly little. Maybe there was something to the myth that the ship's protein mats could repair damaged human tissue.

Rising quickly, he dashed across the small room and checked the hatch to the corridor. It was firmly sealed—for now. Standing there a minute, he became aware of a sickening feeling, and it wasn't from a loss of blood. Avalon was losing altitude.

"Must've shut down the engines," he said to himself. "Well, Mr. DePons, I hope you and Regulus got out easier than me." He knew he wasn't out yet, of course.

There was no sign of recent passage, and he wondered if DePons had decided on a secondary route. For Morvran there was only the door in front of him—an airlock set firmly into the fleshy wall. Rising stiffly, he hobbled forwards and pressed his good hand against the black panel beside the airlock, but it didn't even chirp. Avalon was in lockdown, and it no longer acknowledged his clearance.

This wasn't a good sign. Was this why Lír gave up the chase?

"I don't need you anyway," he said to the AI, and grimacing at the panel he removed a knife from the sheath on his belt. Standing before the door, palming his hands against it, he felt for the slim fissure that marked its center axis. The door was designed to slide open from the center, and Bec had once shown him how to gently coax a secured hatch open using this trick. He ran the knife's blade up the hairline axis, and stroked the surface with his hurt hand until he almost cried. Then, slowly, the door budged open. He thrust the knife deep into the fissure, and the device that sealed the airlock was tripped, opening the door with a pop. He slipped inside quickly and allowed the airlock to seal shut behind him. Then, sheathing the knife, he blinked in the sudden illumination of a large chamber.

An EEV seated only one pilot, and there were three vehicles in the dock. He would launch them all, according to procedure. Choosing the central craft, he entered it without incident, for these were independent of Avalon.

The seat was situated so that his legs were sticking out above him in an uncomfortable way, buried in the nose of the tiny craft. He couldn't see much on either side of the cockpit, but he knew the sounds he heard were the control surfaces of the fins going through an automated preflight check. Seconds later there was another beep, and the small console before him flashed green, then began counting down the minutes to drop. The EEV was ready. After making sure the other two craft cycled through their own sequencing, he jabbed the symbol for automatic pilot. He'd never qualified for flying a ship of any kind. He hated flying—not that what he was about to do was really flying.

The hatch above him sealed with a hiss, and his ears popped. Then there was a sharp rushing noise against the surface of the tiny craft; the outer doors were opening. The drop-ships were suspended from a rack, and this was now slowly easing out of the hatch in Avalon's outer hull. It was dark outside, but that would make things easier for him. He didn't want to be seen—the captain fleeing the sinking ship while his crew lay senseless, helpless among a murderous foe.

He buckled himself in tightly and grasped a steering stick that stood up between his knees. There were precious few controls, and they were really just things to hold onto while the craft made its heart-stopping passage to the ground. A beeping sound warned him to make ready. He snugged the harness tighter across his chest. While he made a second check of the controls, trying not to think of the people he was leaving behind, a sound of static distracted him. It was very faint, and seemed to be coming from a small speaker on his right.

"Kanno," a voice said.

His heart leapt. It was Bec's voice.

He stared out the small round window in front of him into the black night sky. There were no instrument lights to illuminate even a hand in front of his face, so the sound of her voice was ghostlike.

"Kanno."

"I'm here," he said.

"I am Avalon."

"I know Bec. Thank you for helping me."

"You must escape. Qashtu must remain hidden."

"I'll keep it safe," he said. "I wish I could keep you safe, too."

"Your heartbeat is elevated and your breathing irregular," she whispered. "I feel what you feel."

"Maybe I can rescue you. I'll ask them to send me with a whole fleet of Convoy Hubs. We'll raise Avalon—"

"Avalon will not rise again," she answered. "I will never again see the sun of this world, Ertsetum."

"Bec!"

There was a high-pitched squeal, followed by a prerecorded message in a gentle feminine voice.

"This is Equatorial Convoy Hub Avalon to all vessels in the fleet. Our internal systems have been compromised—"

And the com went dead.

"Bec," he said, his eyes tearing.

What an old fool I am.

"I'm still here. They are transporting my Null-body to SARA station to be placed in stasis. I want you to do something for me."

"Anything."

"You fought under the banner of the Forest in the Third Division of the Southern Army. You were only a boy yourself then, and long before you came and rescued me you heard my voice in the Forest. You heard the words I whispered through the trees."

A dim recollection surfaced in Ard's memory. "It was like a dream," he said. "I hardly remember anything of that world now."

"Then let my first words to you also be my last. You will remember them better that way."

He bowed his head, and hardly felt the lurch as the ship was dropped from Avalon. He fought hard, but a tear escaped, sliding down his nose and to his chin. Bec's voice came cold but clear through the small speaker.

These, the Twelve, shall endure apart as one.
Hidden by the Ancients, reunited by the hidden;
May all hold fast their legend until the end.

Slowly, with emotion, he repeated the words. The sound of the ship's small thrusters engaging startled him, and he sat up sharply. There was no falling sensation. Though the craft was dropped backwards, it righted itself flawlessly, the fins extending to their full position with a sharp snap. A brilliant light glowed down suddenly through the small portal above his head, washing his features with bluish light. It wasn't a spotlight or another ship, but the comet.

A holographic screen popped up, distracting him, and coordinates scrolled by in amber symbols—a path straight to the southern continent of the planet's western hemisphere, where the Colonial Government kept its strongholds. Qashtu was there, hidden away with some other treasures in an apartment he seldom visited.

"I'm beginning to remember the rest," he said aloud. "I don't know how, but the words—"

"Words spoken in the forest are not soon forgotten," Bec said. "Teach them to those who come after you."

504

The EEV shook, blasted by high winds, and the comet's light foundered behind gathering clouds. The small craft executed a slight turn. White snow swirled around him, but now he could see the giant shape of Avalon's hull slipping away. She was also descending, though very slowly, and the projecting spikes on her belly were retracting. All that would remain after she came down would be a tell-tale crater in the ice.

"Remember," Bec said, her voice fading into static.

The old warrior's throat clenched. When he opened his mouth, all he could say were the words of the Liturgy spoken to him by the sacred trees of another world.

> *Mul'hungá, Agru the fighter, which is Aries.*
> *Mul'gigir, Narkabtu, Gift to the Gremn-Under-Ban, the Chariot.*
> *Mul'ur, Kalbu, the hound of Great Strength.*
> *Mul'Babbar, Kakkabu Petsu, the blessed White Star of Jupiter.*
> *Mul'hul, wicked Lumnu, the witch of Mars.*
> *Mul'ellag, Bibbu the Lonely, the Comet.*
> *Mul'sipazi-anna, Shitaddalu, Beautiful Orion.*
> *Mul'ashiku, Ikû the Far-Ranging, the Last Pegasus.*
> *Mul'lugal, Sharru, the Hidden Lord Regulus.*
> *Gír'tab, Aban Zuqaqipu, the Scorpion, most precious of gems.*
> *Mul'pan, Qashtu, Gift to the Crodah-Under-Ban, the Heart of Venus.*
> *Mul'dara, Dim Da'ummatu, the Dark Star, First and Last, the Dragon's Heart.*

> *These, the Twelve, shall endure apart as one.*
> *Hidden by the Ancients, reunited by the hidden;*
> *May all hold fast their legend until the end.*

OPERATION
REFORMATION:

"It is good to remember things that once were," Brisen says, though I do not know if all that I have composed herein are things that have happened, or that will happen yet.

I set down this record in the hopes that it will be received in some age hence as more than just a parable. It is the story of Reformation, and of the events that led to Reunification. It is a good story, though only because we have come through the darkness to some good end.

~Introduction to *Reformation*, a testimony
by the Empress of Syrscian.

Aerfen: /iyeur-fen/ *"Renowned in Battle."* Lost in an age of war before the first histories were written, secrets of this fabled weapon are closely guarded by the People of the Forest and of the Wastes, and by followers of an old fanatical religion from the days before the Destroying Fire. Apart from these zealots, traditions telling of Aerfen's glory were long regarded chiefly as myth. Its purpose and form were forgotten in the oral accounts passed on over thousands of generations, leaving us with only the name in a riddling song. Aerfen was supposedly captured and hidden, and the stone that powered it was split into twelve pieces. These pieces were dispersed beyond hope of recovery so that Aerfen could never be resurrected. To this the tale says, *"These the Twelve shall endure apart as one. Hidden by the Ancients, reunited by the hidden; may all hold fast their legend until the end.*"

The Legend of Aerfen also spoke of a pilot destined to employ its power in the reunification of both the stones and the World of Origins itself, and of a song that will awaken this power. Whether these references are figurative of events or actual persons is not clear.

Agru: /Ah-grew/ meaning "Agrarian Worker"; a stone artifact, one of an original twelve, in the shape of a palm-sized bluish black crystal disk. Agru, also called Aries, was inscribed by an ancient symbol: a partitioned rectangle adjoined to the figure of a plow, representing agriculture [MUL.HUNGÁ in Sumerian]. Its name, shared by the ship which bore it to Earth, refers chiefly to what ancient civilizations there knew to be the constellation Aries—a very large region of space. A certain star in the midst of this constellation, too dim to be seen from Earth, drew the stone Agru like a magnetic needle, and then positioned the Gremn for transit. If Narkabtu the Chariot was the stone needed to find the Crodah, Agru was vital for navigation. Once Solar-orbit was achieved, all data regarding the journey was housed in a comet whose trajectory would bring it within reach of Gremn transceivers once every 120 cycles of Ertsetum, just in case a retreat through deep space was deemed necessary.

"Thus," Kabta has said, "the stones given to the Gremn were given for the purpose of reaching Ertsetum, where we had gone to finish our war with Mankind but learned to love them instead." It should also be noted that the Gremn who came to Ertsetum by Agru and Narkabtu also escaped the virus that decimated their world of exile, Iskartum.

Agru's name is of great curiosity to those of the New Council who have studied such matters. It is thought that Agru may refer to the prophesied tasks of the Fomorians, the guardian spirits of the forests of the World of Origins.

"Who holds the power of Agru," the Ancient named Marluin once said, "holds the key to unlocking the secrets of the Forest."

Ancients: *Dyn Hysbys,* or "Wise Folk." A race of people who lived in the World of Origins before any others, the Ancients were gifted in the crafting of wonderful technologies and beautiful art. The tale of their exodus from the World of Origins is a matter of legend with roots in deep history, and is a story committed to the memory of the priests of Gilthaloneth. The full tale, recorded in the Book of Invasions, suggests that the Tribe of the Ancients once ruled the World of Origins, which they named Syrscian, under the authority given them by a powerful creator of worlds, the Master. The Ancients did not consider themselves gods, but caretakers and sub-creators. They were named the Children of Light, and were spirits of the powers at work in the worlds.

The people of the world ruled by the Ancients were of one tribe originally, but they eventually became four. The Ancients loved these lesser children of spirit and ash, and taught them how to craft machines for the ease of their labors. They also taught them song, and about the Master, and gave to them an unwritten testimony of His works in many universes. In that first age, the lesser children lived long; but an evil time followed when the hearts of some Ancients were turned in jealous rage against them, for it was spoken that the doom of their kinds was to rule this universe when the labor of the Ancients was finished among them.

One of the Ancients, proud and beautiful, was consumed by an obsession to destroy the lesser children and restore the primacy of his kind. He became a destructor of life and bringer of darkness, and was named the Destroyer. Many followed the Destroyer when he set up his kingdom in the north of Syrscian. His intent ever outpaced his strength; yet many dark and twisted demons arose among his following, and pupils were taken. Bent and broken, reimagined, they became the first sorcerers, whose purpose was to upset the balance of authority, to gnaw the life from all creation and to claim all power under heaven for their lord. To this end they sought the favor of others by promise and by gifts. Their works slowly spread, darkening the world and dimming its first light.

In this period of confusion and darkness the twelve great cities of Syrscian were raised, with Gilthaloneth as their head. Their foundations were established by the Faithful among Ancients, who opposed the darkness and its sundry minions, and they were all linked by a powerful covenant, the goal of which was to preserve life and resist the Destroyer. The seal of this covenant was the most powerful object ever devised by the Master, a stone artifact that contained all the matter in the created universe within its matrix. This artifact was held by a ruler of the lesser children who was chosen because her heart was pure. She was named Empress of Syrscian, and the stone lived within her flesh, protected by her body. Her life was the life of Syrscian.

Then there was war between the Ancients, between the Children of Light and the Children of Darkness. The twelve cities stood fast in the onslaught as bastions of life. Though the darkness was eclipsed and light reborn for a time, the stain of the sorcerers was too deep, and the wounds they made in the worlds threatened resources. War spread among the lesser children. Anticipating amidst this ruin the nearness of the hour of their departure, the Ancients revealed a protection devised in secret for the preservation of the short-lived innocents: a race of intelligent machines. Among these awakened the only artificial beings the Master has blessed with souls. Very few tales speak of these, who became the fourth race of the lesser children, yet it is said the Ancients gave the awakened ones their wisdom, and gifted them with the ability to reproduce; yet this last was accounted by some a grave sin. The machines were hidden away in vaults beneath the twelve cities; and then, just when they were needed most, most of the Ancients departed. This parting precipitated many sorrows.

Chief among the world's woes was the war between Gremn and Crodah, for during the course of this war the Empress was seized by a secret cabal of the lords of the twelve cities. In ransom for her life, which was the life of Syrscian, she was forced to give up the stone and divide it equally among the nobles. The twelve fragments produced bore powers specific only to themselves, and were given names accordingly; yet these fragments would pass into none, and their powers faded. One by one, the great cities fell into ruin, and the stones were lost or hidden. The war spread, bringing utter devastation to eight of the twelve cities. Deserts consumed almost all of the World of Origins, and many millions perished. The Gremn and Crodah were exiled, and the Empress, defeated, left Syrscian to the governing of the New Council. The world of the Ancients was forgotten.

And yet there were two of the Ancients left in Syrscian after that time, wardens of a plan made in secret. As they carried out this plan, the people continued to wage war on one another, and the worlds became dark. Because of their wars, and because the Ancients abandoned them to the Destroyer, most of the people of Syrscian felt they were betrayed by the Children of Light.

It was for this reason the Faithful selected a few to serve as a priesthood for all Syrscian in place of the Ancients. The priests taught the people, saying, "We are divided, who should not be divided. We were given one to rule over us, who was taken from us. We were entrusted with one stone, which was divided into the twelve. The twelve contain all the worlds, but all the worlds cannot contain our sorrows and strife. Gremn and Crodah are exiled, never to return until the twelve are restored." Though supporting this hope was the stated purpose of the priesthood, laws were soon passed forbidding any to retell prophesies spoken in the Old World—prophesies of the return of the Empress and of the restoration of the stone.

Apsu: /Op-soo/ the Gremn in Ertsetum broke into two factions, and those who followed Lír constructed an undersea habitat they referred to as Apsu, which in their tongue means *waters of the underworld.* Located near Wales, the site of Apsu was guarded with fierce vigilance by Lír's agents. Lír ruled in Apsu many thousands of years, establishing human governments and destroying them as he pleased, all to carry out his long plan of vengeance against the Crodah.

Aries: /Air-eez/ a Gremn starship, the hold of the stone *Agru,* which made transit to Ertsetum from Iskartum, the Gremn world of exile. After his rescue from Avalon, Lír utilized Aries as his mobile command post, and left the ship only to dwell at whiles in Apsu. The ship Aries was immobilized beneath the Irish Sea in the 5th century AD after a failed attempt to acquire a Viaduct, a fate shared by the Auriga, the only other Gremn ship to reach Ertsetum.

Aston, Hannah: daughter of Michael and Anna Aston, who were a near-Eastern archaeologist and nuclear physicist respectively, both employed by the FTI group. After her parents perished aboard a Navy vessel in the Bermuda Triangle, Hannah was raised by her aunt. She graduated UC Berkeley after publishing a study entitled *Sites of*

Ancient Human Cult Activities Established in Association with Natural Electromagnetic Anomalies and with Clear Stellar Orientation. In AD 2004, Aston was hired by FTI to work with Seijung Ford on a project code-named Retrospect, which involved locating archaeological sites which resonated a very specific electromagnetic anomaly. Their first candidate site, Tel Hazor, was accessed in 2006 during the Lebanon War. A spacecraft called *Auriga* was found under the site.

Following the discovery of the Auriga, Aston and Ford were taken into closer confidence with the FTI group, and were moved to an undersea habitat. This habitat was located around yet another ship, named Avalon, laying on the seafloor. Aboard a substation named Geomech, Aston was given the task of locating more technology by the same methods her parents once employed.

Avalon: /av-uh-lon/ originally a Gremn defense fortress protecting the hive at Islith in the World of Origins, Avalon is of a class of city-sized airships known in ancient times as ISOs, or *Isospheric Exploration Vessels.* Avalon was the first vessel of this type employed in military operations in the World of Origins, and is itself very ancient. The fortress was captured by Ard Morvran and the Crodah, and taken to Ertsetum where it joined a fleet of Crodah fortresses classified as Equatorial Combat Hubs. As the new Colonial Government on Ertsetum was established and fuel mining was begun in polar regions, the ECHOs were renamed Equatorial Convoy Hubs. Avalon was named an ECHO, yet retained its original designation as ISO-001. Command was given over to Ard Morvran. The Convoy Hubs watched over the merchant fleets and miners traveling in the northern hemisphere, as Ertsetum was then in an ice age.

Synthesized from plant-life native to the World of Origins, the protein-silicate composites from which all Gremn ships were made continually regenerates. Avalon's capacity for self-healing was directly dependent upon the involvement of a Null-User interface, however, and where such was not present the state of the ship would rapidly degenerate.

It was aboard Avalon that the first Gremn were changed. Though the Gremn do not typically associate sentiment to any place or object, Avalon was meaningful to them as a stepping-stone in their own self-determined evolution. To the Crodah it clearly represented something else.

Ancient human legends on Earth associated with Avalon may stem either from a deep memory of the importance of this fortress and the sorrow of its loss, or from covert Gremn "myth-makers," whose task it was to seed human cultures with conveniently similar stories of their origins. Avalon plays a particularly prominent role in the Arthurian sagas, and is also mentioned as a place from whence immortal beings came. Its name came to be the basis for the word "apple" in several human languages, probably because of the fortress' rotund shape and vegetable origins; and this more than anything else strongly suggests a familiarity borne of true memory rather than the meddling of the Gremn.

Ban: *The Ban*, as spoken of in Gremn and Crodah oral traditions, was an event precipitated by the war known as the *Destroying Fire*. The Ban was announced in the World of Origins by the Empress, and the New Council was given charge of rounding up Crodah and Gremn survivors in the city of Gilthaloneth to be sent away to their respective worlds of exile. As a judgment mediated, its purpose was clearly to punish those who participated in the destruction of Syrscian. Its enforcement, however, was mysteriously linked to the division of the stone, and was an observable phenomenon with horrible consequences.

The results of the division of the stone were Decoherence of the worlds and Displacement Syndrome. These, in effect, were the Ban. Those who attempted a return to Syrscian against the Ban were displaced, incurring further fracturing of the worlds and elevating their risk of a kind of runaway Displacement Syndrome.

The New Council ruled in uneasy peace the entire duration of the Ban, beating down numerous rebellions seeded by those who longed for their prophesied ruler to return and restore the wasted realms.

Bec of Avalon: see *Fomorian.*

Bregon of Gaerith: /Bray-goen/ Lord of House Gaerith after his father was exiled, and Commander of the Southern Army of the New Council. Bregon of Gaerith led the assault of the forest Tarthalion and its seven principal cities a thousand years after the War of Destroying Fire. His appointment as General was pressed upon him, however, and his involvement in the razing of the south was a task commenced under duress. The New Council clearly did not trust House Gaerith, of whom the thousand-year-old son of the lord of House Gaerith was apparently the sole survivor. It is presumed their distrust resulted from House Gaerith's collaboration with Ard Morvran during the War of Destroying Fire, but others believe it stemmed rather from rumors that many of the families of this noble house actually survived the war in hiding, and were plotting to overturn the rule of the New Council.

As it turned out, the Southern Campaign was a failure. Lord Bregon left Army Command and turned against his masters in the Council, thus forfeiting his seat in Gilthaloneth and forever outlawing House Gaerith.

Lord Bregon's reasons for breaking with the New Council's Army Command included a disagreement as to terms of surrender. Whereas the Council demanded total unconditional surrender from the Forest People in Tarthalion, whole villages turned out to fight to the death—women and children included. In their arrogance, the Council refused to hear pleas for negotiation, stating refusal to compromise with "Forest Terrorists." They did this with the full knowledge that these dwellers of Tarthalion had not participated in any of the brutal attacks carried out on the colonies of the Karn River by the northern tribes of Forest People.

Demoralized, the Southern Army fell apart long before Lord Bregon left the battle, following a long trail of deserting soldiers north into the trackless wastes of Ceregor and the canyon lands of Sabiir. Lord Bregon's disappearance and the breakup of the Southern Army sent shockwaves through the New Council, whose members scrambled to spread the rumor that he perished in the wilderness alone. The Council did, however, send out many teams of trackers to ascertain his whereabouts, for they had reason to fear the Lord of House Gaerith, whose lineage once included a strong claim to the highest seat in the Council—that of his father, Cedric DePons.

Black Water: in order to facilitate the implementation of a genetic biometric protocol in machine interface, Gremn technologists developed a method for suspending living tissue within an inert fluid medium for purposes of regenerating allelic termini in mitochondrial DNA. The fluid, which is dark, dense, and oily in appearance, is also capable of stabilizing and repairing tissue damage in injured organs. Where the Gremn saw it necessary to place in stasis enemies whom they deemed useful sources of information, this fluid was also referred to as "stasis fluid", and is used in Gremn stasis pods of all types. Additionally, black water may be introduced in subjects who are using Gremn learning machines, in which case the subject's nervous system is altered by residual fluid to facilitate the formation of new neural pathways in the brain and throughout the body. The effects of the black water are impermanent after the subject has been away from the fluid for an extended period of time. However, prolonged exposure has awakened severe mental aberrations in some cases.

Bringer of Dawn: an office of highest honor in the High Place of Gilthaloneth. The Bringer of Dawn was a singer of very special gifting, whose voice was capable of calling forth the invisible worlds at the break of day. The office was seldom filled, as a Bringer appeared in Syrscian only once every hundred years or more, and not for a thousand years after the time of the Destroying Fire. The unique attributes of the voice of the Bringer, its modulation, timbre, and tone, were of such peculiar quality that the Bringers in the time of the War of Destroying Fire were deployed as weapons on the forefront of battle. Though later considered a profane use of the gift, their songs dramatically influenced the outcome of several major battles of the War, where foes were thrown into confusion and heroes into victorious frenzy.

The most powerful Bringer of Dawn during the war was a young boy of the Forest People whose name was Siru. Siru's Song was so powerful in the battle for Tryst's northern borders that it shattered the mountain ranges of the Ceregor all along the eaves of the Daeradon, the toxic wasteland surrounding the city of Thargul. This Song drove back an advance of the Gremn on the eve of the Day of Fire, when they lost control of Islith to the Crodah.

Collected essays of the *Teachings of the Bringers* were assembled in the long ages before the exile. Among the most important teachings are the contributions of an anonymous bard who says, "The power of voice can

change the world around you when you become the
words of your song. Songs can bend the world or break
it. Some may also restore it."

Brisen: the *Lady in White*, a mysterious being appearing in the
dreams of Null-Users and of the Empress of Syrscian.
Brisen was the sister of the Ancient named Marluin, and
is remembered in old tales as the Ancient who created
the *Null-Navvies*.

Canaan: situated northeast of Africa on a land bridge to Asia
Minor, Canaan is bounded on the east by the Jordan River
and the Dead Sea and on the west by the Mediterranean.
It is the land promised by God to Abraham and his
descendents in Genesis 12: 5–10.

Ceregor: /Ke-re-gohr/ name of the range of mountains running
northwest from the region of Sabiir in the World of
Origins. Ceregor is distinguished from a secondary
mountain chain running south, named simply the Rim
Mountains, and forms the natural western boundary of
the forest Tryst. West of Ceregor lies the sea of Gaerith,
the Troubled Waters, and the cold windy coastlands of
the Great House called by that name. The height of
the highest peaks of Ceregor make it an ideal roost for
dragons, which infest that entire region.

Cnoc Ddraig: /kn-ok thrayg/ a mound in the forest Tryst, the
Cnoc Ddraig, or "Dragon's Mound," houses an unstable
Viaduct aperture that exists between the World of
Origins and Ertsetum. Localized in a cave below the
mound, the portal opens only in the World of Origins. It
was made by the Ancients for their own use long before
the stone existed.

    An ancient sorcerer named Nergal of Kutha
constructed beneath the Cnoc a dark tower, and with
armies of enslaved Gremn he labored through the early

ages in lasting war with the Ancients. The prophecy spoken of this place tells of one who will arrive to lead armies of dragons from the tower against the people of Syrscian, and of a hero who will rise up and break the tower, closing the Cnoc forever.

Combat Mobile Systems: Mobile Suits were first developed in the World of Origins by the Crodah during the War of Destroying Fire. Crodah advanced infantry stood less than toe-to-toe with enormous Gremn warriors, and the Crodah refused to modify their own bodies as the Gremn had done. CM suits were therefore developed with specific human shortfalls in mind, particularly speed and endurance. All suits share a similar basic structure, being a bodysuit composed of carbon-fiber reinforced nanomaterials over ballistic nylon, woven throughout with biosensors attuned to the wearer's body and movements, permitting elasticity or hardness when they're needed to individual sections of the suit. Carbon-fiber and steel armor plating covered vital areas of the bodysuit.

The Gremn were surprised by the first appearance of CM suits in battle; the technology began to even the odds in favor of the Crodah before the end of the war. The boost in speed afforded by the suits permitted long-jumping and short sprints up to 35 miles an hour without damage to the wearer. Load-carrying increased as well, thanks to the exoskeleton, allowing burdens of 150 pounds to be carried several miles with ease. Power to the suit was provided via nuclear batteries.

Though originally intended for Crodah use, the virus that rendered many Gremn in Ertsetum incapable of changing their form led Gremn technologists to collaboration with Cedric DePons, who provided design information essential to the crafting of improved CM suits for their own warriors. CM suits are classified in nine basic models:

CM_1: A form-fitting jumpsuit resistant to ballistics and blades, this early mobile system was also wired to mask the wearer's life-signs from remote-detection.

CM_2: This upgrade of the CM_1 was invisible to infrared, and was the first powered combat suit to utilize artificial muscle-fibers to enhance the strength of the wearer.

CM_3: Another upgrade to the 1, the 3 was designed with powered artificial limbs. The need for this kind of suit belied the fact that the two previous models did not sufficiently protect the wearer from melee attacks of Gremn warriors, who were content to leave their enemies alive on the battlefield humiliated after hacking off their arms and legs.

CM_4: Balanced defensive and combative designs of all previous units were cleverly combined in this simple suit, later favored by pilots of PCUs. The 4's were better armored, but slow.

CM_5: The precursor of the 7, CM_5's were sealed units designed for use in space or deep-ocean environments. Flexibility and strength were the design goals, but the suit's ability to mask itself with its surroundings made it particularly ideal for scouting missions in hostile environments.

CM_6: The CM_6 FPS (*field projection suit*), though only lightly armored, deployed a magnetically reactive field and other anti-ballistic devices. This suit was reserved for Crodah House chieftains or high-ranking military officials.

CM_7: The CM_7 "chameleon suit" flawlessly masked its appearance against any background, making it the best choice for scouting missions, though it was also equipped for light sorties. 7's were also more heavily armored than all previous models.

CM$_8$: The precursor of the 9, CM$_8$'s were designed for flight. Lacking the heavier armor of 7's or 9's, 8's carried long-range sensors, magnetic pulse generators, and jet-propulsion systems in a smaller package, and were invisible to almost all electromagnetic wavelengths.

CM$_9$: Advanced alloy armor covered the chest, shins, and forearms of this unit, with optional shoulder or upper arm attachments or backpack modules. A melee unit designed for battle-line berserkers, 9's put humans on equal footing with Gremn—so long as their power cells were topped-off.

Comet Bibbu: /bee-boo/ the "wild sheep." A lone comet with three tails appeared in the sky during the first recorded conjunction of the worlds in Syrscian, and has ever afterwards carried significance in the histories of the four races. Bibbu is purportedly a creation of the Ancients, a marvel employed by early Gremn technologists as a means of studying and exploring the universe. Alternatively, Bibbu is regarded by many ancient omen texts of the Crodah as a sign of the end of the worlds.

The comet's appearance in the skies of Ertsetum was a surprise to the Crodah and Gremn exiles who landed there; yet its identity could not be denied, for Bibbu transmits the link with which the Ancients endowed it in ages past. This link served the Gremn as a communications network, though they found it more difficult to negotiate a connection in Ertsetum than in Syrscian. Moreover, all attempts to ascertain the comet's exact location in space were unsuccessful, though its near approach of Ertsetum every 120 cycles remained fixed for a period of over 150,000 years.

Crodah: /crō-dah/ meaning "valiant." *Humans,* a race of primitive barbaric tribesmen who lived in Syrscian before they were exiled for their part in a war called the

Destroying Fire. Of short lifespan and prone to disease, their particular strength is in their ability to quickly reproduce. House Crodah was a Great House, but was universally regarded as the lowliest of these, being the one most prone to violence. In the early years of the war, the Gremn corrupted the name of Crodah, naming these creatures *Crodacht,* meaning "the Cruel." The seal of House Crodah displays the emblem of a sword, a blade of ancient origins which figures into early legends of their race.

Dark Stones: those of the Twelve Sacred Stones that were lost during the War of Destroying Fire. As one by one the Dark Stones were recovered and recohered, the Dark Worlds were also.

DePons, Cedric: a man who appears to have traveled in time, Cedric DePons is an agent of Foundation technologies International *(FTI)* who served as an FTI affiliate in the US Army. DePons was in fact the lord of the mysterious Great House Gaerith, and one of the few of his people to become involved in the War of Destroying Fire. Exiled to Ertsetum for his part in supplying atomics to the Gremn and Crodah during the War, DePons maintained that his loyalties were to the Empress herself. He was once recorded as stating his affiliations with the Ancients known as Marluin and Brisen, though Marluin, who presided over DePons' tribunal after the War, refuted this claim. DePons himself insisted that his activities coordinated with a secret plan to end all war, but many believe this plan to be a self-inspired aspiration invented to cover a trail of crimes. During his long exile in Ertsetum, DePons took up with Kabta, the Lord of House Gremn. His effort to preserve the peace between the factions and between the Gremn and Crodah is notable to his defense.

Destroying Fire: a war fought in the World of Origins between the Gremn and Crodah, the Destroying Fire lasted many years, ending with the annihilation of Syrscian. The fighting was precipitated by Gremn who enslaved Crodah for the purpose of mining ore. The Gremn stepped up hostilities when Crodah chiefdoms resisted, and using Ancient technology they modified their bodies at a genetic level, forging a fearsome race of shape-shifting warriors.

Responding to threats that their seats would be removed from the Council, the Gremn attempted to eliminate their foes without a fight by engineering a virus intended to render all Crodah sterile. Long-term plans were to harvest Crodah survivors of the genetically-specific screening the virus provided, and to use this gene-pool for cloning purposes. Crodah clones were then to be implemented into Gremn technology, specifically as memory-allocation resources—living computer modules—needed for their floating cities and sky-ships. The virus failed, however, and mutating, it afflicted the Gremn technologists who developed it. As the virus spread, the Gremn fell to fighting amongst themselves.

Taking advantage of the faction-fighting, a young Crodah chieftain, Ard Morvran, convinced the Empress of Syrscian to participate in a plan to utilize atomic weapons to bring the war to a swift conclusion. The resulting calamity led to the exile of Gremn and Crodah, and to a reorganization of the remaining Great Houses and the Council.

Dragon Slayers: that band of knights of the highest and most excellent order, sometimes called the *Circle of Twelve*, which were pledged to guard the Empress of Syrscian with their lives, and who accompanied her on many adventures. Before the Destroying Fire, Orlim of Gilthaloneth was their chieftain; a thousand years later he was the only one left, for the order was dissolved by the Council after the Empress' departure. The knights of the Circle were originally chosen from among all the four races.

Dwimmer Drake: /dwim-er drayk / powerful chargers the Forest Tribesmen deployed with their cavalry, Dwimmer Drakes were small flightless dragons. Besides being capable of changing their color to match their surroundings, Dwimmers possessed a few other unusual adaptations. Most obvious, perhaps, were their scythe-like forelimbs, which earned them the nickname *Mantis-Drakes.*

The Dwimmers' favorite prey were smaller ostrich-like raptors called Talons, which they hunted in the high grass south of the Karn River. The Talon was a swift and wily breed of dragon, and the Dwimmers' ability to catch the wild Talon long mystified the Galanese. This was due to the Dwimmers' most unusual distinctive: their lack of obvious sensory organs. Dwimmers were completely sightless.

No scientific study of these creatures was ever conducted, as only the Forest Tribesmen would they permit to approach or ride; yet we are assured by the storytellers themselves that only in folktales did a rider of the Dwimmer "lend the beast his eyes and ears." Forest Tribesmen insist the opposite is true. The reason Dwimmers will have no reigns is because of the sacred bond, they say, between the Dwimmer and the one whom it will bear, and through that bond the Dwimmer lends its rider the use of superior and altogether mystical senses. This bond lasts while the rider is in contact with his mount, and sometimes for short periods afterwards. The sight given by a Dwimmer supposedly makes one closer to the forest, and to the Fomorian Sleepers, the Sacred Trees of the Prophecy.

Ertsetum: /ert-se-tum/ *Earth*, the Crodah world of exile. Ertsetum is a rocky world of varied terrain with much liquid water on the surface. The planet is of small size, measuring 12,755 km in diameter, which is why it initially escaped the deep probes and surveys conducted by the Gremn.

Féth Fiada: /feth fee-ah-duh/ "Mist-Lording," the name the Gremn give to their ability to change shape. The name was derived from the idea of making oneself completely invisible, though in reality it just made Gremn agents hard to spot in a crowd. Gremn warriors who were able to utilize this ability were called *Corpán Sídhe*—shape-shifters. Not all Gremn possessed the power of Féth Fiada, and many lost the power upon exposure to a weaponized virus created by the Gremn themselves.

Fomorian: early in the records of the people dwelling in Ireland, a race of large devilish creatures is described, named the *Fomoiri*, usually classified among monsters and demi-gods. The local legends of the Irish obviously have ancient roots in Crodah memory, looking back to the incidents surrounding the fall of Avalon and the beginning of the long Intervening Period, during which Mankind in exile lost their knowledge of the World of Origins.

    The name Fomorian is derived from the language of the Forest Tribes of Tryst in Syrscian, and is associated with the sea, *Fo* meaning "beneath" and *Muire* meaning "sea". In the World of Origins, this naming referred to the spirit-people dwelling under or by the Great Waters west of the Ceregor range, the *Gaerith*, also called the "Troubled Sea." The Fomorians of Syrscian came to dwell in the forest Tryst, east of the Ceregor, and there their powers won them infamy as wild deities of the forests, protective spirits of the woodlands capable of utilizing the life-force of any photosynthetic organism as a defense, a power referred to as "The Green." Bodiless, they assumed the forms of trees, those trees that in the age before the war were referred to by the Forest Tribes as the *Sacred Trees of Prophecy*.

The coincidental carriage of the name *Fomorian* to Ertsetum, where it chiefly signified any kind of sea-pirate, may stem in part from the memory of the loss of Avalon beneath the sea. If so, this memory also retained a scrap of information that assisted the FTI group in the location of what was potentially their greatest asset—a Fomorian princess brought into exile by the Crodah.

It was known to the Gremn in Ertsetum that in the early settlement of their world of exile the Crodah brought with them one of these creatures, in corporeal form, that being the Fomorian Bec of Avalon, who served Ard Morvran aboard that vessel as chief of security and primary interface. Through the recovery of this individual, the Gremn confirmed what was known then to only a few of their own kind—that the Fomorians had taken physical form in order to voluntarily subject themselves to use as weapons during the War of Destroying Fire.

This was the way of it: The Fomorians were sought by the Gremn first, who, having discovered a way to capture them and contain them within artificial bodies called *Nulls*, practiced biomodification on Fomorian captives without consent, the primary purpose of which was to experiment with viruses, chemical weapons, and methods of psychological torture. To the extent that Null-bodies were similar to normal human physiology, this arrangement measured success. However, as a result of their treatment, free Fomorians entered into a pact with the Crodah. Under the pact, Crodah technologists were invited to practice extensive cybernetic modification to their Null-bodies in order to enable Fomorian agents to hijack Gremn technology.

After that, Fomorian agents began to infiltrate Gremn hives and ships. This, however, did not prevent many of them from being captured and implemented directly into Gremn technology by the Gremn themselves. In time, each Gremn ship was granted its special personality via a captured Fomorian drone. The Fomorian Bec was taken early in the war during an operation to commandeer the Gremn city of Islith, and she became the ship Avalon. As a ship entity, the Fomorians were able to regenerate the ship physically if it was damaged, a process mediated by synthetic proteins in the tissue of Gremn ships, and artificial cells derived from plants.

Though they were useful in piloting Gremn ships, the "beautiful killers," as they were sometimes called, were a force to be reckoned in battle on their own two feet. Though the full extent of their powers is not known, it was not beyond the abilities of a Fomorian to easily turn a hundred acres of forested woodland into a dread gauntlet for her foes. The power of *The Green* was lost in desert-lands, however, which is thought to be behind the choice of the Gremn to waste the grasslands of Galaneth with atomics, which effectively prevented Fomorians from escaping the forest Tryst and making their way to the city Gilthaloneth.

It is not true that all Fomorians are female. The male iteration of a Null-body housed Fomorian males, and these were deployed in much the same way as females, but were so aggressive in nature that the majority of them were slain in frenzy before they could be captured. It is not known if any males of the Fomorians survived the War, but if they did they would appear in Null-bodies characteristically similar to those of the females of their kind, with blue hair and distinctive tattooing to facilitate their personal identification.

Ford, Seijung: /say-jung/ a graduate of MIT and Columbia University, Ford pursued an interest in developing satellites that could pinpoint magnetic anomalies from geosynchronous orbit. In AD 2004, he was hired by FTI to work with Hannah Aston on a project code-named Retrospect, which involved locating archaeological sites which resonated a very specific electromagnetic anomaly. Their first candidate site, Tel Hazor, was accessed in 2006 during the Lebanon War. A spacecraft called *Auriga* was found under the site.

> Following the discovery of the Auriga, Aston and Ford were taken into closer confidence with the FTI group, and moved to an undersea habitat. This habitat was located around yet another ship, named Avalon, laying on the seafloor. Ford was to study technology recovered from Auriga in a submersible lab called Lucius Station.

Forest People: the "Fourth House" of the four Great Houses of Syrscian, whose inhabitants dwell in the forests Tryst in the north and Tarthalion in the south. The Forest People are a very ancient collection of tribes, each of which comprises a distinct species. Among outsiders their appearance can be shocking, being a mingling of human and animal forms. The Forest People themselves are shape-shifters, capable of assuming a complete animal form as desired. For this reason the superstitious shunned them, and their villages remained isolated from all but a light volume of trade until the beginning of the War of Destroying Fire. They chose in that conflict to side with the other Great Houses against House Gremn—a sorry blow to the Gremn, whose most valued assets lay in the forest Tryst in the vicinity of the city of Islith.

> After the war's dissolution and the exile, the Fourth House celebrated the prophecy of the return of the Empress and the recoherence of the stones. The

sacred trees of prophecy, trees inhabited by Fomorian spirits, brought forth these words to be carried to all the people of Syrscian. The New Council, however, had reasons to silence the prophecy, so they burned the sacred trees until there were but a few left. This instigated a very bloody conflict.

Responding to terroristic attacks on the colonies along the River Karn, the Council sent armies to deal with the Forest People in Tryst and Tarthalion. These invasions occurred regularly over a span of a thousand years. During this period the Forest Tribes, decimated by war, were forced to retreat deeper into the jungles. Lacking sufficient warriors to guard their outlaying villages, many heavily populated areas were abandoned to a grim fate. Though well-liked by those who dwelt in the Galanese colonies, good neighbors were not enough to stave off the swarms of mercenaries hired by Musab merchants. The bandits burned great swaths of jungle on the borders of the forestlands, slaughtering all the adult males they could find and taking females and children captive. The captured were sold in the markets of Tara and Nara as slaves or pets for wealthy nobles of the Galanese, or were hunted for sport in the Gilat Arena of Nara.

The seal of the Forest displays the emblem of a pegasus, a creature the Forest Tribes regard as sacred above all others.

Foundation Technologies International: FTI is an organization of varied interests and secret purpose. It is an extremely wealthy group with strong connections to nearly every governing body on Earth, yet guards the appearance of being a benign developer of advanced technologies. FTI has dubious connections to two paramilitary organizations: the UAMC (United Aerospace Marine Corps) and the HSA (Human Solvency Army). Its leadership remains isolated.

Gaerith: /Gae-rith/ the Troubled Waters; a sea laying west of the Ceregor Mountains in the World of Origins. Also the name of a Great House, whose lord, Bregon son of Cedric, broke from Army Command during the invasion of the southern forestlands of Tarthalion.

 Gaerith is a Great House shrouded in mystery. The lifespan of its people is shockingly lengthy, with no existing record of mortalities. The Gaerith themselves remained largely uninvolved during the War of Destroying Fire, and afterwards vanished without a trace. It is believed they were hidden away by a prearranged plan somewhere among the Twelve Cities of the Ancients. As they are virtually indistinguishable from the Galanese in appearance, the truth of this rumor would be difficult to test.

 The seal of House Gaerith displays the emblem of an eagle bearing a crest of stars with red and white stripes. The eagle's right talons hold an olive branch and the left arrows. This is thought to symbolize the historic role the Gaerith played in bringing trade, peaceful guidance, and justice to Syrscian.

Galanese: /gal-a-neez/ the tribal people of the Minor House Galanon, who in ancient times dwelt in the rich vale of the Karn River (a region called *Galaneth*) in the World of Origins. The Galanese suffered horribly during the War of Destroying Fire, which they also call the Gremn-Crodah War. Peaceful herdsmen when the war broke out, they could do little but stand by and watch as their homeland was stripped for resources by the Great Houses Crodah and Gremn, then rendered uninhabitable by atomics. Of their many towns and colonies, only the principal city of Cipa (/see-pah/) remained, yet was so damaged that it grew into two new cities. Standing on either side of the Karn River, which Cipa once straddled with shining towers, the colony towns of Nara and Tara struggled on, mining and restoring the technologies of the days before the Fire. These towns are inhabited by the Tenno and Musab, respectively, and are the strongest of the remaining Galanese tribal strongholds.

Though they were considered the least of the Houses of the four races represented before the Council of Gilthaloneth, the Galanese ushered in the age of the New Council that saw the disbanding or outright exile of the former Great Houses. The tragic loss of more than three quarters of their people during the war and their non-combatant role won them support among the other Minor Houses, which banded together to form the New Council before the Ban was enacted. The Ban itself was overseen by the last of the Ancients, Marluin, who bestowed upon the Galanese the favor of his people, naming them a Faithful Tribe who would carry on the promised blessing of Syrscian.

The Galanese, being a tribal theocracy led by priests, installed priests in the most important seats of government in the periphery colonies and over the New Council. Though this priesthood was not recognized among all the Houses of the Council, the number of seats the Galanese controlled grew to a majority. The priesthood of the Galanese treated with scorn the "pagan" tribes of the Forest People, and gainsaid their prophesies that the Empress would one day return to reestablish her rule in Syrscian as it was of old. This led to a burning of the Sacred Trees of the forest Tryst, an act that instigated a war between the Galanese and the Forest People.

It was ever doubtful that success in a war with the Fourth House would win the hearts of the people of Syrscian for the Galanese. The priests were still unsuccessful in bringing the power of the Council firmly within House Galanon after a thousand years of ceaseless conflict. Opposition was strong when the Council debated the prospects of invading the southern forest of Tarthalion. Orlim of Gilthaloneth spoke most strongly against this, refusing the Council's conference of military authority to Galanese Commanders selected by the priests. However, he was unable to prevent the Council from taking control of the army and pressing an assault on the peaceful cities of the south. In Orlim's place, the Council commissioned the last member of the ruined Great House of Gaerith, Lord Bregon, to lead the army. He was threatened that noncompliance would be met with banishment along with his father, Cedric DePons.

Gilthaloneth: /gil-thalo-neth/ the capital and last great city of the Ancients in Syrscian, Gilthaloneth is situated on an island of stone in a large lake called Kethern, which is located along the Karn River east of the forest Tryst in the regions ruled by the New Council. A city of mystery and prophecy, Gilthaloneth is sacred to all the rival races and factions in Syrscian. Its Under-City also houses vaults and crypts of technology left behind by the Ancients, whose secrets are guarded by a priesthood that is as old as the city itself. Those vaults were opened by authority of the Empress during the War of Destroying Fire, and weapons were found there which were deployed without the Council's consent.

When the vaults were resealed after the war, the Empress disappeared, leaving behind only a strange proclamation. She said that the Ancients would permit no return of Crodah or of Gremn to the World of Origins until at least three of the fragments of the stones were rejoined and returned by a combined effort of both Houses. This event, over which the Empress herself would preside, was to occur in the High Place of Gilthaloneth upon a conjunction of the three moons.

Glede: the first of the dragons of the ancient world, which dwelt in the mountains called Ceregor in Syrscian. Glede was made by the black witchcraft of a sorcerer named *Nergal of Kutha.*

The dragons of Ceregor were feared because they were able to attain the look and texture of stone surfaces in daylight, making it easy for them to hide in the mountains and high hills. This adaptation was noticed by the Gremn, who used dragon-carcasses to explore the secret of their abilities. Having discovered this secret, the Gremn developed a technology to change their genome, thereby joining the Forest People as the second House of shape-changers among the four Great Houses.

The threat of dragons was always something to consider, even as far away as Gilthaloneth. A squad of specially trained warriors accompanied the Empress in the Great City, and these were named the *Circle of Twelve,* though most just called them the *Dragon Slayers.* The task of protecting the Empress from dragons was one that kept the Dragon Slayers busy, and many of them were killed in battle. Records indicate that new warriors were being trained all the time, a process that lasted ten years and culminated in an ascent of Ceregor's highest peaks, where a true Flyer must be hunted down and slain. Once sworn in as a member of the Twelve, warriors only had a life expectancy of ten encounters or five years. The only exception to this unfortunate fate was Orlim the centaur, the chieftain of the Dragon Slayers.

Great Houses: the people of Syrscian were ruled in ancient times by four Great Houses, one for each of the four races. These were *House Gremn, House Crodah, House of the Forest People,* and *House Gaerith.* Each House was represented by a powerful and ancient symbol: the Shield of House Gremn, the Sword of House Crodah, the Pegasus of The Forest People, and the Eagle of House Gaerith.

After the War of Destroying Fire, the Great Houses were exiled, vanished, or enslaved. According to the prophecies whispered among the colonies, only the Great Houses can restore the glory of Syrscian.

Gremn: /grāym/ a race of shape-shifting warriors who lived with the Crodah in Syrscian before they were exiled for their part in a war called the Destroying Fire. The Gremn enjoy a lifespan of hundreds of thousands of years and can be destroyed only by decapitation or by being totally consumed in fire. House Gremn, the tribal assembly of the Gremn, was the most powerful and technologically advanced of the four Great Houses of Syrscian before the Ban was enacted. The seal of House Gremn displays the emblem of a shield, for they were once the defense of the people of Syrscian.

Hazor: /hot-sōr/ the capital city of the chiefdoms of the Canaanites in ancient Palestine, long under the rule of kings in the line of Ibni (English "Jabin"). According to Joshua 11: 10–13, Hazor was destroyed by Israelites led by the famed military hero Joshua (/yeh-h -shoo-a/). According to Judges 4, a subsequent "final" destruction of the Canaanite city took place long afterwards.

Hest: a mysterious female warrior of the Gremn and the youngest of all her surviving species, Hest was appointed by her father, Dr. Cedric DePons, to be the companion of Taran Morvran on his journey. She was charged with delivering the fragmented stone Regulus to Taran, and thereafter served as his personal bodyguard. As an agent of the HSA in New York, Hest worked under the guise of a vagabond girl named Drusilla.

HSA: *Human Solvency Army;* an entity created by Cedric DePons in a number of Dark Worlds he passed through while utilizing the stone Regulus.

Ibni-Addu: /ib-nē-ad-doo/ the young King of kings at Canaanite Hazor in 1350 BC, Ibni was caught up in the travails of his time, which included an incursion into the Canaanite chiefdoms by an outside aggressor, a people called the 'Apiru (/a-pē-roo/ or /ha-bē-roo/). It is known from ancient cuneiform texts in Ertsetum that Ibni-Addu was only a royal dynastic appellation for this king, whose personal name was *Abdi-Tirshi* /ahv-dē-tēr-shē/.

Iskartum: /is-kar-toom/ the Gremn world of exile. Iskartum is a rocky world of deserts and fractured sandstone hills. The planet is large, measuring more than 30,000 km in diameter, and it is extremely dry, lacking liquid water on the surface. The atmosphere is acidic with high levels of oxygen. Gravity is also quite high at 1.5 Terran, making it inhospitable to all forms of life except the Gremn. The Gremn, as it turned out, did not survive their sad world of exile.

   After initiating a transit to Iskartum for the purpose of reporting the situation in Ertsetum, Lír's agents discovered that all Gremn on the homeworld were killed by an antivirus designed to control the virus engineered to sterilize Mankind. Returning with this news to Ertsetum, the Gremn unknowingly brought with them a mutated form of the virus—one which rendered Gremn unable to change their shape.

Islith: /iss-lith/ in the deep places of the forest Tryst, east of the mightiest summits of Ceregor, the Gremn dwelt in a city given to them by the Ancients, and they named it Islith. Of old this city was the nexus of their technological revolution, which in turn spurred their genetic augmentation program. When the War of Destroying Fire was begun, Islith became the capital of all Gremn forces, and a hive for the cloning of their warriors was constructed in caverns beneath. This hive was also utilized in the production of Null-User bodies for captured Fomorians, and for the testing of weaponized viruses. Islith was defended by a mighty sky-ship fortress called Avalon.

Islith lies in the northernmost tip of the forest Tryst, looking north across what was once a lush grassland named Darwath. That land was destroyed long before the War of Destroying Fire, however, and was ever afterwards known as Daeradon. In the north of Daeradon was Kutha, where a dark sorcerer lived; and so the Gremn of Islith were charged by the Ancients in peaceful times to be a vigilant folk, guarding the free lands behind them from the threat in the distant north.

Kabta: /kob-tah/ Lord of the Gremn-in-Exile, Kabta led his people from Syrscian after they and their enemies, the Crodah, were banned for waging a war that destroyed the land. He long pursued the Crodah in bitter vengeance, but later turned and became their fiercest ally.

Striving to undermine the efforts of Lír and his syndicate, Kabta relied firmly on the skills of five Gremn lieutenants, companions of his inner circle of trust. These five companions were more than warriors; they were a team of problem-solvers that had carried the plan of a return to the World of Origins for millennia. Their names are:

Abdaya, or *Ab,* a technologist once subservient to Lír and Magan.

Sheb, or *Breaker,* an assistant technologist and trusty warrior.

Hanuta, or *Nuta,* daughter of Nurkabta, youngest and favorite of her uncle.

Hun, or *Attila,* whose blind charges in battle earned him a fierce reputation.

Malkin, once a Nubian prince, Kabta's weapons expert.

Kalbu: /kal-boo/ meaning "Hound"; a stone artifact, one of an original twelve, in the shape of a palm-sized bluish black crystal disk. Kalbu was inscribed by an ancient symbol: a dog's-head facing right [MUL.UR.GI7 in Sumerian]. Its name refers to the constellation Hercules. The stone was one of two kept by the dragon Glede, who knew that it would be claimed by one who became a vessel for his master, a wicked sorcerer and demon named Nergal of Kutha. He found the boy from Ertsetum by the same name, Kal-Nergal, and learned that he possessed a link to the Source, an artificial intelligence that housed the spirit of the sorcerer. Thus the dragon laid his plans to claim Kal-Nergal and bring his master back to the World of Origins.

Kal-Nergal: /kal-noorgal/ Kalbu (/kal-boo/) was the slave of Nurkabta and servant of Nurkabta's son Shubalu, and was renamed Nergal when he entered the services of Morla, priestess-seer of Hazor. The first to personally contact and awaken the Source aboard the Gremn ship Auriga, Nergal was the sole recipient of the Source's knowledge and instrumental in the activation of Auriga's CSR Terminal after the destruction of Tel Hazor. This resulted in the displacement of Morla, Val Anna, and himself. Post-displacement, Nergal found himself in the World of Origins.

Kanno: /kah-noh/ a high-ranking officer in the Crodah Aerospace Militia, *Kanno* is comparable to the U.S. Naval rank of *Captain,* but only in terms of the duties involved. The word literally translates to *Commander,* but may be applied to either a captain of one aeroship or of a fleet of aeroships. The Kanno-rank is also applied to non-military Crodah vessels of any type. The word was used in ancient times in the World of Origins to designate the chieftains of certain tribes, and was later applied to wealthy land-owners in the Galanese periphery colonies.

Karn: /kahrn/ a river running east through the Wastes of Galaneth from the forest Tryst in the World of Origins. Karn once hosted many colony towns of the Galanese, but after the Galaneth was blasted with atomics the river retreated underground for a century, reemerging as a smaller flood. The water was clean, however, fed by the snows of Ceregor and the unspoiled pools of Tryst, and some small towns once again arose on its banks in later days.

Lír: /l yr/ a famed Gremn technologist of Cipa, Mannanan Lír joined in the war after his family was slaughtered in a raid. Vastly intelligent, he also proved a hugely powerful warrior. He accompanied Kabta in his pursuit of the Crodah people 150,000 years ago, but broke from Kabta in order to carry out a personal mission of vengeance against Ard Morvran, the Crodah commander of the fortress Avalon. Lír was captured aboard the fortress, but was rescued a year later in an elaborately preplanned maneuver which left the Crodah defenseless. Though Avalon was lost beneath an ocean with Lír and his warriors aboard, forcing them to endure ages of stasis with no near-term possibility of rescue, the loss of Avalon was a far worse blow to the Crodah, whose subsequent efforts to govern themselves in exile only brought them closer and closer to extinction.

In messages intercepted by agents working for Kabta, Lír was code-named "Oannes." As *Oannes* (the bringer of language, culture and technological knowledge to ancient humans), Lír corresponded frequently with someone who called himself "Berossus." Some speculate this Berossus was none other than Cedric DePons.

Magan: /ma-gan/ underling of Kabta involved in his early plots against the Crodah. Magan eventually turned against Kabta his lord, desiring to heal the wounds of war that had caused his people to be exiled from their homes. In time, however, Magan helped rescue Lír, and then joined his efforts to undermine Crodah civilization on Ertsetum.

Morla: /moor-la/ a name meaning "Lady of the Dark." The King's Seer in Hazor in 1350 BC, Morla was a stranger to Canaan, having escaped an assassination attempt in her homeland of Babylonia, where she served as an Entum priestess and prophet from the time she was a young woman. Morla was able to "see" the immediate future along a path of probabilities, which talent made her a boon to her master—and a threat to the politicians of her day.

    Morla's transit from Hazor to the World of Origins brought her into contact with the Empress of Syrscian, who appointed her Priestess of the High Place in Gilthaloneth. She served in this position until the colonies were overtaken by the War, at which time she was placed in stasis beneath the city of Cipa on the Karn River.

Morvran, Ard: /moor-vran, ard/ the adopted step-son of the chieftain of House Crodah. Ard was a Crodah warrior whose actions led to the Wasting in the War of Destroying Fire. He became Kanno of Avalon.

Morvran, Fain: /moor-vran, fayn/ the father of Thaddeus Arthur, grandfather of Taran and Jon. Fain was a historian and linguist before meeting Cedric DePons at the family estate on Island Aenfer. DePons awakened in Fain a desire to sort out the Morvran family's deep and mysterious history, and turned him onto a path of science that led to the discovery of a stone amulet treasured by the family for countless generations. This amulet launched Fain on a journey around the world, and with DePons' help he slowly uncovered the truth of his legacy.

   While his son was living in America, Fain set off on one last expedition, and was never heard from again. Many believed him to be dead.

Morvran, Jonathan: /moor-vran, jon/ the son of Thaddeus Arthur, brother of Taran. Jon Morvran was his father's oldest son, and the black sheep of the family. At a young age he showed less interest in studies than in hunting. He was prone to violent outbursts, and was generally disposed to loud frolic. Despite his parent's attempts to reign in his folly, Jon became more unruly as he grew older, and took to habits and fashions that were frowned upon in his time.

Morvran, Taran: /moor-vran, ta-ran/ the son of Thaddeus Arthur Morvran. Taran's chief interests were not the historical and linguistic studies that he was trained in, but in aeronautical engineering. He was the childhood friend of Val Anna Naruna, but came under suspicion when Val Anna disappeared after an accident in the Morvrans' barn. Taran ran away from home shortly afterwards, and his whereabouts remained unknown, deepening suspicions against him.

Morvran, Thaddeus Arthur: /moor-vran/ the husband of Margaret and father of Jon and Taran, Dr. "Art" Morvran was a distinguished scholar of astronomy and a professor of Columbia University from 1882 to 1901. He began his studies in the shadow of his father, an archaeologist and linguist who became an inventor late in life. Thaddeus Arthur's descent from an ancient family of some obscure importance made him the sole inheritor of an estate on an island off the coast of England, and of a curious stone artifact, the study of which became the basis of his academic career. With his assistance, Val Anna and Taran were able to construct the world's first flying machine; but following the accident involving Val Anna's disappearance, the machine was disassembled and sold to a couple of adventurous tinkers in Dayton Ohio.

Nara: /nar-ah/ a Galanese colony-town on the south bank of the Karn River, located three hundred leagues east of the Forest, in the dead center of the devastated region of grasslands called "the Wastes of Galaneth". Governed by a tribe called the Tenno, Nara and its sister-colony Tara, which together once formed the city of Cipa, are the central hub of the guild that names itself *The League of Antiquinarian Merchants*. This guild is responsible for the safe collection of ancient technologies buried deep beneath the blasted hills of the Galaneth. Its excavation shafts produce everything from scrap metal and ceramics to working engines, all from the lost civilizations of the Ancients who dwelt there before them.

While Tara was the marketplace for all recovered items, Nara was where the dangerous work of excavation was done. The families who staked claims in Nara guarded their shafts fiercely, employing mercenaries and arming them with some of the more fanciful weapons restored in Tara. The most famous shaft in Nara was named "Old 32," which had reached the level of the grasslands and the basements of the original city before being slated for shut-down because of safety concerns.

Both Tara and Nara suffered terroristic attacks at the hands of the Forest Tribes following their invasion of the forest Tryst and the destruction of the Sacred Trees. The terrorists were led by a man named Taran Morvran, nicknamed *Master of the Wastes*, whose infamous exploits led to an arming of the periphery colonies and the hire of greater numbers of paramilitary forces.

Narkabtu: /nar-kob-tooh/ meaning "The Chariot"; a stone artifact, one of an original twelve, in the shape of a palm-sized bluish-black crystal disk. Narkabtu was inscribed by an ancient symbol: a rectangular frame enclosing a horizontal y-shape [MUL.GIGIR in Sumerian]. Its name in Babylonian refers chiefly to the stellar constellation Auriga. Narkabtu was stowed aboard the Gremn ship Auriga by the brothers Nurkabta and Kabta, and was the power that made it possible for them to traverse the vastness of interstellar space from Iskartum to Ertsetum, hard on the heels of the Crodah.

Naruna, Val Anna: /nuh-rooh-nuh/ [Bal-Ona ("wife of Baal") in Babylonian] adopted daughter of Talia and Colonel Albert Naruna. Talia Naruna's father ran an orphanage in New York City, where the couple met Val. Colonel Naruna pressured his wife to adopt the small child, since they had no children of their own, and bringing her to their home in rural New Jersey they raised her under the tutelage of Dr. Thaddeus Morvran. Her childhood was unremarkable, except that she suffered from horrible waking dreams of living in another world—*phantasies*, as her doctor called them. In 1901, she vanished after an accident in the Morvrans' barn. This led to accusations against the Morvrans, who lost their land and home.

Naruna, Albert: /nuh-rooh-nuh/ Colonel Naruna saw action at manila Bay under the famed Commodore Dewey, for he was a Navy man before transferring at the end of the 19th century. The assistant secretary of the Navy, Theodore Roosevelt—who later became Vice President—commissioned Naruna and transferred him to the offices of Leonard Wood of the Army. There he was instrumental in raising and training the first all volunteer cavalry, nicknamed the *Rough Riders*. That led the colonel to Cuba, through the terrible San Juan hills to risky meetings with General Garcia's pro-independence rebels, and ultimately to Santiago. After all the fighting was done, he went on to Puerto Rico, and to many other adventures.

It was discovered during the investigation of Val Anna Naruna's disappearance that the colonel, her father, was corresponding with a strange man who called himself "Oannes," an ancient form of the name *Jonah*. This character, who had some level of authority in the United States armed forces, had ordered Naruna to personally capture Taran and Jon Morvran and to compel them by force to confess to the charges that they had conspired together to murder Val Anna. By the time this evidence was brought forth in court, however, it had been determined that the Morvran boys weren't guilty of any crime, and that the meddling of Colonel Naruna had caused them to go off and lose themselves somewhere in Europe. Naruna was summarily charged with conspiracy to kidnap minors, but disappeared without a trace. He left behind the Morvrans, whose family was ruined by these experiences, and a mourning wife, who returned to New York to run her father's orphanage.

Nephtys: /nef-tees/ a very rare female Gremn who joined Kabta's syndicate early in their stay on Ertsetum. Nephtys served FTI in the capacity of a medic, though her gifts also lay in maintaining the psychological wellbeing of her comrades. Though a technologist, Nephtys was capable of changing her shape, and was thus granted operational clearance by Kabta. She did not fight in any battles, but her presence kept the core group of Kabta's warriors at peace with one another.

Null-Navvies: /nul na-vees/ the name given to those artificial life forms created by the Ancients, blessed with life and the ability to reproduce their own kind. Essentially robots, the Null-Navvies were of widely varied form, function, and intelligence, but most were indistinguishable in appearance to the other people of Syrscian. The basis for their name stems from their artificial Null-body, and from the program for their original development, the *Null Navigational Construct.* Previous to the War of Destroying Fire, Null-Navvies were employed only by House Gaerith. Afterwards, they could be found throughout the periphery colonies, where in return for living among the other people along the Karn River they were granted employment in colony maintenance or manual labor jobs, though only under strict Guild supervision.

Some Null-Navvies were programmed for more specific purposes, and being unsuitable for menial labor they were granted a loftier societal status than their cousins, even to the extent of being Free People. This group included a wide array of occupational-Navvies, such as the dancers and singers, the hospitalers, and the children. These last, made in the form of human children, were given to childless couples; and some of these retained all the legal rights of heirs. However, all Navvies being capable of reproducing their own kind, and none of them being obviously afflicted by the natural processes of aging, the New Council began managing their personal activities in an attempt to prevent their populations from rising sharply. About the same time, however, censuses indicated that Navvies were disappearing in large numbers from the major cities, concurrently with the people of House Gaerith. It is widely rumored that Navvies and the Gaerith became indistinguishable from the other races to the extent that their "disappearance" could be explained by a secret relocation of their populations. This seems highly unlikely, however, there being no consequent population boom in any of the colonies. Whatever the reason for their disappearance, a thousand years after the War of Destroying Fire there remained only a few thousand Navvies in the colonies, and nowhere else. These survivors were reduced in status to non-beings, machines utilized in Guild excavations at Tara and Nara on the Karn River.

Nunna: /noon-na/ the personal servant of Morla, priestess of Hazor. Left deaf and mute by a childhood fever, Nunna was a prize offered to Ibni-Addu by the vassal-lord of a neighboring kingdom. After her healing, she sacrificed herself to save her friends from the Gremn Nurkabta. Morla laid her body to rest in Syrscian.

NUNNA: *Null User Neocortical Node Actuator.* Nunnas are Null-Navvies created during the War of Destroying Fire to serve in a similar capacity as Fomorian drones. While Fomorians were designed by the Crodah to be implemented directly into Gremn technology, granting them control of Gremn ships, Nunnas were designed primarily to commandeer Gremn PCUs. The Nunnas also differed from Fomorians in that they were completely artificial; yet they were also capable of surprising individuality. Each Nunna was programmed with its own personality, and some were gifted with powerful insight into Crodah or Gremn behaviors. These gifts were granted by the maker of the Nunnas, an Ancient named Brisen, who alone with her brother Marluin among all the other Ancients remained in the World of Origins during the War.

    Nunnas were all created female. Male Null-Navvies created for the same purpose were named Dunnams / doon-um/, *Distance User Null Navvie Ameliorate.* The Dunnams, or Duns/doon/, were capable of acquiring a remote link with shielded Gremn technologies, which ability facilitated remote-piloting of Gremn hardware. Few Dunnams were made, and it is not certain that any survived the war.

Nurkabta: /noor-kob-tah/ Chief of Battle and overseer of the Ritual Complex at Hazor in the 1350's BC. Nurkabta was the father of Shubalu and Hanuta, and the brother of Kabta, Lord of the Gremn-in-exile. His loyalties were with Kabta's rival, the dissident and powerful Lír, and under Lír's directive he was chiefly responsible for placing hurdles in Kabta's way. Nurkabta came into the service of the High King of Canaan by a chance meeting upon the dangerous highways of Mesopotamia.

Orlim: last of the Circle of Twelve, the Dragon Slayers, a band of warriors sworn to protect the Empress of Syrscian. Orlim, a centaur, was an artificial life form constructed by the Ancients via the technology of the Archives in the Under-City of Gilthaloneth. Most of these life forms were destroyed in the War, though a few remained. They were possessed of extremely long life and driven by great passion to follow the purpose for which they were crafted.

Orlim's purpose was to be a warrior, and to this he devoted his entire existence. However, it is notable that he did not support the thousand-years war against the Forest People, and though he was with the Council in most matters politically, he strongly supported the prophesied return of the Empress and the restoration of her authority over Syrscian.

PCU: *Personal Combat Unit.* The nine basic combat mobile systems developed by House Crodah during the War of Destroying Fire were designed to place Crodah and Gremn warriors on equal footing in battle. However, the Gremn response to Crodah CM suits was to produce mobile suits of their own, employing their most advanced technology and limitless resources. These mobile suits were christened PCUs, and they far exceeded the versatility and elegance of any other weapon produced during the War.

The PCU is a combination biomechanical battle armor and gun-platform, usually piloted by a genetically specific Gremn operator. Units range in size from four to more than ten meters in height, are bipedal, and are masked in the bird-man motif peculiar to traditional armor worn by the Galanese in their feudal period. There are two main PCU types: *Seraph* and *Kerub*, the main difference being the Seraph's incendiary weapons systems. *Seraph* units were designed by Gremn to fight rival Gremn in the faction wars. The *Kerub* are mostly networked robotic units; though designed for autonomous military patrols, they are capable of hosting a pilot for brief labor excursions. Common projectile weapons borne by the majority of PCU platforms include Gatling and atomic rail guns. A wide variety of forearm-mounted blades or grappling tools are usually field-fitted to those units prepped for hand-to-hand engagement. Shielding of units sometimes involves electrostatic fields that detonate explosive projectiles at a safe distance, though the power drain on such shielding would relegate its use to those units on short-range patrols. Elsewhere it is more sensible to resort to physical shields or plates that can be fitted to the body or limbs of the unit. Other shielding includes several types of organic nanomesh skins that protect vital subsystems from exposure to electromagnetic radiation, or which are also capable of becoming invisible to the electromagnetic spectrum. Skins are self-healing, which function may seriously drain power. Power sources include H3 quick-charge batteries for smaller units and a combination of nuclear cells and batteries for the larger ones. The significant weight of armaments and batteries is trimmed somewhat by carbon fiber construction. Skeletal frames are molded from super-hard ceramics.

Rumors of an advanced PCU unit began to circulate before the end of the War of Destroying Fire. A Gremn suit called the *Dragon* was referenced in several documents seized before the tribunal and the enactment of the Ban; but if any of these suits were ever constructed, they were taken into exile with the Gremn.

Regulus: /rej-yeu-leus/ meaning "The Little King"; a stone artifact, one of an original twelve, in the shape of a palm-sized bluish-black crystal disk. Regulus was inscribed by an ancient symbol: the reclining profile of a man wearing a crown [MUL.LUGAL in Sumerian]. Its name in Babylonian, *Sharru*, refers chiefly to a multi-star system of four stars in two pairs, which together form one of the brightest objects visible from Ertsetum. In the World of Origins this constellation is similarly visible, and is likewise linked to royalty. The four stars in pairs came to represent the four races, and appeared on banners where each stood for one of the four Great Houses.

Regulus' power was unique among the stones. Besides the capacity for transit, it gave to its bearer the power to locate the other stones. Unfortunately, this special power led to its recurring division in Ertsetum. As many as held Regulus or one of its iterations, there were generated Dark Worlds in their wake.

Qaštu: /kosh-tooh/ meaning "Heart of Venus"; a stone artifact, one of an original twelve, in the shape of a palm-sized bluish-black crystal disk. Qashtu was inscribed by an ancient symbol: a chevron with strokes extended to either side in the manner of outstretched wings [MUL.PAN in Sumerian]. Its name in Babylonian refers chiefly to the planetary body, Venus. The stone was inherited with the family estate by Dr. Thaddeus Morvran. Among many mysterious properties, Qaštu's most notable feature was that it emanated a peculiar electromagnetic energy. First noted by Dr. Morvran and his associate, Cedric DePons, this energy was the focus of secret experimentation by a privately-funded research project called Reformation, conducted at Columbia University in the early twentieth century. Dr. Morvran gave the stone to his son for safekeeping, and Taran unwittingly gave it to Val Anna Naruna as a gift of friendship. The stone disappeared with Val after an incident in the Morvran barn.

Reformation: originally a Columbia University research project financed by the secretive international consortium called *FTI group*, Project Reformation's general aim was to explore the technology of the stone artifact known as Qashtu. Headed by Dr. Cedric DePons and Dr. Thaddeus Arthur Morvran, the project sought more specifically to identify the nature of the heat and light energy exuded by the stone, the goal being possible resource acquisition and development of an independent power source, something to rival or better 19th century steam engines.

Early progress was encouraging. The secret founder of the FTI group even lent Morvran his nephew, a man named Shubalu. Shu provided detailed information about the stones' material and chemical composition, and was permitted by his uncle to hand over a testing apparatus that would assist in the development of simple engines powered by the stone. DePons never told Morvran that there was another stone in his possession upon which all this testing had already been performed, and that this second stone, Regulus, was beginning to attract unwanted attention.

Thus it was that ten years after the project was initiated, research nearly ended when their Columbia university laboratory facility was sacked by a group whose only obvious goal was to seize the stone at all costs. Several lives were lost. Morvran and DePons escaped, and reported the incident at once to the FTI group. It was then that DePons revealed to Dr. Morvran the secret of the Gremn, and explained Project Reformation's status

as a covert military operation. Elements of the United
States Army were closely involved, though all was run
from FTI's hidden headquarters. Morvran and DePons
were employed in a new sort of work. They would be
permitted to protect and exploit Qashtu if they aided
the Gremn faction with which they'd inadvertently
sided.

Caught in the middle of a war he did not fully
understand, Dr. Morvran was hard-pressed, for only
he and DePons knew that before the lab was attacked
the stone Qashtu was given to Morvran's son Taran for
safe-keeping. Complicating matters, Taran had given
the stone to his friend Val Anna Naruna, who had
vanished without a trace. It became obvious that the FTI
group knew somewhat of these events when Morvran's
request was granted for a face-to-face summit with the
founder, a Gremn named Kabta. Meeting in New York,
the founder presented Operation Reformation as the
achievement of a cooperative venture between Mankind
and Gremn, with the purpose of returning both races to
the World of Origins. DePons seemed game to this goal,
while Morvran felt it would be better if the Gremn left
the Earth in peace once they had what they wanted.

A second laboratory, which would carry out the
plan, was already in existence. This facility was begun in
secret by Thaddeus Morvran's vanished father, Fain, at
the Morvran estate on Aenfer, an island off the coast of
Wales. *The Laboratory of the Reformation*, as it was named by
Fain, was abandoned after the stones and their bearers
disappeared from Ertsetum.

Retrospect: an FTI operation that involved the location and
    recovery of lost Gremn and Crodah technological
    assets on the Earth. The unique research required
    for this operation's success, which involved locating
    archaeological sites that resonated a very specific
    electromagnetic anomaly, prompted the FTI group

to contact and employ the talents of two graduate students, Hannah Aston and Seijung Ford. The first candidate site, Tel Hazor, was accessed in 2006 during the Lebanon War, and produced favorable results. Once it was determined the researchers could be trusted, the FTI group brought them to a second-stage of the operation, which focused on the assembly of portions of Gremn technology recovered from the *Auriga*.

Shimeon bar-Kochba: nicknamed Shim; the leader of Lír's security forces protecting the Apsu. Shimeon once served Kabta before going renegade to Lír. Shubalu was trained by this older warrior at a time when he was still in Kabta's favor. Except for one, the five companions of Shimeon served Lír in the hopes of preventing Kabta from uniting his faction with a terrestrial government. Their names were:

> Artakshasu, or *Artax*, Lír's legendary "First of Battle."

> Hiko, a Gremn medic of the first order and of noble pedigree. It was he who unintentionally brought a mutated virus back from Iskartum, the Gremn world of exile.

> Tlaloc and Chaac, twins bred in a facility Lír designed somewhere on the South American continent, possibly utilizing technology left behind by the Colonial Government of the Crodah.

> Shubalu, or Shu, the son of Nurkabta and nephew of Kabta. Shu served his friend Shimeon as a double-agent for a time, though without permission from Kabta himself. Shu was thrust into a grey area between the factions after watching his uncle kill his father in battle.

Source: an entity encountered as a "voice" by the slaves excavating subterranean passages beneath Hazor's Ritual Complex, the Source, which was also called "the

Teacher," led Morla to the discovery of an enormous metallic structure deep underground—a Gremn starship named Auriga. According to Gremn legend, the Source is the actual mind-projection of an intelligent machine, supposedly inhabited by the spirit of an Ancient sorcerer. The sorcerer's name was *Nergal of Kutha*, who was slain in a tribunal of the Ancients for crimes against the four races. The legend does not explain how the spirit of this sorcerer could have come to inhabit a machine. Those who designed the Auriga clearly valued the Source, however, for in addition to integrating it into the computer core they gave it control of a Viaduct Mirror.

Substation: functional name of an undersea facility composed of twelve habitats, created by Kabta and the FTI group. Located in the Atlantic at coordinates 26°58'06.94"N by 69°54'28.80"W, and at a depth of -18,251 feet (nearly 3.5 miles), the extreme environment in which the substation was arranged was more dangerous than space. The construction of the twelve habitats from pieces of Gremn hardware recovered from excavations and storage was a long and secret project, and in its completion achieved something even the Gremn had never before attempted.

Access to the substation was by minisub, though one of the twelve station components was capable of being detached for use as a pressurized elevator. Power for all station systems, including a particle accelerator ring, a quantum computer core, laboratories, hydroponics, air and water scrubbers, and areas set aside for the reconstruction of the engine cores of Auriga and all other recovered technology, was managed by a geothermal power station.

The substation was precisely arranged in a ring-formation around the crash-site of Avalon, each habitat being situated approximately two miles apart and joined to the others via the particle accelerator ring. The location, in the heart of what is commonly referred to as The Bermuda Triangle, was isolated from surface interference and scans. A detailed report of the substation's activities was never circulated. This brief synopsis, and the testimony of the survivors, substantiates all that is known of it after its destruction. To this we may add a list of the twelve habitats:

MAIN OFFICE: Kabta's Atlantic command post.

STOW: Equipment and food storage; hydroponics.

HORUS: Water, waste, and air scrubbers; maintenance equipment.

GEOTHERM: Geothermal power-station and shafts.

REGULUS: Cedric DePons' personal laboratory.

CC: Computer core and servers.

GEOMECH: The geomechanical labs, center of particle accelerator research.

LUCIUS: Large station for storage and study of recovered technology.

ARMS: More than a weapons locker, Arms was a defense post.

UAM BARRACKS: Barracks for UA marines; health office.

SIRIUS: Astronomical data and satellite mission control.

ASSEMBLY LAB: Station dedicated to the reassembly of Auriga's MMPPS engine cores, and of any other salvageable technology.

Syrscian: /sāyr-sē-on/ the name of a magnificent lost world, also called the World of Origins, from which the Gremn and Crodah were exiled after the Destroying Fire. Syrscian is a vast world of varying terrain and unknown diameter. It has not been fully explored by any of its peoples, save perhaps the Ancients. The three moons in Syrscian's sky are Iskartum, Ertsetum, and Luna. Though at no time is the world Syrscian visible from any of its moons, a conjunction of the three is said to open passages between the worlds that were long shut.

Talon: a large domesticated dinosaurian species native to the region of Galaneth in the World of Origins, bred for use as mounts by Galanese cavalrymen. The Talons are classified as raptors, and are equipped with a scaly reddish-brown hide and clawed flightless wings. Feathers are brown or red, and vary in patches from top of head to legs, and in rare cases may cover the whole body. Adults reach about ten feet in height, though often more. The Guildcrest Talon, a species bred in Gilthaloneth, can balance themselves for high-speed charges.

Talons became vegetarians only after domestication. Bearing the beak of fruit or nut-eating birds, they derived most of their nutrition from beans and gourds, and occasionally also from rodents. Before the War of Destroying Fire, the region of Galaneth was rich in vines and low fruiting bushes the Talons exploited for food; the loss of their habitat decimated the species so that it is totally dependent upon the breeders in Gilthaloneth for its existence.

Tara: /tar-ah/ a Galanese colony-town on the north bank of the Karn River, located three hundred leagues east of the Forest, in the dead center of the devastated region of grasslands called "the Wastes of Galaneth". Governed by a tribe called the Musab, Tara and its sister-colony Nara, which together once formed the city of Cipa, are the central hub of the guild that names itself *The League of Antiquinarian Merchants*. This guild is responsible for the safe collection of ancient technologies buried deep beneath the blasted hills of Galaneth. Their excavation shafts produce everything from scrap metal and ceramics to working engines, all from the lost civilizations of the Ancients who dwelt there before them.

While most ancient technology is excavated in Nara, Tara is the home of technicians who are capable of reassembling some of it into useable equipment. By agreement, Tara is also the marketplace for all recovered items—some functional and some curious relics, but all of great interest to the Galanese. A League policy demands that any equipment recovered in Nara that is still running or putting off heat must be inspected by the colony priest. Though a rare occurrence, this rule has preserved some more complicated equipment for careful research by Galanese technicians, including very ancient engines, power-sources, stasis-tubes, intact airships, and weapons.

Tarthalion: /tar-thahl-ee-un/ the mightiest forest of Syrscian, Tarthalion lies west of the Ceregor and Rim Mountains, and is divided into four cardinal "Woods": the North Wood, jutting northwards into the waters of Gaerith, the South Wood, whose farthest extent has never been explored, and the East and West Woods, which are parsed by the winding Aruist River. East of the East Wood rise the mighty peaks of the Rim Mountains, and beyond them lay the sands and poison pools of Urlad.

Tarthalion's Woods are the home of the southern Forest Tribes, who control within the forest seven large towns and numerous smaller settlements. In the North Wood lies Thalion of the Harbor, a seaport. In the South Wood lay Timhureth and its sister-town, Haleth, both located on a southern loop of the Aruist River. In the West Wood lies Keth on the seacoast. In the East Wood lay Belu in the north, Kaleth, and Ulumeneth—this last being a mining town. The forest roads are good, constructed with the help of merchants from as far away as Galaneth in ancient times before the War. After the War, however, Tarthalion was attacked by the Galanese, who sought to dominate the Forest Tribes, perhaps with intent of holding them as ransom against their northern cousins in the forest Tryst.

Teomaxos of Nara: /tay-o-mak-zohs/ priest of the colony Nara of the Tenno people, Teomaxos was long suspected of having secret dealings with Forest Tribe terrorists travelling the Wastes. Despite this, when he brought forth Morla to the New Council in Gilthaloneth, Teomaxos was granted high status. Because of his great knowledge of the ancient legends and the Prophecy of the Trees, and because of the intelligence he had been collecting on the Forest Tribes, he was the Council's man in bringing together the opposing factions under one banner, rallying them for a war against the Forest. Elements of the Council still distrusted him, despite his apparent enthusiasm to put Gilthaloneth in a position to end the conflict with the Forest forever.

The Council's plan, drawn up with Teomaxos' assistance, was to utilize atomics seized after the ancient War of Destroying Fire to burn a path through the forest Tryst to the awakened fortress-city of Islith. There, they would bring forth a Null-User to commandeer the city and employ its cloning facilities, with the aim of raising an army of pilots for mass-produced PCUs. This would swing the balance of power so far in favor of the Galanese that they would be ensured not only an end of war, but the rule of all Syrscian as well. Though seemingly complicit to this scheme, Teomaxos never warmed to the idea of seizing power over the rest of the Council.

Tirshi, Abdi: /ahb-dē-tēr-shē/ Abdi-Tirshi was the personal name of *Ibni-Addu* of Canaanite Hazor, the last king of the Canaanites to rule there during the city's conquest in 1350 BC.

Tryst: /trist/ the forest east of the Ceregor Mountains and west of Galaneth, which forms the northern boundary of inhabited lands. Tryst was ever a forest so deep and dark that few ventured beneath the boughs of its mighty trees who were not of the Forest Tribes. The trees of Tryst are of a type related to the Redwoods of Ertsetum, growing on average 300 feet in height. The canopy ecosystem harbors strange life-forms, including species of talking fish that dwell in still pools of rainwater in the peat and soil suspended hundreds of feet above the forest floor. Of all the strange and varied life in Tryst, that which earns it a reputation as a fearful place are its spirits. Some of the forest spirits are benevolent, being of the Fomorian Tribe, but many are not. There are dangerous and dark things to be found in the mould, where there are no roads, and the worst of them all was named Triath, a spirit in the shape of a monstrous boar, larger than a house. Tryst is also the ground in which the secretive Mugarrum dwell and lay their eggs. Mugarrum, the "Enders", are giant insects that live under the surface, emerging only during times of great tribulation in Syrscian. For this reason, their forms are not remembered by any of the inhabitants of that land, and they are considered legendary to all but the Forest People. It is said that the Mugarrum will one day emerge to consume the entire World of Origins before it is remade.

Besides the Forest Tribes, who have never dwelt in one place in the forest, its only other inhabitants among the four races of Syrscian were the Gremn. Ruins found along the edges of that grassland called Darwath, however, indicate that a kindred people of the Forest Tribes also lived here of old, and they are rumored to have been giants, for the size of their fallen cities and all therein is far beyond human scale. The Forest Tribes called these people in their legends the Nordikus, and said that they were the original inhabitants of Tryst who were defeated by the sorcerer Nergal of Kutha.

UAD: the Foundation's *United Aerospace Division,* headed by Cedric DePons, was a precursor to the militarization of the same unit, renamed UAMC, or United Aerospace Marine Corps. The UAD was composed mostly of Gremn technicians in Kabta's group, dedicated to the task of finding and acquiring bits of Gremn technology scattered across Ertsetum.

Urlad: /awr-lad/ the great toxic wasteland south of Galaneth, Urlad was once a grassland sparsely populated by the ancestors of the Musab people. Lost beneath desert sands was one of the twelve great cities of the Ancients, Ulugrod, which is rumored to hide a great secret. None have been able to locate the city in the desert, however, though Musab merchants claim there are some old storytellers among them in Tara who could be bribed to spell a few clues to the right customer.

Urlad's sands are red in hue, probably from the iron in the soil. The desert was formed by the fallout from atomics deployed in the Destroying Fire, which also brought a subsequent release of gasses and fluid compounds to collect in dense patches or pools across the wastes. Special masks are essential to the survival of any who travel that region; water and food supplies must be carefully sealed, and consumed via valves in the masks. The only known crossing by a large group in recent times was the passage of the Southern Army of the New Council, whose invasion of the forest Tarthalion could not be managed by a crossing of the Ceregor north of Sabiir. The army, under direction of Lord Bregon of Gaerith, donned masks and hauled provisions over a thousand leagues of sand in the eastern lee of the mighty Rim Mountains, making south for a known gap. This army set up camps, and even cut permanent shelters into the mountain-walls along their route, anticipating their eventual return. Though few ever came back this way, the shelters are used by Musab who have established a black-market trade with outlaws of the Forest Tribes.

Urlad's poisonous air can kill a man in minutes, immediately inflaming mucus membranes and causing the lungs to fill with blood. Some creatures, however, have managed to adapt to the poisons by radical mutation. These include a species of flying reptile common in the region, which developed in less than three decades after the war into monstrous winged beasts the Musab call *Kells*. Kell Wyrms dwell in the sand itself, though farther north, closer to the Karn River, they have come to inhabit tall spires of crumbling stone that stud the rocky wastes of Galaneth.

Unsubstantiated reports from travelers and soldiers returning from the south made claim that the poisons of Urlad also changed the dead into living corpses. The truth of the matter aside, Urlad is a place that none travel willingly. When receiving bad news, the men of Nara and Tara say, "It is a stiff wind blows from Urlad."

Viaduct Mirrors: /vuy-uh-dukt/ doors permitting transit of persons in space and time. The Crodah and Gremn developed technology recovered from excavations of ancient cities to achieve time-viewing and time-travel by Viaducts. The abuse of this technology led to a grave event called "The Decoherence," in which all the multiple worlds and times they visited were disconnected from a common vertex. The Decoherence resulted in the displacement of thousands of individuals across time. It was believed by some among both the Gremn and Crodah that this event was the true reason for their exile, and it was said that unless the races brought to Gilthaloneth three of the stones united, the Viaduct would not be accessed which would grant them passage out of exile to the World of Origins. It is recorded in legend that the Viaducts were originally engineered by those people who are called the Ancients, the same who in the Beginning made the stones from the first matter of the universe. As to the manner of their operation, Viaducts were manipulated via terminals in specialized chambers constructed as transit stations. These stations were called "Mirrors." A CSR Terminal (Controlled Singularity Response) enabled an operator to locate regions of multiply connected space, which occurs where the surface of space-time cannot be infinitely contracted to a point. Such areas of space, called vacuoles, commute a passage, or Viaduct, between zones that are separated by a large order of astronomical distance, time, or dimensional variance. The Viaduct passage itself is like a bridge between distant places and times.

The physics of Viaduct Mirrors is actually rather simple, though the matter of the stones makes it difficult to explore to any great depth. Basically, matter has positive energy, and gravity is negative. The gravity of the World of Origins, coupled with that of its moons and the star Sol, is powerful enough to drive negative energy to anomalous proportions. Applying a hydrogen fuel-source to the gravity anomaly makes it possible to identify candidate vacuoles for capture by the Mirror device. This necessitates a CSRT tie-in to MMPPS system circuitry (Mini-Magnetic Plasma Propulsion Systems). Once the vacuole is known, however, only gravitational negative energy harvested from the event horizon of a vacuole itself is enough to create and stabilize a Viaduct, and the only known matter capable of conducting such energy is contained in a few mysterious stone artifacts. There are only twelve known. It is said that the stones contain all the matter of the universe, though how such a thing might be possible is not accounted even in myth.

Before a Viaduct is opened, it was protocol to utilize recirculating plasma to focus a laser for gravitational lensing. This makes possible limited field-projection searches into the Viaduct before venturing transit. This is time-viewing. The actual view across time is preceded by a calculation of gravitational flux on the home world as influenced by the *Dark Worlds*—multiverse coordinate-shifted echoes of the home world in space and time—thus cancelling out their interference from the field-projection. After this is accomplished, it is possible to discern the compression wave of multiply connected spaces interacting with space-time, which leaves a ripple of radiated energy across the event horizon. This energy contains a semblance of the sum-over-histories, a true representation of what is happening in time.

The final phase of transit requires axial shielding to be brought online, which prevents displacement from the point of origin. Though transit through Viaduct Mirror devices is instantaneous, the resulting disorientation accumulating over continued use forces some travelers to restrict themselves to just the time-viewing aspects of this technology.

Watchers: a terrible effect of advanced displacement and atomic radiation on the Galanese, Watchers are an immortal tribe of ghoulish creatures that once were the inhabitants of the Karn River colonies. The Watchers are not a natural effect of radiation and mutation alone, but of the release of quantum energy resulting from the division of the stones. More closely akin to insects than to people, the changes wrought in these beings by the war made them impossible to kill by any means but fire or complete dismemberment.

Watchers are a horrible sight to see, for though their forms are humanoid they have an evil look. Their heads are particularly gruesome, being eyeless bags of clear flesh with broken mouths. The name they are called by, Watchers, is part corruption of *Wasters*, their earliest appellation, and partly the result of the finding that these eyeless beings possess an unexplained keenness of sight.

They congregate in groups, often by the hundreds, and have been observed attacking travelers or merchants in a mob, crushing to death any living thing they discover within their reach. Reports claim that Watchers will eat their victims after mobbing them in this way, often in a frenzy that results in the destruction of a few of their own. Worse, any physical contact with the creatures results in transmission of their condition. Though never explained pathologically, the Watchers' condition was likened to the progression of a disease. They are to be avoided at all costs.

Watchers are dangerous, but seldom encountered by the Galanese or Forest Tribes. They left the desert wastes early after the War, or were driven out by those who reestablished the roads along the Karn, and traveled to the Ceregor as if summoned by one purpose. In response to complaints by settlers, an expedition was undertaken by Orlim of Gilthaloneth after the formation of the New Council, and Watchers were safely captured and contained in a location on the Karn River. There they were studied by Council-appointed technicians, who discovered in these unhappy creatures the strange ability to see across worlds and in time. The technicians reported their findings to Orlim, who hid the Watchers and the laboratory from the Council. His design for the Watchers was not discovered, but they were able to alert him of the awakening of Islith upon the return of the exiles from Ertsetum.